CHAPTER 1
Juniper Park

MW00380675

It is a particularly dark, calm, quiet night; three city patrol cars are parked at the end of an undeveloped cul-de-sac. Four officers meet and discuss how eerie it is to have such a calm, uneventful night. One expresses how he can just about hear the rustle of fall leaves over a mile away. The cul-de-sac is sort of a hide-away when the officers want to meet and be out of the public eye, but still close enough to respond in a moment's notice. The group enjoys the thrill of working nights, and this team has that brotherhood often described in this type of career. A team, a crew, or by many other names given, this group refers to itself as family. They are a unique mix of personalities and quirks.

One is very outspoken and the type to throw his personal stories out for all to jab and joke about. He is slim, has that little boyish look, and seems to have a good way with everyone with whom he comes into contact.. His story this night is of a neighboring agency that was trying to arrest one of the local regular, small-time pot smokers. In city jurisdiction, yet the county guys had come across the local known on the streets as "DoDo."

Officer Tack explains how a twenty something black man who stands six two, about 245, and in exemplary shape gets the name "DoDo."

"Oh my God! I have to tell ya'll now. First time me and Officer Kaybark arrested DoDo, he was only maybe nineteen. I was the FTO for Kaybark, in his last phase of training. Kaybark was all new, and full of fire, wanting to get out and do as much as he could to prove himself. I knew if we went foot patrol in a few select neighborhoods, we would eventually come across someone gambling, drinking in public, smoking some bud, and maybe dealing. Small shit, but enough to get this fucker to stop pestering me about doing something. Over on Avenue H, you know where the old cash for gold shop was? Well, I had Bark tuck behind the trash can."

There are looks and sighs as they all know these trash cans are the worst place to hide. These trash cans are used for much of the trash people don't want in their own cans. Dead fish, dead cats, dog poop, and a variety of illegal waste. Ofc. Tack laughs. He then tells the others. "Bark had the handheld and I would keep telling him, 'Oh, oh, oh here comes one. . . then say, shit!' Went the other way. After hanging this poor bastard out to dry for about an hour, some dude comes walking up to the gold shop. He seemed sketchy as hell. Pacing, kept undoing his belt, then putting it back on. This dude was wiping his head with a bandana, and looked to be full-on stressed. I'm watching, thinking, oh shit, this mother fucker gonna rob the gold shop. I had Kaybark get ready, had another unit en route, and even had dispatch give us traffic and alert County. Just as backup got to me, the dude went inside, spoke to the guy running the place, and then came back out. Dude paced again, and then was yelling at the guy in the gold shop. I couldn't hear what he was saying, but he was pissed. Kaybark could hear the dude outside say, 'Mother Fucker I should just do it right here, right fucking here.' The dude pulled the door again, but the guy inside had just hit the electric lock and the panic button."

Tack laughs as if the story just happened, and continues to finish his story. "Okay, picture this shit. Bark is at that nasty dumpster, me and backup are at my car, dispatch gets the alert from the fuckin' gold shop we just called traffic at, county boys are coming, and off a ways, I even hear the fuckin' helicopter en route. Me and Toby have to drive around the ditch and Kaybark comes around the corner, gun drawn straight down on this guy as the son of a bitch is pulling his pants down. Now known as "DoDo," he squats of?? the front mat, and if I didn't see it myself, I would say a horse took a dump on this gold shop mat. Poor bastard wasn't trying to rob the place. He had gone to ask to use the guy's restroom, and had those shit sweats hitting him. Guy running the place told DoDo only for customers. That was why the belt loosening, pacing, and wiping his head. So DoDo got pissed, hahahaha, or should I say shitty, and walked out. DoDo told us he wasn't going to make it home, and when the guy wouldn't let him use the restroom, well DoDo decided he would drop it at the door! Ha hah. Oh it gets better."

Tack is in tears and Kaybark is just shaking his head. Tack has to give more details of what happened to DoDo.

"Get this, I made Bark arrest this guy for Criminal Mischief, and actually take him down to booking. No tissue to wipe, nothing. Just pull up the drawers, and load him up in the back seat. So listen, you know when you have the bubble guts, and you blast one out and then a few minutes you realize, oh shit, that wasn't the end of it? Yes, DoDo busted ass again in Bark's back seat on the way to the jail. Best thing is, we didn't even give DoDo his nickname. When he got there, more locals were in and they gave it to him, and let's just say it stuck!"

The story breaks the night up, and they continue to take it easy. There is an odd relationship between the night crew and the locals. The four of them know the locals, and share a mutual respect. The ones committing the petite crimes know what they do is illegal, yet in their own way, have many decent sides to them as well. Most closed-minded people could never see this. It's the cultural awareness that makes this group of cops much better.

The most low-key, probably dark-sided of the bunch is Cpl. Valerio Nave. These guys still joke with him, and often ask where the hell he is really from.

One asks in a joking way, "Yeh, where are you from Nave? Close buzzed hair, serious looking all-American white guy, cold-eyed, stern and sometimes you have that deep look, like you could snap a person's neck and not even be phased. And, AND that weird ass name....Valerio Nave"

Nave is pronounced Na-Vay. Nave has moved up quicker than most, and isn't often seen to sit still for very long. A beloved part of the family, he still has a loner side to him. Many nights, like this one, he will stop and chat and then move quickly off to the street again. Usually not long after he departs, the others will take bets on how long before he is arresting someone for drunk driving or drugs. He is definitely a no-bullshit type guy.

Officer Olivia was hired out of the same class as Nave. Oly, as the crew calls her, will randomly tell of a few stories that put the group in awe or admiration for Nave. He was ranked highly in his class, paid his own way through the academy, and no one really knew or had much information on him. He stuck to himself, yet always seemed to help whomever needed it. He studied constantly, and when a few cadets fell back, he went to their houses and brought them up.

He told the class once, "No one here will fail, unless you give up. If you give up, we will escort you out. "He just has that mentality.

Oly is often asked by the guys what the rhino is for. She just can say it was given to him by someone who trained him before he came to the academy.

She tells them, "All he has told me, is it is a symbol of command presence.

Nave had many offers to larger agencies, yet had a desire to work in a smaller community. The upper brass did not truly like Nave. The captain once was heard saying, "That son of a bitch might know someone, somewhere, but he is never taking my job."

So the crew, leaning against their patrol cars, continue to toss the jokes back and forth. They talk of how Florida just doesn't have many dry, breezy nights such as the one they enjoy now. The night passes, and before long they all have nightly business checks to do.

The very next night proves that the calm they relished the previous night would be short-lived. No time for a proper roll call and briefing, they were out of the gates like race horses. First, a domestic in the upper-class neighborhood. A report to dispatch indicated that the wife of the residence had a gun and was threatening to shoot the husband; the woman was found in the couple's kitchen. Oly was the go-to officer for domestics. It helped that she was the only female officer on the night shift. A day-shift female officer was already on scene; however. Oly had special negotiation training. Quickly, Oly had defused the situation and had the wife leave the gun in the home and walk out. Now, Oly would obviously be tied up with this mess for most of her night. This left the crew down to three. The priority call had other calls of less severity on hold. With the situation stabilized, the other officers started taking waiting calls. Tack had a minor wreck to work, and Kaybark was lucky enough to get the call of a man shoplifting women's lingerie. Once on scene, it was noted that the man was still wearing the lingerie. Nave kept himself available for any urgent calls while the others dealt with the minor reports. It was as if the town took the previous night off, and decided to blow up this evening.

Kaybark was quick to handle the shoplifting, and met up with Nave to tell him all about it. Nave waited for Kaybark behind the Target. He could see the anxious eyes nearly three hundred yards away as Kaybark drove into the dimly lighted loading dock lights. The window of Kaybark's, already down, he could not wait to tell Nave this story.??

Just as he stops abruptly next to Nave, Nave grins and asks, "So where is your date?" Kaybark is quick to make light of the comment and says, "Hey, to tell you the truth, she/he might have been better looking than the last few women I have met. Especially that flat
-chested one I met online. Holy shit dude, the crossdresser had bigger boobs!"

He immediately turns the joke on himself as he claims, "I know I shouldn't judge. She is probably telling her girlfriends right now about how tiny my penis is. Anyhow, let me tell you that was some funny shit. The store security had been watching this guy, and seen him come in. He was already dressed like a chick, but the goofy bastard wore a short dress. Okay, Nave, tell me, if you are going to dress like a woman in a short dress, what are you going to do first?"

Nave answers, "Bark I am NOT going to wear a dress."

Kaybark shakes his head as he continues his narrative of events, "Okay, yes I know, you would never wear a dress, but what would you do first?"

Nave looks concerned as he answers, "Get counseling."

Kaybark laughs and says, "Right, but check this out, this dumb fuck didn't even shave his legs. The store security is upstairs, zooming in and laughing as he/she is floating around in pretty yellow high heels, no pantyhose, short black skirt, a tank top covered by a yellow leather jacket, and a black and yellow bag. Hey, at least this guy is color coordinated, right? Now let's break this shit down Nave. Shoes, skirt, jacket, tank, handbag!!!! All doing good. Homeboy is got his colors down. Looking good, he must think. Now we have to look at the not-so-goods—legs, hairy as that wolf spider that scared the hell out of Oly last week. Face—lipstick, done! Eye shadow—yes, had that done! Fake eyelashes—well they were dangling, but had them there. And this goofball had a full beard??? WTF Nave??? Bro, I could hardly keep a straight face. This guy was telling me he was only stealing because he wanted to get something nice for his wife!!!! Holy shit, wonder what his wife will be thinking when or if she finds out? Luckily he had no priors. The store was cool, and allowed me to just issue the princess a NTA for the royal ball being held at the courthouse in his honor later this month."

Nave slightly laughs and smiles as Kaybark **vigorously** tells his story.

Kaybark rests his head back, and then looks at his dash. "Hell, I better go get gas in my ride before anything else comes uncorked."

Nave too heads out to patrol the area of town he had planned to cover.

The night settles, and other than a few minor traffic stops, nothing serious is happening. Now approaching 10:30, the air drifts the distinct aroma of rain to come. Nave parks on the far-sloped end of Juniper Park. The park layout is very picturesque with drooping majestic oaks, tall sycamores, several duck ponds bordering walking trails, and several gazebos for picnics and gatherings.

In the day, it is an absolute dream for families to bring their kids, new relationships to encounter the movie like walks as a man holds a woman's hand while he contemplates what bench he will choose that may earn him his first kiss.?? In the dark of night, the landscape is less than appealing for any romance. There is an ironic shift for any parent wanting their child to be anywhere other than the lighted basketball courts, which are open and visible from the busy street. The many concrete walking trails give access to dirt paths that lead into the backwoods, swamps, and thick scrub oaks. One persistent parent group has pleaded with the City Council to increase foot patrol in the areas of the park, where assumed criminal activity is said to be taking place. As most cities this size, there are no extra cops to spare, and far too often the city operates in a reactive state. As haunting as many dark areas of the park are, it is, as if it is as haunted as a cemetary. We can remember as kids the nonsensical games we would use to scare friends during sleepovers. Saying certain chants in a bathroom mirror, or using a Ouija board. The only time anyone may have seen anything, has been in a movie.

Anyhow, at night the officers try and make it part of their nightly tasks to drive through, spotlight the woods, and even take some time and walk the trails. Ofc. Olivia doesn't much like walking the trails, as she had a rather large banana spider hitch a ride on her shoulder one night. One might have thought a local eight-foot gator had jumped on her back the way she carried on about the event. The wooded area does pose its environmental dangers, and even the officers would be lacking common sense if they didn't take precautions before going in at night on foot. Cottonmouths, gators, and rattlesnakes, are a few of the residents that become more abundant the deeper into the swamps you go. More likely, would be injuries of twisting an ankle on cyprus stumps; sawgrass can scratch you up pretty good, and the muck has been known to trap the legs of many trail hikers. For these reasons, it is not too common that many people even take to the backwoods to hang out.

Nave contacts the others to get an idea of how the night is going. Kaybark is on the other end of town walking neighborhoods and chatting with a few of the neighbors. Oly is still wrapped up in the domestic from earlier, and Tack is in the station printing prep documents for court the next day. Nave decided he would stop off at the park.

Nave:"Unit, ONE. . . TWO. . . SEVEN. . . dispatch."

Dispatch: "ONE. . . TWO. . . SEVEN. . . go ahead."

Nave: "ONE. . . TWO. . . SEVEN. . . out on foot, Juniper Park, basketball courts, contact with small known group."

Dispatch: "10-4. ONE. . . TWO. . . SEVEN. . . at Juniper Park, basketball courts, 23:25 hours.

Nave parks, shuts off the car, and approaches the group. A tall man, appearing to be in his early twenties, stops and turns toward Nave. He holds the ball as he looks over to the others. In sagging black Jordan shorts, no shirt to cover the heavily tattooed skin, and a cigar pinched between one side of his lips, he looks back to Nave and exclaims:

"What the fuck do you want Mr. Cracka Ass Policeman?"

Calmly, Nave walks deliberately in the man's direction. Nave's eyes never leave the returned stare of the man.

Now, at an arm's-length away, the man takes a small step back, bounces the ball between his legs and says, "Nave, you don't want to do this. You better get your badge-wearing, candied-ass back over in dat protective metal heap of patrol shit, with those pretty lights and go play Bad Boys somewhere else. These courts are ours and only for real men!"

Nave fixes on the man, then a calculated glance to the others on the court before telling the taller man, "Drop the rock and let this badge-wearing, candied-ass, Bad Boy show you how to navigate that shit though the net."

Tension immediately breaks; the tall, tattooed guy pulls the ball up, thrusts it to Nave, and both just laugh as this was a common way Nave and the guy acted toward each other.

Nave bounces the ball, and says to the guy, "We can stop all the talk and make us a wager to settle this."

The guy jokes, "You ain't got nothing. What you gonna give me, one of those dopey stuffed animals out of your trunk?"

Nave answers, "One shot. One shot from here, and if I make it, you have to get a rhino head tattooed on your palm"

The guy tilts his head back, rolls his eyes, and bends at the knees as he twirls around with an animated laugh.

He says, "PoPo man, you know you can't make that shit! I want that bet all day. But what the hell you got for me?"

Nave asks, "What do you want?"

His tattooed fingers rise to his lips, pointer finger met to the thumb as a universal sign of smoking a joint as he says, "You can kick me down some of that confiscated dope ya'll pigs take from the hood."

Nave still bounces the ball while answering, "Once you stop dreaming, name something real—unless you are ready to back out. I think you realize the night is just right for me to sink this."

The guy hangs one arm around another near him, and states his counter bet, "Okay, here it is and don't flake your shit out and not come through cause everyone here know you tossin' a brick. I want four large Papa John's pizzas, twelve-pack Michelob Ultra, and a nice jug of Devil's Spit."

Nave and the guy shake on it. Nave takes a few bounces, a few warm up shots closer, and then backs to the bet spot. Some tugging and adjustments on the bullet- proof vest, more bounces, a few two-handed back spins of the ball, and then his knees bend. One hand with fingers perfectly placed on the seams, his elbow bends, the ball now near his forehead, a concentrated laser look to the tattered cloth net hanging from the rim, and with a strong toss, the ball spins free through the thick night air. Passing the glow of the park lights, in line and en route to the intended hole, the shirtless man drops to the court's dirty ground and covers his head. In the brief time it took the ball to travel from just beyond the faded three-point line, to the hoop, the man quite possibly envisioned a rhino head being tattooed on the very tender palm of his hand. Worse will be the witnesses' presence to tell of the bet, and that the rhino was given to him by a cop. He would be eternally linked to the same cop who sent him to jail for a year, took over $20,000.00 in heroin, and confiscated his paid-off, custom 1974 Impala.

There is then the sound of leather clashing with steel. The folded up man hears the ball hit the metal backboard, and seconds later the sound of the ball bouncing off the concrete court. He did not have to wait long, as the others were far too happy to start calling out orders of what they wanted on the pizza, and how Nave better make sure those Ultras were on ice. One man even makes a point to slowly spell out and use some sort of sign language illustrating Devil's Spit. He was a smaller, older man with short, tight nappy hair. His hands position to each side of his head with pointer fingers up to mimic devil horns.

In his smoke-rasped voice, cleared by random deep chuckles, he closes his eyes and announces past his prickly mustache, "D.E.V.I.L.S. MUTHA FUCKIN S.P.I.T!!! Hell's yeh, Devil's Spit be good on my lips!"

You might gather that this is one of the funnier ones in the group.

Nave extends his left hand to help the relieved man off the court. He assures the man the bet would be honored on his first day off. Nave was the by-the-book type, and to go buy alcohol in a patrol car would be way beyond protocol. So the men realize they would have to wait.

The dismay of the small raspy-spoken man was all too tragic as he pleas to Nave, "Come on cracka', you can't do a brotha' like that. Had me already tastin' dat hot whiskaaay. Dat some bullshit, somebody betta hook me up or I ain't play no mo ball, till I gets mine!"

The tattooed man takes the ball, and hits the small man in the back of the head. "Play no ball, nigga. Yo drunk ass can't play no way. Nave told you true, he be bringing that shit his next day. Too late now anyways."

Nave asks how things have been in the park lately. One speaks up and says he saw some older dude heading back on the trail with his daughter or some young-looking girl—said the girl didn't look like she was in danger, just thought it was odd.

He asks, "Why go walking with your kid this late? Maybe a school project or something like that" He nods his head to indicate the direction the man and girl headed.

"Well, I may go take a walk and see what they are up to." Nave told the group.

Nave: "ONE. . . TWO. . . SEVEN. . . DISPATCH."
Dispatch: "ONE...TWO...SEVEN...go ahead."
Nave: "Dispatch, just be advised I am going foot patrol on the Autumn Trail west of the courts."
Dispatch: "Copy, show you foot patrol Autumn Trail."

Nave takes the concrete trail, and soon is among the dark. The lights of the courts only offer a faint glow in the distance. There is a natural beauty in the shadows challenged by the sway of trees and soft blue rays of the moon passing until terminated into the thick fern-covered ground. He walks the length of the Autumn Trail, and decides he may have just missed the people, or perhaps they had left during his humiliating defeat on the court. There is a shortcut that would give Nave a chance to take a deeper look into the woods. The trail is solid, and has many clearings along the way. Just off one path, he is sure he heard a young girl's voice. Nave, always skeptical and not wanting to relinquish his element of surprise, begins to walk lightly. He wants to hear the man's voice.

Another ten yards in, he clearly hears what he believes to be a young girl say, "No!" in a quiet, low-crying tone. "I don't like doing that. Please, I don't want to again. It hurts."

Nave's emotions calm. His head slowly tilts forward. His eyelids drift easily to rest closed. His chest expands with a smooth, long, deep breath. With a slow exhale, his eyes loosely shut, his right hand firmly and steadily removes the Glock 45-cal. from the black-molded holster. His piercing blue eyes focus into the woods. The limbic region of his complex brain takes over. He approaches swiftly and cautiously. In the same delicate sway of moonlight through palms and drapes of willows, he sees the back of a large man's silhouette in the shadows. With a slight move to one side of the man, Nave saw the crying eyes of an undressed girl, who appeared to be no older than ten. Nave slowly walked to the man's left side. He sees the man wearing only a black golf style shirt. His khaki pants lay gathered near his ankles, and he had just placed a condom on his penis. A cold stare, and authoritative stance, Nave is much of a surprise to the man.

Fifteen yards to the man's side, the half-naked man holds his hands out and attempts to reason with Nave. "We haven't done anything. I wasn't going to. I was just teaching her a lesson" Facing Nave, the man is frozen in guilted, disbelief. Tears channel past his thick glasses; snot now collects on his greying mustache, just above his quivering lips. No words exit Nave toward the man.

Nave posed and almost statuesque, has his right hand gripped around his gun.

His left hand cradles against his other fingers, and in a light, assuring voice, Nave tells the girl, "You will never have to see this man again!"

The group on the court still excited about the bet and telling each other how good it will be when Nave shows up with the goods, sits along the courtside bench. Each seems to be breathless as they first hear one echoing POP come from the Autumn Trail—this followed by the scattering noise of birds fleeing the trees. Disbelief in the silent eyes of the men, one holds his jaw in a wide-open gape.

The smaller, funny black man looks away, springs up, holds his right hand on his head, and in his quiet, drunken whisper says, "Maaaaan, Nave done popped a cap in that perverts ass ya'll."

Another discounts, "Bullshit. Ain't no way. He must a come across a gator or one of those bad-tempered cottonmouths. If Nave found that old dude doing anything, he would just have to arrest him. You can't just go droppin' mutha fuckas these days. Holy shit, Bro,what if the dude got spooked and dropped Nave?"

The tattooed guy is quick to stand and even pace as he tells the guys, "Hey man, Nave put me away, but Nave my boy ya'll. That cop a straight dude. That pervert come out this way and Nave not with him. . . I tell you true, I taking that mutha out!"

As they speak, they hear the rev of high-output police motors, sirens, and ambulances converging on the park. Time appears not to progress; the shadows become clear of a man and small girl. In the clarity of those court lights, Nave walks slowly and determinedly, arms curled like a hero under the small girl, who hides her face in his shoulder. Her arms clinched, and will surely not release from Nave's neck. He passes over the court, says nothing to the men, and looks as if his focus was beyond the world itself. He passes his patrol car, walks between two other units, and arrives at a parked ambulance. The doors are open, and Nave and the girl step in. As he sits, the first droplets of the girl's tears roll off his badge. EMS realize the girl would not be releasing her grip off Nave's neck for some time.

The Sergeant, Oly, Kaybark, and Tack are all starry-eyed at the back of the ambulance as the Sergeant asks, "Calls came in shots fired in the park, you are holding a small child in an ambulance, and still I don't know what the hell is going on here! Are you or the child hurt? And just what in the hell is going on here? Is there anyone still in the park?"

Nave, still gripped by the girl in shock, looks out of the back of the ambulance, which is framed with curious, concerned faces. His trusting glance is direct toward Oly as he says, "The threat has been terminated."

The doors close, and the ambulance pulls off. The Sergeant orders the Sheriff's K-9 deputy to lead a team toward the trail.

Tack nervously asks Oly, "Did I get that right? Terminated?"

Oly mutters, "Shit Nave."

" Tack, Kaybark, and Oly quietly gather near Nave's patrol car. The Sergeant goes in with the deputies. Moments later, another deputy opens his trunk and walks off with yellow crime scene tape.

As more bystanders gather, so do the vans of local news stations. Quickly, satellite antennas are up, lights are blinding the crowd, and the eager journalists are attempting to get anyone to offer information about the incident unfolding. Of course, there are the camera whores who want to simply be seen on TV, blunder misinformation, and project many false assumptions, which the news channels thrive on. An eruption of reporters fight for their spot as the K-9 and other officers break the shadows of the trail. Yellow tape is being stretched as if a few more inches will matter to these reporters lunging for any bit of information. A calm, yet almost sorrowed-looking Captain stands and waits as he looks over the reporters. He looks straight forward, and addresses no single person of the group. Once the barrage of questions stops, he takes a step toward a mike. After all, they all want to know the same thing as the Sergeant, "Just what the hell is going on in Juniper Park?"

The Captain's right hand covers his left hand, as they rest near his belt line. With the many hand held devices outstretched toward him, he offers a statement, "Tonight one of our officers was on foot patrol here in the backwoods of the park. That officer came into contact with an adult male and a minor child. It appears an altercation of some sort took place, and the officer was believed to have fired a single shot. The unidentified adult did not survive the shot. The child was rescued, and is being attended to by medical personnel as we speak. These events are still unfolding and we simply do not have any further information at this time. I can say the officer involved sustained no injury and is with the rescued child."

One reporter after another blurts random questions, yet the captain calmly walks to his car, and leaves the area. The Sergeant and other patrol officers stay to contain the crowd, and secure the integrity of the crime scene. The Sheriff's office continues the investigation as protocol in any officer-related shooting.

The news reporters then turn to the crowd once again. One lone reporter saw the group of ball players, somewhat out of the scene. Inconspicuously, she departs from the rest, and is careful not raise any awareness from the flock of vulture reporters taking in the nonsense of many, who were not there to begin with. She approaches in a nervous manner, yet boldly; she will not turn back. The young men stand silent. One leans against the silver metal pole of the hoop, another stands staring toward the now silent woods. The others pace, and scuff their black and white Chuck Taylor Converse on the court.

The slender, tall woman looks more like she should be reporting at a hippie parade. She is simple with long, thick hair and soft, natural curls, and no make-up. Her feet, covered by woven, flat-bottomed shoes and a loose, free -flowing blouse that lifts in the wind, reveal a dull yellow daisy-flower belly button ring. Her voice delivered in a soft appreciative tone, makes clear why the men feel comfortable speaking with her. These men seek no attention, nor do they huddle among the reporters.

With only a handheld recording device at her side, she comes to be there with them on the court. In a timid gesture, dipping her head to one side, she does not ask the men anything. Just the opposite, she makes a statement to them, "You were here when this happened. You guys know what went on, and you seem to have a particular concern. The officer, the one who had to shoot the guy in the woods. . . he is a good cop, isn't he? I have heard of this stuff going on in the park and something finally happened, didn't it? I am not recording now, but I want to know and let everyone know the reality of why this happened. I want to turn this on, and I believe you guys have something real to say, unlike all those there in the parking lot"

She turns to face the crowd in the distance, and as she looks at the many reporters sucking in the useless misinformation, she says to the group, "Not one of those people was here or know anything, do they?"

The tattooed one leaning against the pole folds his arms and asks, "Do you have a camera, or do you just want it recorded?"

From a hemp-knitted bag, she retrieves a small video camera and uses the recorder that she held at her side.

Hours later on the local news channel there is a banner of BREAKING NEWS.

The lead news anchor breaks in over the weather report, and has an excited, surprised look as he begins:

"I am being told we may have an exclusive report of actual accounts of the moments just before and after the shooting in nearby Juniper Park. This is the story we have been following of the officer involved in a shooting. Our field reporter, Lynn Grace, spoke with a group of men, who claim they were with the officer moments before he went into the wooded area. I understand we have that footage, and we advise that these are only accounts stated by those at the scene. Our station takes no position on any statements, as there will obviously be further information to come. Let's go now to that footage."

[The TV then shows the video from the basketball court]

Lynn is out of view and can be heard, "The officer's patrol car is still parked here near the courts. Now, you advised the officer came here first and actually took a little time to talk with you guys. Sort of just hang out"

The taller, tatted man offers his words first, "Let me tell you all, Nave is a stand-up guy. He come up and chill with us; we shot some hoops and the man is real. I tell you that straight. We just a bunch of misfits, did some not-so-legal shit (station bleep), but Nave not like most. He gives us respect. We told him some dude looked like he was walking into the backs with some little girl. Thought it could be his daughter doing some school project, like catching frogs or some shit" The man speaking takes long side-to-side swoops of his head as he continues, "I tell you, if we thought the perv was doing some shady shit, we would have gone in and busted his ass up, true!"

The shorter, usually funnier black man comes in and adds, "Hey, we alllll know why that man got his ass shot. The fact is, they was somes bahaaad stuff go. . . in. . . down back in dem woods. You axe me, if all is how we all know it to be, dude done got what he had coming, period!" He strikes a sideways, arms-folded, half- backed lean, and exclaims, "Nave should be held up and given a damn metal or whatever the damn PoPo place be giving the good cops."

Lynn calmly allows the men their time to voice their thoughts. She then asks, "You all saw the officer come out of the woods. What can you tell me about that? Did the officer say anything?"

The tatted guy places his palms on his forehead, and then with his elbows upward and hands now cradling the back of his neck, he takes in a breath and twists in the direction of the path. His pause shows him likely resisting his thoughts of what he saw and he speaks, "We just chillin' here, and heard a POP. Everyone round her know that sound straight up. We first wondered if our homeboy, Nave, was down. I tell you, I was so glad when I first seen the shine off the keys on his belt. As he come out, we all just stared. Nave come slowly holding that poor girl. I could see the knuckles of that scared girl, white as your teeth. That girl been abused, and we all know it! She wasn't letting go. Like some wrong shit out of a movie I tell you. Nave didn't say a word. He was in a zone. On focus I believe. Just take care of that little girl. Just get her away from whatever bad shit happen back in them woods. Nave held tight all the way into the ambulance. Give us a few more like that guy. . . well, we might not have the crap going on with these pervs like we do now. But you know (as he looks directly into the camera as if he knows he will be looking into the eyes of everyone watching this now),this will all be turned to make the officer look like the bad guy. Damn child molesters and rapist seem to have all the rights. You ask me. . . close the case. closed case. . . justice served!"

The video stops and now. Lynn is behind a desk talking to the live camera in the news station. She explains that once the man made his final statement, they were done. Lynn tells the anchor, "I will tell you from the short time I spent on the court, the guys there have a deep respect for the officer. Now, I should also express that these were the accounts and opinions of those men. We have no information from the department verifying any of the acts stated, and an investigation will take place. Obviously, that investigation is already underway there in the park."

The anchor asks, "Do we know if the men there on the courts heard several shots, any type of altercation, or if they knew the man who was shot?"

Lynn answers, "The guys on the court were sure there was only one shot. They did tell me they had not seen the man or the girl before, and did not even pay particular attention to offer any description."

The anchor looks to the monitor and says, "That is Lynn Grace, field reporter with our exclusive Channel 13 coverage of this late-breaking story there in Juniper Park."

The next morning the loop is constant of the men telling their story of what Lynn Grace recorded. The upper brasses at the department worry, as the other stations are now heavily focused on only one shot. The national news media are now piggybacking on the accounts, and political volley of right and wrong.

Several days later, the Chief of Police makes a call to the networks advising there will be a news conference in two days, knowing that all stations, local and national, will surely gather.

A well-dressed woman comes to the podium lined with microphones. She is stern, has her pancake holster to one side of her belt, and her clip and badge to the other side. She advises she is the lead Internal Affairs officer assigned to the investigation. She addresses in more of a dictation manner, "The shooting, which took place in the backwoods path of Juniper Park, is and will be thoroughly investigated by an outside agency. Our department policy is to place any officer on administrative leave while the investigation is ongoing. Cpl. Valerio Nave is a highly respected law enforcement officer, and believed to have acted with-in the parameters of the law. This department is supportive of the officer, yet will also cooperate with all facets of the investigation. Upon the completion of this independent investigation, there will be notice of the appropriate actions to take place. This is all we can advise at this time."

The press feels that this was no more information than assumed before the press conference. Still, it gives the department a break from the frequent calls and media push. Nave is in the department to discuss the matter. With much coaching, he has been instructed to stick with a particular scenario of that night. It is the department's view that it was dark, the man was obviously in the shadows, and the girl was in imminent danger.

The questions asked of Nave are almost scripted: "So when he was there in the dark, he reached for his pants, right? When he reached, you thought he was reaching for a weapon?"

"Nave, this has to be just right. If we do not show you had cause to use deadly force . . . (a long pause). . . you could be facing some serious and hard-to-fight legal issues." The conversation and coaching end.

CHAPTER 2
Investigation Report

Two months have passed, and Nave receives a call from an inside friend at the agency doing the investigation. ."Nave, it's Mike. Hey buddy I wanted to call you as soon as I saw the final report. It will go to your department tomorrow, and then press will be anxious for a release soon after. Are you prepared to address the media? You know I am always there beside you, bro. Our department will release the findings and its recommendation. The press wants to hold a major bullshit public release on Wednesday. They expect to hear from you at this thing on Wednesday. I tell you, what a fucking circus show. Just sucks really. Well, don't forget, we all have, and will always stand, for and next to you."

Nave tells Mike he has no regrets, and that he will address the press as he is. He advises he is not the type to take the cautious route, and believes the people should hear the truth.

The early morning sets the tone as an area is cleared for the media; the podium is placed, and the news vans have their antennas lifted to the clear skies. There is a growing crowd of reporters, who want the closest position possible. A parameter has been placed to handle the crowd that has gathered. The majority of spectators seem to support the actions of Cpl. Nave. There are a few who have the stance that the police use excessive force, and are just willing to shoot and abuse their power. This particular situation of a child molester and a little girl, lends much reactive support with little to no sympathy for the man who was shot.

Now, minutes before the scheduled time, shoulders touch along the front row of the reporters' section. Lynn Grace has a center spot, and has been given almost special treatment. It was her footage that overshadowed the many useless blunders of the other stations.

The doors of the Sheriff's headquarters open, and one man comes out holding a brown legal, docket-style folder. He is in a light grey suit, balding, stands tall, and has an old-style, hard-nosed cop look. He is not of the new college-placed, upper-level brass. He served his time in the streets and gutters, and survived the early years on the beat. It is fitting that he is the one assigned to investigate this case. He addresses the crowd and press:

"Let me state my name from the record, Investigator K. Dean. I was assigned a very difficult task to investigate the officer-related shooting at Juniper Park. No fellow brother ever wants this task, yet it is a necessary function of our legal process. Our many officers, deputies, and troopers are asked to perform the daunting task of protecting our innocent, and not- so-innocent. We have a legal structure in place that has to be followed, no matter how unlawful the act. Our emotions, our gut feeling, or just that sixth sense, cannot be a deciding factor when we are to uphold the rightful action of our citizens and our officers. (The investigator pauses. He looks to the thick file, and he then grasps the edges of the podium.)

"On the night Cpl. Valerio Nave entered into the dark-wooded path, the officer had information that there were at least two people who could still be in the place he was to patrol. He knew one was alleged to be an adult male and the other a minor child, assumed to be a girl. Cpl. Nave also had just been with a group of men, who stated previous to entering the wooded area, he was in good spirits. Cpl. Nave found the two unknown individuals in a deep, unmaintained area. It was there, in the secluded area, that Cpl. Nave witnessed an act of great criminal circumstance. Cpl. Nave was in an unimaginable situation in which he was forced to take an action most officers should not have to endure, yet have been trained and prepared to do so (His stern gaze captures direct eye contact from each reporter.) As investigators, we have a controlled environment to evaluate and strategize that which an officer only has a split second to execute in the real world. Through our investigation, we found the adult male had and was attempting to continue the sexual assault of the minor child. The adult male had a previous record of aggravated sexual assault on another child. The adult male had forcibly taken the child from a parking lot of a nearby neighborhood. We also concluded the adult male was unarmed.

(Quiet sighs, to almost speculate the findings would not be in favor of Nave).”

"Cpl. Nave did willfully and intentionally fire one fatal shot. It was also determined the adult male did not comply with Cpl. Nave's direct orders. It was determined, through witness testimony that the victim was in fear for her life and believed the adult male was attempting to reach for her. As the witness described, 'to twist her neck off.'"

(The noise rustles like a bed of crickets being disturbed, as the crowd feels a shift in the investigation.)

"Our investigation on-site of where the shot took place and where the victim's proximity was to the adult male, we have found.

(Inv. K. Dean closes the file. He looks to Nave, looks at the reporters, and looks particularly at Lynn Grace.)

". . . . We have found that the child's life was in imminent danger, which would likely have resulted in serious and even deadly harm. It is the final conclusion that Cpl. Nave acted lawfully, and the use of deadly force was justified to protect and secure the life of an innocent child. Our department will support these findings. A complete report has been delivered to the State Attorney's Office, and a recommendation of justified use of deadly force is this department's final suggestion. We do not expect, and will not support, any charges to be filed against Cpl. Valerio Nave. Furthermore, I will not take any questions. My word and report are final, and all you reporters have the information I am willing to offer. This concludes my report."

As Inv. Dean stands at the microphones collecting his file, reporters still fire questions: "Will we hear from Cpl. Nave?"

"Has the family of the diseased made any comment as to any lawsuit?"

"Can Cpl.. Nave return to work and continue to protect the community?"

"Will the residents finally get extra patrol of the park at night?"

As another question is hurled toward the investigator, who is now turned and walking toward Nave, Nave stands, absorbs a relieving calm, deliberate stare from K. Dean, who leans in to Nave, and asks, "Are you sure you want to talk?"

No answer, just a concentrated stare assures the man, Nave will do what he feels to be right. In almost disbelief, and a black Friday type rush to get their recorders closer to the podium, the reporters are amazed Nave is walking towards the microphones.

You can hear the mumbles of reporters advising, "Nave is giving a statement. Can you believe he is fucking going to give us a statement? He just got cleared and could just walk off."

Nave clearly knows he does not have to address the media. He could simply allow public relations to handle the press. However, a look of a man, who must exhale and rid himself of the trapped emotions, stands before the hushed crowd. Nave has no paper, no file to review, or reference material. He only holds a worn, black leather-folded badge wallet.

Nave speaks, "There is a tragedy in our world, and we see this each morning as we turn on the news, log on to our computers, or sit with our families at night watching TV. Around our state, and every other part of the country, we host another fragment of loss, and worse, the lasting burden on a young girl's life. The girl may get help or counseling, yet the scars she has cannot be healed. This matter also damaged a family unrelated to this girl. The victims are many, and if we take a minute to think; how many closed doors block our view of the next one? What mother sits quiet, protecting a man whom she knows has abused another? How many are watching, listening, or will read this and wonder if they will ever get caught? This sickness has no rehabilitative success!"

Nave pauses, standing straight, and has a calm, stern, almost aggressive look as he collects his coming words:."I was told what to say, how to say it, what is better in the department's view and many more politically correct ways to address the media, if I decided to speak. Well, you are going to hear it from me, the way I am, period!"

A public relations officer rushes to the podium, attempts to pull Nave aside, and pleas to speak away from the microphones.

Nave is direct as usual; in few words, he tells the woman, "If you wish to give a statement, you can do so. You can sugarcoat every detail, and fill these reporters full of the usual department-issued crap; however, I am here to address the community who stood behind me, and more importantly, supported that little girl. So I can do this here, now… or I can do it in private. You tell me, which you prefer?"

The woman laces her fingers and whispers to Nave, "Don't hang yourself; you have a daughter who needs you."

Nave repositions himself to the microphones, and continues to speak."I have no script. I have, however, had the same time to replay every second of that night. There would be no benefit to escort this crowd through every horrific detail. Instead, I want to give you the trail of thoughts I have had to assemble in order to have peace. First; *I have no pity or remorse for terminating the life of the sick individual who was abusing that child!"*[

(Oh the shuffle of the department staff sitting near, the clicks of cameras, and low mutter of agreeing voices in the crowd).

One outburst was clear, "Damn right! You ask me; put a god-damned bullet in all them perverts. Hell, I will donate the ammunition myself!"

(Several other comments project.)

Nave continues, "I have no difficulty in resting, as I know what I did was as I would hope one would do for my child. We are almost brain-washed anymore in the academy, in remedial training, to find a resolution. To seek the least force. To reason and take every possible step to allow the courts and justice system to work. Well. . . *I don't believe in the justice system any longer."*

Now the gasps, the sighs—the reporters salivating with each comment—Cameramen clashing to get the next shot—shots of the crowd, to the staff, and then to Nave. It is unheard of to have such a candid, honest response.

Nave continues with disregard to the commotion in the crowd:

"The department wanted to order psychiatric evaluations. Pending the outcome of the investigation, the department wanted to determine which mental restructuring classes I would attend, and only then would they determine when they felt I could return and be assured that I could be reasonably safe to continue my duties as an officer of this city. So, in my own evaluation. . . . (His trusted friend, Oly, smirks and grins. If you can read lips, you would know she said, "F IN 5150 Nave, you son of a bitch. I love the standup mother fucker you will always be!")

". . . . I took the time to consider what the so-called professionals would ask me. They surely would ask if I felt like I could have done anything different. My answer would be. . . there is nothing different to do in that situation. Then they would ask, if I felt as if I would take the same action if I had it to do over. Well, I stand here before all of you and ask, if it were your child (He looks to the Chief, the Captain, and back to the crowd,). . . . If it were your child that night, what would you have me do? The department doesn't want honest. The department wants to counsel the offenders. The department now wants to counsel the officers. Yet, the community continues to suffer. I truly do not feel I can continue to act in the role of a public servant with the restraints and stipulations, which will be a condition of my return to work in a full, official status. As of today, (He slides the worn black badge/ID holder to the front of the podium, and loosens his grip of it,) I resign my position with this agency. I believe it is unfortunate and pathetic that an officer be subjected to a stigma of guilt until evaluated innocent. This evaluation, no less by a book-educated therapist, who has never worn a badge, never attended an academy, and surely never faced a dark alley with the duty to enter the shadows and not have a pre-test before leaving the lights of safety. This community has been a driving force and I am grateful for each of you."

It looks as if he is about to walk off, and then he stalls. Along with his hesitation, are the curious on-lookers wondering why he stopped. He looks over to the Captain, who in private, told Nave he believed he murdered the guy in the park and personally would not stand behind him.

Nave turns back to the crowd, and particularly Lynn Grace. He states, "This year there will be an election. There is a particular Captain who seeks your vote for a higher office in the city. If you believe in true justice, . . . be sure you do not pull out the seat and welcome this cavity into a position to make vital decisions for your city."

The cameras zoom in on a disturbed, seated captain. Nave walks to his night family. They all knew the end result, and honor his choice. As family will, they try to keep him, yet know he cannot continue, as his view of justice is in a way out new society doesn't quite see.

The nightly news-cast ends with a quiet fade of Nave's frayed wallet resting atop the podium.

CHAPTER 3
Judge Grace

A month passes, and Nave is actually enjoying the fact he doesn't have court, doesn't have the mounting stress of the investigation, and finds that he and his daughter are becoming much closer than before. He and his ex-wife share custody of his daughter, Amanda Dean.

While out teaching his girl how to place her fingers on the laces of a football, she expresses she is determined to be the quarterback of the girls' football team.

Nave jokes, "Good thing you don't have to wear a helmet on the girls' team. You would never get all that hair in there."

He had always known Amanda Dean was not the Barbie doll, prom queen, pretentious type. She would often express her appreciation toward him, as he allowed her to be who she was. He simply enjoyed having her close. She liked to get dirty, loved her go-cart, and yet still had her stunning looks. She just didn't display them for gain or favor.

In the small neighborhood, they know everyone. It is easy to recognize whose cars belong, and if anything is out of place. So when a 69' Dodge Charger slowly comes down the street, they stop throwing the ball, and curiously admire the classic car. Someone had spent many hours restoring this muscle car. It is slightly lowered, painted a deep black with several coats of hand-buffed clear to give it that mirroring reflection as you often see on commercials. The engine forces a lobbing sound produced by a high-octane heartbeat. As they stare, the car slows and eventually stops in front of the yard. The limo tinted windows hide the identity of anyone inside, and Nave orders Amanda into the house. As his right hand maneuvers behind him and under his shirt, he grasps the handle of his H&K 40. Amanda is at the window, Nave in the drive-way, and the long driver door opens. One black pump touches the ground followed by loose, black business slacks, and a light lavender top covered by a dressy business jacket. Ray-Ban sunglasses and a mild frosting of lipstick are very familiar to him now.

Amanda steps back out and asks her dad, "Are you gonna shoot her?"Obviously, this is yet more of Amanda's sarcastic flare. She then asks, "So who's the girl with the really cool car?"He looks to her, and quietly answers, "Oh Dean, this is Lynn Grace."He walks to the end of the drive where she silences the deep rumble of horsepower, and asks, "Okay, are you going to tell me this is your car?"

Lynn caresses the rear quarter panel in either a teasing way or like a car show model would, as she smiles before saying, "Well, I'm not in any hurry to see my daddy kick the bucket, but I am the only child and his sweet precious little girl. So when his time does come . . . .this sweet monster of real American steel and horsepower is all mine!"

A few minutes of gawking at the car, and then Nave asks Amanda if she can leave him to talk with Lynn alone.

As she walks toward the house, she tells them, "You just better not go hot rodding without me"

Lynn removes her shades, and leans against the stone mailbox. She tells Nave, "My dad knows you are a damn good guy. He asked if I could come by and see if you might come and talk with him about some work. He has a friend, who needs a reliable hand, and who can run a portion of the company. He can only have a very trustworthy person. See, the clientele are very well-off, and someone like you has the integrity that my daddy trusts"

He looks to her and asks, "What sort of company or work?"

Lynn doesn't provide much detail. She only knows they deliver parts and even deliver vehicles to very wealthy clients. Stuff you can't get at a local parts store, and she advises for some reason that the clients do not trust shipping companies. She knows enough to advise he would have to travel at times.

She tells him, "If you think about it, please come by when you can."

He assures her he will consider it, and on a day he doesn't have Amanda, he may swing by.

Her thumb depresses the door handle, and she stands between the open door and roof. She hesitates and looks to Nave."It's good to see this side of you."

Amanda sees that Lynn is leaving, and hurries back out. She rifles a bullet to Nave, likely to show Lynn how tough she is before waving good-bye.

Lynn eases out of the neighborhood, echoing a steady growl of the exhaust. The two listen, as the motor opens up, and the bellow of rubber devours the newly paved asphalt.

Amanda asks why she came by, and Nave advises, "Her father wants me to come talk to him about a job."

Amanda appears excited, and replies, "Dad, that might be a good idea. You know savings isn't savings when it becomes more of spendings."

Nave tackles Amanda Dean and they lay in the leaves, as he asks her how she became so smart. They have a solid connection, and she has never had a doubt when it comes to her place with her dad. She also endures the frustration of a father, who is way overprotective, and frequently has officers stop by her lunch table at school. She doesn't realize that his only fear is his daughter. This man could part with any possession; he could vacate anything at a moment's notice. He knows his life is that girl.

A few days pass, and Nave drops Amanda off at school. He drives back, as The Howard Stern radio show goes into a fart monologue. This is a portion of the show in which he finds no humor. He turns the radio off, and in the silence, his mind returns to a possible meeting with Lynn's father. When he returns home, he calls and leaves a message with Lynn to set up a meeting.

Hours later, a return call:."Valerio Nave, this is Judge Grace."

Nave answers, "Judge? Lynn didn't tell me you are a judge."

Judge Grace laughs as he continues, "Well, to her, I am just her old dad. Retired actually. Nave, I am a straight shooter. I have a particular liking for you, and pardon the expression, I would say a damn good judge of character. If you don't mind, when could you come by the house?"

Nave advises he can come the next day at 10:00 a.m.

The judge says, "You are precise and definite. I like that. I will see you tomorrow, and introduce you to Robert. He is the operator of the work you will learn of. Nave, thank you for the call."

Nave spends hours on a manicured lawn and soon Amanda returns home."Padre, it is so nice outside today, don't you think? Being a week day, I'll bet there isn't anyone on our beach."She is not so subtle with her hints.

He gathers a few loose shrub branches and tells her, "Dean, Dean, Dean, your surfboard is already in the truck, and all we need to do is stop at Publix and grab our sandwiches or some fried chicken"

They frequently drive over to the beach, as it is only thirty-minutes away. She wants so badly to be a cool surfer; however, he still has to hold the board for her as she stands. Many times, it is only a few seconds before she is underwater. Nave cherishes the quiet, uncrowded times when he can allow her space to try each ride. They soon sit on the sand, and share the ends of their bread with the many gulls, which dine and dash. Ironically, the birds chant the call of the free meal, and then battle the new arrivals for each piece tossed in the air.

On the Atlantic side, the sun will never drop into the sea and scatter the changing color bands of blue, pink, red, and purple. The night just comes, as does the thunder this evening. Those in Florida have the frequent gift of fascinating lightning shows in the night skies. They travel back and watch high-voltage fingers of nature, energize the night.

The next day, damp, grassy yards produce a steady release of steam in the early sunlight. The retention pond is awake with a few turtles, some cranes, and a clutter crowd of gnats that hover just over the moss. The waters are calm, and only a ripple trail of a single duck, parts the glassy surface.

Amanda sits quietly in the car as Nave drives her to school. As they pull up, he comments on how it is hard to believe the school allows some of the students to wear some of the clothes they do, or the lack thereof.

She looks to him with a quick head flip, and advises, "Oh my God, the clothes are one thing. What disgust me are the nose rings, the eyebrow studs, and tattoos. Padre, some parents just don't care. No worries, I have no desire to have any. . . ANY needles impaling my tender skin. Ha! Too much like a shot, and I don't do shots!"

He kicks her out of the car, and begins his drive to meet Judge Grace. He will likely be at least fifteen minutes early, as being late is not acceptable to him and surely the Judge feels the same.

A long, oak-tree-lined drive is the forefront of the double-crossed, dark, horse fences. It winds through the picturesque fields of well-groomed grounds and horses scattered throughout the property. A final turn up this mile-long, private drive, and he arrives at the home.   Rockscapes, fountains, a small archery lane, and between the detached four-car garage and home, he sees a well-maintained boathouse at the lake's edge. As he stops near the gravel guest parking area, he notices one of the nine-foot entry doors open.

An older, yet very fit man, stands at the door and motions for Nave to come. The man tilts his head down, looks over his half-cut glasses, and tells Nave, "We have a lot to cover, and you being fifteen minutes early has already made the appropriate impression. That which I expected"

The man turns and walks through the door; Nave follows. As they walk through the home, singing can be heard. The clank of a glass on the marble countertop, the opening of a refrigerator door, and more singing of a woman's voice. She is over singing to the radio, and she attempts to match the deep tone of Josh Turner's song, "Eye Candy."The two enter into the sprawling, gourmet kitchen. It is Lynn in a sundress, sandals, and her unkempt, free-flowing hair.

She laughs, takes a drink of cranberry juice, and sings her way into another room.

"You know my daughter, Lynn,"the judge states.

Nave is polite, yet decisive and answers, "No. I actually don't. She covered the story in a remarkable way, she came by the house, yet I can't say that I know her"

The judge raises his eyebrows and agrees. The judge enters an office, sits on the edge of a desk, and folds his arms. He tells Nave, "She sure knows plenty about you. So she thinks. I will say, through this whole bullshit investigation around you, all she did was work on your story and the energy of the public. Honestly, I was glad when it ended so she could enjoy some free time again"

Nave redirects the conversation. He asks in more of a stated manner, "Judge Grace, I know you were a Supreme Court Judge. You handled several high-profile cases in which the defendants were found not guilty because of technicalities. You, by all accounts, have a bold reputation of questionable outcomes. It is unparalleled to my case, yet you sought me out for a job delivering parts and vehicles for very wealthy individuals. I have to be blunt in my wonder of what is it I am truly here for. And who is this Robert guy, who is not here?"

The judge walks over to a window, turns, and answers, "Robert will be here at 10:30. Intentionally, I wanted a few minutes alone, as I needed to get a feel for you myself. He will be very particular in my approval. Yes, I have reviewed everything about you. Nave, everything! So on paper, if you will, you are a solid fit for the trust he needs. Nave, the clients Robert caters to are probably the wealthiest in all the world. If they need a part, or the entire car, they are not going to risk a common fifteen-dollar-an- hour courier, who may likely return later to steal their shit, or worse! It is just another luxury service the wealthy see fit to pay for.""And yes, there is quite a bit more to this, as you are about to discover."

A side door opens, and a Hispanic man comes in."Robert, this is Valerio Nave."

Robert is as straight to the point as Nave would be. He advises, "Nave, the judge likely has told you the one side of our business. The fact you are still here tells me the judge is assured of your trust. Now, I am going to go a little deeper into our range of services."

The side door is still open, and Lynn sits in the breakfast nook. Robert closes the door. Lynn stands, pulls her hair back in a single ponytail, and under her breath and behind a smile, she says to Nave, "Welcome to the family."

CHAPTER 4
Paying Up

The grasses of Juniper Park have been recently mowed. Footballs and Frisbees sail through the humid air. A small toddler is ambitious in her chase of a mallard duck, and the birds rest quietly in the trees. The echoes of that single shot have long parted the fear, which caused the abrupt awakening many dark nights ago. What remains of that night, are the men on the basketball court. Nave pulls into the same parking spot he did that night. He sits looking through the window. Silent, no radio, engine off, as he sits in a thought-provoked pause. Moments later, he opens his door and then the rear door of his truck. His hands full, he has to nudge the door closed with a swift abduction of his right thigh. He walks toward the court, and is quickly noticed.

One of the players spins the tall, tattooed man around as he says, "What the hell boy, look what we have here. Damn hommie, can you smell that! The guys had just arrived there, as they have always on Monday afternoons, just before the night. Nave knows this well. The funnier, small black man, known as, Tyree, stands inside the free throw key. His legs wobbly, he holds the basketball between his ribs and right arm. His left hand is straight out to his left at about shoulder height.

As Nave sits the pizza boxes down, he looks at Charlie. This is the smaller black man's street name.

The man's head tilts back, he closes his eyes, his right arm extends out, and the ball drops to the ground. He speaks to the Lord, "There is a god. This god is good. He is real good. Today is going to be a good day foe sho!"

He walks toward the others licking his fingers one by one in a very dramatic manner. Each finger pops and he says, "Yup, gonna gets mines."

After each finger pop, he then asks, "Okay, Okay, Nave man. Let's see how you done hoooooked a nigga DA, I says DA fuck up! Show hopes you dent fogets the Devil's Spit!!!"

He does a quirky dance in a circle with his finger off his head like devil horns, and he proudly sings, "Pizza and wiiiskaaay, pizza and wiiiiskaaay, pizza and wiiskaay, wiiisakaay, wiiiiskaaay, Fo dis nigga!"

One of the other guys asks Nave, "Yo, ain't bout that Devil's crap, tell me that cooler has some dim Ultras.

Nave opens the white cooler top to reveal just the shiny twist caps of several Ultra bottles bathing in ice. The party has now begun.

The tattooed guy sits his beer down. He looks serious, and tells the others to sit theirs down as well. He gathers the crew and then addresses Nave: Yo, Nave. You a stand-up dude. Had no doubt you would show up and what you did. . . That shit was full on vigilante shit on the true, bro. But like in the right way, you feel me? I tell you true, bro, you ever need a word on the street, you need some real backing, we got you. That's for real. Check this."

Each of the men extend their left hand. There, on their palms, were the outlines of rhino heads. And on the outline of the main rhino horn, was the date of the incident.

He somberly states, "Way we see it, that night, that single shot was for one girl, one community, and justice for so many who still have the pain."

He holds his palm up, and advises he will never forget, never.

The next day, Nave balances his time so he can pick Amanda up from school.

She enjoys him home, yet he has so much more time to be around, more than a daughter her age wants her dad around. She is joking as they drive off, "Padre, you know there are these things that a bunch of kids get on, it then moves magically from street to street, and something amazing happens. Yes! The kids exit right near their homes. They learn this, as it happens every day. Oh, don't worry, it's totally free. Yes, can you believe it? Oh guess what else. Okay hold on, this happens in the mornings too! I know it's hard to believe, and you are probably totally stoked by all this."

He drives, and offers up his thoughts, "Dean, do you know I actually love to pick you up? If I were closer, I would walk you to and from school. Hey. . . there is a great idea. How about we move closer so we could walk each day?"

She banters in return, "Dad! You better not. I am going into the 9th grade. I'm practically a woman now."

He laughs as he says, "Whoa, whoa, Dean! A woman you are not. You have about fifteen years to go on that one. Anyhow, how was school?"

Amanda answers, "Ugh, there are some sick people out there. I am so glad you left the department dad. Yeah, it was cool and all, but the real world is scary. We saw this thing where a guy was trolling the school in Marco Island. He was trying to pick up elementary kids. One kid said the guy did some stuff, but the perv got off. We had a debate on it and even some stupids in the class don't get it. I wish you were in class today and could have set them straight"

He advises, "Well, just be sure you always, ALWAYS stay alert. I can't always be there to watch over you."

Amanda looks, and tilts her head to the side. Her left cheek crinkles toward her eye, as she looks at Nave when she tells him in a joking way, "Seems to me you or your friends are! Like I am in the witness protection program." She laughs, and advises that he should take her to Amigos for chips and salsa.

Sitting at Amigos, she asks how the meeting went. He explains to her if he were to take the job, he would have to travel. He gives very little information on the particulars. He only advises he will be taking cars and parts to very wealthy people.

She likes to express her common sense side in a humorous way. She then mimics the wealthy: "I just won't go to that dreaded O'Reily's and get my own parts."

Then, with a salsa-soaked chip balanced on her tongue, she playfully says, "Oh dearie, could you please pauuusss the Grey Poupon? Also, I am simplaaay way to rich to dunk my own chip in the salsa. You wouldn't mind, so I don't get my Rodeo Drive gloves messy, now would you? That would be simplaaay maaavalous."

Yes, she has a unique perspective of the world, and she is well beyond her years in maturity. She has never had any admiration for pampered types. She is happiest out back shooting her BB gun, playing football, and lying in the hammock. The hammock is her usual location to sit and read. She says the sway under the cypress trees is therapeutic. She has known that sway from an early age. He used to hold her on his chest as an infant, and many times they were found both asleep as night terminated the day's light.

Later that evening, Amanda has her headphones in; her right leg dangles over the edge of the khaki-colored hammock as she taps her toe, giving just a slight sway back and forth.

A perfect opportunity is presented for Nave, as he quietly comes behind her. She is catching every other verse of a No Doubt song, and Nave just kneels behind her head. A few minutes pass, and she stretches her arms above her head. Her hands are near the D ring of the hammock. Nave pokes her palm with a twig.

She jumps and blurts out, "Dad . . . you know I hate . . . well I do not like it when you sneak up on me." She intentionally stops her expression of the word hate, as he has always urged her not have hate. He has her scoot over, and they share the extra wide hammock.

He tells her, "While you were out here singing, and watching stars, and yes the stars sound much better than whatever you were singing, I was chatting with my new boss. Yes, I am taking the position. Do you remember the woman who came by with the cool Charger? If you feel comfortable with her, she may come hang out overnight when I have to travel out of town."

Amanda sits up, and tries to impose her demand: "I am cool with that. But be sure to tell her she isn't babysitting, she isn't telling me what to do, and she better not be weird."

He advises, "I already told her you were capable of taking care of yourself, and I mean that. She would be here just in case of any emergencies. My first trip, I have to go to Jacksonville, pick up a new Bentley, and deliver it to Bal Harbor.

I am not sure, but I will likely have to stay overnight. But I will be back the next day."

The first trip Nave is to take will be with Robert. Robert wants to drive Nave up to Jacksonville, and spend more time getting deeper into the services they provide for the clients. Robert spends time explaining there will be times when he may simply deliver a car, get specialty parts, and even drive these clients to private air strips. Robert lets Nave know that another careful consideration he and the judge had of him was the fact Nave was highly trained in arms and hand to hand combat.

Robert then asks, "You are armed at all times, right?"

Nave looks out the window toward the coastal drive and asks, "Is there a particular reason I need to be armed?"

Nave then looks to Robert and tells him, "See that pull off up on the right? You are going to stop there. And Robert, I am not asking you to stop there. You are going to stop there."

Nave remains silent as they reach the pull off. Once stopped, Nave steps out, and walks over to the old, wooden railing. It is weathered and overgrown; sawgrass sways against it as the sea breeze comes against him.

Robert walks over, arms open, palms out, and his sport coat blowing back in the same sway as the saw grass. He tells Nave, "I only ask for your own protection. Do you realize this is a fantasy land of people who drink bottles of wine that coast more than your truck? These people are backstabbing mother fuckers, who generate a lot of enemies and envy. You go pick up a guy in Bay Hill who is taking a private jet to the Super Bowl, who just fucked over another guy for millions. Next thing you know, you're being followed by some dickhead, who has it out for the guy in your backseat. That is why this pays so damn well."

Nave leans on the rail, and looks toward Robert. Nave is the type who lacks expression, shows no remorse, and gives no indication of his intent or feelings. He advises, "Robert we covered a lot with the judge. I will tell you right now, every person, every car, every package, and anything I handle, will be searched. You must not forget what I stressed in our meeting. I trust no one . . . EVER."

Nave returns to the passenger seat in the Audi A8L, and Robert follows. As he pulls out, Nave looks to Robert and quietly gestures, "Your clients will always be protected."

They arrive at a prestigious, gated entry. The security guard greets Robert, and inquires who Nave might be.

Robert says, "Jason, you do realize my position with Ms. Bennet? You do know her trust in me and what I am to her? Now would I bring just anyone through Ms. Bennet's Gate?"

The guard turns and walks back to the guard house.

Robert looks to Nave and says, "Jason is a solid son of a bitch. He did exactly what Ms. Bennet would have him do. I'm going to have to call her to let us in. Hey, can't blame this dude for keeping her gate secure. Told you these people are a no-shit deal."

On the dash, Robert scans a screen and selects a code. It doesn't show any names, just a six-digit number. Soon, Robert speaks, yet Nave cannot hear the woman. He tells Ms. Bennet of his arrival and that Nave is with him. After a few words, the safe-like, steel pins dislodge from the heavy, square stock framing of the gate. The gate parts, and the guard monitors the area.

After a private meeting with Ms. Bennet, Nave is given the Audi A8L to return home with. Robert takes a liking to the Bentley, and decides he will deliver it to Bal Harbor. As Nave exits the gate, he awaits a classic VW 16-window van loaded with young kids headed in the direction of the beach. He contemplates getting a head start on his return home, or taking a diversion to see the waves just a few miles to the east. The wheels turn toward the memory of his youth, when his toes often went days with no shoes. The sands would cover his feet, and the cold, open rim of a Michelob would wet his lips.

The laughs and sounds of youth have been in his past for many years, yet the true gift of a memory can bring us back when we just allow it to come.

Nave finds a local Publix Supermarket, and then a quiet pullout along the Jacksonville coast. Nave is particularly partial to handmade subs from Publix. Leaning on an old wood beam, bare feet just off the first step of a beach access, he enjoys his sandwich and ice cold Michelob. He finds his solitude in nature–undisturbed, pure, and not dictated by the molestation of human ways. This sanctuary is full of life and sounds. He looks over the berms of sand and dancing sawgrass. It is as if the rolling waves are pushing the wind to embrace the grass and mix the sounds of the water being welcomed by the sands. He listens closely to hear the fizz of sea foam, and the soft coos of overhead gulls seeking a portion of his sub. A few long boards rock under the surfers enjoying the warm Florida waters. Nave knew of this equitable freedom he shared with nature. As a teen, he was that long-haired beach bum sitting atop a fiberglass vessel of true freedom—not knowing, nor caring of the future as he embraced the now. Happy was that moment. As the gulls follow the jet stream, glide through the air, and not have the stresses of reality, he too would allow the ocean to take him where nature decrees. His detour is often necessary to balance his choices in life. Choices many could not fathom or excuse. Knowing that the oceans never stop embracing the beach, and the gulls will migrate to the next feeding hand, Nave absorbs this moment and returns to begin his drive home.

It is dark as Nave pulls into home. Dean comes out, as she notices the different car. Nave goes to close the door, and she stops him as she wants to check out the inside of this "classy ride" as she puts it.

Nave holds a hard-locked briefcase, hugs her, and tells her, "I don't know what all those buttons do; the car is not mine, and unless you want me to sell you, I cannot afford to replace that car. So don't mess anything up! She laughs and as she admires the interior, Nave heads into the house.   He is so pleased to learn that there is baked chicken, potatoes, and his favorite sweet tea.

Dean comes back in and joins Nave. "That is like really nice inside, and has a bunch of cool stuff, but on the outside it looks like a grandpa car, dad."

Nave, quickly replies, "Let me tell you right now. . . if I am a grandpa, you are going to be a widow before you even get married!

"OMG dad, what worries me is I almost believe you! So dad, are you heading out of town? Ms. Badass came by in the Charger, and said you may go down south. She is actually pretty cool. She said she was in the neighborhood, so she decided to drive by because she knew you were with some guy in the Jacksonville area. You better have not gone to the beach without me. How is the chicken? I guess the empty glass means I did okay with the tea. If you go down south, is she coming to stay here? Are you going to be all night, or all week there and back?" Nave calmly looks, as he quietly laughs, "Dean, you're rambling. And when you ramble, you usually want something, want to go somewhere or need to tell me something.

Her head slowly tilts to the left, her thick hair drapes over her shoulder, and she makes slow side-to-side movements as she says, "Okay, so tomorrow is Friday, and there are a few of us, well hopefully I am part of the us, going to the Square for a snack and movie."

Nave is never quick to permit her to do anything. He seems to have a rule to take time to think of all the probabilities for each scenario. It drives Dean nuts, as it does many others, "If I am not here, and something happens, I would not be close enough to help you."

"Dad! If I am home and you are not here, what if someone comes here, what if I fall, or choke on a colossal olive?"

He thinks, he reasons with his counterargument of, "Lynn will be here and she can save you."

"Oh no! I do not need a babysitter."

Nave laughs, "Okay, then take Lynn with you to the movie."

Dean squints as she says, "Right, so take her with me. And how would that work? Do you not think I would look a little weird with a grown-up tagging along?"

"Oh Deanie, I'll tell you what. Let me think about it, and I will leave instructions with Lynn tomorrow."

She slumps back and says, "Great, there is a 50/50 chance of boredom at home."

Nave points a piece of chicken pierced on his fork, "More like a 60/40 chance. Just don't be surprised if I am waiting in the parking lot after the movie. . . IF and only IF you do luck out on that 40 percent chance. This was really good to have dinner with you, and that you thought to do this. I hope you know it means a lot to people when you do things like this. I have to leave early, so I will get my old ass up, see if I can make it to the 'grandpa-car' without a walker, and drive you to school. Then I have to head down to Deerfield Beach and Bal Harbor. If I end up staying down there, I will call you. Lynn will come over at some point to chill here. I put her number on the contact list for you."

Dean is the direct type, just like her father. Her directness is often lightened with a splash of humor. She knows her limits of banter with Nave, and doesn't cross them. However, she also knows she can joke and do it respectfully. She stands at the desk where the contact list is, and as she is turned away from Nave, she asks in a silly tone, "Hmmm Lynn, so she is pretty hot papa. I'm sure you noticed that, didn't you? Simple, almost chill, beach, hippy type. Oh wait that is your type isn't it? Funny, she didn't mention any boyfriend, or guy in her life. And wow, all the sudden she is around. Around the house, watching over me, driving by. Makes me wonder about you two. Wonder, wonder, wonder."

Nave dismisses Dean, "Listen little smarty, she is a reporter who did an amazing job for us, she is fully vested into her career, and. . . AND she is my boss's daughter. Is she attractive? Yes. However, there is a professional relationship here. So you behave and get those ridiculous ideas out of that young, impressionable head of yours."

He tells her he has to check over tomorrow's work, and plan out his day. He takes the briefcase in with him, and sets it on his desk located in his office just off his room. The room is dimly lit by a small desk lamp. The dark red briefcase— still shut. He sits deep into the chair, and eases slightly back. His arms folded, his look, intense, he unfolds his arms, rocks forward, grasps the case, as his right index finger taps a selected set of numbers. Once done, the front of the briefcase flashes with a small, LED, red light. He takes his left thumb, and places it on a small, smooth pad near the metal latch. The red light turns to green, and the latches slide to the side. Nave opens the case, and makes a fist with his right hand; his left wraps over his right, and his nose and lips land against his combined fists. His eyes cold and unblinking, he looks inside of the case.

Nave closes the case top. As the top touches the bottom, the latches slide, and the red light again flashes for a few seconds before going out. Nave takes an odd-looking, flat pad with only a few buttons on the back. He deliberately selects a sequence. On the glass-type pad, an icy blue light slowly illuminates. Nave holds the pad, intensely looks through the dark, gently raises the edge of the pad close to his mouth, and clearly, deeply, says, "The parts will arrive tomorrow."

He lowers the pad, again turns it over, and presses a determined sequence of buttons. The icy blue light on the glass side of the pad then pulses in a quick, rhythmic beat. . . pump, pump. . . pump, pump. . . pump, pump. . . .

The night is quiet and dark, as he lies still with his continual thoughts as repetitive as the pulse of the faint blue light

—dim, yet noticeable on the ceiling. His eyes closed, his mind unrested. Sleep has never been a luxury, and his habits of police work and his past have made this pattern of unrest the norm. With little rest, his performance has never been compromised. The pulse of the blue lights continues as the night passes, and Nave fades to sleep.

CHAPTER 5
Deerfield Beach

Chuck Taylor's in red, jeans with an intentional knee hole, a long-sleeve, jersey-type shirt, a hint of mascara, and a ponytail. And one girl is dressed, ready and done in less than 20 minutes.

Oh how lucky one dad feels that his daughter isn't as many of the tramps in high school; she isn't afraid to be herself, she is casual and bold. He has an admiration for how well she has turned out in light of her mother being absent for the most part. As they drive to school, she again brings up the movies and "hanging out."

"Dean, Lynn will be over, and you must first see if she has an agenda. That is the respectful thing to do. Oh, and if Lynn ends up being a psycho, then call me. Don't worry; I have already had her checked out. After all, you didn't think I would let anyone come here, and me not know her past did you?"

Dean's mouth drops, as she turns to Nave, "Dad, you are a mess. Do you check everyone out?"

"Dean, just make good choices. You are not always in control, and I know that. However, much of your life, you can do the right thing. Not always will that right thing look right to others. Not always will it even seem right to yourself. There will be a part of your limbic brain that will take over, and help you make those decisions. Now, first go to school and get through that mess, and then worry about tonight. If I do make it back, it will be very late."

Dean gets out, and as soon as a friend is spotted—poof! Attention is gone with the slam of the car door. Her world of catching up with friends has an importance far beyond the attention of the guy driving her to school. After all, he is in a grandpa car.

Nave pulls to the end of the parking lot, and takes the pulsing pad from where he had placed it in the center console. There is a modified dock just to the right of the navigation screen. He places the pad with the pulsing blue light to where he can see it. The navigation screen changes to eliminate the normal mapping usually seen. There is a direct route and two markers to indicate an ending location. Now in sync, Nave heads south on the Turnpike. Traffic is light; there is a glare as the overnight thunderstorm has left the road wet. The inconvenient spray off of the tires of large trucks makes for a bothersome need for window wash and wipers. Nave is focused, and in full control. The dangers of the elderly in many areas are ever more evident as a Buick Regal abruptly slows in the fast lane, and then turns sharply to make the exit near the over-55 community neighborhood. Now past the populated areas, Nave can make up time. The Audi A8L is smooth, and comes to a cruise as Nave levels the speed at one hundred and twenty-five mph. He periodically slows for traffic, then quickly accelerates back to one hundred and twenty-five mph. Nave nears the Deerfield Beach cutoff, and the navigation system directs him to a vacant lot in an undeveloped business park. Nave is calm and backs in; his eyes are in a fluid motion checking the mirrors, and scanning the vast area beyond the windshield.

The Navigation system suddenly alerts in a more realistic voice, as if it were a cell phone or intercom: "There will be a white Lincoln Navigator occupied by two. It will arrive in two minutes. The right, back door will come to your side, and will be unlocked. Signal 44 has been secured. Complete delivery is authorized."

Nave is unfazed, and obviously aware of this method. As alerted, the white Navigator stops; Nave enters the rear door, and the Navigator quickly departs the location. With no words, the two men are separated in privacy by a limo-style partition. The navigator calmly makes its way, and then stops at the back of a strip mall in a depressed area of town. Nave exits the SUV, and goes to the rear. The rear lift gate has already opened, and Nave takes a small black bag from the cargo area of the Navigator. The Navigator rear gate closes, and Nave walks away with the bag. There is a swampy, wooded area with thick cover across the way. Beyond the cypress clusters and swamp, is a canal, then a fence, and an open field that is wetland until it reaches a main road approximately a mile away. Nave enters the cluster of trees, and opens the bag. He is wearing gloves, a black ball cap, turned-backward, shirt covering his arms and neck, and slick shoes that are a size and a half too big. He places the pulsing pad in a clip holder around his right upper arm. The pad then pings three times. . . ping. . .
ping. . . ping. This, immediately followed by a one-way message:

"Green Chevy S-10, match subject visual, enter backseat, message match with profile, deliver non-weapon elimination."
The rear of this strip mall is not used, and trash has built up. There sits an abandoned 1986 Toyota Celica with gunshot holes in the side. Old washers and dryers, mattresses, yard waste dropped by the neighboring track subdivisions, and the litter of small, clear, crack baggies and broken crack pipes are scattered

about. There is the sound of tires on wet asphalt, and soon the sight of a green Chevy S10 slowly drives in Nave's direction. The S10 slowly drives past the buildup of trash, slows to a near stop, and creeps along to go around the other side. The S10 then fades out of sight beyond the other side of the abandoned buildings. His patience tells him to stay out of sight, and remain in his location. He continues to be on alert of his entire surroundings.

A dog is rummaging through a black trash bag, and as the matted brown and white dog has the reward of a Church's fried chicken box, it scampers off. Just as the dog clears the drop off behind an old transformer pad, the S10 again slowly approaches, this time even slower. The S10 comes to a stop closer to the trees. There is a white T-shirt on a stick, which has been deliberately secured into the dirt just over the curbing. The S10 parks right at this shirt. A well-dressed man, longer hair, yet well-groomed, looks toward the trees.

Nave exits the wooded area, and comes to the open window of the S10. The man wears a business jacket, button-up shirt, and has white boxers on with his erect penis coming out of the fly.

Nave tells the man, "I'll get in the back."

Nave opens the door directly behind the man, and then closes it. The man reaches over to the passenger seat, and gets a bottle of lotion. He tips the bottle, and dispenses a small amount in his hand. The man reclines the seat, and with his head closer now to Nave, he begins to masturbate. Nave reaches into the black bag with his right hand and with his left hand, reaches up and applies firm pressure under the man's nose just above his lip. The man opens his mouth, and Nave's right hand comes from the

bag and covers the man's mouth then forces it shut. The man's
eyes expand, his body twitches, and in a matter of seconds his
tense body collapses in rest.

The man has the energy to ask, "What . . . what. . .uh . . .
uh—

I . . . I . . . I. don't, I don't understand. What did you do?

Nave is still at the back of the man's slumped head, and
softly tells the man, "I am not a fifteen-year-old boy; I am not the
fourteen-year-old from last year. You will not have to struggle
with your demons any longer. You can rest now. This time, you
will not have to find a way to get off on a technicality. This will
be where and how you will be found. In a few minutes, you will
expire."

Nave leaves the bag, and exits the S10. He walks calmly
along the tree-lined drive, and reaches a path through the trees,
and finally to an old service station. A taxi pulls up, and Nave
simply gets in. The taxi drives off, and the driver never asks,
"Where to?

The taxi has no meter, the driver is unknown, and soon Nave is
back to the Audi A8L. Nave exits the taxi near the rear of the
Audi. He removes the supplied clothing,and it is left in the trunk
of the taxi. Nave removes a change of clothes from the Audi
trunk, and the taxi drives off. He enters the car, and the
customized navigation activates. Nave clips the small pad into
the slot, and the voice activation communicates once
again:"Enter code for successful delivery."   Nave sees the
navigation screen offer a twenty-digit number display and six
letters. He enters a selected code, and the display fades to a blank
screen. The small pad pulsing of the icy blue, stops. A short
delay, and the icy blue round pulses, turns to a flat line, bold,

blue, and constant tone. The tone and display are constant for approximately thirty seconds, and then closes to an inoperative blank-off device. Nave starts the car, and departs the location.

Back at home, Dean is home from school and at the kitchen island with a few friends. She had the feeling she would not be able to go out, and decided to have the friends over to hang out. Typical girls, they have music on, talk about select boys, and then the not-so-usual is Dean discussing playing football.

The other girls discuss the boy on the team they would hope to date or see at the Square, while Dean talks about which one is a decent player and which one sucks. Dean doesn't play on the boys' team, yet is allowed to participate with their practices at times.

The other girls don't realize that Dean is a shoo-in, and on a friend level with many of them.

One girl starts the more inquisitive conversation: "Hey, hey, hey, wait a second! Dean. . . you are playing this all cool, but you know all the guys. So, you better be coming clean. This is some truth-or-dare shit. And the dare is not an option other than if you dare to hold back, we are all jumping you and making you wear a girlie dress and makeup!" This is a real threat as Dean just isn't the dress and makeup type. There is a smaller black girl in the bunch; Talia, she has hazel eyes, tapioca-colored skin, is very high maintenance with salon- prepared hair of curls and color, and clothes that would make many women jealous.

She offers her request as well: "Now Dean, you know I have a certain level of living I enjoy. And even though I am earning my own muuulla, and paving my own path, this girl still needs to know her man is going to have it coming in. Some SERIOUS ends, coming in, so's this girl has ends to spends."

Talia holds her to hands up; her fingers touch her thumbs and create a rubbing motion to indicate the usual illustration of having money. This causes the others to erupt into laughter.

Talia holds one hand up, as her eyes roll shut, and she looks down just as she speaks again: "So, let me ask you this. Darin, the hot chocolate star that stands in the back. Is he doing anything back there? Cause I will tell you, it seems like all the bunch is in a pile while my hot chocolate is back watching. Yeah, once in a while he runs after someone, or chases the ball, but tell me, should I be looking somewhere else? Cause if my hot chocolate is all pussed out and afraid, ain't going to work. I mean, if the boy is good can he be makin' some NFL-type cash?"

Dean displays a friendly, playful smirk, and attempts to explain: "Ughhh, okay, he is a free safety."

"Whoa, Whoa, Uhh, No. What do you mean, FREE? The girl quickly interrupts.

Dean continues, "Listen, meaning he is like free to watch over the quarterback, and track the ball. He is a very important player. Darin is a stud! He already has several colleges scouting him, and he will have a free ride to college. So, your hot chocolate is ALL THAT! Good thing he is getting that scholarship because, sorry to break your money-grubbing heart, his parents are dirt poor."

The small black girl frowns and slumps into a seat.

As the girls compare stories and wishes of what boy they would like to talk to them, there is a knock at the door. Dean looks to a monitor in the kitchen area, and sees it is Lynn.

Dean seems to speak to the monitor and tells Lynn to come in. She indicates that she is in the kitchen.

Another girl very cautiously asks Dean, "The TV was on music, and when the lady knocked, it showed her. Does your dad have the whole place under some high-tech surveillance? And how did it just automatically show just the front door?"

Dean pours some more tea, and loudly and energetically expresses her doomed life in the house of surveillance: "You guys have NOOOO idea. He has this super Sci-Fi system that whenever there is motion anywhere it interrupts the TV, and shows the area."

"That is way cool," one girl says.

"NOT cool when I'm watching something and I have to see a sandhill crane land by our gate. So yeah, if you ever think I am sneaking in or out of Alcatraz, it isn't happening!"

Lynn walks in, as this conversation is taking place: "Oh, girls, just know daddies will always do anything they can to keep their girls safe. Just really sucks when we girls don't always want daddy to know everything! Hey, I grew up with a dad who is a judge, and let me tell you, when a judge says you're guilty . . . when that judge is dad . . . there is no appeal process."

This immediately breaks the ice with the girls. Dean explains who the woman is, and why she is hanging out:

"So girls, what is the big plan for the Friday night?"

Dean politely, yet in disgust, replies, "We wanted to go to the Square and see some friends, eat stuff that is bad for us, and see a movie. However, papa didn't exactly say I could. And if he didn't say I could, that means I can't. I know he is just overprotective, and honestly I have to say, I really like it. OMG do not tell him I said that."

Lynn Grace sits her bag next to a couch, and joins in at the island. She looks at Dean and says, "Your dad told me I was in charge, and if I felt good about it, you could go as long as you contacted me every thirty minutes. He also said something about giving you a ride to meet your friends. Well, it looks like your friends are here so I guess you all need a ride?"

Talia says, "My mom dropped us off, and I have to call her to let her know the plan."

Lynn looks at the girls in an inquisitive manner and asks, "Who drives? Wait, let me be clearer. Who has a valid, unrestricted full license?"

Sarah speaks up and advises that she has had her license almost two years.

Dean leans back against the counter, and asks, "Drive? We don't have a car, and thought you were supposed to come with us if my dad said it was okay."

Lynn states, "Your dad told me I was in charge. He said if things seemed right to allow you to go and make sure you had a ride there and back. He was very precise in his words and clear that you were to have your own ride back, and never to rely on someone to bring you home. So I am just doing what he said. Here are my keys because there is no way my old ass is going to the Square to hang around the adolescent nonsense. I had my trip in that world. This girl is done with that shit. Plus those little fucks will get me in trouble when they gesture stupid sexual shit they can't back up. Girls, I will say this. You burn me, and you lose. Done is done with me. I give respect and if you. . . if you screw it up, that is on you."

Dean and the girls are silent yet cannot remove the admiring grin from their young faces. Lynn hands the girl the keys, and instructs Dean about the thirty-minute check in.

"Every thirty minutes! If you are in the movie, you better still check-in. I don't give a shit about the crap of not using your phone in a movie."

Dean tells the girls they should get going. As they head near the door, Dean says,,"Just wait until you see what we are driving. Believe me, the attention will totally be on us when we pull up. She has this badass Charger."

They are all giddy and excited, as we all remember when we first started driving and finally scored a hot ride to be seen in.

Now at the driveway, four young girls stand in a still disbelief. The small black materialistic girl shakes her head and says, "Uh I just don't do this, Dean! I am not super big on these types of cars. . . well, unless they are foreign. . . however, I am pretty damn sure a

badass Charger does not have a sliding side door, seats eight comfortably, and has Town and Country on the side of it!"

The girls laugh, and in that unexplained phenomenon, say the exact same thing: "Park it in the back!"

The night has been good for the girls, and the atmosphere is upbeat at the Square with young, budding adolescent energy. The language is more than the older generation can often tolerate. This generation has seen the scars of the past and with education and simple mature growth, anyone could come to the Square and see the future has a leap of equality beyond what many would expect. The night has gone by quickly, as it does for younger people, and the crowd begins to thin. The girls finish the movie, and say good-bye to some friends. Dean decides to run back to the restroom quickly, and tells everyone to wait until she gets back. The Square is more of an outdoor-style promenade. The restrooms are just down a hall, and down a concrete staircase. Dean runs over and enters the restroom.

As she comes out, a guy is waiting. He smiles and says, "I saw you earlier and was too shy to come up when you were with your friends. I am not really from here, but want to get to know some people."

Dean tells the guy that he should just keep coming, and he will fit in. It is obvious he is a little older, and not anywhere near the age she is; yet, he is still a younger man.

She attempts to walk away, and he grabs her arm and says, "Wait a second, I didn't get your name. Can't we talk a minute?"

Dean is quick-witted and direct: "End of the night: 1. Creeper outside ladies bathroom; 2. Touching me; 3. These are all strikes, and you are OUT!"

She is keen to all her dad has taught her, and takes the stance of being bold to show no weakness, and seek a way out. She turns to face the guy, and backs away. There is a planter box to her side, and a wall to her other side with a little room to maneuver around him. Her choice is to either squeeze past, or go back into the ladies' bathroom. The ladies' bathroom is an obvious danger area, so she decides to try the squeeze past. The man, approximately six feet, is well-built and wearing a shirt that is at least a size too small to promote the man's excessive time spent at a gym.

As she is about pass him, he stops her. Dean can smell the wreaking odor of whiskey pass through his slow slur of words:

"Oh come on, I really like you, and I just want some time to chat. Maybe give me your number. I'm really a good guy."

Dean feels he isn't really a threat, yet she breaks it down: (end of the night, drunk guy, desperate last attempt to meet a girl type). She tells him, "I'm going back to my friends, and I am going home. You go sleep this off and be a good boy."

He takes offense to this, and replies, "Listen you little bitch, you think you're too. . . ."

The man stops his words, and as he does, Dean looks to her left.

She looks back to the guy, and says, "You're night just went real bad!"

Nave walks toward them, and as he seems to look into the dark soul of the man, he instructs Dean, "Wait at the steps; do not go to your friends yet."

Dean is at the steps, yet cannot see her father and the young man. She hears a faint thud and a noise similar to something being slowly slid along a concrete surface. Nave comes to her, and sees she is not so much shaken by the man, as vulnerable. She expresses her concern for being in trouble for being at the Square and the situation.

Nave looks at her, and she is surprised by the half grin yet still cold stern look. He stands with her and tells her, "Dean, you see now why I have my concerns. I did not come here to spy, to drag you home, or to embarrass you. I had just gotten back into town, and decided to swing in as I had a pretty good feeling you and the other brats would be here. I saw Jessica, and she is the one who let me know you ran over to use the restroom. First off,

I thought it was against the girl code to ever go to the restroom alone."

She interjects, "Dad you know I am not that girl."

"He continues, "Still, listen to me. ALWAYS pair up. Now, here is the part you must do now. You and I will go back, and you speak nothing of this to the girls. More so, do NOT mention this to Lynn. She trusted her judgment, and for her to be a factor in this part of watching you—that has to remain in good standing. Some things, Dean, have to just be."

Dean hugs Nave tight, and with her face buried, she mutters, "You are an amazing dad. I will never forget."

As they walk up the steps, she inquires, "Dad, can I ask you something? The guy, is he going to be alright?"

Nave answers without looking at her, and says in a soft, deliberate tone "No."

As they walk toward the waiting girls, he asks how she is getting home. Dean tells her dad that Lynn let them use her car, and with a quick, surprised look, Nave begins to make a comment about the Charger. As he does, Dean stops walking and displays a comical, disgusted look as she explains the fact they were sporting the minivan. Nave walks the girls to the van, and of course delivers a short lecture about parking in the worst area, and how it could be a prime spot for someone to be waiting for them. The girls drive off, and as Nave walks back toward the building, a deputy's car pulls up. An older deputy sits behind the window with clear safety glasses on. The officers often wear these even at night to protect against people spitting in their eyes, body fluids, etc. The deputy is older, yet in great physical shape; he has a tattoo on his left forearm that has a United States Marine logo, and words that read, "Some only return in our hearts."

He stops and gets out. His hand is extended in a firm handshake as he advises, "Well I had a few of the newer guys go pick up the ass basket near the restroom. Thanks for calling. One of the guys, who does bike patrol here, said he has seen him a few times but never caught him doing anything. He said he always had a weird feeling, and wondered why the guy just hangs around."

The deputy folds his arms, leans against the car, and tells Nave, "People wonder why we don't trust any of these bastards. Hey, when I was younger, sure I would chase the girls until I had no energy left. But this dumb ass is twenty-two years old. I never went scamming on high school girls. What a desperate fuck. Well, they said once they were able to wake him up, he freaked out scared. Oh, he wanted to file a complaint about some guy who caused his injuries. David, the deputy doing the report, told him it was obvious he was drunk and fell down the steps."

Nave tells his old friend, "Hey, I will be doing some private stuff out of town at times; I need you guys to keep a look out for Dean."

Well, this is good for Nave— however, not so much for poor Dean. She already feels like she is watched way too much. Perhaps after tonight, she has a new understanding of why.

"Well buddy, I have a daughter to go hang with. Hope your night is calm. I'll catch up with you down the road," Nave says, as he yawns and cups his forehead.

Nave pulls into the drive, and sits for a second looking at the comforts of the car. He enjoys the elegance and craftsmanship of the interior. Now that work is done, he has a private moment to play with the buttons, and see what the car has to offer. Impressed, he mutters, "It's nice, but you would never get me to pay what they want for these things new.

He grabs the briefcase, and heads in to find Dean. He drops his stuff in his room then heads to the kitchen. The kitchen is the usual gathering spot. Dean is looking through mail, and over on the couch is one sleeping babysitter. Bare feet dangle over the edge of the couch, rough pads that give evidence that her feet don't often have shoes on them. She is wrapped in a San Diego Chargers throw blanket, and next to her long, flowing hair is a cell phone.

Dean asks, "Do you want me to call her?"

Nave walks toward the back sliding door and says, "Nope, I have learned it could be dangerous to wake a strange, sleeping woman. Let's go listen to the night, Dean."

It is a regular thing for them to spend time at night on the hammock. Nave grabs another large blanket, and near the back door, there is a table where he grabs a clicker lighter. There, near the large hammock, are tiki-style candle burners. He lights those to keep the mosquitoes away, and crawls onto the hammock. Dean pulls her hoodie on, covers her head, and rests next to her dad. This is where the majority of their talks take place; it is their place to bond, and to know they are connected. Nave knows one day this hammock will be just a memory for her, yet hopes that the times they spend swaying side to side and watching the night turn darker will be like a moral storage closet for her to open in times he cannot be there for her. Perhaps times when he doesn't have to be, as his investment in his daughter was fortified when it needed to be.

"How did the first job thing go today?" Dean asks.

Nave has his right leg off the side so he can keep them swaying. He replies, "It was really simple and quick. The drive was the longest part."

She laughs, "Well, from what I could see, it was a pretty cushy drive."

"And what about the movie and your night, before that idiot bothered you?"

She gives some info, and discusses a little about the movie, until she realizes her dad was already bored of the ridiculous plot of yet another hip-hop dance challenge movie. It is clear that this wasn't her favorite movie either, but there is simply not much else to do.

As they sway, there is a guest in a dark living room just now opening her eyes. Lynn looks at her phone, and calmly gets up, she sees her keys on the counter, and through the slightly opened vertical blinds, is the orangish flickering of burning citronella candles. She gathers her stuff, and walks over to the sliding door. Still, she watches in admiration, two people who know they are in each other's' lives. She takes a moment concentrating on the look and expressions Dean has. She sees security, a young woman who has faith, a person who is real, and has become that way through an open guidance from a parent, who simply gave her time. Lynn knows Nave has never been excessive in gifts or material things for Dean, and is looking through the glass knowing she is witnessing a rare interaction, where a father is giving his child time—the one gift that cannot be purchased, or have a price. It is a simplistic act that has a value greater than one can calculate. She smiles, and quietly excuses herself to go home.

Nave and Dean will not know Lynn has left for several hours, as they catch up on everything from football to how one of her female teachers dropped a condom out of her purse in class.

Early the next Monday, Nave sits at the kitchen island waiting for his spiced chai tea to cool. His computer is open, and he is reviewing the weekly and monthly work schedule. The back door is open; it is becoming warmer each day. The faint pink and blue clouds are the telling signs that morning is near. Silence is only challenged by the gargled chirps of a few frogs near the pond. A shuffling girl is unwilling to even offer the slightest smile, as she makes her way to the kitchen. She attempts to compare the stress of her school day to come to that of Nave's work. She, like most teenagers, does not have the foresight of how difficult life may become after school.

She comes to her dad's side, and flops her forehead in the middle of his back. "Night school would be soon much better!" she says as mornings are not her strong point.

With incredible effort, she lifts the enormously thick head of hair, and looks over his shoulder. His screen is open to his work task. She looks puzzled. Almost like she doesn't want to believe what she is looking at.

She asks, "Is that what you are really doing this week?"

She looks closer, looks at her father, and then walks to the edge of the island counter. "That is where you are going, and you are doing that? Oh, oh, oh, and you accept money for it?"

Nave doesn't look at her, yet he does answer. "You know I have to work hard so I can give you lunch money."

She takes her yogurt, Simply Orange orange juice, and banana, and walks away. In stride, still lazily, she calls back to her dad, "I don't like it at all!"

Later, a car pulls up, and Dean is off to school. Nave has already left and started his travel. Today, he has to take a rare, solid gold, clock insert to a client in Sarasota. The clock will be installed on a Rolls Royce limited sedan. On the order, it advises this clock insert was valued at $57,000.

On the drive into school, a boy sitting up front asks Dean about what her dad is doing now. It was no secret--the shooting case that went so public. Dean is an open book on most things— sometimes too open. She decides to elaborate on what her father is doing for the week. "My dad is so bad! Today he is going to Sarasota. He is staying the night in a nice hotel then he will have to go to Marco Island on Tuesday. He is leaving a car there, and then as a favor to the client, he is driving a Cadillac Escalade stretch limo back to Daytona Beach."

The boy looks back and asks, "How did he get that sweet gig?"

Dean explains just a little about how her dad knew people, and decided he would do this thing.

"Yeah, so while I slave at school, he gets to play and get paid."

The girl driving looks to Dean in the mirror and jokes, "Looks like we are cruising a Cadi to the dance, hey hey hey!"

The boy is rummaging through his bag while commenting more, "Okay, why don't they just have a car hauler service bring it? See Dean, I told you, your dad scares the shit out of me. That is why I would never date you. I know if I ever did anything wrong . . . missing Jake . . . I would be buried in that pond you have."

He has a pack of gum, and asks everyone in the car if they want a piece and jokes to Dean, "I don't even know if I am allowed to offer you a stick of gum. Just don't tell your dad. I don't want to be killed by choking on gum."

Dean and the rest are just laughing as she tries to dismiss his humor. "OMG, my dad is so nice . . . okay well maybe not to other people, but to me. Plus, the reason he is driving it is because it's too long and the last limo the guy had hauled was messed up after."

"Probably so they can transport a shitload of bodies!" he jokes. Jake seems to like to keep the group laughing.

Chapter 6
Marco Island

Later this day, Nave enjoys a beautiful drive over the Sunshine Skyway Bridge, as he leaves out of St. Petersburg. The mastery of a span four hundred and thirty feet above the passing inlet is almost a peaceful thrill ride for Nave. At the top, is the ironic twist of beauty and tragedy. Placed every so many hundred feet apart are the eerie blue telephones. Not placed for the stranded, they are offered to the lost–for those individuals lost in grief, despair, or the many downfalls brought on by life or by themselves. Each time he passes over this bridge, he has a deep empathy for those who have reached the top and found their only remedy in the step over the rail. The effort it took just to reach the edge was not enough for some to find the will or reason to turn back. To see such a majestic view of life from a height only achieved by the will and bravery of many workers, and the result of perhaps one who could not find the work to keep from leaping off this architectural piece of art is both humbling and awe-inspiring. Each pass reassures him of the gift of a great life, and the ones he has near him. Nave continues smoothly and as usual, way ahead of his appointment time. Time is allowed, as he reaches Sarasota, to explore the town. He finds a small seafood restaurant where he can take a break from his drive, and enjoy lunch with a view of the Gulf Coast.

The walk deck is splintered; the door handle is made of a large Mangrove root and is well-worn over by the many hands before Nave. Inside is bright, and to the right of the hostess podium, with a captain's steering wheel, is a high top table situated perfectly to watch over the car and the Gulf. Nave is particular to keeping a close eye on the car and the gold clock that is in the back seat. There are wall-mounted TVs to each side of the open shutter-style windows. There are few workers; one cheerful girl comes to the table, pulls up a chair, and takes out her order pad. It is unfortunate that service has really suffered in the restaurant industry, so to have a lively, energetic server is a positive start to this lunch break. She has a few suggestions, and one is just what Nave was set to have anyhow—a simple grilled shrimp linguine with garlic butter and oil, and a side of garlic bread.

A couple of state workers are a few tables to Nave's left. There are a few people at the bar, and an older couple at a small booth sharing a platter of bright red snow crab legs. The channel 9 news is continuing a week-long special report on how horribly the state system is at keeping track of the registered sex offenders and pedophiles. The female news anchor shows her emotions as her professional stature is weakening, because there are more discussions on the severity of some crimes committed by a large number of these missing persons. She asks a spokeswoman of a regulatory department, "How is it that a registered offender can be entered into the database or your system, and just vanish?"

The state official attempts an answer, "There are such a large number of individuals in the system, most of whom abide by the requirements and do just as their assigned stipulations dictate, yet we simply do not have the available resources to monitor every offender at all times. If a person is in the system and decides to leave the state, move, or simply vanish, we likely will not know until they miss a probation visit, have a situation in another location, or are alerted in some other way."

The news anchor looks puzzled and says, "It is a known fact that a large number of these offenders, whom our state department cannot find, are serious offenders, repeat offenders, and are suspected to have a tendency to repeat the same, if not more serious acts in the future."

The state official is quick and even interrupts, "I will tell you now and will always stand by my expressed plea that not only in Florida, but on a national level, we simply must pass strict laws, allocate funding, and find better ways to assure we do not allow this to continue."

The anchor is more sympathetic in her expression and agrees with the woman's plea. The anchor then asks, "Do you believe many of these offenders who are missing, are camouflaging themselves in the homeless population, and also fleeing to other states that also don't keep track?"

The state official offers her thoughts, "Many do migrate to small areas where little is asked; some enter into the homeless masses and either direction is alarming. When with the homeless, they are often among likeminded and cannot or do not continue with the mental help they really do need. Regarding those who relocate, we see many continue for a long time with no incident until their inner demons and illnesses are just too overwhelming and they assault once again."

The anchor cues up a fresh, local story out of Dade, County. "As we do this special week-long report, we now learn of a man who apparently committed suicide in the Dade, County area. That report when we return."

The men sitting near Nave openly comment on their aggravation regarding these offenders. The men are not hesitant to state how they would handle it, "I will tell you now, I am all for a fair trial, make sure the person did what they say. But some of these, where they full-on catch the mother fucker . . . no trial, just take um out, pop pop, done. Save the tax payer money."

A woman sitting at the bar is bold to chime in, "Killing the wrong?? is just another wrong act. How do two wrongs make a right?"

Another man in the group debates, "It doesn't make it right, it doesn't make it go away; however, now just hear me, if the person is that sick, and messed up, there is no rehab for this mental illness . . . do you agree?"

She nods and says, "I do agree with you. I am sorry. I just oppose the death penalty and think there should be a way to retain them in a facility to finish life in a more humane manner.

The first man slides his chair so he can face her, "The woman just said how the government doesn't even have the money to monitor them now. Why do you think they are not locked up longer? The government would rather dump them on the street, and just hope they don't do it again. This government is like that with a lot of shit. Waste our money on bullshit Washington crap, and let these baby boy fuckers out here for me and you to have to worry about OUR kids. You tell me Ms., don't kill them, do you have kids? How will that change when your kid comes home and you have to go take that trip down a road no kid and no parent should ever turn down!" He turns around just as the news report is coming back in from commercial.

The news anchor calls back to her lead out story, "Before the break we mentioned a breaking story out of Dade, County where a man who Deerfield Police have identified as Alan Park, was found in his SUV dead from an apparent suicide. Park was one of the many registered sex offenders, who had gone missing for over two years. Park was in the center of a very public case a few years ago when he was found guilty only on lewd conduct of a minor. Park was a cook on a private yacht of an oil tycoon, who lived in the Fort Lauderdale area. Park had failed to register and update his living status as required, yet the State never followed through with locating Park. Yesterday, Deerfield Police issued this statement,

'The Deerfield Police bike patrol was patrolling the abandon strip mall area on the east section of town when they observed a suspicious vehicle. Upon closer investigation, a white male, later identified as Alan Park, was found deceased behind the wheel of his vehicle. Park was alone and initial indications are leading this office to believe Park died of a drug overdose. We are investigating additional clues that have evidence to show Park was arranging to meet or had met an underage male subject. We have no information on the subject, and there is no reason to believe the correspondence of this individual had any contributing factor in Park's death.'"

The news anchor is back on camera, and gives her own opinion then dismisses the afternoon news, as she turns it over to the weather.

The few people eating continue the debate how they would fix the world, what government official is crooked, and objections to having a weather reporter, as one patron feels the weather guy just guesses anyhow. Many feel this way until there is adequate warning now of devastating hurricanes. Yet, not often do we hear praise for saving our overly critical Floridians.

Back en route, and Nave listens to a replay of the morning's Howard Stern radio broadcast off of Sirius radio. Nave often listens for entertainment with rough, sharp realism often disguised with vulgarity and crass, lacerating truths. The navigation is directing him through a pristine almost unreal neighborhood. As he drives slowly, he is taken back by the clean streets and curbs that look as if the HOA must pressure wash each morning. Foliage is manicured, and the homes sit back like framed art work in a gallery. A few more turns and there is a rock arch, an iron gate, and a key pad. Nave activates the intercom, and when asked, he advises of his business there. The gate opens, and Nave carefully drives to avoid the many terra-cotta planters. Nave parks and after getting out of the car, he locks it behind him. Nave stands in the entry patio and finds a decorative pull rope that has indications of being the door chime. A slight pull and a low tugboat-type horn sounds. The door slightly opens, and a tall, slim woman speaks in broken English asking if Nave is here for Mr. Alice. The woman is in an open nightgown; her skin reflects the sun and has an olive, creamy tone. Her midnight black hair ends straightly at her neckline. The gown lies freely open as the woman's perfectly manufactured breasts show they are free to soak up the Florida sun with no tan lines exposed. Light pink panties wrap comfortably around her hips, and her eyes look like the waters of the Caribbean Sea. She elegantly takes Nave's hand and says, "Come, we go to patio. Mr. Alice always in patio on the Mondays. Not on the Tuesdays."

The woman, half exposed, holds Nave's hand as they pass through the hall to the patio. The patio is sculptured in the replica of the front of a ship. Anchors decorate the railing that has uniquely carved pillars. The entire patio offers a view of the marina and inlets. They enter the patio and the six-one model-type woman advises, "Mr. Alice, the man come. I bring him to here. Now you need more drink?"

A small man, no more than five foot five, stands and is abundantly happy. He approaches Nave as if he has been a friend from ages. Nave tells him he has brought the clock

"My clock, you have my clock. Oh, oh, oh, you have no idea how long I have been waiting for that thing." The small man does a weird, funny shuffle and just chuckles as he comes to shake Nave's hand, "Do you have any idea what it has taken to get that clock here and made? There is one guy, ONE, who lives in Switzerland, who does these. Every single piece is solid twenty-four karat gold. It had to be absolutely precise in order to go into my baby. Okay, well, where is it son?" the man says, as he leans back and opens his hands.

Nave has his briefcase, and sets it on a patio table. This briefcase is simpler, and needs only a number code to open. No thumb scan. The case opens, and a small devise is in the case. Mr. Alice asks, "What the hell do you have there? That does not look like a gold clock."

"Nave informs him, "This is a palm and finger scanner. I will need identification and a scan before I release the clock to you. I am absolutely secure, and the reason you have someone like me delivering your clock from Switzerland is you will have the security of knowing all measures are taken to guard your possessions."

The man laughs and says, "Goddamn son, do you have one of those we could guard Tana with? Hell, I guarantee she isn't scanning anyone's cock before she hops on it. You met Tana; she helped you in. Son, let me tell you, it is nice being rich. Did you see that tall amazing creature? Picked her up in Morocco a few months ago. Took the yacht for a little cruise, and brought back a souvenir. Oh, like the rest, she will enjoy the ride for a while then she will get tired of having to sleep with an old man. Then I will be out looking for another. I just have one rule: I keep it over thirty years old. I may be a rich, dirty old man, but I have a daughter who is twenty-five. So I try to keep it five years older than her." He chuckles again and says, "Damn, what am I going to do as she keeps getting older? Hell, I'm sure the Cialis and alcohol will knock me off one of these days." He just smiles and laughs as they scan his information and palm.

Nave receives confirmation that he is Mr. Alice, and returns to the car. He retrieves the small box, and hands it to Mr. Alice. Prior to the arrival of the box, Mr. Alice was sent a special key. He eagerly inserts his key then Nave also has a key he inserts. The box unlocks, and there lay a solid gold Swiss clock to be installed into Mr. Alice's Rolls Royce "Mr. Alice, enjoy your clock, and thank you for the trust you have in our service."

Mr. Alice reaches into his Bermuda shorts, and removes a roll of paper money. "Here, this is for you son. And don't even squawk at accepting this. You did everything just right. The security scan thing was kick-ass. Your boss will know about how you just secured a regular customer."

Nave thanks Mr. Alice, and while standing at the open door of the Audi, Nave sees one of the four garage doors open. A black convertible Bentley exits with a very classy-looking Tana. She waves to Mr. Alice, and he asks, "I wonder what cost me more, this gold clock, or what she may buy on this afternoon shopping trip?"

Nave leaves the questionably happy little man to his purchased life, and departs toward Marco Island. A smooth ride south with his first assignment complete, he is relieved the gold timepiece is gone. Along the coastal horizon, the towering thunderheads form in the afternoon sky. Dark bands of grey under roll the clouds, and distant flickering of lightning chase boats inland. He later arrives at The Marco Island Beach Resort. The moody storm has since past, and the freshness seems to drip from the crisp, swaying palms lining the guest entry. His meeting is early the next morning, and Nave has planned time to run the pristine, sandy shoreline. His balcony door is open; white curtains whip softly behind him, as he sits looking down to his waiting track of sand. Donning a loose black shirt, board shorts, and sandals, Nave leans back, takes in a deep breath, and heads down to the beach. A long wooden dock with spaciously draped trees provides a postcard-like view. A true perk of Nave's new career. With his sandals left at the edge of the wooden walk, grains of sand comfort each step, then each gallop, and soon each expanded stride, as he has an infinite path to run. He has no fancy gadget to tell how far, or how long. Nave runs, and takes in the many views across the ocean, the hotels and homes on land, and the few remaining tanned bodies walking against the sunset. His return, still in stride yet more relaxed, rhythmically continue in the growing dark; he looks to the glow of lights that come from the many boats rocking with the calm waves. The hotels are well-lighted, and there is no person more aware of direction and surroundings than Nave. He slows to walk the last three hundred feet to cool down and relish in the luxury of such a beautiful beach. Given a choice, Nave would take the night beach over the day. He often explained to Dean how the night gives a person a truer sensation of all the wonder of the beach. You have to hear the foam of the receding waves. You can listen to the buildup of each wave, and see the moonlight guide each swell. In the light, it is all just there. You don't have to be a part of the ocean, as you do at night. Talk to a moonlight surfer. He or she will tell you how you have to have a trusting relationship with the water. Nothing taken for granted. You absorb the natural power and beauty. Nave stops to collect his sandals only to find he is too late. Apparently, there was someone who liked them just as well as Nave, and decided to acquire the sandals as their own. Nave shows no frustration nor does he take any time to search for the sandals. Instead, he finds the pleasure of walking barefoot along the wooden pathway, and rinses his feet in the poolside shower. Towels provided at poolside were a good find so he doesn't have to slop through the hall and elevator.

The handcrafted interior of the hotel attracts a very fitting guest demographic. As Nave confidently walks to the elevator, many affluent patrons, superbly dressed, show their peers how easily they can spend a half week's wages of many regular folk on one divine dinner.

While the elevator ascends, an older couple enters with Nave. The woman might believe she has improved her wrinkled and leathered face with the excessive plastering of face paint, and a framed haircut. Her hands, weighted by the gold and rocks the aged man next to her likely bought for the many cover-ups of coming home late from the strip clubs in which he surely pretended one of those poor girls "working her way through college" actually thought his hair plugs looked real, and couldn't-wait- to-see-him-again type nights.

The woman deliberately exchanges places with her husband. She smugly and so ineffectively brings one hand to her nose, careful not to touch it. After all, who knows how much that nose job cost? She mutters rudely to her husband, "I do wish they had strict dress requirements here. I most surely would have waited for the next lift."

Her cowardly husband stares straight so as not to make eye contact with Nave, or his wife. This ridiculous manner of those who self-deem their position in life is comical to Nave, and he takes no offense, yet takes full notice. The doors open at Nave's floor. Nave quietly exits, and hears the woman still mumbling her displeasure of Nave sharing the elevator.

Back home, Dean and Lynn are comparing the importance of a sports scholarship or an academic ride through college. Dean asks Lynn what it took for a reporting gig. "Dean, let me tell you something. Life is not something I believe we can script. Moments change, people change, the technology of life in general is a constant change. The roots of who you are might lay a lot into how you think and what you want to do, yet you have to at some point ask, am I happy?"

Dean replies, "I would be happy to just be rich!"

Lynn looks in a deep, understanding way and tells her, "I love nature, the woods, the unimaginable rising walls of Zion every seventy-two miles of Lake Tahoe, the way the Everglades float with a different ecosystem than almost anywhere, and yet I went through college to major in Law. I am still a very good lawyer, and yet I do not make one penny from my major in Law. I did find through those curtains of uncertainty a gift in helping tell the truth." They both laugh, and Lynn opens the comment of irony that an attorney would seek the truth.

Dean questions, "If you have such a love and passion for nature, the outdoors, and simplicity, then why not work in that field?"

"I do," she answers Dean. "I found that every part of who I am is part of what I do. If I am happy in life, then what part of which pays me is just as much a part of that collective happiness, as in turn, if I don't have that energy from nature, then no matter what I do . . . I would not be successful."

Dean is now totally drawn in to what depth Lynn is sharing. Dean asks, "How do you equate your passion to your career in a way that you feel you are doing what you love for a living?"

Lynn shuffles back deeper in the couch, crosses her abrasive bare feet over her lap, and in perfect posture holds her hands out, palms up. "Okay, here in my left hand is my love of nature. My right is my career. I know what my heart enjoys most, and I also know how to obtain the necessary ways to enjoy that love. I do greatly enjoy reporting. I get to be outside often, and I can take fun stories that deal with outdoors and incorporate the gritty stories, which most stations feed off of. So I earn a living to pay for real-life needs with that, and always know I have a separate fund. That is the 'me fund.'

Dean perks up and expresses how she wants a "me fund."

"Well, yes everyone should have a 'me fund.' I know in order for me to, well . . . be me, I have to encounter new places, see life, places full of people, and some that have seen little to no people. So I plan a few things each year; I set a goal, and decide how much it will cost. I work, pay my 'me fund,' and when I escape on a new adventure . . . okay here is the weird part, and don't laugh . . . I actually pretend I am working as a naturalist." Lynn even offers a little laugh and confides in Dean, "I even write myself a check, and YES intentionally put it in my left hand."

They continue talking about living out dreams with a little fantasy mixed in as well. The respect Lynn shows to Dean makes this more of a casual situation where Dean has all but forgotten Lynn is by label, a babysitter. It was a nice touch when they shared organic tomatoes and a salmon filet at the kitchen island. It was there when Lynn timely expressed that Dean should look at Lynn as she was watching over the house and not Dean. It would not be seen so much as that by Nave, however.

At Marco Island, Nave receives a call from the owner of the limo to be taken back to Daytona Beach. The owner requests to meet for dinner, and they decide to eat at the restaurant in the hotel. Nave joins Mr. Layne, and notices the elevated attention afforded by the restaurant staff. Mr. Layne passed a criminal check, and the usual background safety stuff. Nave privately investigates any contacts. It is apparent the staff likely knows only of the clout and prestige of Mr. Layne, which allows for an immediate walk past many waiting for seats. Mr. Layne and Nave discuss the plans for pickup in the morning, all of which can be done over a phone or email, yet good personal contact is a parallel both men share regarding business. Mr. Layne is one hundred and eighty degrees opposite of Nave's earlier client. He is a large man with white hair receding back from a lightly tanned forehead. His beard is white and sharply groomed. He is a well-spoken man, even with the staff clamoring over his every need. Mr. Layne exhibits a deep respect for each person serving him. Nave quickly takes in that part of the attention of the staff is quite possibly admiration. Seated near a window at the back of the guest area, Nave can see the woman and man from the elevator a few seats to his right. He notices the couple is about to leave when the man looks toward Mr. Layne. He and his wife walk over and indulge in a pretentious gush of nonsensical conversation with Mr. Layne. Politely he smiles, listens, and maintains a demeanor indicating he would be just fine if they had not come over.

The woman clutches her handbag, straightens her back, and looks at Nave, "I don't believe I have had the incredible pleasure of meeting you. I am Mrs. Dawkins." She extends her bent, right hand in Nave's direction.

Nave coldly looks to her husband, who now has tiny sweat beads magnifying the reddening of his forehead. He looks to Mrs. Dawkins and tells her, "Ma'am, the only pleasure you find in me is the company I am in. If I were just in from a run on the beach and someone had stolen my shoes and we shared space in an elevator, would you extend your hand or simply bring it to your nose in disgust?"

The cowardly man quickly excuses his wife, and begs of her to leave Mr. Layne to his dinner and guest. Perhaps not the classiest avenues to take, yet that is just Nave's direct way. Nave lets Mr. Layne in on why he responded as he did; Mr. Layne lets Nave know he likes dealing with people of integrity.

"What do you think of the hotel, Nave?" Mr. Layne asks. Nave and Mr. Layne sit outside while the man has a few drinks. Nave looks over the pool, the trees, and the details of the hotel and answers, "I will let you know something about me, I am pretty opinionated in the good and bad of many things. The landscape, the interior, the food, and no doubt the view are pretty damn exceptional. It doesn't mean a damn thing if the service is crap. I have seen many places that are just like this. Everything looks great; however, the service sucks. I went to Amelia Island with a girlfriend once and yes, it's a beautiful place; however, I have never been back. The people acted as if they didn't even want you there. So, I didn't return"

The man breaks in, raises his half empty Tom Collins, and asks, "Is that how you see this place?"

"Completely the opposite," Nave continues, "I arrived and every person I have had any contact with has been full of life,—helpful, and has just a general sense of wanting to be a part of your stay. I am sure one day I will drag my daughter back down to show her the place. We live near Orlando so we have a quick shot to the beaches there. It's just nice for a road trip to head down to a new place."

Mr. Layne smiles and says, "Well, Marco isn't such a quick jog from Orlando. You might have to make a weekend of it. Do some fishing, and just take it easy. We like it eeeeasy down here," Mr. Layne says still soft spoken and casual.

Mr. Layne stands, as does Nave, and shakes Nave's hand. "Nave, I will have the Cadi here tomorrow at nine a.m. Leave the keys to the Audi at the desk. You tell that girl of yours I want to see her reel in a real fish when you make it back down."

Nave agreeing says, "Well, that girl of mine would be too stubborn to allow anyone to help, especially a guy."

Nave stays on the patio after Mr. Layne leaves.

A woman walks toward him. She is holding two glasses of a dark wine. "I didn't want to interrupt guy time, but I saw you earlier rinsing your feet at the pool. I was with my kids. We just finished dinner, and they went to grandma's house for a few days, so I thought I could come say hello."

Nave smiles and politely explains, "Sorry, but I don't drink on school nights."

Her long black hair falls to the right side of her face, and she mildly laughs, saying, "These are both for me. What kind of girl buys a man a drink to say hi? Okay, yes I was going to offer you one, but I will surely drink both now." The woman is stunning. She has silky, long, straight, thick black hair—light eyes, and bold Italian/Greek features. She is wearing loose black pants, and a fitted top that exposes her dark skin; it is difficult to avoid seeing no need for a bra as her cleavage dips firmly into her shirt. Slightly above that, is a distinct neckline caressed by a black and silver necklace. Her manner is light, classy, and possibly a slight bit flirtatious. She tells Nave, "I am not from around here. My Mom lives here, and once in a while me and the kids come up to visit."

Nave leans against the half wall near the steps and asks, "Where are you from?"

"We live in Key West; however, I spend a lot of time in Miami. I am a designer, and most clients are over that way. What do you do? Do you live here or on vacation?"

Nave finds himself in an awkward moment, as this is the first time he has had to think about what it is he does, and how different it is to say he has a career that isn't law enforcement. He does not want to sound like he is hiding anything. "I work all over the state. I live near Orlando, and have a few clients I needed to visit down here. I guess you could say I am an independent contractor, who specializes in services for wealthy people."

She finishes glass one, and says, "In a way we are doing the same thing. I help rich people design their home interiors and you do whatever it is that you do for rich people. I can't complain though. It has provided a really good life for me and my two tinies." She is now standing closer to Nave. She sets her glass down, and asks if he ever gets down toward Miami or even The Keys.

"Just last week I was near Deerfield Beach. I think I will be heading toward Miami Gardens soon. I don't have a set route or schedule. One day I may have to head to Ocala, then Saint Pete, and then back over to the East Coast. All depends on who wants what, or needs a special part."

She looks out and closes her eyes. "I love the beach at night. Do you want to take a walk?"

Reluctantly, as they reach the very spot the sandals walked away on their own, Nave and Andrea take off their shoes. Andrea holds her designer high heels; Nave puts his shoes under the wooden walking deck. When he explains his earlier situation she says, "Oh my god that is sucky. I just thought you were like this rough, I don't need shoes at the beach, macho guy. Which I have to say, was sorta sexy!" After a long walk, and each divulging of themselves a very minimum of their personal lives, they make it back to a now quiet hotel. Nave finds a chaise lounge and pulls a second close to offer Andrea. He sits down, and reclines back. The second lounge rests empty as Andrea reclines on her side with her thick black hair near Nave's shoulder. "Nave, this has been a nice night. You seem like a decent guy—a little hard to read however, but still a good guy."

He closes his eyes, and lands his nose on the top of her hair to smell the scent of a woman, who is very particular in her appearance and hygiene. His hands know a delicate touch as he follows the curves of her cheek, her eyebrows, down along her ear, and flow between her hair and neck. She exhibits acceptance with a hand over his shoulder and her leg locks over his. She quietly asks, "Can we just listen to the night for a while?"

He is in a place he surprisingly did not expect to be, and tells her, "I would be just fine if we stayed here all night." The night passes into morning, and both decide it is unfortunate they have to get some sort of sleep.

Up early, and Nave goes to check out. As he had expressed to Mr. Layne, the service was stellar. The woman behind the desk brings Nave's hotel information up on the computer. She smiles and asks, "Sir, can you give me a second? I have to get my manager." Another woman comes from the back section with an envelope. "Hello Mr. Baine. (Part of Nave's job and cover is to have fictitious identities.) I was advised to fill you in on the details of your next stay."

Nave looks at her and asks, "My next stay? I am not sure when or if I am coming back. I mean, I love the hotel and the service is amazing so yes, someday I will, yet I am not sure when I can."

She smiles and tells him, "Well, Mr. Layne wanted to be sure you and your daughter hurried back to enjoy a weekend or weekdays of your choice. Totally complimentary as a private guest of Mr. Layne. He also wanted to be sure you advise when you come so he can take you and your daughter out on the fishing boat. So just hold on to this information, and when you do decide to come, just call me; my info is on the card, and we will have everything all set up for you."

Nave is surprised and asks, "So he is going to pay for me and my daughter to come stay?" She looks at Nave and asks, "Did Mr. Layne not tell you he and his wife own this hotel.

CHAPTER 7
Jason Dal

Dean is beyond thrilled as she listens to her dad fill her in on the Marco Island Resort. Even with it being a Tuesday, she feels they should go right then. He explains that could not be possible with the workload he will have for the next few weeks to come. "Dean, I have a lot of travel, and the good part is most of the trips are quick turn arounds, so you don't have to have Lynn stay."

Dean is tossing a football just in front of herself in a simple, spiral action. She advises that it isn't a bad thing to have Lynn around. "Don't get me wrong Padre, no one can take your place, but given the fact you have to be gone at times, Lynn has turned out to be pretty kick (Dean snatches the ball with both hands, bugs her eyes out, and overdramatizes) BOOTY!"

It is no secret that the language in the schools and among youth is more derogatory than a rap song being edited by a drunken sailor from Jersey. Nave has made a great effort to instill a level of strength in Dean, and to exhibit that with class. Dean has her moments, yet finds a respect in herself to speak with a higher level of dignity.

"How are you on your homework?"

Dean looks at him, rolls her eyes and laughingly says, "Dad, it's so easy in school. They give you time to do it in class. Plus the college classes I have are easy." Dean doesn't seem to realize she is a rare student, who just breezes through school. Her mental aptitude is uniquely high, and school has never been a challenge. Sometimes, Nave worries that common sense might be lacking.

Nave grabs his keys and tells Dean, "Amigos shouldn't be too crowded right now. I wonder if I have to eat alone?"

Amigos salsa is perhaps Dean's favorite snack food of all. When she was younger, Nave didn't think she would like it, let alone handle it. As she literally took a straw and drank the juice, after a dare from her dad, he realized she had no problem handling the salsa. Nave and Dean have a favorite booth away from the front; it is more private, yet they are able to see everything. Nave always likes to be able to watch all around. The booth is like another place where they catch up—either the hammock or Amigos, and it is their time.

They walk in, and are quickly greeted with a usual smile of a Mexican woman who is always observant of Dean's growth. The small Mexican woman—yes Mexican as she is from Guadalajara, Mexico, is a small, medium-built, older woman. She has been there since they opened. She has seen the top of Dean's head, and now looks up to see Dean look back down to her.

"Hola, my friends." She comes to them, grabs Dean's hands, and looks at Dean, "I no belieb jew growing too mucho. Ebery days jew coome and more taller. I no more grow for me. You . . . you more growing ebery days." The woman, expressing a true joy, smiles steadily as she takes them to their favorite booth.

"So what do you have coming up?" He opens the conversation.

Dean dribbles salsa from her chin, holds both hands up in a way to stop his words, closes her eyes, and almost whispers past the tortilla chip, "Wait . . . a moment of silence for my mouth is in pure ethnic bliss." She quickly comes back to reality, and lets her dad know she doesn't have anything major. She asks when it gets to summer or on a holiday if she can tag along to see more of Florida, and see what he does.

"There might be a few times I can bring you. It all depends on the client, if I am transporting a car, or just delivering parts. It would be awesome to have you come down south on a Friday or Saturday, and then we could sneak over to the Keys maybe."

Dean agrees and inquires as to when he thinks that may be possible. "Well, these few weeks are out. I have to run all over, and I'm not sure when I have a special meeting with the main guy. I think I have another training thing soon. We want to hook some hi-tech computer up in my truck—also streamline the communication avenues."

They enjoy their early dinner, and head out to Cocoa Beach before sunset. They enjoy another few hours of Nave holding the surfboard as Amanda practices her balance.

Over the next few weeks, Nave is steadily busy with usual business. The feedback from well-established clients is increasing the frequency of business. He now is making his own route schedule with the upgrades in the computer-based, client request format. Nave has it functioning to reduce too much time away from home. This week Nave has his route mapped to pick up a custom leather seat for a Maybach Mercedes. The seat has a Tampa Bay Buccaneer Logo specially made for one of the pro players in Tampa. After that, he will travel up the turnpike to a horse farm in Ocala, Florida to get an antique bridal that had belonged to the very first Kentucky Derby winner, and bring it to a collector in Tallahassee. From there, he will take a trip over to

Destin, then work his way back toward Jacksonville and Saint Augustine.

Nave has already had the advanced systems installed in his truck. After his drop in Tampa, and pickup of the priceless bridal, he heads toward Tallahassee. A little way past Gainesville, the blues of B.B. King silences, and the center dash slides to the right. A navigation screen opens with a small, flashing red dot that is just east on the mapping screen. A woman's voice, live and not of a computer advises, "ES 1912 disregard target."

Nave takes the next exit, and as he pulls off the Turnpike, the woman sternly demands, "ES 1912 10-XT! I repeat, 10-XRAY TANGO.!"

Nave stops in a gas station parking lot, and as he picks up his phone, it rings. Nave sees it is Robert. "Nave, you might have noticed a few upgrades in your truck, which I regretfully did not know were activated. When you arrive in Tallahassee, stand by until I call you. I am headed over to get on the private jet now, and will be in Tallahassee soon."

Nave replies, "The tracking devise I have, this feature is not for normal deliveries obviously. Should I rip this shit out of my truck, or are you going to fill me in here?"

Robert advises, "Nave, this is my fuckup; however, I can't discuss anything in regard to this on a phone. If you want to park the truck, fine. If you want to meet me in Tallahassee, even better, as I don't have a car there. You know what, even better, can you go get lunch, and I will fly into a private airstrip just out of Gainesville."

Nave agrees, and goes a few blocks finding a small, local hamburger stand.

There is a steady line; many local college-age kids order with ease, and there is no need for a menu. After all, as he gets closer, he realizes there isn't a menu. If you know what you want, you ask for it. If the woman doesn't make that, you don't get what you want. So a simple burger, mushrooms, lettuce, tomato, and BBQ sauce is what Nave asks for. The woman is happy, maybe in her early fifties, a faded circle is around her finger to indicate she is likely married, and several photos of what may be her kids are inside. As he waits, he realizes this is not a typical fast-food place. The woman reaches into the refrigerator, grabs a presorted ball of meat, and places it in a steel hand press. Once in more of a traditional hamburger shape and it is slid onto the grill. She takes her plastic gloves back off, and slices a thick section of tomato, pulls a few leaves off the romance lettuce stalk, and then a bowl out of the fridge. In the bowl is a dark, soupy sauce with sliced mushrooms. Soon, Nave is handed a true handcrafted burger. He sits on an old, dirty picnic table. The catsup is hardened into the splintered grainy wood table; the younger crowd clusters near their cars as they listen to Eminem.

Before Nave is finished having lunch, his phone rings. It is Robert. "Here is the GPS ping of where I am. How soon can you be here?"

Nave goes to his truck and advises, "It says I will arrive in twelve minutes." Nave enters a neighborhood where there are signs indicating that aircraft have the right-of-way. Down a long road/air strip, he arrives at a home that has two private leer jets parked to the side. He sees Robert waiting at the side of the closer jet. Nave parks on the grass and joins Robert and one other.

"Nave, this is Jason Dal. This is his home, and he is a trusted friend"

Jason Dal is slender, about six feet tall, expresses a slight friendly look, yet is also very intense as he folds his arms and asks Nave and Robert to come in. The wind blows Dal's long, dark hair as he walks toward a side door. Inside the garage, hangar, and office area, he offers Nave a straight scotch. Nave declines. Jason Dal looks into Nave's eyes, squints, and in a low sway of his head, looks over to Robert. He then turns to the liquor hutch and with his back turned openly states, "I don't know if I trust a man who doesn't accept fine scotch."

Nave still has not had any real explanation as to the codes, the alert on his navigation map, who the woman was talking to him through his truck, or what the red icon was about. He boldly tells both the men, "I don't need you to trust me. I don't know or care who the fuck you are. I do know my truck had some woman talking to me in codes, which apparently I have not had any study sheet for, I am in a hangar, and I have to say if there are any trust issues . . . well, I think me being here is showing a hell of a lot more trust than your glass of fucking scotch. So how about you slam your drink, tell me what you need to tell me, or find a drinking buddy and I can head back to Orlando."

Jason Dal slams his drink, walks over to Robert and gives him the glass Nave declined, and as he looks at Nave, tells Robert, "You did tell me this guy was direct and all business." Jason Dal sits on the edge of his desk and smiles as he talks to Nave. "Nave, I used to be in your shoes. I just wasn't cut out for the fieldwork. I would get nervous, I would back away too soon, and honestly just jeopardized too many critical and, well, profitable situations. However, I have some very valuable connections; I have a brilliant knowledge of satellites and computers. So I found my value to stay in this unique family, and still feel like I am a positive asset."

Robert breaks in to advise that Jason Dal is absolutely vital to the operation, and has been practicing his craft for over twenty years. He explains that the advancements in the company and the military access of tools available are so far advanced, no private entity even has knowledge of it.

Jason gets more excited, and waves the men into the house. In the house, they walk into a large study room. Jason uses a remote and the blinds close. Now, with all windows closed, Jason enters a security code on the screen of his flat-screen TV. It is a normal looking TV with the music channel tuned to classic rock. Now the screen is a real-time satellite view of his home. Two additional screens slide out the sides of the first screen. There on the left, is one geographical area, and the screen to the right shows a menu of several functions. Jason stands at the screen, and in an educational manner begins to tell Nave what he is doing. "Okay, your truck entered what we call a target zone. The target zone is preset to capture an alert ping at random. The ping you noticed was an alert we did not anticipate. That subject was funded, and then moved to California. So now he pops up here, and my team has been doing a full research of his moves. So when your ping hit, we immediately had an alert to pull you off. The woman on your intercom is a member of my team. No one ever knows who she is."

Nave asks, "How do you set these alerts, pings or whatever they are, and what does it do, and why did it show up in my truck?"

He excitedly answers, "There are hundreds of thousands of registered sex offenders across our world. However, most are simply in the system. Could be that some dude was twenty-one, had sex with a seventeen-year-old at a dorm party who was carrying a fake ID, and BAM poor fucker is on the list. Not the best choice, yet is he really a pedophile? So we do not mark those types. The sickos we do mark are the ones clients advise us to research."

Nave adds, "Clients, like Deerfield Beach? Okay, so how do you track the ones you decide to track? I can see if you did it by phone, or a car trace, but what if they don't have a phone or something you can scan?"

Robert is sitting in a richly stitched mahogany-colored, leather chair and gives his input. He tells Nave, "This is where our connections in the judicial system, the world of medicine, and the long list of high-ranking individuals proves very beneficial to our operation. This is in large, why a small, simple mission as Deerfield paid you $125,000. Our organization made slightly over one million for that bag of crap." He continues, "We can access records to see if they have been to a doctor for any reason, if they have been arrested, stopped, have a utility in their name, vehicle records, etc."

Jason is eager to continue his show, "Okay, yes, he is right. I have a team who does nothing but work on ways I can keep track of these pervy fucks! Typically, we are contacted by the client. Once we know they are funded, we can start our process. Yes Nave, I could go on and on about every little detail; however, here it is simply:

First: Client funds the operation;
Second: My team does recon on how to locate;

Then: My team evaluates the subject for a minimum of sixty days;

After that: Evaluation and recommendation for assignment are submitted to this great man in my comfy chair;

Lastly: Assignment is in cue determined on experience, geographical proximity, and risk.

The equipment you have in your vehicle is simple. As time progresses, you will receive more sophisticated technology. If you think the slide navigation, target ping, and system override were impressive, your head will spin as you progress."

Robert calmly adds, "Nave, Jason gets way too excited when he gets to play with his toys. The main focus here is he keeps you safe. He keeps you undetected, and this whole operation is a way to provide closures when the judicial system fails. When we covered the scope of this operation at the Judge's house, you recall the progression process. Not everyone can do what you can do, Nave. You have an impressive background and your ability to have balance is what sets you apart. In time, your assignments will become more direct. As we discussed, you will at times meet privately with the funding client. The risk is greater for you, yet safer for the operations."

Jason opens a new window on the computer, "Nave, or as you may have determined, you are ES 1912. The ES is Elimination Specialist. I am printing out the codes; I will also have you back here next week to spend a few days getting deeper into all I do, what your truck will do, and the vehicles you transport for assignments will do. We have no intent to keep you in the dark. You're the one who keeps this service a reality."

Robert stands and tells the men that there will be a schedule sent to get Nave back next week; however, a scheduled drop for an antique bridal still has to be made.

Nave is back on the road, and quietly absorbs the beautiful Central Florida horse country. After having the moment of muddy clarity, he feels a calm. The drive is now effortless, and it is as if the path has opened for his travel.

Chapter 8
Tallahassee

    Approaching outlaying Tallahassee, his GPS shows his arrival to be in approximately fifteen minutes. There are long, tree-lined roads, winding, with very few homes. Nave slows to be sure to not miss his entry to the house. Night has the area pitch black. A few sparkles of raccoon eyes dart behind the shadowed trees. A few more turns, and he is stopped at the end of the road. To proceed, one must pass through the fortress of rock and heavy timbers comprising the impressive security entrance. There is not a key pad, nor a call box. Only an official sign stating in bold black lettering, "All guests must be escorted in, AND must exit with the same escort! NO EXCEPTIONS!"

    His contemplation has his wheels turned and about to backtrack to a point to which he might get a signal to call, when a Clydesdale pulling an antique carriage arrives at the gate. The carriage is brilliantly restored with tucked upholstery, deep black glossy paint, and gold leaf, hand-carved, large wooden wheels; Lanterns also adorn the corners of this work of art.

    Stepping off the carriage is a stern, yet very attractive woman. High boots, tight mocha paints, a long-sleeved black blouse, and well-brushed, long blonde hair pulled tightly into a single ponytail. To the right side of her tucked in shirt, is a worn leather holster stuffed full of an antique six-shooter. She walks toward the gate and then behind the right portion to be out of sight. The gate begins to vertically raise straight up, along the enormous walls. The woman comes to Nave and with an outreached hand, states, "You don't know how glad I am to see you. I, well we, have been waiting to have this bridle back for longer than I have been alive." She is pleasant, smiles with ease, and has a welcoming manner. "You're just in time for dinner. I am Jann, and that is what I would expect you call me. Not ma'am and surely not Ms."

Nave is not one to impose, nor is he quick to just sit down with anyone he doesn't know. He replies, "Ma'am, I am only here to deliver the bridle. I am sorry my arrival has me interfering with your family's dinner. If it be better, I can wait here with no problem, and you can send for me once you are ready."

She turns, and as she walks toward the carriage, she clearly advises, "Follow me in, your place is already set and out here we honor those who visit us. Besides, you just called me ma'am and now you owe me!"

Arriving at the stable area, she stops near a covered outdoor entertainment gazebo. Nave parks, and goes to where she walked through the flower-covered entry. There are a few ranch hands seated, a small child is feeding two dogs hotdogs, and an older woman is opening a foil-covered tray of smoked meats. "Hope you are okay with real, home-smoked brisket and all-natural, farm-grown veggies?" the older woman directs to Nave. The aroma of hickory is thick in the air. Real butter is soaking long green beans, golden cornbread steams in a pan, and a large glass pitcher sweats a ring on the tablecloth as the sweet ice tea waits to dive into everyone's glasses.

"Just the look of what you have created here is impressive. I wouldn't even think of skipping this," Nave says with a lighter sense of emotion. They all sit and eat; the family chats about farm stuff, tractors, and all the time they waited for this bridle.

Jann is lighthearted, funny, and obviously the forefront of the family. The child, a girl who could only be about twelve, has a guarded attachment to her mother, Jann. The girl seldom makes eye contact with Nave, and finds random entertainment in the available decorations nearest her. Nave pays particular attention to how the girl will dash a small layer of salt on an empty saucer. She takes her index finger and slowly and very gently swirls designs often with one hand as the other loosely clings to the inside of Jann's forearm. Her head rests against her mom, and occasionally the young girl will gain a half smile. All the while, others continue to chat, and decide who will tackle each task on the ranch tomorrow.

Jann raises her glass, as the melted ice lightens the color of the sweet tea, "Well folks, dinner has been a treat; however, Mr. Baine and I must take care of this bridle that I must have in my hands ASAP!"

Nave stands and heads out to get Jann her prize. The two meet near the stable office, and in a secured office, Jann has a wall mount which has been constructed just for this item. She examines the bridle, and carefully compares the tangible antique with many photos. "It is absolutely flawless," she exclaims.

Nave has her enter a code into a small, handheld device, and then scans her right index finger–then her left thumbprint on the printed copy to take back.

She is seated in a light buckskin business chair, and as Nave places the documents and handheld scanner into a secured case, she leans back, and says, "Mr. Baine, we have another matter to discuss." " It's about your daughter. I know she has gone through something that has scared her and your family." Nave exclaims. The woman looks to Nave and says, "I am aware of your unique abilities. I was told you are very secure, and that you will not discuss anything until you have the utmost certainty that any detail is 100 percent classified. I have a basement wine cellar that you may search, scan, and do all the high-tech stuff you do in order to feel secure to discuss our other matters."

Nave and Jann walk across the dirt drive, and they come to the back side of the house. A brick stairwell descends to a knotty pine door. Heavy buckle-style hinges and hand-bent black bars decorate the door window. She depresses a few numeric buttons and then inserts a large key into the lock. On the way over, Nave had stopped to collect a rectangular case, which he brought inside. She advises she will step out while Nave scans the room for any recorders, bugs, vents, or other devices which may be used to capture any part of their conversation.

Nave grabs a chair, and places it in the center of the room. "Ma'am, I will need you to stay and sit still in this chair as I scan your room." Over the next ten minutes, Nave sets up small, solid black cone-shaped objects in different areas of the small cellar. All have peel-back strips adhere-able to the surfaces which he places there. He places several on the ceiling and many throughout the cellar. Then on a tripod, Nave screws a silver box with a dark glass-like top onto the tripod. Visual inspections are done, and now Nave again tells Jann, "This is very important that you do not move for just a few seconds. I am going to activate the sensor, and turn out the lights. You will see green beams. They are completely harmless, and only used to detect anything electronic which can be used to transmit, record, or collect audible tones." Nave turns out the light, and turns the sector on. One beam instantaneously flashes to a ceiling mount. One by one, the beams connect to the small receivers Nave had placed throughout the cellar. After all connections have been made to the sensors, the unit on the tripod gives a light-toned chirp. A red beam goes directly from the unit to the right side of Jann. Nave is not concerned, and goes near Jann.

She looks to Nave and cautious asks, "Is it my phone?"

Nave tells her to take her phone out and notice that the red beam will precisely follow the device." See Jann, there can be absolutely no conversation until we are BOTH protected."

The cellar is secured, and now Nave and Jann are able to talk about the matter which Jann has requested him to stay for. Jann sits on a small bench. The fabric is red velvet with gold fringe tassels lining the bottom of the seat.

Her hands are palm- to palm and wedged between her knees. Her shoulders are slightly lunged forward as her head tilts back. "I will tell you from start to present, and I hope you will decide to help us. A few years ago, we had a man working horses and doing a lot of work around our ranch. As with anyone, the maids, the gardeners, anyone who works here, we run full background checks and check references. My husband could not speak any higher of anyone we had ever had working here. Over time, Jason became closer to the family. He would run the horses more than anyone. He would offer his help even past the times we would pay him. He would often join us for our patio picnics as he would be here late. During the busier season, he was here before the sun and after the moon had broken the sky. We worried about his drive, as he lived nearly an hour away. We have an outbuilding with power and hook ups often used for guests, so we decided to suggest that Jason haul his trailer up, and just stay on the nights he was too tired to drive. That year, he usually would come in on a Monday and stay until Friday—

sometimes even Saturday when Mark—sorry Mark is my husband." There are obvious signs of sadness, as her eyes are now red and glassy. "When Mark really needed to get ready. Toward the end of the summer, there was a little more occasional free time and Jason loved to fish in our private lakes." (Jann stops, and her head drops. As rain on the concrete sidewalk shows the first drops of a cloud soon to open, the dark wet spots appear one by one on her mocha colored pants.) "This is hard, yet I know you will bear with me. Our daughter loved to fish; and many times she would come running back to the house with a fish. She would be smiling and almost singing, 'I caught us some dinner, I caught us some dinner' with her head bopping and ponytail just dancing behind her. That little girl loved to fish, and if her daddy wasn't around to take her, once in a while Jason would drag her along. Just a few weeks before the heavy work would have been done, Mark had to take a few horses down to Ocala and then to Miami. Mark was going to be gone for just over a week. He left on Sunday, and on Thursday our daughter had complained of being sick. She was drawn, very unusually quiet, and said she had a stomachache. I took her to the doctor, and in the office she told the doctor some of her pain was in her private area." (Her hand cups her chin now, and a quick puff of breath as she continues the story of the time in the doctor's office.) "I never even thought it was anything bad. I thought, our poor little girl has a UTI and needs some cranberry juice and maybe some medication."

"The doctor examined her, and looked concerned. He asked if we could speak privately. He sat down, crossed his hands and told me, 'Jann, there are many things that could be the scenario with your daughter, and I want you to bring her in and really talk to her. Your daughter's hymen is not intact; she has likely been hiding the bleeding, and we need to find out what has caused this. Now do NOT jump to any conclusions, as I have seen this happen when young girls have accidents, explore at an early age, and yet we just cannot ignore the unimaginable that your daughter could have been sexually assaulted. I need you to talk to her, and if she has been, we have to notify the police immediately.'"

"I was in shock. I am not sure even how long I just stared at that doctor, who is a family friend, and just attempted to process what he just said. Mr. Baine, I had taken my daughter in to see why she was sick and it hit like a brick— this morbid conversation of what the doctor just told me." (Jann completely breaks down and sobs, muttering through her draining nose and tears.) "I had to sit in a doctor's office, and see my little girl cry telling me how that fucking animal put his dirty fingers inside her." (She sits upright, and uses another tissue on her nose.) "We went directly to the sheriff's office, and they took her statement. That night, they came and arrested him on my property. I had invited the wolf right into our home, and put my little girl in his reach. For so long, I had deep guilt and always will. I have found ways to get past it, and I and my little girl never part unless my mom or sister is with her. That night, I sat with my phone in my hand trying to push the buttons to call Mark. There was twice when Mark had called when I was holding the phone, and I could not answer. Finally, when all my energy was evaporated and the sadness had just breached all my walls, I called. Every aspect of this assault on our family was just compounding more and more. First, I could not protect my only little girl. Second, she had to face a doctor and relive this over and over with the police. Now,

I am on the phone with her daddy and I can't be there for him. I did know enough to have Jason arrested before Mark came home. No doubt Mark would have killed him, and I didn't want to see her lose her daddy too." (Her head gently tilts, and she looks to Nave.) "Well, that didn't work too well. See, when the hearing was scheduled, Mark decided to show up at the courthouse, and tried to get in with a gun. I will say, the security scanners at the court are all that saved my husband from being in jail for five years as opposed to life if he had made it to Jason. Yeah, it's been a shitty few years for us around here. So that year, I spent much of my time hoping one man goes to prison for life and another is found not guilty. I guess you know as well as most, the legal system is a corrupt, unjust pile of crap!" (She stands and pours a merlot. One hand holding the glass, the other rests on her forearm.)"My daughter could not testify; she was too scared and as much as I tried to comfort her, she still could not do it. She has shut that part of her memory down after the interview with the deputy. The deputy, and she did all she could, I will say that for her, was not able to show enough evidence from the interview, and there were also the bullshit technicalities. Nave, how can a jury possibly not see who this guy is–a piece of shit? They came back a hung jury, and later the prosecutor stated until there could be clear and decisive evidence, they could not proceed with the case. He was free to go and likely prey on another child."

She tilts the glass back, sits the empty glass on the drum to her side, and says, "Mr. Baine, I can't lose my husband when he gets out next year. More than that, our family, my precious little girl, could in no way handle reliving this horror for years in court. We are not pursuing the case. The judge, the judge you know well, is who connected us. We don't want to know the man could ever do this to anyone's child and surely more."

Nave depresses a button on the unit. All the beams extinguish, and he collects each sensor. He closes his case, walks to the door, and before he opens it he tells Jann, "The judge will be in touch once I confirm the legitimacy of everything." He walks out, and she sits in the dark room on the red velvet chair sobbing.

Chapter 9
Dean Finds Bugs

A day later, Amanda is in the garage with a few of her friends looking for Nave's old skateboard. She has been bragging how her dad used to be a rebel California wild child. She is on a ladder trying to reach the garage ceiling door, which gives access to the attic. Two young girls are holding the ladder; as Dean is close to the top, Nave pulls in.

With a curious concern on his face Nave asks, "Just what are you doing and what are you looking for?"

Dean pushes the popcorn ceiling cover-up to one side as she answers, "We all decided to skateboard up and down the street, and I remembered you had that cool, old skateboard up in the box you keep all your collectables in."

"Dean, you understand what collectable means? It usually means one who has collected, preserved as original, and placed in a box or other container so others will not gain any use of such, intends that such collectable not be used, and certainly not be subjected to any risk of damage."

At first, a drape of hair falls past the ceiling opening, then Dean's smiling face as she smiles and asks, "Okay, I will not ride it, but at least let me show them how cool it was."

"Dean, do you know that game, hot or cold? Being up in the attic is probably hot, yet in your search you would be cold," he jokes with her.

"Dad, there is some cool stuff up here." She tells the other girls to come check some stuff out. Nave holds the ladder and in firm voice tells the curious girls to be extra careful and not to come down until he comes back to hold the ladder for them. The space above the garage is tight, yet has a floor and is well-kept. Random, neatly placed totes and boxes line the edge of the walls, each marked to hint what is inside. The girls are looking through a box marked, "Old school art," another "misc collectables," and one girl sees one marked, "spy equip."

"Dean, can we look through this one?" one girl asks. The box is old, and has signs that the tape has been removed and reapplied many times. Dean has her friend slide it to her, and begins to open it. She carefully removes a small black box with a plug-in and a meter; she has no idea what it is used for. Then one girl pulls out a black plastic disc that has a handle on the bottom. The disc is very similar to a modern-day, small satellite dish, yet only eight inches in diameter. There is a c-cup shaped holder directly in the center of the disc, and on the bottom of the handle are two metal receiver-type jacks that wires would be plugged into.

"What is this, and how do you use it?" one girl asks. "Maybe your dad goes out back and gets signals from E.T."

As they laugh, the second friend gets on her knees, holds her right hand out, extends her index finger, and begins to mimic the movie, E.T. "E.T., phone home, E.T. phone home." As she has the disc in her other hand, she stumbles and topples over. Dean continues to look through some clear, Ziploc-type bags. She opens one, and inside she finds small, hard, round pieces with needles protruding from them. There are different colors with "Hz" just after the numbers. She rummages through a few more packages, and finds one with an order pamphlet and basic instructions.

Dean tosses it over to her friend and says, "Hey, nerd geek, read these and translate what it says so us regular earth people can understand it."

The girl flips a few pages, and then examines the very small objects with sharp needles coming from them. As she looks over these, Dean pulls another piece from the box that looks very similar to a flashlight; however, one end only has a mesh-type cover and the other a single metal receiver jack like the one on the disc. "I wonder if this is a microphone," Dean tells the girls as she holds it up to her mouth and starts singing in her comic, deep, funny voice, *"I'm too sexy for this shirt, for this shirt, so sexy it hurts. I am a model, you know I'm a model, I do my little dance on the cat walk, on the cat walk, on the cat walk, I do my little dance on the cat walk."* Her hips over-exaggerate to each side, her shoulders pounce in a jerk from side to side, and she has a very animated sexy-girl look on her face.

The girl, who has been studying, interrupts and in a whisper-type shout declares, "Dean, Dean, stop. Do you know what this is? Oh my God Dean, your dad is like CIA, FBI, or some sort of spy. This is all high-tech spy stuff. These little thumbtack thingies are bugs. The disc is high-powered; listen to the bad guy microphone. Yeah, the flashlight with no light . . . that is the microphone."

Dean drops over to where she is, and looks closer. "Shut up! This is so cool." Dean then tells them they should probably not say anything, and just put it back. She diverts their attention to the skateboard down in the regular area of the garage.

The girls place the items back, and Dean hollers to her dad, "Padre, Padre, save us. We are trapped and need to be saved. Please don't keep us locked in the attic forever."

Nave comes out and holds the ladder, and the girls come down. He asks if they had found anything good and they quietly just reply as if they didn't see much.

After dinner, they take a walk around the neighborhood. Around one corner, are a few farms and one has very large Clydesdale horses that love to come to the fence as there are not many times Amanda Dean hasn't brought a few cut apples for them. "Dad, isn't it amazing how such a powerful animal can be so calm? They will do as we train them, work to no end for man, yet they could easily overpower even the strongest man on earth." She rubs the firm nose of the horses, and the deep brown eyes of the animals glimmer as they soak up the attention. After a brief stop, they continue to walk. Two of the enormous horses slowly follow along the fence line to the end of their property. Their majestic heads lean over, and snouts flutter with noise from their noses. The sun now seems to have sped up its decent to drop into the western horizon allowing a color pallet of pinks, pastel purples, and hues of many oranges. A race car blue smoothly darkening into the higher skies, clear and a bit cooler than normal.

"Dad, can we just chill on the hammock tonight?" Both of them have to be up early, and Amanda Dean has really wanted to catch up with her dad.

"I will make you a deal, Ms. Dean." Nave grabs her around the neck and pulls her close. He tells her the deal: "When we get home, you set out the Hagen Daas chocolate, chocolate chip, I will start the fire, and we can kick back for as long as you want."

The night is clear, there is no moon, and the stars are brilliantly twinkling in the many clusters. Away from the city lights, their neighborhood allows for amazing views of the night skies. The fire pops and crackles. Small smoke heat funnels wisp from the fire pit. Aromatic natural wood hovers around the yard, and in the distance, the sound of small green tree frogs sing back and forth. The hammock sways; Nave holds the pint of ice cream with a small washcloth, and they each have their own spoon that often clinks as they race to get the next scoop. Sitting facing each other, Nave in a San Diego Chargers pullover and Amanda Dean wrapped in a Tampa Bay Bucs blanket, they trade stories about when she was young, and how Amanda always made him lie on the couch to watch Barney the dinosaur. "Dad, I can't believe I liked that."

Nave's right hand taps her nose with his spoon and he tells her, "Not only did you like it, you made me sing the stupid thing to you all the time! 'I love you, you love me, we're a happy family, with a great big kiss and a hug . . .'"

She interrupts telling him to stop, and that he is not allowed to sing that song anymore.

"Oh you think it's silly now, and YES it was torture to sit through it, however, you were little and little kids love those shows. Plus, it always seemed to have a good message." Nave slides his spoon around the bottom of the container and comes out with the last spoonful. "Look here Dean, the last spoon of the best ice cream ever. Now if I were a nice dad, I would pass this right over and give this creamy, chunky, sweet mouthful of pure chocolate heaven to my angel of a girl."

Amanda Dean tilts her head as she usually does, and smiles in her reply, "Awe my daddy does love me, and will give me that last bite". The spoon's course abruptly aborts the path toward Amanda Dean, and is redirected by the power of Nave's will to be headed hastily back in Nave's direction.

She has her mouth open in shock; her eyes open just as wide, and she makes her final plea. "Padre, you would not dare!

In a swift snap, the spoon is ejected clean and shiny. There is no trace of the last scoop, which Amanda Dean truly thought would be hers. "Oh my Deanie, I do love you, yet giving you that last bite is not how I decided to show my love tonight. You know what though? Seems that last bite lasts longer. Hey Dean, it's like the chocolate chunks are just embedded in my taste buds. Wow, it was the best bite of them all!"

She does not seem to share his amusement and tells him, "Wow, hope I don't remember this around Father's Day. Maybe I will wrap up an empty carton and a used spoon, and see how you like it!" She can't help but giggle over her humor.

They lie back, and Amanda Dean cautiously enquires about the stuff they had found earlier. "Dad, can I ask you something?"

"Dean, you know you have always been able to talk to me about anything"

"This job you do, it isn't really what it seems is it? When we were up in the garage, we found stuff we probably were not supposed to find. I think you work for the government or military and are some super, under-the-radar spy or something."

Nave gives a crooked smile, and quietly laughs as he tells her, "Oh Dean, the young mind does like to wander. You are talking about the old box of outdated stuff with the handheld mega ear disc?"

"Well, yeah. Look dad, you go on these trips, you have secret cars, and speak in codes on the phone. You say you are just going for work, but I bet you are flying off to some foreign country, doing some covert ops stuff, and hurrying back. I just want to know so I can be safe. Plus, I don't want you to forget to come home . . . if you know what I mean."

"I can tell you I am not a spy. Plus, did you happen to see the dates those antiques were made? Not likely I would be a very good spy if I had to use old shit like that. I got that stuff from a yard sale years ago. I thought it was cool and who knows, maybe there are more of those bugs planted all around our house? Hmmmm, just what do I know?"

"Dad, you better not! Oh, I am going to check everything now."

He covers her face with his hand, and jokes as he tells her, "Silly girl, I would rather listen to all those Barney songs before listening to you and your friends' drama all day."

Amanda laughs and agrees that it would not be so good if he used old, outdated gadgets. They douse the fire, and head in for the night. She gets a drink, sets the glass down, and jokes, "Oh I know . . . you're a hitman for hire."

As she imitates a person holding a gun and laughs it off, Nave walks away and tells her to stop imagining things. "Dean, you're going to end up having nightmares".

Chapter 10
<u>Horse</u>

A few weeks have passed with Nave enjoying regular work. Today, Nave receives an alert to keep next week's calendar open and await a notice. Nave goes into a whole different mode when he anticipates a special assignment. Each day is two trips to the gym, and often extra time in the garage on the heavy bag and jump rope. In the gym, he usually keeps to himself and just gets in and out. The afternoon trip is hard as he has to go at a busier time in order to be home for Amanda. This day he pulls in and the parking lot is not only full, but several cars are parked sideways, covering two spots this likely due to the owners' self-egregious belief that their car needs to be recognized and deserves extra space. Nave takes great pride in not having his truck scratched. He also takes pride in the fact that he does not crowd others' space; thus, he usually will park well away from others. So around the back of the gym and clear of the cluster, he is fine with the extra walking. As he approaches the door, he sees a woman a few feet away. Politely, he holds the door. High-dollar yoga pants, designer top, matching Nike running shoes that look as if they have never been used, fresh makeup, hair freshly done in a fancy pulled back braid, sunglasses on, and headphones in, she slowly walks past Nave with no acknowledgement of the kind gesture. The woman stops to talk with the girl scanning the members as they check in. Nave also hands the girl his scan card.

The girl behind the check-in desk is always upbeat and inviting. "Hey, Mr. two-times-a-day, whatta ya know?"

Nave looks at her, looks at the rude pampered woman, and replies, "Oh I know a decorated woman who ignorantly believes she has or is everything, but really has nothing if she lacks the class and appreciation for what others do for her."

The girl behind the desk laughs and tells Nave, "You have no filter, do you?"

As he walks away he lets her know, "That was filtered!" It is one of those crazy days where it is almost counter productive to even try and get a good workout. Between being busy and the fact many are in the gym to socialize, Nave has to repeatedly wait or change what he will do. Some meathead, who seems to have a diet of energy drinks, steroids, and frequent trips to the tanning booth, is grunting, slamming weights, and only stops to study himself in the mirror. After coming back several times, Nave finally notices the guy has moved on. Of course, he left the bar completely loaded as many dip shit bodybuilders do so everyone can see how super incredibly strong they are. Nave takes some of the weight off, and slides the flat bench out of the way.

Moments later, the guy comes walking back. "Whoa, whoa, bro. Sorry, man I have a few more sets here. I am in super set mode and gotta hit this shit hard, man. Let me knock a few more sets out, and you can have it. You know how it is, right bro? Not quite done my man." The guy's eyes are bugging, and the fake tan is darkly lined to highlight his bleached white short-spiked hair. One arm is decorated around his bicep with a tattoo that reads, "All about being ripped." He has an enormous, clear-studded earring likely to be mistaken for a large diamond. The poster child for a gym rat stands at the bar, as if Nave is supposed to simply succumb to the delusional idea that the entire gym is this guy's personal training facility.

Nave is on the other side of the bar, leans in closer, looks at the guy, and tells him, "I am NOT your bro, or your man, and you are done on this machine for about ten minutes. You know how it is . . . right?" The guy goes off to the other seated machine he came from; several other guys are with him, and he makes it noticeable that he thinks Nave is a dick for jumping in on the other machine. Nave could care less, goes on with working out, and soon finishes up with what he wanted to get done for the day in the gym. He knows the guy is still suffering from his steroid rage, yet has no interest in even letting the guy feel he is a factor.

He walks past the desk, and the girl calls him over. "That was the funniest thing when you made that chick feel like a pretentious little snot. She lives down the street from my parents' house up in the foofoo area. Her husband is like this old, creepy guy who owns a ton of property and she just spends the money. She totally comes in here just to push her fake boobs out, and find young guys to sneak off with because you know, even the little blue pill isn't getting her old geezer man excited."

Nave tells the girl she is a mess and turns to walk out. Well, Nave's new friend is puffed up, and giving some girl advice that clearly the girl had not asked for. It is more that these guys feel they have to impart their bodybuilding knowledge upon poor, helpless girls who already have great bodies.

The girl is working hard to be polite and struggles a few smiles, a head nod, and as she attempts to slide away, the guy notices Nave. "It just gets hard in here to get a decent workout when ignorant dickheads fuck up your supersets. Like this fucktard!" The guy is holding a gallon water jug, and points directly at Nave. Nave is just to the right of the girl, who seems to be a little inquisitively shocked. Nave looks back into the gym area,looks back to the guy and tells him, "Looks like YOUR machine is free; you can get that superset all done and see if that might impress someone."

The girl laughs, and the guy steps closer to Nave. He is not quiet when he says, "You are going to think you are pretty funny when I kick your ass." The guy gives a stupid smirk, and puts his left hand on Nave's shoulder. "Listen fucktard, I suggest you don't get in my way again. You might get yourself hurt." Now a few more have loosely gathered, as the scene has become more noticeable as a real confrontation.

Nave's eyes are cold, direct, and the small black hand towel he holds drops quietly to the floor. "You are going to take your hand off my shoulder, you are going to step back, and I am going to peacefully walk out that door. If you don't . . . you are probably going to have a broken arm." Nave was quiet in his brief warning, yet as calm as the crowd was, many could hear what he said. The forearm of the guy shows defined muscle flex; his lips clench, and just as he starts to say something, Nave's left hand speeds to grasp the man's hand, pulls it in a reverse motion, Nave's right hand then slams the other side of the guy's same hand, and pushes it backward against the natural way it would normally bend. The guy spins; his left knee drops to the floor, and in a quick jerk, Nave snaps the guy's wrist. A loud pop is heard, and sudden gasps of onlookers as it was undoubtedly clear that the guy was in agony. "Right now, you are in a lot of pain; however, I just broke your wrist. Here is where you get a second chance to not be a total dumb fuck. I can release your hand; you go get it fixed, and move on. Or you can be stupid, keep trying to fight me, and I will snap your arm. That will not heal so well. Your choice." Nave is calm, and emotionless. The guy is embarrassed and humbled, and Nave drops the guy's hand which flops painfully to the floor.

A guy close to the small, gathered crowd mutters, "Damn, that don't look right. Homeboy's hand is pointing the wrong way. Hope that isn't his jerking hand." Another in the crowd talks to her friend, "Oh my god, so glad I was here to see that. That muscle head is a total tool. He had that coming." Nave picks up his towel, gets his keys off the hook, and calmly walks out the door.

He sits calmly in his truck. Just then, the echos of thunder vibrates the truck and dime- sized drops of rain terminate their fall along his window. As he pulls away he says to himself, "Yeah, pretty much that sort of day I guess!"

A few miles down the road, his radio silences as it did in Gainesville; the screen slides, and the woman's voice announces "ES 1912, advise 10-40."

Nave replies as he pulls into a parking lot, "10-4; 10-40."

The woman continues, "ES 1912, confirm information sent to signal 09-06. Confirmation allowance, six hours. This announcement is 10-17 at 18:15 hours."

Signal 09-06 is the assigned identifier for Nave's deep red briefcase, which is used for his targets.

He pulls in to the driveway at home. Amanda is home and deep into a book. Lynn Grace is parked in the open grass just off the side of the drive.

Nave gets out, and Lynn opens her trunk. "I guess it is no coincidence you are here, Lynn."

She smiles, reaches into her trunk, and pulls out a small, worn duffel bag. "Well, I sorta been missing that cool girl of yours. I figured we would catch up on girl talk and you could run off and *deliver a special package!"*

She runs the bag strap over her shoulder, closes her trunk, and leans against her car. "Nave, I never interfere nor could I ever advise you on what to do. All I can express is I want you to always, always, ALWAYS, come back to us." She shakes her head, and quickly corrects her words, "I meant to say come back to her, Amanda. She needs you. Not us, that was weird to say." They are both leaning against her car and looking at the scattered thunderclouds ease off into the night. "I don't think I could ever get tired of a good lightning storm," Lynn says. She closes her eyes, and her nostrils open to take in more of the night air. "The aggressive power and ability of danger is almost poetic. It always reminds me how delicate I actually am. Perhaps that is why I am still single. I guess I want the thunder, lightning, and warmth of the rain on my skin to remind me I am not always so bold or tough."

Their shoulders are touching side to side, and Nave slides his hand past a small gap between her arm and the bag's strap. It falls, and Nave takes over holding the bag. "Here, I will take this in." He walks up the walk, and she pauses at her car.

She looks down past her long tan legs sticking out of cut off denim shorts, to her feet, slides her hands in the pockets of her hoodie, and she smiles. Her eyes watch over him and as she follows his direction, her eyes meet Amanda who is sitting on the park-style bench near the front door.

"Ohhh, that was a sweet moment you two just shared." As Amanda cups her heart, and speaks in a higher effect and tone. Nave says, "Dean, your young mind wanders and lost is not a good place to be." Nave heads into the house.

In his private room, Nave sets the red briefcase on his desk. He taps in the six-digit code; the red light appears, and then he puts his left thumb on the latch. The light illuminates, and he opens the case. The computer comes on, and there is a new feature he had been advised of. Near the top left, is a clock. Next to that icon, is an icon that shows, "Start Review Timer." He clicks this and a message is prompted to read, "Enter ES number here." Once the ES number is entered, review is terminated precisely in ninety minutes. ES must accept target delivery within 6 hours of original announcement." Nave enters, "ES 1912," and immediately a video has a prompt to start.

Robert Faye is seated in a plain black room, and speaking to the camera. He has nothing in his hands, no other informational items, and his hands rest at the edge of the clear glass table.

His message is brief. "The target delivery has been evaluated. All information is accurate. A beacon has been activated for this target. This video will play one time. Once you accept the target, the existing details and constant update feed will then be sent to the ES which is assigned. ES 1912 has priority until the six-hour decline is extinguished." The video then stops, and a new window opens. Nave watches as the new window is more of a PowerPoint format:

Target Bio: Jason Lion

DOB: 03-05-1970

Geographical Known: Jacksonville, FL. Atlanta, GA. Key West, FL.

Last Known: Jacksonville, FL.

As his information is displayed, there are several photos of Jason. There is a virtual photo that allows Nave to zoom in, rotate the subject, and examine any needed details. The nude photo is so precise, it shows Jason is missing a left, lower molar.

Just below his virtual photo, is another casualty chart. It lists particular information which is crucial to an ES to evaluate their interest in the target:

Caution Level** 3 (Caution levels pertain to the risk level of each target). One is low risk, and 5 is extremely dangerous and often requires additional support.)

Accessibility** 4 Accessibility pertains to how easily the target can be located. One would indicate a target leaves himself open, or can be easily lured in as the target in southern FL. Five would be a target which is nowhere to be found, escapes detection, vanished, or is in a country which could jeopardize an ES to have a safe escape.)

Weapons: AR15; Glock 45 w/ target laser; Ruger 9mm; Hoyt combination bow, knife variety.

Special Combat Skills: Army honorable discharge; Survival specialist; Hand combat educator.

Known Vehicles: 1. 1997 Lincoln Mark VIII LSC Black edition. Vehicle tag FL. 8TY 866

2. 1992 Chevrolet Silverado Blue over Silver Vehicle tag FL 33R 4TG

The photos show 360' views of each vehicle.

The informational PowerPoint goes into great detail regarding the situation which Nave had already heard from his client. The information also has classified documents that show prior incidents of concern while in the Army. Downloads of websites to include fictitious fantasy roll play, BDSM, searches of sex in churches, and one which is particular—a search for farmers' daughters. Along with the investigative material, is a full audio and transcript of the trial which Nave had discussed while delivering the bridle.

After Nave reviews the entire target delivery, there is a final window which has four empty boxes—one in each corner. In the center of the window, is an acknowledgement. It reads, "ES 1912, you have reviewed this target delivery and have priority to accept. Enter your ES ID in each box before the indicated expiration time." The box in the top left corner pulses. Nave enters slowly, "ES1912." That box fades. Now the lower right box pulses. He enters, and it fades. The top right pulses, and after his ID, it fades. The lower left is bright red. He enters,"ES 1912."
A bold lettered scroll develops across the screen.

"ES1912 ASSIGNED JACKSONVILLE DELIVERY **HORSE**"

He closes the case, detaches the glass pad, enters the combination, and brings the pad to his face and announces, "Deliver the Horse." The icy blue light once again pulses calmly through the night.

The dew shines across the grass with a trail of footprints left by the early squirrels running from tree to tree. Nave is in the driveway with a cup of hot tea, and two bagels. One has cream cheese, the other plain. There are two sandhill cranes that often stroll near his front gate. They are calm and meet Nave often, just as common as a neighbor stopping to say hi on a morning stroll. Standing tall, the crane lunges its large beak slowly and gracefully to accept frequent stabs of the bagel. The other sees there is no harm and shyly approaches. The evening left the road wet, and the rise of the morning sun now warms. Steam floats in the humid air, and gives a hint of the balmy day it will be. The bagels are gone and feathered freeloaders slowly roam away.

An unfamiliar aroma seeps from the window of his house. It is uncommon that there is such an inviting smell to escape his kitchen so early. As he opens the front door, there is a sizzle and a crackling sound coming from the kitchen.

She wears her hair up in a loose, thick ponytail. A thin, strapped tank top can be seen just over the countertop. Nave cannot see anything below that from his point of view. He pauses, and in his mind he adores the pleasant thought of seeing a beautiful woman in his kitchen. "Good morning," he tells Lynn.

She replies, "Hope you don't mind, I sort of jumped in and started breakfast." She turns and the light purple, very small tank top struggles to contain the ample breasts that are free to move very naturally in her top. She had not bothered so early to worry about a bra, and Nave even wondered how often she even wears a bra. There have been several times when he noticed she likes to be free. Now facing him, she slices mushrooms on a cutting board. "Okay, so my all-natural omelet, spinach, fresh mozzarella, mushrooms, spices, and crispy bacon." She laughs and looks at him "Cause I know you like that awful pig belly stuff. Can't believe I even touched it. Yuk!" She smiles, looks at him and asks, "Can you think of anything I am missing?"

In his mind he is thinking . . . a bra! However, truth be told, he is quite okay with that. He does joke with her, "Um, I don't know. You have the eggs ready, mushrooms, spinach, bacon, spices . . . (He cautiously enquires in a light and humorous way.) Lynn, I can't really tell, but you do have some sort of bottoms on, don't you?"

She laughs, and says, "Well yes, I made myself at home, but not so much I am going to bounce around with nothing on." She steps to the side, and shows proof that she indeed has shorts on. Barely! They are white, thick-topped, elastic band shorts with a tie on top. The very loose shorts rise along her thigh line, and as she turns back to check the bacon cooking, the back reveals her hamstring tightly joining her lower butt cheek. "You go take a shower or whatever, and I will get this all done. I have been here enough to know where everything is. Give me about fifteen minutes, and you will have the best all-natural omelet."

Amanda wakes, and looks at what Lynn has made. Amanda opens the refrigerator and grabs a single pack of string cheese, orange juice, and sits down. "Why are you putting a plant in that gross egg and fungus mess you are making? At least you have bacon. Is that so you can smell something good and pretend you are not eating that melted yard food?"

"Amanda Dean, this is so good. And it's all organic," Lynn tells Amanda with a fun, light-hearted sentiment.

Amanda is slumped over the counter, bites a slice of bacon, and says, "I am not eating anything that comes out of a chicken's butt!"

Lynn goes to the counter and sits beside her. "So you like bacon but not eggs?"

Amanda takes another bite and comments on just how wonderful the crispy, hot bacon tastes.

"Have you ever been to a where bacon is made? Oh let me tell you about the time I visited the hog plant."

Lynn is stopped by Amanda who makes a horrible face and states, "Eww, eww, stop. I swear, I am just going to survive on chips and salsa."

Nave comes back to the kitchen and joins the two girls. Lynn quickly gets up and goes to the stove. She drizzles a little olive oil and butter in the pan, and pours the seasoned, whipped egg into the pan. As she stands at the stove, Nave sits at the counter and looks over to Amanda. She is holding her head over and down into her shoulder as her eyes look out the top of her eyelids. He gives her a scowl squint as to quietly ask why. Amanda widens her eyes, looks at Lynn's tiny shorts, looks back to her dad, then back to the shorts, and to her dad. He just shakes his head and says "Dean, you are a mess."

Lynn looks back and joins in a conversation in which she has no clue what they are talking about. "Why is my girl Dean a mess?"

Nave tries to discount his words and says, "It's nothing, let's just eat this good breakfast."

Dean is fully awake and spunkily engaged with this conversation. "Oh no, no, no, Padre. Let's hear this. See, Lynn a few weeks ago I came out and had some shorts on and Mr. Proper here was quick as last night's lightning to direct a U-turn and make me change."

Lynn looks down and with concern asks, "Oh, I'm sorry, should I not have worn this? I'm so sorry. I just feel like home here."

"You are fine, and you should feel at home," Nave expresses.

Amanda says, "So I remember hearing you say, YES I actually do listen sometimes, that shorts that don't cover your butt should be worn as underwear, and UNDER something else."

This is friendly and light as Amanda and Lynn joke with each other like sisters. "So, mister, I always have a good reason; tell me why Ms. Sexy legs is allowed to saunter around the house, all cooking breakfast, and showing off?"

Nave looks to Amanda and says, "Dean, let's see. Lynn you are how old? Oh wait, I guess that is one of those don't ask things. Lynn, you do have your own house right? And you pay your own bills? Let me guess, you have graduated from high school, and college! And I am pretty sure you are not my daughter, you are not wearing those to go hang out with your guy friends, who are overloaded with hormones which cannot be controlled, AND, AND . . . the boy who was in MY house eating MY food was literally foaming at the mouth when you walked through, Dean!"

He thanks Lynn as she sets the plate down. The golden yellow peeks through the melted white mozzarella; sliced cremini mushrooms lay across the top of his steaming omelet.

"See Deannie, once again I do have a good reason, and a very valid point."

"Lynn! Help me here. Tell this man it is not a sex thing; it's a comfort thing."

Lynn dries her hands, and goes around and grabs Amanda's shoulders. "Deannie, I got your back. Stay here I will be right back."

Amanda looks at her dad in a cocky, joyous flash as she says, "Looks like the tables have turned in my favor—the odd man out."

Lynn comes out of the guest room wearing baggie Guess sweats, and a Predator's jersey. "You are right Dean, I am so comfortable now. And this way we can wear similar stuff around the house when there are boys here." Lynn winks at Nave as she takes a mushroom off his plate.

Amanda stands, straitens her arms to her sides, looks up to the ceiling and grunts, "I think I must go now. Horrible morning!" A smirk and twist, she shuffles off with a last note, "I could have sworn you said I got your back, not stab you in the back! Traitor, you are."

Nave finishes, and tells Lynn he will have his phone with him if she needs to reach him.

"How long will you be gone?"

Nave stands against the counter and tells her, "This is normal business stuff. I have some deliveries, a transport, a few escort drives, and anything could come up in between. If you could be around for a week or two to be safe, that would be great."

"Well, I guess I will just settle in to the guest room for a while. And I want you to know I actually really like being here with your daughter. She gives me so much life and energy. I look forward to times I have to be here."

He looks to Amanda's room and replies, "That means a lot to know she has someone to show her a different light and way. Thank you so much."

She picks up his dish, and from across the kitchen tells him, "Sorry about the tiny clothes. It's probably better you see me in this rather than the other pajamas."

He laughs and says, "Too late, I can still see the other outfit. Gotta get going."

He puts his case in the truck, and then slides his suitcase into the backseat. He runs through a check of the oil and lights, peeks under the truck, and then heads out. Across the Beeline Expressway toward Interstate 95, he then uses a remote to activate his inboard navigation and secret voice guidance.

There is an announcement, "ES 1912, verify 10-10." (10-10 is code for alone and can receive all classified material.)

He holds the new remote close and states, "ES 1912; 10-10."

A reply announcement confirms, "Voice verification acknowledged; access granted ES 1912."

He then requests a variety of information. Included in this information, is the last known address for Jason Lion. The information is displayed on the pop-up screen, and a red alert banner is scrolled. Nave continues to be surprised by the unknown technology in relation to his alternative career choice. He pulls to the side of the road to see exactly what the banner is advising. The red scrolling message notes that the last known address is not the last known location of the target.

Nave changes his request per the information, "ES 1912, request last known location HORSE."

Audible reply advises, "ES 1912 new target information available." The screen now displays a satellite view of Key West, Florida and a stickpin icon to illustrate the last known ping for the target. There is also a date that allows Nave to see it was only three days ago that Jason Lion was near the southern edge of Key West. He thought he would be traveling north to Jacksonville, and now he heads south on I-95. He relaxes, and settles in for an even longer drive. He slides in Alan Jackson's CD, "Drive." He sings along, and knows every word. Sometimes, he replays a song as it reminds him of a time in life or someone close. He never sings around anyone else other than his Dean. With her, it is more to annoy as she despises his country playlist. With a wide-open drive, he nears Jupiter, Florida.

The CD mutes, and the usual person announces her message. "ES 1912 already verified, 10-10; confirm no status change."

He formally and directly responds, "ES 1912 status is signal 10-10."

She then begins her information, "ES 1912 your nav screen will be redirected to vehicle acquisition location. Location is verified, secure and of nonpublic access. You will receive coded intel once arrived by GPS guidance, and correspondence will be validated per policy as you acquire temporary vehicle for target HORSE. ES 1912 verify nav redirect." The screen has been updated and there is now a mapped navigation displayed with audible guidance. "ES 1912, does have redirect and audible function for vehicle acquisition." She no longer is on his audible messaging, and he now studies the route he will be following. He notices he will be detouring to West Palm Beach to what appears to be a residential area.

He exits I-95, and with his window down enjoys the breeze and view of the palm tree-lined road. Turn after turn, the homes seem to grow with each neighborhood. The many landscape companies are parked with trailers and drop ramps to make maneuvering a challenge at times. There are four different landscape outfits in just a mile stretch and all seem to have more than enough business with the yards that need to be kept, the medians of plants and flowers, and several small offices in the area. He nears a final turn and reaches a side drive with a single wooden gate.

The screen displays a message: [Enter Code 4455661 now] on the silver keypad. The code is entered, and the gate rolls into the thick ivy. The ivy lined brick wall leads straight back for two hundred feet; and as he reaches the end; there is only a left turn, and now he sees six large bay doors. One door is open and he is directed by his computer to enter the Number Three door. The door immediately closes once he is inside. "ES 1912, vehicle acquisition is door Number Six . Close current vehicle status and re-advise in target vehicle."

Nave holds his remote and advises, "ES 1912; 10-7 POV re-advise in acquired vehicle. Dissolve correspondence and access until voice verified."

The screen displays a brief acknowledgement; the screen closes, and the truck is shut down. He looks over to Bay 6 and mutters, "I think I am going to enjoy this trip." Glossy, black chiseled lines, rough and nothing sexy about this target car. Unless you find brute strength and the rarity of the 1987 Buick Grand National GNX sexy. He carefully lowers his suitcase in the trunk, and places his case in the front seat. He fits himself behind the wheel, and takes a single key from the center console. Like a nervous but excited boy who has his first attempt to slide his finger in the wet panties of his date after a high school football game, he presses the silver key into the slot and pauses to take in the reality of what is about to happen—the anticipation to know when the fingers grip, turn and twist, there will be an orgasm and eruption—all at the power of his hand. The key turns, and his ears open; his eyes close, and he listens to the sound of the faint click of a key in an ignition. Depleted, let down, and like many high school boys, he experiences a feeling of pure rejection as he did not receive the audible foreplay he had worked himself up for.

Instead, a voice comes through—the same female voice he has in his truck, "Acknowledge identity. You are in a protected government vehicle and must acknowledge identity immediately."

Nave quickly replies using the remote to his mouth, "ES 1912."

She replies, "ES 1912 granted access target vehicle acquisition; vehicle is now operational. HORSE delivery target information has been transferred."

He again holds the key, and tells himself, "Oh the moment is gone. It just isn't going to be the same now." He starts the Grand National and says, "Wow, still sounds good!"

The computer screen slides open, and the navigation is set for Key West. The bay door opens, and the car is posed to pull straight out. He eases his way along the ivy-lined brick path and has to re-enter a code to exit. The streets he has to take to work back toward his main route are narrow, crowded, and busy. He has an abundance of power just under his right foot, yet is restricted by the overpopulation of white-haired, tanned, elderly drivers in huge Town Cars and Cadillacs. He comes to a street, and realizes small miracles do come his way at times. The impending cluster of snowbirds and retirees seem to have vanished and a byway in front is clear. The light is bright red, the sky is deep blue, and the road is clean and dry. The red light extinguishes and his right foot buries the accelerator; the green light is a momentary blur as the perfect GNX leaves only the whitish-blue cloud of tire smoke in the distant past. Only enough distance to see the needle cover 105 mph, Nave has to back off the joy of what most will only imagine as they recall one of the true muscle cars that Buick built "Oh SHIT!" he says to himself when he looks to the gauge and notices the mint condition collector car has only rolled 1,225 miles and has never truly been broken in.

The bright flicker of sun-glared waves are almost blinding as he arrives in Key West, just in time to see the sunset. Green plants, wet walkways, and an old tub sit to collect water as they have in the long past for the Hemingway cats. Nave calms himself by taking in the history of this inspiring house. The casual atmosphere and friendly vibes of Key West are such a detachment from the hustle and chaos of Miami. It is understandable why many in Key West are happy, polite, and dress up for dinner by wearing a shirt and often even shoes. Nave finds his hotel, drops his bag, and heads out into the warm night on foot. He walks along the outdoor patio restaurants, down through the boat docks, and finally over to the Sandbar Grill.

At the long woodgrain bar, he is greeted by a young girl who wipes her beer-soaked hands, hands him a drink menu, and asks, "What am I pouring you today?"

"Well, is your water filtered, tap water or just pumped out of that bay?" he replies.

She laughs, and tells him, "If you noticed, I have a bottle of Dasani under here. If you are looking for something non-fueled, I would say your best bet is the iced tea. I brewed it, and it is so good."

He notices an open, small table near the patio edge and takes his tea. There is something admirably relaxing about the lights of swaying boats, the subtle noises and sounds of the water clapping between their hulls and the docks, and night birds darting from pylon to roof tops. Random conversations, couples walking hand in hand, occasional bikes with shirtless, long-haired men who may never release the youth they hold onto, and one elderly couple at the lighted entrance to the boat docks are the particular visions Nave ponders as he enjoys the aura of the southern-most tropic in the United States.

His walk down Duval Street allows him to hear and see the difference of the locals and those on vacation. He wanders off the main drag and through a darker path back to his hotel ,not completely isolated as there are others who have chosen to use the same street. Some on foot and some with big smiles behind the colorful, rented mopeds. Near a small convenience store, a few men who seem to be in there early thirties are gathered on and near a wooden bench. The bench is in true Key West fashion, painted bright tropical colors with random, happy notes and quotes left by the wisdom of those who felt compelled to share. A woman and two younger girls are just ahead of Nave and approaching the group of men. Clouds of smoke billow as the men pass a tightly rolled white paper joint from hand to hand.

The woman and girls are very enthusiastic, and singing, "Montego, Key Largo, come on why don't we go . . . FLORIDA KEEEEEYS."

Many people have sung the words not exact, yet the tone and tune are easy to recognize as the popular, happy vacation song, "Kokomo" from the Beach Boys.

One man wearing faded grey cargo shorts, OP flip flops, no shirt, and thinning, long brown hair, steps out just before the three on the sidewalk. "Hey, hey girls. Wanna see the fun side of the Florida Keys?"

The woman is confidant, direct and even understandably polite as she holds her hand up and tells the men, "MOM, daughter, and daughter's best friend. I don't think we are the catch you are looking for tonight fellas." The younger girls are probably fourteen years old at best, and lock arms as they just laugh.

Still blocking the way, he holds his right hand to his lips with the joint, takes a deep, long drag, and slowly blows toward the woman. He sways his head almost as a snake would in a dramatic cartoon, and says, "Momma can tuck the baby chicks in the nest, and come back to enjoy some nightlife."

Another lanky man rolls his tongue out, and flicks it sharply, and with his one index finger lightly touches the shoulder of the daughter's friend. He looks back to the other two remaining men and says, "Hell, I say they all hang out and get an education on what is really important in life. You know how it goes, old enough to bleed, old enough to breed."

Thinking he has impressed all his friends, the lanky man swaggers, holds his one hand up, and receives high fives as they all laugh. The mother, now visually shaken, shields her daughter and friend just as Nave reaches them. Nave has seen and heard the entire assault.

The tall, lanky man notices Nave, and tries to make light of what has happened "Yo my man, these your girls? We just messing and having a little joke is all."

The woman looks to Nave, and can easily tell he is not associated with any of this trash. She just begins to speak as Nave steps slightly past her, and strikes the tall, lanky man on the side of the neck. The man flinches, his hips twitch, and then he collapses..

The other man holding the joint raises his arms and says, "What the fuck, homeboy?" As he walks toward Nave, he is stopped by the left sole of Nave's shoe against his shirtless chest. The joint dislodges from his grip; he stumbles, the right foot of the man slips off the curb, and he lands ass first in the street.

Nave looks briskly to the other men and advises, "Unless you want to join these two bags of shit in the sexual assault charge, I would sit down right where you are and don't say a word." Headlights guide a speeding car around the near corner, then another from the other direction. Both cars aim in the direction of the store bench, and Nave lets the mother know, "When I saw the first guy step out to block you, I had already called the cops."

She is shaken, yet still very solid and protective of her two girls. The girls huddle next to the mom, and with a scared yet relieved look begin to thank Nave. With his cold, deliberate stare, he tells them, "Never let any man get away with touching or treating you wrong. This trash likely does this often; and remember, it is in no way any fault of yours." Still intensely focused on the girl who was touched, he says, "If you do not press charges, he will do something worse to another girl. Be sure you make the police take him to jail and more importantly . . . press charges!" The first man is placed in the back of one patrol car, and the officer advises they will at least charge him with Disorderly Conduct and Possession of a Controlled Substance. The lanky guy whom Nave struck in the neck, is revived and made to stand up.

The guy acts bewildered and curses at the mom, "Are you fuckin' kidding me lady, you are going to try and have me arrested? For what? I didn't do a fuckin' thing to you, bitch. To you, or your jolly, singing, goofy daughter." The guy then looks over his shoulder to say something to his buddies detained on the bench.

It was not until he felt the athleticism of the mother's skills as a soccer player (She delivered a solid, direct blow to this man's crotch) that he knew she would answer his sarcasm in a way a mother would see appropriate in this situation.

He doubles over, and through wincing pain, asks the officer, "Aren't you going to arrest her for that? She assaulted me. You saw that!"

The officer lifts the guy and tells him, "I am sorta new here on the force. Let me ask my partner. Hey Scott, isn't it actually legal for a mother to blast a dirtbag in the nuts if said dirtbag has touched the mother's daughter and said dirtbag is a thirty-year-old pedophile piece of shit?"

The other officer raises his eyebrows and answers, "Yeah, sorry dude, it is covered under the don't-touch-the-little-girl statutes."

Nave fills out a witness statement, as does the mom and two girls. The other two guys are released, and information is recorded regarding their lack of involvement compared to the two taking a ride to jail.

"You girls put this away for now and enjoy the Keys. Don't let this ruin your trip here. You go ahead and I will be right behind you until you get to your hotel," Nave advises. The daughter tells Nave he should just walk with them. He sternly tells her, "For some reason, I was in this place to protect you. I am fortunate to have been here for that, and I will be right behind you until you get to your hotel. However, this is your time with your mom and your friend. You should get back to that, and just know I will be close enough to make sure your night is safe. And by the way, the Beach Boys sang it, 'Key Largo' then' Montego.' You all had it way off."

This is just enough to return the smile that a group of men stole from these girls. The mom motions with her lips, "Thank you," as she places her hands near the bottom of her chin in a universal sign of prayer. Still, the mood has been darkened; they walk closely together. Every so often, there is a glance back to be sure Nave is still near.

The woman and girls reach their condo door, and the woman walks to Nave. "You are a good man, and I am very glad my daughter could see that exists. I am certain my husband will want to contact you and express his gratitude for what you did." She turns and joins her girls. Nave walks off and finds a bar and grill. It is now time to focus on his real target.

The crowds thin, and on a half wall over-looking the Gulf, Nave watches the night as he prepares his mental stamina for the task he has been chosen to carry out. He has to see the streets, the boats, the shops, and clubs in the night. He knows daylight may bring difficulties, which he is too brilliant to risk. For several days and nights, Nave studies the neighborhoods. He tracks who leaves, who drinks. He knows locals and those who will be leaving. A moderate boat is being restored and sits between two other sailboats. Nave has noticed the two sailboats have had no activity, yet the boat being restored has had lights on, and a man working until nearly twelve midnight each night. The fourth night, he walks to the sailboat next to the boat being restored. The sailboat is yet again dark, gate access locked, and a realtor-type sign is professionally displayed across the entry of the boat just past the gate.

A shirtless man has a cordless drill in one hand and a Corona in the other, as he comes atop the boat that is being restored. "You looking for a boat?" the man asks Nave.

Nave, still inquisitively looking over the boat answers, "I am, yet I am not sure I want a sail or have a regular inboard type cruiser."

Friendly and almost charmingly gracious, the man hops over the rope of the boat he is working on and stands near Nave. He walks to the front of the boat, and tells Nave, "I have only seen the owners once. He is an older man with not much time left on the clock, if I understand it right. Heard they are looking to dump this to help prepare for final-life type stuff. No kids or family, so he wants to be sure his wife is comfortable after he sails away up top, if you catch my meaning there."

Nave walks to the back of the boat and tells the man he appreciates the information. He walks back to his hotel, and stands on his balcony as the crescent moon plays hide and seek with the fast moving clouds. An evening storm is predicted to move in overnight, and an advisory is issued by the National Weather Service for small marine craft to anchor or dock. He slides the balcony door closed, and turns out his light.

There are a few palms across the highway leading out of Key West; the sky is dark purple with hints of pink and blue, and the lamps that hang over the road are still lighted. Nave has an open road and the Grand National brings sudden fright to the many birds which rest in nearby patches of bushes by the turbulent waters. The overnight storm lingers, and he is now headed east across the bridges that take him away from Key West. He drives in silence to simply saturate himself with the brisk freshness of the air just after a storm. A few hours later, he reaches Homestead, Florida, which makes it clear that one is no longer in paradise. He turns on the local talk radio and catches up on the current topics. Already the talk is of the minimal storm with scattered trees that have sprinkled limbs and leaves. There was not much rain, and callers complain about neighborhoods without power.

A radio host team breaks the topic of the storm, and covers a local story. "Okay, is it just that we are more aware, or is it that things are getting even worse? Last night two hood rats, YES I said hood rats because these punks are just that. Anyhow, they are down on the beach and messing with an older couple who just finished dinner."

Another DJ breaks in the conversation, "Oh, I know exactly the thing you are going to talk about. Oh my God, it is getting to where you can't even eat and walk to your car without being harassed by these baggie-jean-wearing thugs. And they are like twelve years old."

The first DJ jumps back in, Yes, yes, yes. The police came, and the report is that one was thirteen—the other sixteen. This poor couple was just out for dinner, trying to go home and then they had to deal with this. It is going to get to where people who spend money are not going to go down to the boardwalk for anything anymore. Doesn't even matter if it's day or night either."

A third DJ offers a lighter side, "Hey, we all know I am no young spring chicken, and pretty quick I am going to be that old dude. I'm telling y'all now, I am packin'. Also, I am taking classes on how to use one of those new walking sticks. You come at me . . . bam! Old man wood right in ya head!"

The female DJ laughs, and plays on his wording, "Old man wood? You can't get wood now, what you going to get at that age? You better be using that old man wood walking stick just to keep that young stuff you like to chase around."

All DJs crack jokes and carry the fun out for a few minutes. The main host calms them, and segue ways to a new story. "Speaking of wood and storms and all, did anyone hear the news just about an hour ago from down in the Keys? I think actually in the marina in Key West? Some dude, let me see her if they have a name, no don't have a name released yet. I guess he was a handyman working on a boat, and this morning the boat owner went to be sure her boat was still tied and what ever. She knew the guy was staying on the boat but . . . let see what they said, oh yes she said she just needed to check and couldn't find this guy who was staying there. The doors were open, lights on, and his little Coleman boom box like radio was still on."

The female host jumps in, "Was it on our station? I hope so because we need more listeners down in the Keys. I like it down there, and we just got a stronger signal so I can totally hook up my peeps down there with our channel."

The host sounds almost disgusted as he tells her, "Laynee, I'm trying to cover a serious topic for once, and you are worried about a clear signal."

"Hey, the Keys need to have better music, and they need to hear ME there. I bet they are listening to ME right now. Hey y'all call in, and let Marti know I am right."

The host again restarts, "Anyhow, this lady can't find this guy, and notices a rope tied off the front of the boat really tight leading to the dock. But not like tied, like a boater ties off. So come to find out, this guy got tangled up apparently and wrapped around the dock pylon and drown." The host seems to be reading and talking and he tries to offer any information and the other host says,

"I wonder how bad the storm was there. I know a few years ago some dude was found tangled up in his ropes on his private slip. He lived, but hung there until a neighbor found him."

The more professional and serious host adds, "See, I have a boat and I admit I have just run down to check if it was tied good before a storm or hurricane, and I really should have someone with me. You just don't think of it until you read this stuff. Well, we will follow this if we hear anymore. I know the police won't release much until they notify family, and all that stuff. Here, all it says is he was a handyman, doing work who lived on the boat alone.

The morning passes, and in the humid afternoon Nave stops for lunch in Fort Lauderdale. The restaurant is simple, yet it is his favorite chicken place, Popeye's. Always the same thing, three legs, red beans and rice, with a biscuit and real cane sugar sweet tea.

An older man sits at the table just in front of him, and comments on the car. "I almost bought one when they first came out. I thought it was a great car, but the wife bitched about wanting a four-door. So we got a Continental."

Nave smiles and says, "So has the air suspension gone out yet?"

The old guy laughs and says, "Oh let me tell you! When those bags went out and burned up the pump, I showed her an old ad I had and might have pointed out that the car I wanted didn't have that crap." He shrugs his shoulders and continues,

"Do you think that made a difference, hell no!" He looks out the window, holding his chicken leg, and with a point and shake, says, "If she just so happens to drop out before I do, well her life insurance is just enough to cover the expenses, and a little left for this old guy to get behind the wheel of one of those." The guy finishes his chicken, walks over, and refills his drink. He stops near Nave, and thanks him for the conversation.

Nave asks the guy, "Do you have a driver's license in that wallet?"

He laughs, "I'm a little older, but not that old buddy."

Nave tells him, "Here, you leave me your license and while I finish this up, you take a joy-ride down the street and back."

The man looks bewildered, looks out to the car, and asks, "You serious?"

Nave holds the key to the man and tells him, "Your tattoo is real, you served in the Marines, and I see the Purple Heart on that Continental out there. I am pretty sure you will be right back, and you will respect the car. Now get your happy ass in that car, and I will see you in ten minutes."

Nave stands drinking his sweet tea when the man pulls into the parking lot. Nave had entered a code to lock out the automated secret alert and information system when he parked, so the man only knew it had a modified navigation installed.

The retired Marine smiles as he steps out of the car. "Well, my good man, here are the keys, and I left my balls in the passenger seat as I don't need them to drive that Lincoln." They both laugh and head their separate ways.

Nave activates the system, enters his ID, and continues up the coast.

Several miles up the coast, the computer comes on and the woman provides information. "ES 1912 advise status."

He replies, "ES 1912; 10-10, able to receive information."

She states, "ES 1912 follow GPS route; do not divert and return to original acquisition location. Be available, additional alert has been periodically detected on satellite. Subject is Level 5. Case is open to all ES, and target payout is $500,000.00 cash in full."

The route is quite a diversion from the quickest and most direct route, and Nave is focused as he is aware the route is following an erratic path. Nave reaches a road that runs along a private airfield community.

Then as in Gainesville, the NAV screen alerts and a red dot pings sharply and immediately; the woman advises, "ES 1912 is affirmed in proximity of Level 5 target. ES 1912, you are receiving full details and will need to secure a location to access your case. Advise when able to engage."

Nave quickly finds an open lot then opens and activates his case. Once all codes are verified, a full file opens for this Level 5 target. The red dot is fast and frequent. Nave is calm and not rushed by the pings, as he is studying the many photos of the target. Each photo has random information, and statistical information. The airfield is just beyond the high hedge of where he is parked. He looks over to the runway, and the doors of a leer jet fold up and the plane heads toward the runway. Nave is intently locked into the plane and writing at the same time.

The plane rushes into the open sky, and then the woman comes on, "ES 1912, target is at 1,000 feet and climbing. Beyond 10,000 feet, we will lose tracking. Target Level 5 "'GHOST' is in the air, and no longer detected." She advises to all, "ES 1912, proximity no longer in range and delete trace."

Nave answers, ES 1912; 10-100." "GHOST" 10-100 is code for new information related to a target.

The woman advises, "ES 1912 will deliver Level 5 update now."

Nave informs the team, "ES 1912 update information of Level 5 GHOST. Last GPS - 26* 11 50 N / 80* 10 15 W FAA FXE. Known possible group, five white males enter leer jet Gulfstream tail number N11771. Photo upload will be sent by 2100 hours of this date. ES 1912 no further information."

The alert is canceled, and Nave returns to where he has his truck waiting. He decides to drive along the coast, as it always has a way of bringing his mind back to a peaceful place. He sees the diversity of those who travel from modest neighborhoods to visit the few places for which the fortunate have taken ownership. There is little envy, yet there is pondering of how something so rightfully given to all can be gated by the power of money. Still there lay many areas which families park and allow tiny feet to scamper in mystique, as the family dog whips the sandy waters from its fur coat. The beach holds memories for these children as it does for Nave. For many who may never feel the humid air clam their skin, he is left to believe he is most fortunate to have had a grandfather who made sure he left his tiny prints in the sand. Nave's memories often drift like the winds. Soon, many miles pass and he is turning off the coast highway and across the BeeLine back home.

Nave pulls into the drive, and can see Lynn and Dean are just around back in the hammock. Quietly, he walks closer and calls out, "Now, there are a lot of stories in the threads of that old hammock. Something tells me there might be a few more weaving their way in."

Dean rolls out, and heads over to her dad. "Padre, you are finally home. Guess what? Lynn is taking me to work with her tomorrow."

Nave looks over to Lynn who holds one hand up and says, "You left me in charge and the school assigned a work-study project so it is all legit!"

Dean asks, "So where were you this time?"

"I had to take care of some business in Jacksonville, which turned into Miami and the Keys," Nave tells her.

Dean is wide-eyed and asks, "Did you get caught in the storm? It was crazy I heard. OMG! We saw on the news some guy around a boat got all caught up in some rope, and the storm caused him to get trapped. The say he was all tied up around a wood post or something."

Nave somewhat in a dismissive manner responds, "I heard it on the radio, but I was already on my way to Miami by that time."

Amanda tells him she has something in the oven, and walks to the back door.

Lynn rolls out of the hammock, and as she folds Amanda's Tampa Bay Bucs throw blanket, she looks deeply at Nave and quietly says, "I'm really glad you didn't get wrapped up around that pylon."

Chapter 11
Colorado

The days are getting shorter, and even in the Sunshine State the temperatures are becoming more tolerable. The crowds are thinner around the beaches, and Amanda and Nave enjoy more time to themselves on the sand. They are walking over to RonJohn surf shop and come across a guy sitting alone. He is tattered with leathered skin and quite sad in his manner. A pair of couples walking to the restaurant on the pier smugly pass, and make several comments about the man who asks nothing of them. After Amanda grabs a few stickers from the counter, Nave asks if she wants to eat something at the pier. He intentionally asks to be seated next the couples who demonstrated such ill-judgment of the man earlier.

After being seated Amanda whispers to her dad, "DAD! What are you going to say to those people?" She knows her father well, and knows he has a deliberate intent because of his request to sit in this spot.

"Don't worry, just take in what is right or wrong. And don't forget the message."
The restaurant is quiet enough that Nave can easily interject his intent to join their conversation. "Excuse me for stepping in to your night out; however, I wanted to offer to buy your dinner tonight."

Amanda just looks stunned, and wonders what is happening. She thought her dad was going to scold the pair for how they spoke of the man outside.

One of the women who seems to take interest and is classier than the others asks, "That is unusual and a very nice offer, yet I am sure we must know why you would randomly ask to buy our dinner."

Nave shifts his chair, and gestures with a slight squint, "Yes, nothing is free. I only ask that you allow me to tell you a short bit of information. Nothing I am selling, just something you may find interesting."

One guy replies, "As long as no preaching starts, I will listen for a few minutes if you include my bourbon as well."

Nave smiles and says the drinks are included. Nave looks out the window, and starts by introducing Adam. "See Adam out there doesn't mind anyone casting judgment upon him. He knows all too well the many sides of life. A few years ago, he was at work and his wife called his office to tell him he was supposed to be home to join her and their two kids for a play they were to go to. He promised his daughter he would sit right next to her, and she could have those candied almonds. Yeah, the ones that stink up the arenas and shows. Well, when his wife called him, he explained this client's case was huge and the law firm, HIS law firm, had to take care of the clients. He explained to her this was their livelihood, and he just could not drop the ball on this case. Upset yet understanding, she told him she would take the kids and let his daughter know daddy would be home to tuck her in. Maybe even make it there late. See, no one knows what the next turn in life will be. Less than an hour later, he was called again. The Orange County Sheriff's Deputy told him he needed to hurry to the ER, and they did not know if that would even be soon enough. That man you passed and thought was some worthless bum who would never amount to anything has more money than anyone knows. There is still a home over in Bay Hill that is paid for, and even though it is his, he never goes back. That night he did not make it in time, and lost everything that should have been a priority. He never went back to work; his firm still handles cases, yet he will talk to no one. Too late for him, yet maybe before we cast our prejudices, we should stop and talk to the person. The person and not the object we believe is worthless."

The woman is in tears; the one man lowers his drink, and quietly says, "Thank you. Humility is ours to have tonight, and perhaps we all have grown by your words. I believe we owe you dinner."

Nave says a deal is a deal. He repositions his seat and looks back to them. "Don't be down. Be grateful and enjoy your night. Live life, and think of those you should make your priority."

Amanda is also glassy-eyed, and looks at her father saying, "You are such a powerful presence, and I hope I can capture that trait of yours."

The coastal wind echoes the sounds of the waves slapping the wooden pier, and they walk out from dinner to the truck. "Padre, why do you always open my door? I am grown!"

He closes the door, and when he is pulling out of the parking lot, he tells his daughter, "Expectations you should have, are by example; I hope these will resonate with you of how I expect any young man to treat my daughter. Yes, you can open your own door. The door is not which one should be opening yet, it is a respect that a young man should be giving that will open your heart and help you see a difference in the ones who do not deserve such a wonderful young lady, like my daughter." He grabs her head, and shakes her as she laughs. He looks and notices he has a message from the judge to call when convenient.

Now back at home, he goes to his office and calls the judge. The judge requests that he meet with Robert tomorrow for lunch. It is arranged to meet for lunch at Houston's. Nave has no hesitation, as he has been a full supporter of their French dip. He proclaims Houston's French dip to be by any reach, the best ever made. He would not have to argue this much, as many would agree.

Rain sprinkles the windshield, and thunder mumbles in the distance like a garbage truck several blocks away. Dark skies invade the taller buildings in the distance, and the radio host tells the listeners to avoid any downtown, outdoor lunch patios unless they want their water refilled by Mother Nature. Houston's is away from town, and he is more than happy to avoid the crowded streets of Orlando. He arrives fifteen minutes early, which according to Nave, is on time.

He walks in and the hostess, dressed in a classy, all-black outfit, with pants neatly ironed, shirt pressed and tucked, a thin flat black tie, and her hair tightly pulled back, makes eye contact, and professionally asks, "Hello sir, how will I be of service to you during your time here at Houston's this afternoon?"

He tells her he is meeting someone for lunch and simultaneously notices Robert in a separate room. The hostess sees him look and says, "Mr. Nave, I will be sure to remember you on your next visit. I was advised you would likely be arriving soon."

She escorts him to where Robert is seated, and Robert looks to the hostess. His expression is polite, yet motionless as he tells her, "Jennifer, thank you. Will you have Hanna come over in five minutes, and we will order then?" Robert rests back into his seat, and rests his large battered hands at the edge of the wood table. He lowers his head until his chin is near his chest. He has thick, black, and gray eyebrows, and one slightly rises while his eyes slowly look to Nave. "We had a good feeling you would be a great asset to this operation. It is always unknown to what level any _elimination specialist_ will perform. After the unprecedented performance in Key West, it is becoming very transparent this operation would benefit greatly to advance your geographical territory. There are less than five who have the accuracy, perfection, and pure balls to eliminate the targets in the fashion you have. After lunch, we will take my car for a drive and I have some new avenues I think you might . . . well, I am sure you find very exciting." The two compare the facts they each present to justify why a French dip or a steak at Houston's is so much better for lunch. Perhaps Robert's analogy is best said: "Nave, let's agree in this sense: if there were two models, one blonde, one brunette, both look great, smell amazing, and (Now he grins and chuckles.) AND we would eat um both and leave satisfied. Hell, we might even ask for a take-home box!" He laughs, and they finish up at the restaurant.

They walk out, and Robert goes to the black Bentley. As they drive in no particular direction or to no particular destination, Robert fills Nave in on why they are meeting at the restaurant. "Have you ever been to Colorado?" Robert asks.

Nave, tells him he hasn't.

"It will be best to intently study the terrain, the people, the logistics, and the ins and outs. All this, of course, if what I tell you fits into your desire to expand. See Nave, when things get hot, or suspicions creep up, many specialists reinvent themselves in a whole new way. It is actually very beneficial for longevity in this profession. If you decide to progress into a

National Elimination Specialist, your rate grows, your target access is broader, and you will enjoy more of what you may miss from the work you did before leaving the military." He looks toward Nave and exclaims, "Let's face it Nave, you were a bad ass in there!"

They pull into the parking lot of the Jai Alai arena. There are few cars, the rain has slowed , and Robert explains a strategic episode. "You may be in the middle of a parking lot like this, and receive a notification on your alert system in your truck or any vehicle we assign to you. There will be less than ten minutes, usually less than five. You will ALWAYS have your tack bag with you. That is a must. ALWAYS! You will drop who you are with, you will grab your bag, and you will either be driven to a departure site, or be met on top of a building and lifted by a chopper to depart. These are critical situations and very unlikely. Will it happen? Yeah, I would say at least once or twice a year. Hell, Nave with your expeditious turn time and accuracy, maybe more. Local police, fire, even federal will be deterred by our team and the judge's contacts. You will have access to some fancy shit, and if you are an NES or GES, you will NOT be interrupted. These targets are deep contracts. Some, many are government-assigned."

Nave listens with no cross-examination, and allows Robert to saturate the information to cover every detail to this point. Robert has now spent over two hours passing details to Nave when he asks, "Can you take this on?"

Nave calmly looks to Robert and simply replies, "No."

Robert looks back. They now are looking directly at each other, and Robert smiles. "No . . . No because your integrity must study each target. You must dissect every pore of your subjects and find your own knowledgeable facts in order to eliminate any target. Am I right?"

Nave still looks to him and states with bold, stern, directness, "One mistake, one omission of fact, the target is a victim. I will never eliminate a victim. I do not eliminate any target for you, the operation, or grudge one may have. I see my justice in those who are and have suffered. When I have certainty this is accurate . . . (His eyes seem to have become stone.) I will effectively eliminate any target!"

Robert hands Nave a black case. He tells Nave, "Tomorrow you contact me, and I am sure you will be advising me your new status as NES 1912. See Nave, we already anticipated your demand and I will tell you, your elite brotherhood also demands the very request you expressed. Our operation becomes more about the specialist, well, being the specialist they are. You will often if not always, meet with the victims or the clients we accept. Any specialist who would take this offer and not have the response you did would have immediately been removed from the operation. It is that simple. So here is your package. Call me tomorrow and tell me your thoughts." Robert speaks to his stereo and requests Billy Joel's greatest hits. They listen as he takes Nave back to his truck.

Through the night, Nave studies the case for **Colorado**. He is particularly enraged at the judicial connection of the predator and the gross scrutiny that was publicized against the victim. In examination of the fifteen-year-old student, Aspen Lorn, she was repetitively accused of seducing the thirty-four-year-old man. The suspect's attorney was the brother-in-law of the sheriff and long-time country club friend of the judge. The attorney for the man accused, Orin Young, was permitted to badger the fifteen-year-old who agreed to testify.

Nave reads portions of the court transcripts. Att: "Young lady, did you know Mr. Young before the night you claim he forced you to have sex with him?"

Lorn: "Yes."

Att: "Did you meet him at a park? At your school? The skating rink? Did you meet him at a playground?"

Lorn: "No."

Att: "In fact Ms. Lorn, was it a pool hall which my client was at having a few beers in? The bar where you approached him?"

Lorn: "Yes."

Att: "Ms. Lorn, you wanted my client to do something for you, didn't you? You wanted him to buy you drinks. You in fact whispered to him if he bought you drinks, you would pretend to be his girlfriend. Did Mr. Young buy that drink for you?"

Lorn: "Yes"

Att: "Yes! Yes he did. And let me ask this, did he ever ask your age?"

Lorn: "Later"

Att: "Stop there! We are only talking about the time you walked up to him and you two now have your drinks. This moment only at the bar. Then and only referring to this time, that YOU approached him, did he ask you your age or did you even tell him you were fifteen?"

Lorn: "No."

Att: "Ms. Lorn, you have been noted to have admitted, and let me read your words here to you, 'I have done this at the pool hall many times, and never had a problem.' So Mr. Young is not the only adult man you have approached. Isn't that correct?"

Lorn: "Yes"

Att: "Is it true, that Mr. Young really never knew your age?"

Lorn: "That is not true! Not true at all! I told him when I went to his house!"

The judge interjects and orders the girl to calm herself at once.

Att: "Yes you claim you told him, yet don't you find it possible given your history of lying to so many adult men, you could have maybe left that detail out?"

Lorn: "I told him. We do it just to get alcohol."

Att: "Alcohol you say. Is that all you were getting? Weren't there gifts?"

Lorn: "Yes, but he did that on his own."

Att: "Oh, you never maybe hinted . . . after all you were a young yet not-so-looking young lady who wanted to be pampered, so you did ask for things."

Lorn: "Only once, a pair of shoes."

Att: "Do you expect this court to believe you now, as you already changed your story in a matter of minutes, that you only asked for shoes? Ms. Lorn, aren't you in fact making this whole thing up because once my client found out your true age, he cut you off? He in fact did the right thing and made you leave."

Nave examines the document further to objectively see the flip side to this, and tries to see the fact as they have been reported by the family who is seeking his service.

The State-assigned prosecutor, David Hardy, had a very different line of questioning for Mr. Young:

Hardy: "Mr. Young, what do you do for a living?"

Young: "I own a small ice cream, lunch spot called Frozen Lunch Times."

Hardy: "So are all of your employees older?"

Young: "Not sure what you mean by older. You may want to be more specific, sir!"

Hardy: "You want specific? Oh I can be specific. You have five employees who are sixteen, and all female. You have one who is seventeen, a female, and one who is thirty-two, who is your manager for the later shift.. Is this accurate?"

Young: "I guess you better check your facts, buddy. Lindsey is actually eighteen. So I guess you don't have your facts straight!"

Hardy: "Well, I guess I must. Anyhow, let me ask you this. Your manager who is (and let me say approximately thirty-two), and the five girls who are sixteen, can you not tell a difference in those girls?"

Young: "I don't see the girls dressed up."

Hardy: "Just answer the question, Mr. Young."
(Transcript shows a sustained objection which did not require Young to answer.)

Hardy: "Mr. Young, have you ever taken your staff to dinner, to an appreciation event or say a night dinner to the Chipped Rock Country Club?"

Young's attorney objects: "Objection, staff and employment are not a part of this case."

Hardy: "Judge this is a vital part of our case, and leads to past conduct of the defendant."

Judge: "Mr. Hardy, we are not having a trial for the past. Objection sustained."

Hardy: "Mr. Young, you still claim you never knew of the victim's age until that night you made her leave?"

Young: "I never knew her age; if I had, I would have done the same thing far sooner."

Hardy: "Do you recall the time Ms. Lorn asked if she could come to work at your restaurant?"

Young: "Well, she mentioned needing a job."

Hardy: "In order for her to legitimately work and be an employee, she would have had to fill out an application, file documents, and report taxes. Isn't that correct?"

Young: "Like I said, she only asked but never came to work."

Hardy: "Mr. Young, were you aware that Ms. Lorn actually went to the same school as five of your employees?" The audio transcript erupts with courtroom gasps, muttering and a judge's gavel echoing as he orders the room to silence.

Young: "I don't recall that!"

(Nave advances to read, and listen to another portion of the transcript.)

(Hardy now calls Lindsey, who is the seventeen-year-old.)

Hardy: "Lindsey, you have worked for Mr. Young for how long?"

Lindsey: "Just over two years."

Hardy: "And are you a shift leader now?"

Lindsey: "Yes, I make the schedules and cover if Mandy can't make it in."

Hardy: "And just for the record, Mandy is the now thirty-three-year-old manager, correct?"

Lindsey: "Yes, Mandy sometimes calls if her kids are sick or she and Mr. Young are going to be out."

(There is a pause in the audio.)

Then Hardy is heard asking, "Now you say she, being Mandy, and Mr. Young are going to be out. Can you clarify what you mean by out?"

Lindsey: "Well, Mandy told me Mr. Young takes her to dinner, the movies,"

(About this time audio of the other attorney objecting as to hearsay.)

Hardy: "Okay, I guess I have to rephrase my questions. Lindsey, have you yourself, in person, ever seen Mr. Young doing anything that you would believe to be inappropriate?"

Lindsey: "Well, OH GOD YES! See, there was one time I went into the office and her, oh do I have to say her name as we are in court and all? Mandy's computer was open. Now me being nosey and the like, I had to read and look. Oh good lord, let me tell you I still haven't seen two people do anything like what they, Mr. Young and Mandy did with ice cream. Good thing he didn't get frostbite on that thing!"

(The audio gives clear indication of some laughing and some in deep sighs.)

(Mr. Young's attorney again objects while the attendants settle.)

Hardy: "Okay Lindsey, let me just ask you one particular thing. In that office, did you ever see an application from Ms. Lorn?"

Lindsey: "Well, I hope I saw it. Aspen filled it out there at the shop while I was sitting with her having some chicken fingers."

Hardy: "Who did you give the application to?"

Lindsey: "I handed it to Mr. Young."

Hardy: "Wait, you are telling this court, with all certainty, you physically handed that application to Mr. Young? The same Mr. Young seated here?"

Lindsey: "Yeah, but he just looked it over, and put it right in the little shedder."

Hardy: "You were there when he shredded it?"

Lindsey: "Yes."

Hardy: "I know I said that was the last question, but I have to ask for the record. Did Mr. Young tell you why?"

Lindsey: "He said he had enough teenagers working already."

(The audio again indicates shock in the crowd.)

Nave carefully listens to ever portion of the transcript. He reads the deputies' report to find one very peculiar discrepancy. The deputies who initially took the report and took the photo did so exactly two days prior to the written report filed by the department. This was one more issue simply dismissed by the court as a typo. The court refused to acknowledge the computer-generated reporting system does not make typos. After all the facts which the Court and State Attorney's office ordered removed from the trial, the final charge was merely Contributing to the Delinquency of a Minor. The defendant flooded the trial with fictitious witnesses who claimed damning character traits of Aspen; two jurors were suddenly removed for unexplained reasons, and in a huge change of events, Hardy's closing statement encouraged leniency for the defendant. This was still a shock to the family and many in the city.

In a portion of his closing, Hardy stated the jury should look at only the facts.

Hardy closes: "Oh I remember being fifteen, wanting to skip the next six years and be twenty-one. After all, most kids are finding ways to get alcohol and of finding whatever drug they want. It is no different for boys or young ladies, who perhaps have a desire to be grown. Here today, we have laid out a lot of information. Information that is supposed to give you, the jury, some sort of guidance to make the right judgment upon another person. That task is no task anyone generally wishes to have. So when I come to this final argument I tend to lead myself to not argue at all. After all, you have sat through three days of that. (He leans against the wood banister next to the jury. Aspen is seated crying, as she has betrayal soaked through her every nerve.) Even we, who are closest to that evidence, can be misled or even avoid the reality of what is the true crime. I can't tell you now what to decide. You have all you are going to be offered to make the outcome you collectively make. Let me remind you first what the defendant must answer to in his charges. One: did he contribute to the delinquency of a minor? Two: Indecent Exposure toward a minor? Three: Rape!"

Now after three days, nearly thirty hours of figuring out what one person believes, what another knows, and what the true paralleled facts are, we have this; the accuser said in fact she went into a bar and the defendant agrees in fact he met the same female in this bar. The defendant admits he purchased alcohol for Ms. Lorn, and admits he did so on several occasions. Those are the two paralleled facts that both sides state are true. Now here is the hard part you must sift through: Did the defendant know Ms. Lane was a minor when she was in a twenty-one-and-over bar? You must decide if you believe the defendant truly knew the woman's age. And perhaps the most difficult with the hazy testimony is whether or not Mr. Young ever committed the aggressively accused rape, and on several occasions as one person claims. I will sympathize now with each of you, as in the many cases I have tried, I can easily say I would expect a quick and guilty verdict. However, in this case . . . I wouldn't be so sure. What I do have faith in, is those of you here today, will hear me and make this man, Mr. Young, answer only to what you know those facts are.

(The audio clearly sounds one man speaks out, "Holy fuck, this crooked-ass town, that son of a bitch was bought! Jury, do the right thing, You ALL know he did it, you know!" He screams as the judge orders the man out, and the bailiff escorts him away.)

After Nave listens several times, he sets the tape in the case, and looks over the photos that were taken by the mother of Aspen. Nave reaches for his phone, and calls Robert just after midnight.

Robert answers, "Yeah, I guess you reviewed the tapes and photos."

Nave says, "I am flying to Colorado tomorrow morning. There are a few details missing, there is more to this."

Robert enquires, "What do you mean, more to it? It is all right there. What more do you need to know? That guy is foul and you have the tapes."

Nave simply replies, "Tomorrow at 11:45 I will be in Colorado Springs. I will need a car and a place."

Robert agrees and tells him it will all be worked out.

The temperature is quite a change from Florida to the high Rockies. He walks to the rental car counter and waits to be greeted. The woman sits on a chair that is made of heavy steel to support the girth of the woman. She has dark pants on, and a badly wrinkled shirt that has no chance of staying tucked in. She stares at her computer as he can hear the frequent alerting computer-generated system announcing "You've got mail."

Still, she has not looked at Nave, much less stand to do her job then in a heavy breathing tone she expels the energy to ask, "Do you have a reservation?" This barely understandable between the smacking of her gum. He does not answer. She continues to read her email as he stands there waiting for her to actually do her job. She then leans closer to her screen, and in Nave's direction holds a finger up, the curled purple and green nail is nearly three inches long and tells him, "Oh honey, you have to hold on just a second. I HAVE to take care of this, cannot wait, cannot wait!"

He looks over to the Enterprise counter, and a young man, approximately in his early twenties, is printing reservations, sorting keys, and checking vehicle stock once washed. Nave walks over and asks if he has any available cars.

The young man says, "First, let me welcome you to Enterprise. I take it you may not have an existing reservation. So let me see what I have for you to select from."

The woman apparently finished her priority emails and calls out for Nave. "Excuse me sir, are you going to pick up a car or what?"

Nave only slides his eyes in her direction for a second and then back to the man helping him. "She is lucky I didn't take that computer and smash it on the floor. Customer service is so lacking anymore. Gabriel, I am glad you take pride in yourself and your job."

"Well thank you sir and here is what I can do."

Now Nave is set up in a rental, and heads toward town. He calls Robert and gets information regarding a car. He takes a portion of the day to admire and become familiar with the surrounding area. The unusual aroma of different kinds of wood being burned in the many homes is like a mountaineering experience to him. The calm has a sense of wholesomeness as the frequent scents that seep through the lowered window are compatible with the fragrant pine trees. There are many childhood memories that reoccur from the days he would drive up to Wrightwood and Big Bear California during the winter. The objective difference here is the lack of a dirty brown layer of smog that infects the valley below over the Inland Empire around San Bernardino and Riverside Counties. His direction takes him further up the winding roads lined with tall markers protruding out of the snowbanks created by plows that have cleared the roads after the last snowfall. These markers allow drivers to know where the edge of the road is. The day has traveled past the Rockies, and night pushes the horizon colors to quickly darken. The dash indicates the temperature has now dropped to a frigid 7 degrees. Small, crystal-like flakes dance freely in front of the lights of a small mountain diner. A gift shop shares the large walking deck, and Nave finds a parking spot near the side of the diner.

Even though he is not a dark, olive-toned man, with skin damaged, as many from Florida, the gracious woman who greets him at the hostess counter takes notice.

"Well, either you have had yourself a nap in one of those fancy sun capsule tanning thingys, or you are not from these parts mister. Is it just you?"

"Just myself tonight," he answers.

She has her hair sliced hard in the back, stiffened with hairspray in the front, and sharp points that follow her cheeks just past the bottom of her chin. Her eyebrows of magic marker are like paint and in a high arch. Her baby blue eyes seem very light in-between the thick black eyeliner. Amber metallic brown lipstick also lined in black, and a small, diamond-like stud don her nose. She wears a short, cutoff-style skirt that makes it easy to see the insides of her legs do not part until her knees. The woman has a blue, white, and pink country-style shirt that buttons up the front. She grabs a menu, and asks Nave where he would like to sit.

"I need to be over near this window so I can keep an eye on my car," he requests.
She returns with a glass of ice water and sits across from him. The button-down top she wears now has one less button fastened; she leans forward only to have the table give her a little more cleavage to press up and out of the now open top.

"Now being that I am always working here, I know I have not seen you in here before. So let me guide you through what we do good and oh I will be honest, what the cook CAN'T cook! I'm seeing you might eat pretty healthy, and you need some real food to fill up all that, mmmm, all that man body you have." She flirts in a way as if she has mastered a comfort in being playful and boldly aggressive. She opens Nave's menu, and with her wild-haired troll pen, points out his options. "Any steak is going to be a winner. Hand-cut, rubbed in a house seasoning and thick!" She drapes her hands over his menu, looks at him from the top of her eyes, and smoothly tells him, "You can trust me, some things thick around here may be very good. You won't be disappointed!" After her attempt on sexy, she continues,

"The chicken fried steak is big and amazing. The B.B.Q. chicken is one of my favorites. Now we have some pastas, but let's be real. Look, country cabin, smoker to cook, and every table have three different B.B.Q. sauces. Do ya think there is some Italian lady in the back hand-stirring some pasta dishes? You ain't gettin' pasta if you ask me."

He goes with the ribeye, and she more than reassures him she will be right back to check on him and is going to personally make his salad. She brings him the salad and a glass of sweet tea he asked for. As she sits his salad plate down, she friendly plays and touches his shoulder with her left hand.

She raises her right hand and makes sure Nave watches her, "Oh looks like a little of your ranch got on my finger." She takes her finger to her amber lips and gently removes the ranch as she tells him, "Now you enjoy that salad mister."

He has a moment to himself, and sits among the louder families, and not too far from the small bar. There are stories of the past few months of hunting, of who has cords of wood for sale, if Aunt Jenna is going to make that flaky pie, and when the next storm is to come in. The decor supports the conversation as the many fish, deer, moose, bobcat, and elk are mounted throughout. The tea is a fresh brew; the salad had hand-cut tomatoes, carrots, in-house baked croutons, and a ranch like he had never tasted before. He wonders if the dairy cow and buttermilk used in the ranch was from that day. His experience so far was of being impressed with the small mountain restaurant. Looking around, he can see a community of happy, close people. Real people who enjoy meeting up and sharing their time. A few people leaving pass his table and offer a genuine hello or good-bye. Some even a welcome and wish to stay a while. Obviously, the hostess/waitress is very kind. She returns with a large plate covered in a slab of ribeye, and a pile of hand-mixed mashed potatoes. Beautiful marbling and the fatty edges still sizzled when she landed this plate in front of him.

"Ain't gotta ask you if it's okay, cause my daddy only hand-cuts the best. All I have to check on is if you can handle all that," she jokes.

A tall man in Wrangler jeans, a huge rodeo belt buckle, grease-stained cowboy hat, and worn black boots comes by Nave's table. "Welcome, how did we do on that steak for ya mister?"

Nave offers a few words to the cook and owner of the place, "I have traveled many places often to see steakhouses spend a lot of time and money to show those passing by how great their steak is. Sure, a few times I had to go find out. All I found out is their wrapping paper is better than the present. Here, you have a simple sign out front saying, 'Oxford's.' I will tell you; this is the best ribeye I have had. For that I will remember the name."

The man laughs and acknowledges his confidence in his food. The waitress meets up with them and her dad reaches over to her, and as he buttons her top says, "Missy, the only breast being served around here is a chicken breast. Don't much care if you are thirty-five years old. Still whoop your ass if you get outta line!" With friendly and simple conversation he asks, "So I take it you are just passing through. Where do you call home?"

Nave quickly answers, "Southern California. Near San Clemente."

Back to his drive, he finds his way to a location provided by Robert. The road was recently cleared, and yet very choppy.

Rutted, the many grooves pull the car to one side or the other. Darkness has a new depth in this area, and now two miles in he sees a faint blue reflector. He turns left, and travels another mile over worsening roads. A hunting cabin sits alone, and a single garage is unattached behind the cabin. When he gets out, he notices nearly a dozen solid red lights in many areas of the woods surrounding the cabin, mounted at varied levels in the trees, and pointed in all directions. The door has a metal box with an opening just large enough to slide a hand in. Nave reaches in, and then enters a numbered code. The garage door automatically opens, and only a few canned floor lights come on. Thirty-eight-inch tires hold up a white International Scout. He sits into the upgraded, aftermarket seats, and takes notice that the interior has been completely modified. He pulls the Scout out slowly, and is more than pleased one upgrade was power steering. Thirty-eight-inch monster mudders would have been a nightmare to steer on the roads he will drive. He stores his rental in the garage. He has arranged to use the cabin during his stay. Of the many luxuries in his line of work and the clientele, he could only expect what this cabin, hidden deep in the Colorado mountains, would be like. He parks the Scout near the front door and steps right onto the rugged porch. He opens the door, turns on the light, and stands to take in the interior of this cabin. The wide open entry allows him to see his accommodations. To the right, is a single burner stove. A small window above has a hand crank opener. To the left of the room, is a single bed that had an oversized mattress, and just next to the bed is a door. Beyond the door is a toilet, and a stand-up shower. One wall has a floor to ceiling clothes cabinet, and on a small dresser sits a fifteen-inch tub television. Between the cabinet and bed is a wood-burning stove that will be his only source of heat. He realizes the stacked wood on the porch is not Shabby Chic decor.

A fire burns, his briefcase is under the bed, his gun is on the dresser next to him, and silence. He lies peacefully in the absence of spoils which seem to be the necessity in life now. Sounds he had not heard in many years are now all he has to listen to. A tree sways and its leaves sing the night wind's songs. The heat of the stove melts the icicles causing a few to shatter on the frozen dirt. Just in the moments before he sleeps, with his eyes closed and he lies still, he hears the nothing of sound can ring like softly humming horns.

Is the sun brighter at 9,000 feet, or does the thinner air simply allow the rays to find the earth faster? Waking just in time to put another log in the stove and catching the beams of sunlight through the small window over the single stove, he realizes he is not walking out the front door and feeding sandhill cranes as he did in Florida. He could, however, try to feed the animal that left the large paw prints just to the outside of the Scout he parked near the front door. Today, he will begin his work. After seeing the size and span of the tracks near the truck, he wisely takes his H&K compact 40 with him for his morning run. His run is quick and short, as he soon becomes reacquainted with the high altitude and two-degree temperature.

After his run, truck exhaust echoes through the barren wilderness as he fires the Scout up. He awaits it to warm, as he has a large cup of hot, spiced tea. He packs his briefcase and a milk crate of supplies just in case he gets stranded. He is always prepared for any situation. In the cabin, is a coded, locked box. From this box, he retrieves a map, and a specialized device with three buttons. Also in the box, is more contact information for the victim's family. Robert had advised there would be areas in which cell phone service would be lost. The device he is using would be linked directly to the agencies advanced recovery team. At any given time, the agency has a recovery team that is on call. If a NES is in imminent danger, the mission is compromised, or the NES has to be recovered, he can activate the device. The three buttons are in particular order. One, "Alert! Do not send recovery." Two, "NES needs recovery immediately." Three, "Cancel recovery, NES is no longer in danger."

The map is encrypted by code which would lead Nave to a secure meeting place with the family of Aspen. He travels through a challenge of snow-pack, old hunting trails, across open fields, and over steep terrain. Four hours of testing the rugged craftsmanship of the International Scout, he comes to a cell tower that overlooks the valley below. A service room adjacent to the large cluster of weather satellites, cell towers, and power supplies has a custom Jeep Wrangler parked in front.

Inside, Nave meets with Aspen's father. Nave brings his briefcase, and again clears the room of any recording access. The man is stout–likely able to handle the task of Mr. Young himself. Nave explains the logic that such actions would be further harming his family.

He explains, "I don't know who you are. I don't know how you know the judge, or where you come from. I do know I have a lifetime of history with the judge, and trust in him as my family. See, I was in Vietnam with the judge and together we saw too much for two young boys out of Georgetown, Illinois. After what we went through, it seemed we could only trust one another. So with that said I know if he sent you, I will be as he would be in trusting you." The man looks out a thick glass window lined with frost on the top and sides, while a layer of snow covers the bottom. The city in the distance below is his focus as he tells Nave, "It used to be a solid place to live. Now it has nothing but corruption. I have always had money, my family was from old money and yet we were always humble. Always the ones who would give and sit equal aside those who had less. Now, seems money for these no-good, greedy fucks is all about how they can take and take and take. Who can be bought. Who can flaunt. I have nightmares of why did I not buy that spineless piece of shit attorney before they got to him. Hardy, I wonder what it was that got to him. I'm sure you reviewed the case and can see it sure changed in that closing statement. They fucking bought his ass, I tell you! Oh I will have my day with that son of a bitch! Here's the thing: I know damn well my daughter crossed the line. I can live with that and would deal with that. She is a kid and that dirty bastard has done this before."

He folds his arms, leans back against the windowsill, and slightly hunches forward as he emphasizes, "Aspen isn't the first one. Hell as I hear it, he is so cocky that he was just seen with another girl he supposedly just drove home so she didn't have to walk in the snow. Her mom came to me asking what I noticed about Aspen as her daughter is suddenly acting very strangely. Five girls in this town. Five! Yet, they are all afraid after one showed up at the sheriff's department, and the next week her dad was killed in what was called a freak hunting mishap. We all know damn well Young caught wind she was going to say something, and held true to her when he said if she told anyone he would hurt her family. Let me tell you, I don't have the skill of getting information that you may have. I'm sure once you start diggin you will find the foul odor of the shit a few high-ranking fuckers are tied into."

Nave pulls into town and stops at the small Ace Hardware.

"Hey there hun, you need any help? Those are some really good axes, and if you need a wood splitter, we have those in back," the woman tells him.

He asks, "Do you have a chipper? One that will chop even really hard stuff? You know like frozen limbs, sections that might have knots, and won't get jammed up if there is any wet material like sap?"

She looks puzzled and asks, "Noticed your truck says you come from Arizona. Do ya'll cut and chip in the winter down there? Hun, you wanna wait until at least spring before you go too crazy, you know choppin' things up and all."

He smiles and replies, "I guess I better just stick with the axe and splitter; right?"

The splitter and axe loaded up, he gets a feel for the town. Even reviewing the case, speaking with Robert and Aspen's father, he still needs to have no doubt in his task.

Across from the Ace, Nave stops in to have lunch. A young woman comes to his table and says, "Welcome to Frozen Lunch Times." She wears a name tag showing her name is Lindsey. Same straight forward, matter-of-fact personality that was portrayed in the transcripts.

With light conversation Nave asks, "This seems like a fun place to work. Are you making a career out of this, or are you in school?"

Lindsey replies, "Oh hell naw, matter fact, one more week and I'm outta here. Start my nursin' school up in Denver so no more scoopin' and grillin' for this girl."

She returns to grab an order and comes back. Nave asks, "Are you planning on staying in Denver or just getting school done there? I only ask because my mom is the HR director and recommends candidates for the Life Flight, ER Nurse program in Utah. She says they are hurting for ER, cardiac therapy, and pediatric nurses."

Lindsey, now very attentive asks, "What does Utah require, and is there a way I could keep in touch? After all, any inside help is good to have. So many people in school fighting for the same jobs."

Nave hands her a business card and tells her, "I will be in town for a few days. Call me, and I can give you my mom's office info after I find out myself what her address is. I don't carry that stuff with me. After that, you are on your own young lady. So do well in school."

She looks at the card and asks, "Mr. Bork, what is an off-shore geologist out of California, doing in our little town of Colorado?"

"Well, I bought a truck in Arizona and decided to take a little winter road trip," he answers.

The next day she calls to ask if she can get the information in regard to his mom at the hospital.

The business card, number, and name was all prearranged with the agency along with the altered appearance of Nave himself. He would not risk identity while doing the leg work for his investigation. When talking to Lindsey, he knew she would be off work at the time he would be in town.

"I have to stop at the mall to get some warmer shoes. So if you are near the mall I had her fax me her office letterhead, and she said that way when and if you complete the program, you can have her letterhead. She is very tough and persistent on wanting to see if you will be disciplined to hold onto the letterhead until you complete your training." Lindsey agrees to meet at the mall.

He comes out of the sporting goods store, and sees a small green car next to the Scout. He had told her what he drove and the unique truck wasn't hard to spot. He walks up, and sets his bag inside as she gets out. He hands her the letterhead, and directly addresses her, "Lindsey, I'm only going ask this of you one time. You are leaving town and that may be very good. I am investigating the Aspen Lorn case. It is a private firm out of California, and we have more information that this Young guy is getting more out of control. You know more than what you were asked in court. I also know your father wasn't such a great person to you before he died. Our firm helps young girls be safe. You are grown now, and I know you have a lot to tell me."

She sways to hit her right hip against her car, and the first of many drops run down her nose and over her lip. A brave sniffle and whip of her hair and she says, "I'm done being quiet. Where can we talk?"

They drive to a secluded spot just out of town in the Scout. The darkness this time of year does not wait for the clock to indicate nighttime. Along a dirt ridge, they overlook the glow of the town which she is anxious to forget. There, she finds more courage to focus on the past, perhaps with the promise of the future ahead of her. She brings her feet up beneath her legs, holds her knees close, and with power, she begins to explain.

"In a small town, girls are always looking for hope, a way to be someone, something, anything that will be better than the typical, helpless food server or cashier. You know sir, we don't learn these signs in school. Our parents either ignore, or are simply ignorant of the facts. It really isn't too hard for a guy to figure out which ones will go along or fall starry-eyed for a chance for what we think is the good life. Ridiculous to see now that there were many eyes gazing back at the hope, that they would be the one girl to land that catch."

She turns slightly to face him more directly, lowers her head, yet confidently looking through the tops of her eyes, expresses:

"Do you have any idea how perfectly fitting it is to be compared as predator and prey even as a human being? A child navigating her way through emotions, biological changes, economic uncertainty, peer pressure and for a few . . . finally being someone. Sure there are those who say, '*Oh these girls nowadays ask for it, they are the ones enticing and provocation lays upon their own doing!*' Sir, the fact is. . . well the sick fact is, the predator is all too cunning to lure its prey in."

Nave wants to allow her the open release to continue, and asks, "Lindsey, you're not the only one. Aspen wasn't the first, was she?"

She takes her sleeve and wraps it over her fingers to then dab the tears. "We think we did something wrong. We think we caused it. At the time, it seems harder to face your family rather than just hope it goes away. Each day is different yet just as scary. You know the girl working right beside you is going through the same thing, yet we fear the unknown. When it happens . . . well those dreams of being a 'big girl' are gone. You immediately have guilt, which is not like cheating on your math test. It is a guilt of which makes you wonder if your soul has abandoned you altogether. Just like prey, you feel trapped. Days when one of the girls doesn't show up, your stomach drops, your mind wanders not knowing if she is okay, and at the same time just as much wonder if he selected her as the one who will in some sick irony be the **lucky** girl. See, there is a perpetual flow of desperation on our side, and an infestation of sickness on his side. He became hungrier and found it to easy."

She rests her elbow on the window edge, cups her chin, and looks out the window. "I was fifteen. After my dad, shit I figured this was normal, yet so unsettled, made me an odd kid really. No idea of a normal boyfriend and probably looking for a way to escape childhood altogether. I started seeing the signs with the others and eventually, he even began to make me read books on how it was right because of how the old Mormons accepted it. I had no idea what polygamy was even about. He even showed me a video he had hidden of a few of the girls. He assured me he had video of me and if I ever said anything he would show it to everyone."

Nave sits and listens. To interject would only take the release of tension away which this girl had kept inside like a festering cyst. Then she offers him something he would have not imagined.

"One night, he passed out and I noticed his safe was left open. I only dared to take one tape. I have never been more scarred in my life. I hid it outside, and returned so I would be there when he woke. He hurried me off as his wife was to return the next day, and I watched him go close and lock his safe. I honestly don't think anyone will ever believe me, and even in the video it is hard to see me. But look closely, and you can see my name tag, my school lanyard, and a scratch I had from hitting the oven at work. In another part of the video, you will see Janie. She worked only a few weeks, and after her parents felt like she was acting funny they made her quit. She doesn't do anything in the video but you can see the deception and manipulation how he starts it."

"Please if you have any way to stop him, please, please, please do it!"

She adds a few more facts of different girls, some speculation of others, and then when they return to the parking lot, she opens her car door and turns to him and asks, "How long do you think your agency will take to do whatever you can do?"

Nave boldly assures her, "We are swift and don't exactly play by the rules."

Days go by, and Nave spends more time watching the town, studying the people, and spying on the habits of not only Young, but also Hardy. One day the skies are clear, the air warms slightly, and a nature path is partially clear of snow. Hardy parks his brand new truck, which was said to have been paid for by a family member, yet Nave's sources indicate is an acquisition of the town and given to Hardy. Hardy releases a golden retriever, and sets off toward south on the trail. As Hardy comes up to a trash can on the trail, Nave meets him as he walks the other way. Hardy pleasantly greets him.

Nave replies, "I suppose it is a nice day. Let me ask you Hardy, do you think the clear sky and a little warmer sun on your face makes it a nice day for everyone?"

"Hardy pulls his dog closer, and says, "Look jackass, I don't know who you are, but my right hand just took a firm grip on this Ruger. I suggest you move on, or it is you who will not be having such a good day!"

Nave takes a step closer and tells him, "It is a really nice day today. Cherish that which may be gone."

Nave walks off and leaves Hardy to contemplate the stress he now feels. A brisk pace back to his truck, and dirty snowmelt is slung behind the tires breaking loose as he hurries away from the trailhead.

Hardy pulls into his garage, closes the door, and walks into his kitchen. He tosses the keys on the counter, twists open a beer, and paces in his kitchen. He brings the cordless phone to the kitchen bar and sits it there as he finishes a second beer. He dials a number and once answered, frantically exclaims, "Goddamn it, you son of a bitch! You promised me this would all go away!"

He listens to who is on the phone, then replies, "I don't like being ambushed in the fucking park by a stranger asking questions. Never seen this fucker, no idea where he came from, and now I have to look over my shoulder." Again he listens to whom he has called before retracting angrily. "Don't worry? Don't worry? You know what motherfuckers, the truck, the money, that hot whore who would have never had anything to do with a guy like me in the first place, is all SHIT if you can't keep me from having strange fucks popping up out of the **thin mother fucking air?**"

He listens and seems to calm. His drinks come more slowly; he softens his tone, and once more replies, "I guess you are right. Probably was just some bastard sore over the trial and you're right, gonna be a few that want to express their anguish at times. Sorry, just on edge and all."

Parked outside of town, Nave has an earpiece in, his briefcase open, and as Hardy hangs up, Nave gently depresses the stop button on his tap. He removes his earpiece, and closes his briefcase. He winds back through the hills, and returns to the cabin.

For several days he lays out plans; he studies times, locations, habits and the activities of the town. After the fifth day, he returns to town. He walks out of the grocery store, and passes Hardy coming in. Hardy stops, turns and looks.

Nave needs to fix a hinge at the cabin, and returns to the hardware store just to pick up a replacement.

A very happy clerk comes around the counter. "Well, well Mr. Arizona has come on back in. You come to get a rake, or weed whacker hun?" She jokes about, and then shows him to the hinges. She sends him off with an ample amount of flirting, and today even a wink. He sits the hinge down on the seat, pulls out, and just past the stop sign he sees blue and red lights behind him.

The assigned Scout was equipped for his task, and no sooner had the cops lights activated, the truck's navigation unit alerted, "NES 1912 continue straight at safe speed and await direction."

His delay in stopping prompted the sirens of the patrol car. In the patrol car, the officer calls in the plate and description. Dispatch first advises no record found. After Nave continues and the siren comes on, dispatch recalls the officer on his radio and advises, "County unit 147, discontinue stop. Vehicle and occupant is federal; do not interrupt." Nave monitors all this from his truck as well.

Nave leaves town using a route completely obscure from his normal route to assure any tail or curiosity would be diverted.

A friend of Young and now Hardy, the officer meets with them at Young's house. It was almost as if this officer was on trial himself for the stop earlier in the day. Hardy and Young grills the officer over and over in a frantic manner after knowing of the dispatch transmission.

Young asks, "You are telling me even though your dispatch told you to disregard, you didn't even stop and see who the hell he was? GOD DAMN IDIOT! Fuck Hardy, do they get these fucks from the retard school? I don't get it. You turn your lights on, stop the car, and at least, AT LEAST get his fuckin' ID!"

Hardy tries to mediate between the two. "Orin, could he have stopped the guy? Maybe I guess, but if dispatch says he is a Fed, well frankly we have more to worry about than stopping him. Hell, are you not more concerned why this Fed FUCK is snooping around and more, why he come up to me? You already had your trial, you walked. What about me? Tell me, what about me?"

The officer can only offer even less information letting them know he ran the plate out of Arizona and it was flagged. "Sorry guys, I just can't magically create information. The guy is protected, and pretty freakin' deep."

At the county station, the sheriff called the dispatcher into his office. "Do you see this fax? This reply came from the FBI, this reply from the state office, and this reply from the Colorado Department of Law Enforcement."

She looks at it and responds, "Pull the tapes. Before you come down on me, pull the tapes. I can see your faxes are advising no one from those offices has any knowledge of interfering with the stop, but I was following what I was being advised. I mean, who would know so quickly we were stopping that vehicle and all the related information? The tag itself is flagged and we can't even request a record of it."

The sheriff holds the paper firmly in his left hand as the page wrinkles, he shouts, "Did you read this part? Our Agency does not interfere, request, or monitor local dispatch communication. It would be the best practice to effect the stop and ascertain the identity of all occupants and forward to this department immediately!"

The sheriff throws the paper on the floor and leaves the room.

Nave returns to Florida.

"Welcome back troublemaker," Robert tells Nave.

Nave has his briefcase, and Robert goes to the door and motions someone in. It is the tech from Gainesville. "So you had a boot tryin' to stop you in Colorado? Dumb rookies."

Nave smiles and asks, "So I take it you were the one on the dispatch diversion?"

Excitedly he answers, "Holy crap, that was too easy! Hey, just fair warning, not always that simple. That dispatcher was an airhead." Robert asks, "So what do you have, and what sort of timeline are you thinking? I would guess a few months."

Nave takes a water from the mini-fridge, sits on the barstool, looks first at Robert, then at Jason, the tech. "It hasn't stopped. We don't have a few months. Robert you keep the briefcase, I will pick it up in two days and you let me know if I missed anything. I am going home and thawing out for a bit, "Nave tells them as he shows himself out.

Jason laughs at Robert and says, "Holy shit, I hope you guys pay him well. I am thinking we want to keep him on our side."

Robert pours a drink and replies, "Jason, we have no worries about him. He isn't on a side. He is more of a rogue out to justify his existence, and this is his way of mattering to serve."

Nave drives up the street, and sees Lynn on a ladder and Amanda on another ladder, and as he pulls up Amanda waves. "Padre, I know you have an exact science to putting up Christmas lights, and I know all the bulbs have to light and be pointing in the same direction. Just relax, cause we are just getting the lights in position. You can perfect it once we get it in place."

He playfully scorns a look her way and then to Lynn and tells them, "I will go change, and come supervise."

The window nearest them opens, and he has Christmas music playing. He comes out with his ugliest Christmas sweater, and they all sing to the songs. Of course Dean has to over-affect the twang as she makes fun of his country Christmas CD. He allows them to drape the tree in front, and as they twirl the entry posts, he surprises them with hot chocolate and whipped cream. The sun drops, and the neighbors walk over to share in the first house to have lights up. Nave, Lynn, Chris and Josey, their little girl, and Amanda stand talking out at the end of the drive.

Amanda, anxious to see the lights, tells Nave, "It's dark dad, go flip the switch."

He looks at her and says, "Hey Dean, you started this, you finish it."

Very excited she asks, "Seriously, I can do the first lighting–the almighty event that you usually have to do?"

He smiles and says, "You deserve it. Besides, you and Lynn ran most of these lights so if someone gets shocked, well it isn't going to be me! Hey Lynn, go hold her hand as she plugs that in."

"Lynn slaps him and says, "You hush, mister."

Amanda plugs in the box and the house comes to life—simple, yet crisp and precise. The eaves are straight with lights, the windows glowing, each tree has a different geometrical shape, the fence is wrapped, and the entry is like a runway to a happy home. The neighbors join them, and Nave has been outvoted to now have a traditional CD of Christmas music while they sit outside around the fire.

The next week, Nave spends time taking small jobs throughout Florida, and makes up for time away from home. As it is Amanda's Christmas break, Nave takes most of that time off to be with her. There is one job that has to be done near Fort Lauderdale, and she wants to go with him. A customer with a Rolls Royce needs a set of side mirrors, and the iconic hood mount. Not to be trusted in the traditional mail, it is up to Nave to get it there before their Christmas show. Amanda goes with him, and after the delivery they stop for lunch. Amanda is an open girl, no judgments, yet still has not seen all there is to see in life. As they sit near a window, as per usual Nave positions himself to watch anyone enter the place. He can see a rather interesting person coming into the restaurant. Amanda has not noticed as of yet, and Nave just sits back and waits to see how she will react. The woman, WOMAN? Is all of six foot three" hair well done, and a slight curl over her shoulder and down the front. Tight leather skirt, dark pantyhose, and shiny patent leather high heels make a perfect outfit. Her hands large, forearms skinny, and defined thick veins similar to an athlete, hold her purse. Amanda, uncertain, looks more intently, looks back to Nave, yet doesn't say anything. The woman has done a fine job to have herself in top order. With the pantyhose, it is not clear if she has shaved her legs. The curious look of Amanda likely comes from the dark shadowing of the woman's chin, strong chiseled jaw, and upper lip. Amanda may still have the confusing thought of: Why does this woman have facial hair? Amanda starts to take a drink from her straw just as the woman orders. The masculine, baritone voice is proud and confident as HE orders his lunch.

Amanda slightly chokes, looks intently at her dad, and says, "Dad" shyly and cautiously dragging her eyes in his direction.

Nave just smiles and says, "Welcome to South Florida."

The Christmas season passes and it is now the first week of January, Nave begins to re-engage in his work. He expresses to Amanda how January and part of February will be extremely busy. The first week, he does more local, quick work as he begins to secretly orchestrate the elimination of Colorado. On Saturday, he meets with Robert. After reviewing the information Nave presents, Robert lets Nave know any assistance will be readily available. In the secure room, they brief all details, and Nave leaves with the suitcase. He stops at home to spend the remainder of the night with Amanda. He tells her he will be on a long turnaround again. He says he will have to go clear up to Pensacola, Florida and even into Alabama for a day.

Early Monday morning, he drives north on the turnpike long before the sun has cast any ray over the chilly meadows of the horse fields through Ocala. By the time he can see his truck's shadow in front of him, he has already passed Tallahassee. He stops in, and makes reservations for a later date at Destin, Florida. After that, he continues onward to Pensacola. He spends the day there, and once night comes he secures his truck in a private hangar, and meets Robert in a remote area of an airfield.

Robert first talks to Nave alone. "Nave, we have the jet set up and there is a pilot who is a GES. Much like you, he doesn't talk much; he will not ask you anything, he doesn't want you asking him anything. You two will get along great."

About this time, a short, stocky guy comes from a side door. He says, "In twenty minutes, I will have the jet in front of this door. The lights will go dark on the building for ten seconds or less. That is all the time we have, and we will be cleared for takeoff."

There was nothing more to discuss. There is no room for error, and Nave's timeline is critical on this flight to Colorado. Robert goes one way, Nave is in the hangar, and the pilot walks off as well.

The plane maneuvers to the hangar door, the lights flicker and go dark, then the lights come back on and the plane seems to have never stopped as it turns to approach the runway. In minutes, they are in the air. In his seat, Nave reads a script of exactly how to exit the plane, which vehicle to get into, and a GPS coordinate of where he will need to be in order to have an escort back to Florida. The plane lands on a military base in Colorado, and Nave is hurried into a Suburban. The truck takes him directly to the cabin, and there is no conversation or communication of any kind. The silence, direct order, and swiftness is in place and followed precisely as Nave requested. Now in the cabin, he sets his briefcase on a table, opens it as always with codes, and takes a small vial from a side pocket. The vial is plastic, capped, and a yellow tape seals the cap. He then slides another small, locked box from under the bed, and sets it on the bed. He carefully looks all his items over, and turns out the light.

Orin Young finishes his work at the restaurant, and heads home. Seemingly exhausted, cold from the icy wind that is channeling through his breezeway of his porch, and struggling with his key while he balances a six-pack of beer under one arm, he finally opens the door. The house is warm; his dog is old yet still sits near his feet as he sinks into his couch. His right hand tires of turning channels until he decides to leave it on re-runs of *COPS*. Still in his khakis and restaurant polo shirt, he struggles to bend over to take his shoes off. As he slumps over, he stalls. His eyes swollen, his mouth lightly opens and the first dribbles of slobber moisten the leftover powder from the mini-donuts he had eaten. The TV is now the only light and he lies heavy into the arm of the green leather couch.

Unable to move, he has a sense of delirium and disbelief as he hears Nave speak to him. "Orin, it doesn't matter who I am, and it doesn't matter how I got here in your house. See, I know on Mondays your wife goes to Grand Junction to see her dad in the nursing home. I also know it is always a Monday when you would bring one of those poor girls back here to your house and even hide a camera, so you could have nights like this to come home and watch what a sick, disturbed monster you are. Oh don't worry; your wife is just fine. She is probably asleep on a side chair as her father lay still in his medical bed. You can also be assured you will never have to have your wife sit next to you in a hospital bed."

Orin's head twitches, as he struggles to generate the control to lift his head and look at Nave.

Nave still sits in a wood chair he brought from the dining room; he is in a full body Lycra suit with nothing exposed. He continues to inform Orin Young. "The donuts you have every Monday night with your beer as you sit your pathetic lump of sick flesh on this couch made my work very easy. Here is what you are going to experience, Orin. You already know you can't move. You will sit here slumped over until you fade off. You may drift in and out a few times; you may or may not feel the horrific pain of defalcating through your pants and then possibly violently vomiting. In this position, you will likely not move much and just be a huge mess once anyone finds you. Ironic, don't you think? After all the times you scolded your wife for being heavy, for being stupid, for all the times you embarrassed her in front of those girls and customers at your restaurant . . . now you will be the disgusting one who is a pile of perverted shit. However, just so you know I am not a cold, cruel empty soul, I am going to take your dog and set her outside. I don't know if I could feel right if she happened to eat your vomit and died. After all, you have a shitload of poison in you. It is probably starting to really set in about now. So before you shit yourself or spew bodily fluid everywhere, I better get going. By the way, I took your safe and destroyed the tapes. You already got off, and those images would only open the scars of those you already cut. If you wonder about the other items in the safe, well it went to a few girls' college funds." Nave replaces the chair, and takes the dog to the garage.

Nave walks to Hardy's new truck, and calmly drives off. He returns the truck to Hardy's house, and takes a short walk along the wet pavement until he comes to a cut in the trees. In about a hundred yards, he reaches another street. Not more than five minutes of walking in the street, there is a glow in the wet distance. He continues to walk toward the approaching car; the damp road spray almost sounds like bacon cooking in a diner. The sizzling of the tires on the wet road slows, and a car stops across from him in the opposite lane. Nave reads the plate as it comes closer, and then notices a sequence of lights on the dash. He opens the back door, and is taken away. An hour's drive in, Nave is pulling into an airstrip; the pilot has his plane waiting. He exits the car, goes to the trunk, and carefully slips the suit off, and leaves it in the trunk.

Now warm, he sits in the seat of the private jet and opens his case. The announcement is made. "NES 1912; Colorado package has been delivered."

The next day Nave is set to travel back, and makes it to Destin, Florida. He finds a marina, and notices how much happier the locals seem to be when it is not clustered with Spring Break students. There is a normal walk of life this time of year. He finds a small diner, and sits on the porch looking out to the Gulf.

A younger man, maybe nineteen or twenty carries a bucket and a hose. "Not too bad a day is it?" he asks of Nave.

Nave sips his spiced tea down and answers, "Not sure there are too many bad days with this view."

The young man sits in another chair and informs Nave, "Well, true; however, when you see those waters trash your family business, or watch a swarm of college assholes trash your entire city, one wonders if paradise is a target."

After a decent conversation, Nave heads over to the hotel he had made arrangements with before.

Even being cool for Florida, it was still quite a bit warmer than where he had just been. He drives across HWY 98, and pulls into the Bayou Country Club. He speaks with the golf pro there to see how tee time runs, and as the pro looks over the book, Nave pays close attention to only one name. He returns a few hours later, and heads to the driving range. He sets a bucket of range balls on the ground, props up the rented clubs, and strikes up a conversation with the gentleman in the next driving slot to his right.

Nave first says, "Wow, it sure is cold out here today."

The man snickers and tells him, "You must be a local. Let me tell you buddy, this is paradise for me. Every year I come down here for a few days then keep going south for a week. I fly out of Del Ray next week and will head home to a shit pile of snow." They are the only two driving balls, and the man introduces himself."Muh name is Mark Hardy, I'm from Colorada, and sneak down here to warm up a bit after the holidays. The wife is over gettin' her face done, and some new paint on the finger and toes."

Nave leans the club against the post, and says, "My name is Orin."

Hardy has no suspicious thought and quickly says, "You don't say, I have a good buddy back home who is an Orin."

Nave loses the casual demeanor and eases in close to Hardy. Hardy has more of a concerned shyness, and Nave explains to him, "Hardy, you don't come here every year. You didn't even pay for the week here in Florida. And you may have guessed by now, my name isn't Orin. You really feel good about a new truck, a fancy trip, and your house paid off to be such a coward and let those girls suffer?"

Hardy now twitches, and looks around as if someone will come to save him and tries to reason with Nave. "Hey I don't know who you are, and yeah, maybe I am a piece of shit for what I done. But understand, it was my career they threatened. I ain't no top-notch lawyer who could go anywhere. That was my last chance and that town has a hold on everything. Yeah, maybe it was wrong, but you don't know those girls either. Those girls in that town just about ask for it. So why should I throw my life down the drain on a lost cause?"

Nave takes the largest driver out of his bag. He explains to Hardy the force generated by a professional golfer and then in a twisted reality advises, "But Hardy, I have never been a great golfer. I would have no idea how much force I would generate in a swing, especially since I don't play much." He looks at Hardy, who is physically sweating now. "See Mark, I am not a golfer. I am more into chess. Planning, strategy, counter moves and prediction. Sure, along the way there are a few casualties and some pieces are eliminated, but it is the checkmate that is the reward."

Nave wipes off the club he held, slides it into the bag, and looks to Hardy as he tells him, "Mark Hardy, tell your wife to take a lot of pictures. Enjoy this vacation. Pretty sure you may not be back for a long time."

Nave walks off, gets into a Lincoln Town Car, and drives off. He had the rental set up and left his truck at the hotel.

Hardy sits down for a while, wipes his face with the golf towel, and then goes into the pro shop insisting to know who had been out there with him. The counter person looks over the book, and says that no one else had scheduled any times. Almost hyperventilating, Hardy hurries to his room.

The next afternoon, Mrs. Young presses her garage door opener and is irritated when she sees her old dog come slowly from the garage. "Orin . . . why is . . . Orin?" She calls as she walks into the house. She drops her keys, as she has a clear view of her husband slumped over. There is no asking if he is okay and his mere appearance is immediate evidence of his death.

The sheriff, the county coroner, and CSI are all at the house, and one young investigator says, "I have a hair, and don't anyone walk anywhere in this house, especially the dining room." The sheriff asks what he has.

The investigator explains, "Well, this is not going to be too hard to figure out. We have a foreign hair that is not too dry and old. Can you see how the chair legs have been drug back to the dining room? And when I was picking up this hair, I saw a well-soiled path of footprints from the dining room to the door."

The coroner later takes Orin's body; Mrs. Young is questioned, yet quickly released and the house continues to be processed.

Late Sunday night, Mr. and Mrs. Hardy are weary, exhausted. They look to each other and smile as they turn the last corner to their street after traveling all day. She looks puzzled; he has formed a few beads of sweat. As they near their home, they see a patrol car, an unmarked car, a van, and yellow caution tape blocking off their home. Neighbors stand out front, and as he slows their car, two marked units appear behind them and turn on their red and blue lights. Over the PA radio, they are ordered out of the car, and Mr. Hardy is quickly taken into custody.

"What the hell is going on? I didn't do anything wrong. That jury entered their own verdict!" His questioning likely in thoughts brought on of his guilt and the outcome. He obviously believes the arrest is for his taking the bribe or making a deal.

He will soon be hit harder than a golf club when he has the homicide investigator at the scene tell him, "Mr. Hardy, we have evidence sufficient to effect a search of your residence, vehicles, and your person. In relation to that search, we have probable cause to place you under arrest for the murder of Orin Young." The investigator smugly reads him his rights, and asks if he would like to speak freely or invoke his right to silence. Hardy, being a criminal attorney, is at least smart enough to remain silent.

Several weeks later, Mrs. Young drives slowly up the street, slows, and then stops near the restaurant her husband used to own. The parking lot is covered in snow, the windows fogged over, an unlighted sign sits idly that would have normally been flashing, "OPEN." Loose, tattered yellow tape ends lay strewn about from when investigators had taped the building off during the search. After a brief pause, she continues to the courthouse to sit in on the discovery arguments to determine all the charges to be brought against Mr. Hardy.

A prosecutor stands confidently behind the old wood podium. The prosecutor proudly informs the judge of all the evidence which the crime lab has processed. He carefully advises the State has a hair sample on Mr. Young which matches that of Mr. Hardy. The footprints are an identical match to those taken from Hardy's home. Hardy's truck was seen, and tire impressions taken are consistent of the timeline that would place Hardy's truck at the scene. One odd yet distinguishing item was a missing chess piece. Mr. Young had a crystal, gold-layered chess set in his home, and the king was missing from the display. There was a crystal and gold king chess piece found in the seat storage of Hardy's truck.

The trial drags through the winter months. In mid-April, Nave is taking Amanda over to Islands of Adventure and he always likes to listen to The Monsters of the Mid-Day on a local radio station. During a station break, a national newscaster reads of some national stories. One in particular makes Nave smile.

"And out of Colorado, a jury found a former attorney, Mark Hardy, guilty of the murder of a former defendant whom he had prosecuted in a messy child sexual assault case. He is awaiting sentencing." The newscaster presents the stories with no prejudice or change in the reflection of his voice even though one national story was incomparable, as it was about a family of ducks that had mysteriously wandered into a Clanton, Alabama church.

The radio bunch comes back on, and the leader of this afternoon radio mess asks about the national news, and if anyone had heard of the Hardy thing out of Colorado.

The one female of the group who seemingly fronts as a dimwitted, carefree, yet very opinionated member of the group loudly exercises her command of the mic as she educates the rest. "Oh, oh,, oh, wait, wait ya'll, I read about this when we were on our Christmas break."

A wingman of the group sounds frustrated as he reminds her, "It isn't Christmas break anymore. It's winter vacation or something. You can't call it that. You know that because I tell you every year now!"

She sounds less than convinced by the huff in her voice "UGHHH listen! It is the last two weeks of December, I have to listen to Christmas, or should I say F'ing, winter music in every damn store, I eat way too many candy canes that make my ass fat . . ."

The head guy interjects, "Candy canes, waffles, red velvet cake,"

"Okay, well maybe not just candy canes, but you know what I am saying. Plus the fact I go broke buying my son a shit load of presents that he opens on . . .what day does he open them? You're damn right, Christmas, not winter people, he opens them like all you do, even the fakers who cause this stupid crap of being politically correct and not saying Christmas, Christmas Eve, or Christmas Day. So ya'll can kiss my candy cane ass because I am always calling it Christmas break!"

The main host brings her back on track about the story. She continues to give her input on the story. "So, when we were all off on our CHRISTMAS break, I read this story. The dirtbag guy who had some ice cream shop was doing some bad stuff to the girls that worked there, as the story says, cause you all know we can't give out any bad info and get our ass sued right? Anyhow, one of the girls told, and they had a trial and all. Well the attorney guy, you know the one on the girls' side, he totally was bought off, allegedly, and the crazy thing, a few months later, he killed the guy that got off."

The wingman personality clarifies, "Okay for you listeners, and probably all of those listening, I will clarify what she just butchered. The guy who allegedly molested the girls went to trial. He got off, no pun intended, and the attorney for the state, later went and killed the guy."

The leader of the show adds, "I did read more as you two were butchering radio as it is, and found that many in the city say the attorney, this Hardy guy, intentionally threw the case, and they believe just so he could go off this guy later. Here is the crazy thing; in the investigation, they found that this attorney was given a truck to drive, and a huge bonus during the original trial. A lot of shady doings out there in Heehaw, Colorado if you ask me."

Amanda looks over to her dad, and in an inquisitive manner asks, "You think the guy got what he deserved, don't you?"

He looks at her as the approach the parking attendant and says with a smile, "Seems to me two people got what they deserved."

Chapter 12
Agent Suspicion

Federal Agents, Calvin Morrow and Mike Holcomb, make a visit to Hardy after his trial. Morrow is still unsettled by the dispatch events, and after speaking with Hardy cannot rest his suspicions even though his partner Holcomb is at ease to let it go.

Morrow discusses the information with Holcomb, and agrees that Hardy is linked in some way, yet as he drives into the sheriff's station he stops the truck, turns the key off, pauses then looking out the window, tells Holcomb, "What if Hardy was set up?"

His partner turns to him, his right hand is on the dash; his left arm rests along the center console. He answers, "I can't retry the case; I won't say Hardy did it alone, with someone, or not at all. I do know I reviewed every word of that first trial, and there is one guy who faced his final judge last winter. We were sent here to look into some jackass impersonating a Federal Agent, NOT to solve a child-abuse-turned-murder case. Is it weird that some hillbilly confronted Hardy, and then when stopped, there was the interference? Yeah, maybe. But there isn't any more to go on. The truck out of Arizona hasn't been found, and no records are available."

Morrow opens his door, steps out, and says, "No records, immediate contact to dispatch, and now one dead guy and one in prison. Something . . . someone knows a lot more." He shrugs his shoulders and raises his hands as he walks to the door of the station.

Back in Florida, Nave is staining his fence when he hears the deep, hollow warning of a Charger coming up his street.

Amanda asks her dad, "Does this mean you are going out of town for a few days?"

He assures her he is going to finish this fence before any other tasks are taken on. Lynn walks over and looks at the amount of fence that is left to do, and jokes, "Yeah, you might be a while doing this."

Nave laughs as he tells her, "You know, as much of my food you have eaten over here, I think a little free labor might be justified." Nave doesn't know Amanda and Lynn had talked earlier and Amanda had already mentioned how lucky she was that she got to help with staining the entry post and fence. Nave sets the spray gun down, and asks what brought her over.

Lynn goes to her trunk, and grabs a sack and a big blanket. As she walks toward a tree, she says, "I figured if I was going to come help get this fence stained I should grab some chicken. So get your butts over here, and take a few minutes to have some lunch."

Nave asks, "Dean, would you . . .

Amanda stops him before he can finish and says, "Yes Padre, I will get some sweet tea."

"Did you get Publix by accident, or do you just know they are the best?" he asks.

"Your daughter might have been in on the lunch idea a little."

After a quick lunch under the tree, he continues spraying the larger sections while Lynn helps Amanda hand stain around the entry post. He looks over, and sees that Lynn is awkward with a brush. Her hair is pulled up, and poking through an old Buccaneers hat. She has a sharp, tan jawline, and a little muscle tone to her shoulders that are free because of the thin tank top she wears. Small black cuffed shorts look even shorter when long, thin, tan legs extend down from them. Old running shoes and ankle socks finish off her outfit. She did come to work, and Nave has to hold back on his OCD to go touch up the areas they are either missing or not done as he would have liked. One of the things that pleases him most is that his Dean is happy to have an older female figure to be close to. His work makes any serious relationship unlikely, and there have been many times he questioned his path. This day he looks to the two and one he admires for her strength and what a strong woman she will be one day. He never questions her love for him or the connection they have had. In the other, he finds an attraction that he cannot allow to become a distraction. His eyes and desires lead his mind to think how grateful he would be to have her visits more often and even permanent. As easy as he visualizes this fairytale life, he quickly shakes his head of the unreal possibilities. Still no man, even of blurry or no sight at all, could find Lynn anything less than exceptionally attractive.

The two girls put in a good day's work, and Lynn walks over to Nave near the far end of the fence. She has no idea of the thoughts that Nave has struggled with earlier, and to make his head even more abruptly embattled, she playfully demands, "Now Mr. Slave Driver, being as I have brushed these here posts all day, the sun scorching my tender, hot, and now dusty skin, I must demand you stay clear of your wash room for a moment. See, I am in dire need to cool myself under the shower and rid my body of this awful dirt. Why yes, I could simply have my master hose me down here outside; however, it would be visually inappropriate amongst the neighbors and especially the young eyes of your daughter. So I do warn you to not wander beyond the doors of your guest bathroom until your labor girl has emerged fresh and clean." She laughs, and blames her provocative nature on the fumes of the stain. As she walks off, he looks over to Amanda. She has been fixed on them, and just smiles. He gives her a look, and goes back to finishing the fence.

At the station in Colorado, Morrow sits at a desk as the night passes, and he welcomes the morning crew who arrives. One asks, "Been here all night? Still trying to figure out the whole thing with that white Scout?"

Morrow acknowledges that is what still troubles him "I have been doing this all my life. Well, at least the last fifteen years as a Fed, and this just doesn't add up. There is more to this truck, and how is it no one knows who, or where it went?"

The deputy tells the agent, "You are in the wrong place, looking at the wrong screens."

Morrow rolls back, folds his arms, and eagerly asks what the deputy meant. The deputy advises that he should try looking at a few of the store cameras, and even the ones that have cameras on the outside. "I thought they taught you Feds all that shit in your *advanced* super cop schools."

Morrow and Holcomb start later the next morning and try to reach as many stores as possible to see customers, cars, and anything that will bring any peace to Morrow. After two days of discovering many stores don't keep recordings after a few days, they have all but given up on this idea. They have already spoken to the shopping mall security, who advised they didn't patrol the parking lots and any video they had would have been erased.

Morrow stops at one of the mall anchor stores to grab a new belt. As he is about to leave, he notices an off-duty cop and asks, "So is this an overtime gig, and how often do they have you guys in here?"

The city cop stands around and talks a little, and through conversation Morrow discusses the dead-ends he has been running into.

The city cop at one point laughs in disgust and says, "I will tell you now, if you are looking for any cooperation from that county department, you are going to only find dead ends. Hell, just hope you don't find yourself dead in the end. Corrupt shit over there." He also lets Morrow know that the store operates its own cameras, and even has a few mounted on the exterior. After the usual outcomes he has encountered, he shrugs it off at first saying he was sure the tapes have been long erased by this time.

The cop, who stands about six five, is a football player type, often grasping his hands along the collarbone area of his tactical style vest, looks down to Morrow and says, "This store is no bullshit, bro. They are all digital, and back up everything. It is all stored on a hard drive, and their loss prevention catalogs every week. They are in between eight and four. May be worth a try."

The next night, Morrow calls Holcomb who has already returned to Virginia. Holcomb is in bed, His wife is a small, petite woman. She rests atop him as the dancing light of an off - balanced candle illuminates her creamy skin. Her short black hair allows her thin neck to be as exposed as the rest of her body. Given her naturally small frame, it would be understandable to believe the solid, round, directly forward-facing breast were a later addition to her body. Her eyes are dark, her nose is solid, and her pouty lips seem to be quite fitting for this Argentinian goddess. The seduction of a South American woman is the pleasure of Holcomb this night.

As he lies amazed, the phone rings. She smiles, lowers her face to his left ear, and tells Holcomb, "I am going to answer that. I am going to tell, (you know who) what I am going to do to you and if you talk to him, then you better hope he is better at doing you than I am." He resists nothing and allows her to pick up the phone.

"Hello, Cal. Listen to this. Right now, Mike is lying directly under me. Now, I know you have seen my body because I catch you looking all the time. This body is still gleaming from the body butter lotion I slowly rubbed into my skin when I was waiting for him to get home. Oh I rubbed it deep, hard and let me tell you, I did not miss one spot. My breasts are silky, my hard, flat stomach is smooth; my round, hot ass is almost glowing as the candles shine on it. And yes Cal, I made sure I waxed everything. See, you have had my man for a long time and now I have him. This is MY time. And after days of just being alone with only few porn vids to watch, well I am about to unleash myself on your partner. Oh Cal, there is nothing we will not cover tonight that I watched while he was gone. Plus a little more. Now Agent Morrow, I did tell him he could take the phone and talk to you; however, if he does then you are going to have to do all the naughty things I am about to do to him. So Cal, are you willing to do that? Because right now I am holding him in my right hand as I talk to you. I might struggle to keep talking once I take my thick lips around him. Oh Cal, your partner seems to be a little stiff. Should I hand the phone to him, and you two can talk and plan a little date so you can finish him off? Are you on your way over now, or should I just tell him to call you tomorrow? Oh dear, tomorrow may not be good either because I saw a lot on those dirty videos that I plan on trying. Cal? Cal? I can't hear you. Didn't you want to talk to Mike?"

He simply replies loudly, "Mike, you lucky fucker. Just call me when your exotic wife is done with you!"

The next afternoon, Holcomb meets with Morrow at the office. Morrow immediately flew back to Virginia. After the expected hazing of jealously from Morrow, they look over what he discovered in Colorado.

Morrow explains how he was able to review the videos, and that the white International Scout was there. He elaborates the details of seeing the man meet with the girl and them leaving together. He was even more excited as the zoom was able to capture an image of the girl. Morrow had already checked the girl's photo, and discovered it was in fact Lindsey who had worked at the restaurant. He adds that whoever was in the Scout never allowed a clear camera shot of him, and it was too difficult to see inside the truck. Morrow urges Holcomb to go to Denver.

"We, have to talk to that girl and see what the deal is with Mr. Scout." Holcomb seems to be onboard, and throws a brown file over to Morrow. On the case file tab, Holcomb has used a black sharpie to write, "SCOUT."

Morrow and Holcomb have a meeting with their senior case advisor, who has looked over the information they collected. Morrow asks this to be assigned a full investigatory case, and seeks financial and personnel support. Their supervisor is not so impressed and more so, not willing to allocate funding for this— what he calls meaningless goose chase.

The supervisor practically scolds the two, "What the hell do we have here? Some jackass calls into a Podunk sheriff's office and tells them to disregard the stop. The vehicle is not found because the fucking plate was a fake. Now you want me to allow two of my guys, OH WAIT not two, you want a whole goddamn army to chase down this mysterious INTERNATIONAL SCOUT. Am I missing the punch line? You have some hunch this Scout is involved in the murder. A goddamn, mutha fuckin' solved fuckin' murder! A solved fucking case. Someone got over on Andy and Barn, and you want me to allow you to go find Opie who is driving this white Scout. Ohhhh wait, Opie picked up some girl at the mall and she went away with him, came back, and drove off. Hell, let me call the NSA, CIA, and get a tactical team for extra firepower. DO YOU SEE HOW GODDAMNED ASININE THIS SOUNDS *MORROW?* Holcomb, why do you let this dip shit drag you into this crap?"

The supervisor stands up from his desk and stands near a water stained window overlooking a common area. He lightens his tone and asks, "Okay, I realize you may see something in all this. I like that you want to go after everything with a passion. Hell, you have been doing it for a long-ass time. But guys please understand the other issues we have take precedence, and we can't afford to have two good guys chasing this stuff. Right now, I have a stack of pressing cases, and you two should already be in California working on a guy who is scamming people out of their Federal income tax returns. That is real crime. Poor, hardworking, everyday folks not getting their returns and somehow we can't trace where the funds are going. Go help those folks."

They walk out, and in a way come to agree with the level of importance of the other cases. Morrow still goes to his desk and sits staring at the closed file which simply has ""SCOUT" scribbled over the top tab. Almost like saying goodbye, he clutches the file and releases all his held air as he drops it into the file drawer.

Chapter 13
New Technology

Over the course of the next year, Nave has eliminated three other targets while the continued guise of the high-end service career has been steady. The targets have been lower level, and swift.

The first of the three was an alert form the tracking device. He was on a routine job taking an all-numbers-matching 69 Z/28 with only four hundred original miles in a padded and temperature-controlled trailer from St. Petersburg, Florida to a Miami Dolphins player. After dropping off the trailer, he had decided to drive through a deprived and crime-stricken area of town.

The alert announces, and the women on the in dash computer advises, "NES 1912 confirm status."

Nave confirms, "NES 1912; 10-10."

She delivers details, "All ES, 1912 is 10-19 target. Details in twenty seconds." Target information is sent to all cases with positive photographic ID, fingerprint verification, and case information. Mandatory subject study should have been done by each ES prior. "NES 1912 is now locked in, and four miles from target. ES 4422 is thirty minutes, and locked in. Assist with diversion at Martin Luther and Interstate 95. GES 2006 is locked, and ten minutes to the south. GES 2006 will stage and await NES 1912 assist request."

As she finishes coordinate details, Nave advises he is in visual sight and proceeding on foot. This is a dangerous yet necessary practice to obtain more detail and confirmations. GES 2006 advises he is arriving, and has visual on target and NES 1912. GES 2006 has a vehicle grill-mounted, high-powered camera recording the event, which is being immediately transmitted to tech support and watched by Robert. The cameras record the event.

The street is cluttered with trash; several homeless shuffle carts along the sidewalk, often having to kick and move the sleeping from their path. One woman finds a paper coffee cup with a black lid resting near the top of the other trash, and takes the lid off. She peers inside for a slight moment and tips the cup back as she drinks the remainder of what is left. Another man leans against a half concrete wall that has broken iron railing atop of it. He appears more alert; his shirt is worn, his tan slacks wrinkled and smeared with dirt along the calf areas, and upon his feet, Avia sneakers. The sneakers have good, solid soles, and the bag nearest this man is more of a backpack/computer type. No cardboard around him, no alcohol bottles, no shopping cart that contains any belongings. Walking in his direction from the other side of the overpass is Nave. As Nave nears, he drops a pack of Pall Mall cigarettes. The pack lands at the man's right extended leg. Politely, the man picks it up and hands it up to Nave.

"Wouldn't mind having one of those if you could spare one," the man says with squinting eyes, and one hand acting as a sun visor cupped around his forehead. Nave tells him, he only has two left and can't spare one. Nave turns the corner, walks another block, and climbs into his truck.

Carefully, he sets the pack of Pall Mall on a scanner that is linked to Robert's tech support, and in less than sixty seconds the woman announces, "NES 1912; 10-19X." (10-19 with the added X is a confirmation that the ES is with or contacted the target and all ID including fingerprint and tracking device are a match.)

GES 2006 is still parked with direct sight of the target. The camera shows the man lean back, cradle the back of his head, and now extend both legs out and flat. He is about ten minutes into the shady portion of the overpass, and in the glare of sunlight he looks to his left. Nave has returns, and asks the guy his name.

"Man, out here we ain't got no names. Just another poor black man held down by the system."

Nave has a paper sack under his left arm and that pack of Pall Malls in his right hand. He baits the man by offering him the last cigarette and shows him a very cold bottle of Miller Lite. "See, I walked away and it got to me. I am in no rush; I am done working for today, and I was simply walking around the area as my car is being worked on around the corner. Car wasn't done, and I figured I could have been better to you. So what do you say, we could take a place on that table over there, and you can have this last smoke and drink one of these beers so you don't have me driving drunk when my car is done?" Nave tells him as he holds the beer by the bottleneck and starts to walk over to the concrete table that is on the edge of a park.

The park likely has not echoed the shrills of kids on the merry-go-round in many years. The rusted backstop fence and weed-covered ballfield may only be a memory for a few long gone or even now sleeping against the chain-link fence. It is quiet away from the overpass, and random pigeons hop over to see if they too can get a free bee. The twist-off cap releases with a popping hiss and the smoke-like vapors that escape greet the recipient with the aroma of the crafted beer inside, which swirl from inside to dissipate into thin air. The man takes a brisk appreciated drink, and sits the bottle on the table.

He asks for that cigarette, and Nave holds the pack with his left hand. He flips the top up, and shows the man the pack truly only holds one single cigarette. "Look, I am not a wealthy guy. Damn cops seem to harass me for every little thing. Can't ever get out of the system once them bastards have it in for you. But I figured, hey at least I have a job and all this poor dude wants is a smoke. So here you are. I can get another," Nave tells the guy.

The guy has his own lighter, and through yellowed, largely squared teeth begins to philosophize his wisdom upon Nave. "My man, you ain't shittin'. But let me tell you. Listen to me when I say, this is freedom. See, I don't be like these normal homeless. It all bout being free, and staying under the radar. Them cops don't wanna get close to this area; they afraid of the one on the street. Plus look here, who want to handle someone livin' on da streets? Me, I got my reasons. I lay low. Teddrick don't play they games. Smarter than that," he says in a boisterous way as he holds the cigarette like one would smoking a joint. Now holding the beer in his left hand, cigarette in his right he continues to educate Nave. "I don't pay taxes, I do as I want, get free shit all damn day, and get this, I tell you true. Hear this . . . my ass wanted in four counties. Miama, Dade, Martin, and Broward. But shit you not, they would rather a man live on the street than feed him in jail. Jail ain't no place for me. No Sir. I can't do being shacked up with nothing but men. I likes me some women. Good puss fo me. Likes um young and firm too. Mmm Mmm, and check this. No don't get me wrong, I would never do anything but, BUT damn just bout mile up this way, high school. Outdoor pool and they always out there."

He stops in the midst of getting carried away, and takes a long, good, slow drag of the cigarette then bends that same hand to rest against his hip. He takes a quick sip, and tilts his head heavily back; his bottom lip presses his upper lip in a half smirk and he asks Nave, "Now let me axe you. What you do? What a cracka doing in dees parts? Bet you ain't gone be hangin' once it get dark up in this mutha."

Nave sits his beer down; the guy now finishes the cigarette and listens. "See Teddrick Russell, (a very alarmed, inquisitive look from Teddrick), I am not afraid to find shit bags living on the streets hiding among the homeless. Oh don't worry, I am not a cop, I have no interest in putting you in jail. That would be too civilized, and a total waste of my tax dollars. Instead, I hunt you and your type down and finalize your sentence. Oh, it's starting to make sense to you now. You are remembering how you were a teacher and got away with what you were doing. See, you have reached the end of you freedom. And gadging your small frame, lack of decent nutrition, and how quickly you smoked that cigarette, well you will not even make it to that high school pool today."

Teddrick's eyes struggle to stay open, the beer slips from his hand, and he looks surprised. His bottom lip quivers, his knees begin to buckle, and Nave walks off. He now leans against the concrete seat of the park bench, and his left hand just sways as if he is trying to point to Nave.

The camera again sees Nave walk along the sidewalk and around the corner. Five minutes later, "NES 1912; 10-04. Target 10-07 (eliminated). ES 4422 10-12 (diversion no longer needed) GES 10-01, resume normal operation, and submit information."

The second target was confirmed and later found to have been fatally bitten by a cottonmouth.

The third target was enjoying a gambling night out after coming into a large amount of money by a racing sponsor. The man had a very affluent group of constituents, who served beneficial in getting him off. The man was drinking heavily while the boat was about to return to Cape Canaveral. The medical examiner confirmed he had a high BAC when retrieved from the waters. Drowning was determined the actual cause of death.

Technology continues to develop, and Robert calls Nave to come in. Jason and Judge Grace are also in Robert's secured room.

Jason is asked to explain the newest technology, and how it will be of great benefit.
"Nave, we have always been working toward developed technology, and this is something that will not yet be mandatory; we are looking for a few NES and GES levels to give it a shot," Jason says in a much more reserved than his usual excited nature. He hands Nave, the judge, and Robert, all of whom have not actually seen the work he is presenting, a very small device. It looks to be made of a screen-like material, with a solid titanium flat disc. It is no larger than Nave's thumbnail.

Judge Grace comments, "Jason, if this is a bug, and I have to say it looks like a bug, it isn't very inconspicuous."

Jason smiles, and the childlike excitement just can't be held back. He holds one, and goes to his computer. He tells Nave to hold it to his ear. As he does, Jason uses his computer, and soon Nave hears the woman who is usually on the specialized dash informational computer. Not convinced, Nave asks if this will just be a small headphone, and how he is not going to wear an earpiece."

Robert adds, "Jason, I have to agree. I don't think a single NES or GES will ever agree to a visual and probably uncomfortable bolt-on like this!"

Jason answers, "No, no. Wait and listen. Nave, this is Surgeon Ian Tork." Ian Tork appears more like a MMA athlete and unlike the white coat, passive, yet deliberately concerned type doctor many are used to. He stands a noticeable six feet four inches tall with a tailored sport coat over a bright burnt red and black fitted dress shirt, casual dress pants, and a very confident look in his eyes.

.Jason adds, "He handles our guys if anything should happen."

Robert steps in and reassures Nave, "Nave, Dr. Tork is who I told you about if we have to take care of you in-house. Obviously, if you are on a private mission and get shot, cut, or even slightly injured, Dr. Tork will be the one who will be taking care of you. Reality tells us, at some point you will need to see Dr. Tork."

Jason explains why Dr. Tork is there for what would seem more of an IT or surveillance matter. "The onboard communication will be a thing of the past. You will be upgraded with a new tracking device for the vehicles; faster and more elaborate electronics will be installed and this little bug is not a bug. It will be your communication. Dr. Tork will make a small incision behind your ear. This will be surgically attached. All audible transmissions will only be heard by the ES fitted with the device. Benefits to this: We can communicate with you anywhere, anytime, even if you are lying in bed with some hot, spicy Peruvian goddess. You will speak as you normally would, and that is where this mesh portion comes in. A high intensity receiver will be able to hear you as clearly as we talk now. I have to tell you, we have been developing this for over seven years, and worked through all possible scenarios—flight pressure, underwater, impact, frequency interference, you name it."

Jason seems to have more to say when Nave interrupts. "Dr. Tork."

Dr. Tork stands confidently and answers, "Yes, Mr. Valerio Nave."

Nave walks over to him, holding the device and asks, "Do you have 100 percent faith in this, and that you can do this without fault? And that it will not fail?"

The doctor simply assures Nave, that the only thing that will blow the transmission communication capabilities is a direct blast, which would be fatal by all accounts anyhow.

Nave looks over to Judge Grace and Robert then walks over to Jason and says, "Well if it is surgery, I am out for today. I have already eaten lunch. Dr. Tork, Jason, where should I be tomorrow, and what time?"

There is energy in the room as the uncertainty was a factor going in for Jason. Jason then starts to run Nave through the particulars of how it will work also adding what changes will be done to his truck.

Then Robert tells Nave, "Nave, you will start to get dump cars periodically. These will be completely synchronized for our operation and seem completely normal on the exterior. When I say dump car, these cars are untraceable. If stopped, our team will intercept the local request and it will show FLAGGED. Much like Colorado. Jason and his team have some very elaborate connections that have made our level of success so valuable. Your first dump car will be ready. Jason, when is that car ready?" Jason looks up, and advises it is just being painted now and then the tires and exhaust will be taken care of. He advises the hardware has been done for several weeks.

Nave leaves ,and Robert sits next to Dr. Tork at his bar. Dr. Tork questions Robert, "That Nave, he is a bit different, isn't he?"

Robert swirls his ice around in the glass of brandy. He gently sits it down, and his head turns to the left as he gives an answer in what could almost be felt as a worried response. "Ian, you have seen most of his file that you need to see. There is much more that most will not know about Nave. He is a freak of nature, and how that man can go from being as delicate as the thinnest ice on a shallow pond in the early morning, to a force that will crack an iceberg and rain hell upon those who cross him is beyond me. His precision and pure ability to know exactly what every countermove will be is beautiful." Robert pauses as he stands. He places his hand on Ian's shoulder as he expresses, "For those who live life right, have good intent, do no harm to that man's family, or sink below the greasy levels of righteousness against children . . . well they will never know of a relentless, masterful hunter like Valerio Nave. As you have seen, those who cowardly take advantage of children will at some point find that side of this man and exit this life. Scary thing, depending on the circumstance, it may be a brief preview of the hell they face after he finalizes their time here."

The powerful Dr. Tork stands and with relief in his expression states, "We are very fortunate we have him on our side."

The light is blinding as it is directly aimed at Nave's face. Behind his right ear, there is a smear of yellowish brown as Dr. Tork has cleaned and prepped him for the implant. As Nave is under, the doctor spends four hours placing the device under his skin, and linking it to his inner ear canal with the mesh that will allow him to hear the transmissions. Then on the earlobe there will be a small puncture that most will believe to be an old earring hole. That will be the receiver or microphone. Jason spends time running tests and calibrating the unit to Nave's skin thickness and exact distance from his mouth to the receiver. On Jason's computer, it shows the implant to be 100 percent. The main dispatch for all ES confirms audible transmissions are clear and proper for being placed in service.

It is dark; the room has no windows and as Nave begins to regain consciousness, he intentionally remains quiet as he wakes. He has not adjusted to the dark room, and his head is very cloudy. He notices the shape of a person near the only crack of light, and can barely focus on the faint illumination of the person's cell phone. As his vision improves and he is more aware, he notices it is Lynn. He feels a warm appreciation to have her there and not just a nurse or even worse, Robert. She is close, and as he can see better, he lay still and just watches her. He admires her comfort to fold her legs under herself, or recline. She talks softly into the phone. She answers the person, and advises that it would be best if the person she was talking to was home by eight.

Lynn is startled and drops the phone when Nave barks out his opinion, "Tell Dean, she BETTER be home by eight. Not should!" He laughs and tells Lynn how he had been listening to her and soon put the conversation together, and knew it was his daughter Lynn was talking to. Lynn is seated by Nave, and is on his left side. She asks how he is feeling, and has a warm cloth which she lightly swashes over his forehead. She is delicate; her fingers run the line of his eyebrows, and she questions if he has any pain. She moves her chair, and sits next to his side now. He is slightly elevated in the recovery chair, and he can still only see the slightest outline of Lynn. He can feel her. Like the times a man can close his eyes and dream of a woman, he can see her in the dark. There is a slight fragrance she delights with. Her tone is safe and caring. He holds his thoughts captive, yet no part of his mind is quiet while it chants the pleasure he has at this moment to have not just someone there with him, he has Lynn. The words will not pass his lips of his thoughts—his deep, emotional struggle as he is embattled against the desire to know Lynn as more than just a professional partner. He reaches to her, and takes her hand as he thanks her for being there. As she keeps her hand in his, he feels her hair along his neck. The fragrance swims through his senses, and her moist lips take the place of the warm towel on his forehead. She kisses him so slowly he feels as if he fell asleep and woke even happier.

   In her smoky, sultry voice she tells him, "No one asked me to be here. Actually, I was told to stay away. I am here for you. And I also realize I am here for me. There are fears I have of losing you, and there are reasons I cherish each time you return. Perhaps I am too close; however, I don't feel close enough. You have to always know, I never want to be disconnected from you." She tells him she was glad to be there as he woke, and that she has to get going. She walks out, and he stares at a door. The door has a way of being a projector of the many times he has seen her; in a way, he wishes things were different. Admiration and fantasy reflect off that door. As the lights of his mental projector burn out, he realizes the dark reality of being alone in a room once more. He lies in a single bed; his dream was brief. Grateful he is, and regretful he is challenged. His vices haunt him as he knows he has a self-inflicted dedicated responsibility to continue his work. He also ponders the possible acceptance Lynn may offer to promote a healthier home life. As his thoughts are running sporadically in his head, he drifts back to sleep.

His next awakening will have a much different aroma, and the silhouette will be much larger. Robert steps in, and the two walk outside. They see a large, colonial-style porch; the railings are as white as a new notebook paper. Hanging flower baskets are still trickling from being watered, and duel wide staircases lead to the yard below. The greens of a private golf course are just beyond the eight-foot wall that surrounds the backyard. Nave and Robert sit and watch the passing golf carts driven by stuffy men in ridiculous bold and pastels of that look like a color wheel. Robert projects a deep yet quiet distain for the irony in of the business they find themselves in. Robert admits he could be just fine without the income that comes from the clientele they have, and yet he knows there will never be a time when the specialist will only be a secret of history. Robert and Nave decide the relaxation has to come to an end and it's time to get back to work.

Nave finds Jason, and they spend many hours working with the new unit. They cover how to shut the unit off remotely, or on their bodies by depressing an area behind their ears. There is a whisper mode and also an amplifier. Nave especially has an interest in the amplifier which will allow him to hear people from up to seventy-five feet clearly, and one hundred feet if conditions are ideal. There is no discomfort, and the child-like Jason decides to talk to Nave the entire drive home. Jason informs Nave that he is to never have an X-ray or MRI—no harm to Nave yet the unit may fault out.

Chapter 14
<u>Utah Relocation</u>

The judge contacts Nave, and asks for a meeting. When Nave arrives, he is met at the door by the judge.

The judge is very upbeat, dressed down, and says, "There was no mistake it was you. After all, that barreled billow of a supercharged Hennessy powerhouse being forced through that exhaust is quite impressive."

Nave looks back, and tells the judge that he will not be so happy when he has to dump this car. Nave had always wanted a '69 Camero Z28, and the custom restoration of this beast is a perk he is very pleased with. The deep, dark black cherry paint, black windows, and the tight lowered suspension over wide rear tires, are of no falsity to the performance that comes with 702 HP. Not the car one would use to sneak up on anyone. The judge feels his youth urging him to live life in the fastlane again, and he suggests that the two take a ride to Dixi Crossroads for lunch and a talk. A black tight leather seat will hold him in place. Smooth black cherry accents across the dash, and a glass flat center dash piece covers the intricate electronics that has to accompany the dump car. The solid silver finger grip Hurst shifter awaits a firm hand to either gently glide it through the gears, or be brutally slammed from each position as the tires heat with angry force against the road.

With a greedy smile, the judge tells Nave, "Nave, now if I wanted a luxurious stroll through a tree-lined prairie, we would have taken my Town Car. The wife would kill me if she saw me in this car . . . *with you at the wheel* so let's get the hell out of my driveway!" The lope of roller cams grunt like a mean dog stalking its target, as they ease out of the judge's home. The gate closes behind them, the rear of the Camero prowls slowly down the quiet street. Tinted taillights, a black chrome bumper, and a license plate that reads, "DMONRYD" sinks. The gargle of supercharged power is heard through the moan of rubber burning, and the rich smell of tire smoke will soon creep through the noses of the boys sitting on their bikes near the corner, who encourage Nave to "Light um up!" Bigger than those boy's' smiles, is the smile of Judge Grace. Thrilled is a term normally misused until one discovers the truest relation of a thrill. To be scared—to challenge oneself to overcome that fear, or live the fear as a conquered bout with mortality—or the difference of emotion that one person shares all at once. Judge Grace grips the armrest with his right hand, and he reactively places his left hand on the headliner; his ass clenches the leather, his feet smash the carpet, and his face shows a euphoric sensation of happiness. Reality, doubt, fear, and hard life experiences tell us the pleasure often comes at a high price. The judge has few words during the drive, and even shows some concern at times. Nave notices the occasional glance over to the speedometer. Across one section, Nave knows of an undeveloped neighborhood where there are wide, empty streets. Perhaps the test of the judge's nerve level because some corners put the view sideways as they drift several hundred feet before he brings the front of the car, back to the front. Then a smooth fast pace up Interstate 95, and finally an arrival at Dixi Crossroads. The car comes to rest as many admire. They step out, and the judge gently closes his door.

He walks near Nave, and tells him that he isn't sure if he even took a breath that entire ride. "I know one thing Steve McQueen, I need a hard double Crown and Coke."

They sit down and order. The judge explains to Nave that his time to relocate is near. This is an aspect which all specialists know is a precautionary step that has always been a standard practice in this operation. One thing they talk about is how the West is undermanned, and the move could be beneficial as Nave's family lives in Utah. Judge Grace has an entire new cover job which Nave can either accept or await a new move.

"Nave, we will place you with a company that has traveling work groups. You will be as any other employee, and carry on as life would be. That is the simple part. A nice factor is you will actually be paid; you will have a secondary retirement to accrue, and will be closer to your family as you have often mentioned. The workers, higher-level management, or any HR will of course have no insight into who you are. There are two close contacts who will know you, and make sure your application is accepted. After that, you will retain your employment as anyone else would. The group you will work with will cover Utah, Idaho, Nevada, all of California, Oregon, Montana, Wyoming, and the Dakotas. There are often targets in the Las Vegas and Reno areas. To have you there would increase our success rate on those with monitor, implant chips. I have a folder with the company information, and will need your answer within two weeks." He goes over more menial details and as usual, Nave asks few questions. He will first analyze all the information, and see what may be missing or may have been unanswered. He is very optimistic in regard to being closer to family.

They finish lunch, and when they get into the car, Nave tells Judge Grace, "Don't expect the same ride back. That all-you-can-eat Rock Shrimp is not coming out in this car."

Later that day, Amanda pulls up with a few friends as Nave is out front catching up with Oly from his old department. Oly explains how several people have left for other agencies, and she is even considering going to the county. The mayor and the chief are refusing to budget for even the smallest of necessary equipment for the patrol guys. Oly laughs as she asks Nave what kind of hassle is he going to give the poor boy, who is driving. Amanda tries to play it cool and says she was just getting a ride, and the boy is totally nice.

Nave walks over to the window and asks, "Who are you?" The boy nervously answers his name, and questions if he was supposed to give her a ride. Nave is less than hospitable in tone, and advises it may be okay if the boy is legal to drive and doesn't drive like a dumb-ass. He requests the boy prove he has a license. Amanda half laughs as one other girl in the car tells the boy she had to show her license too. Amanda stands with Oly, and knows Oly is going to run it for her dad.

Oly walks back over and says, "So young man, is there anything you want to tell us now that I already looked at your driving record and your other records?"

The boy is confused, looks frightened, and tells the other girl in the truck and Amanda that he doesn't know he did anything wrong. He swears he has never been to jail, or even stopped by the cops. The close proximity of Nave at his window motionless and glaring at him likely isn't helping his anxiety at this point. Oly stands at the passenger window where the other girl is seated.

She begins to offer her thoughts and concern. "See Nave, there is not a squeaky clean record here. And this young man just drove your daughter home. Oh Mr. I-don'-t- have-anything-to-hide, you sure do play the innocent guy pretty well."

In front of the truck, Amanda is just shaking her head and slightly smiles when she says, "Oly, why do you encourage my dad to do this stuff? I know you two are messing around."

Oly looks through the car to Nave, and tells him how this innocent faker thinks he is above the law, and can just park his car anywhere he wishes. "Yeah, last year this car, this one that is registered to this driver, was left standing in a NO STANDING zone at the movies. Oh and let me express very clearly, AND left running with no one in the car. So my perfect driver friend, how does that match up?" With Nave peering into him, he stammers to explain until Amanda comes and drags her dad away, and tells the boy that her dad and his friend are just trying to scare him.

The girl laughs and says, "Well they succeeded; hope he didn't wet his cargo shorts. Bye Deanie."

Oly leaves and Nave tells Dean there are popcorn and a movie on for tonight. After the movie, he explains the probability of moving to Utah. Amanda Dean misses her aunt, and is torn as she also is at a point where friends are important. Through conversations with her aunt, a few days later she comes to her dad and makes a very mature decision to support the move. She will be out of school soon, and knows there is so much to being with family.

A home has a weird grasp of the memories after the material pieces are packed up, and the shell of the home sits bare. Nave walks the property line, remembers the trees he had to cut after Hurricane George, and others. The pond has as few fish with hook-holed lips from when he taught Amanda to reel in a line. He looks at the fire pit that crackled and glowed as the smoke carried the many conversations up into the trees to grow on for many years. One last time, he and his Dean will drive through the rock and wood fence pillars they built. He remembers a few days ago, seeing that long-haired hippie girl lean against her macho Charger, and noticed the sunlight sparkle through a heavy, slow running tear just before he hugged her.

Lynn Grace is not ready for him to move on. She assures him there will be a time when he will have to pick her up at the airport so they can go play in the snow. She has a list of places and activities that she has always wanted to visit and do. She and Amanda have an equally hard time knowing she cannot simply cruise over for a movie, hang out, or offer face-to-face advice. Sitting in the moving truck next to her dad, Amanda rolls the cuff of her sweater to again dab her eyes. The same sweater that dabbed those big blue eyes, is the reason for her sadness. It still has the perfume Lynn wears; it is a loose, knitted hoodie with a big hand warmer pocket in front. Lynn wanted Amanda to have it for those cool days in Utah. So she said. The warmth of a person's soul makes the fabric of any sweater closer to another's heart. They both understand the sweater is a way for her to feel a hug from Lynn when days get tough. So she looks over, and tells her dad that she is ready to see family again.

Then she asks, "Are you serious when you say we are going to be driving for two or three days?"

He laughs and replies, "No, if I decide to sightsee it could be at least a week!" The moving van turns out, and they both look back in their review mirrors. Soon the porch light fades, and they are heading in one direction, not to return.

There is an abundance of change to come for the two of them. Amanda has not lived anywhere but Florida all her life. On cold days, she has enjoyed being able to finally wear a hoodie, and on rare occasions, an actual jacket. The perception of cool, cold, and absolutely freezing doesn't resonate with those who have not dealt with such temperatures. As fairly comparable, would be one going from the dry, moderate temperatures of Northern Utah to spending a summer in Florida.

Coming into the high desert in the spring will offer them a wonderful introduction to the stunning landscapes, colors, mountains, and waterfalls. Florida does have a mountain; it was built and placed at an amusement park. It also has waterfalls, those which are part of the elaborate landscaping of a few golf courses. Being so flat, water simply flows or stands. So Nave does have several amazing places he will be anxious to show her. There is another change which will be of a greater challenge. Nave is not a religious person, and Amanda Dean has a harsh opinion of the hypocrisy of many organized religions. Utah is highly influenced by the Mormon religion. Nave has spoken of the judgments she will encounter and swift prejudices that will be cast against her. He encourages her to be true to her beliefs— to be firm regarding the opinions and education that have made her who she is. There is a warm conversation about the way he has respected and admired her for the young woman she has built in her own skin. There is a repetitive notion; he has always stressed that her strength is her ability in not conforming to the norm. He has brought her up to be that girl who will debate her position, and in a prideful manner be who she is and strives to be.

The headlights of the moving truck finally illuminate a sign welcoming them into Utah as they leave Evanston, Wyoming. She sleeps as he steers the truck down the Weber

Canyon, and exits onto Highway 89. His hands are tired; his shuffle of feet and stretching of legs are more frequent as this long trip is now heading toward the finish line. A few turns, a couple of lights, and finally the truck stops at the house that will be their new home. That is until he is relocated again. Likely, this will happen after Amanda has graduated and moved on. The moon has long past; there is a blueish hue over an unusual outline to the east. His door opens, and the interior light awakes Amanda Dean. Her thick hair is thrown to one side as she stretches out her arms. He comes around and opens her door. Her bare feet, loose sweatpants, and thin shirt were sufficient along their trip, especially when they left Florida as the night temperature was a cool sixty-eight degrees. Her stunned look, and those outstretched arms quickly react to give herself a hug for warmth. This is her first encounter with the spring Utah air.

"OMG Padre, Noooo, I don't think I can do this. Did you decide to go to Alaska instead?"

He laughs and hands her, her shoes.

She steps down and when she walks on the walkway to the house she looks to the yard.
"Whoa, what? Is that snow? There is snow!" She goes inside and then looks out the window, where she now expresses how beautiful it is. This admiration is with just the slightest dawn light. He has two air mattresses ready as he knew it could be hard to set up beds upon their arrival. They drink some juice at the counter, have a little snack, and walk through their new home. Excited, yet very worn out form several days of travel, Nave closes the blinds and goes to sleep.

The days to follow will be busy with unpacking, showing her around, and catching up with family. A trip up to Park City, where they went shopping at the outlet mall, allows her to find clothes for this new world she has encountered. There is a noticeable excitement that she was able to buy things that would be a total waste or ridiculous in Florida. In all, she shows an enthusiastic optimism for this change. It will not take away the sadness of leaving friends, yet a valuable experience is change. It can be a fragile moment that must be met with care and reason. He understands this, and has already built a fire pit next to a place they will have that hammock set up.

Nave heads in for his first day at his new job—a railroad contractor who replaces apparatus used in the rail industry. The group he will join is from all over the Northwest. The group has a lot of work in the Salt Lake area, which is nice to keep Nave near home while they adjust to the new area. After introductions, and a lot of construction-worker-type banter, they load up in the trucks, and are off to see what this work is all about. One guy is more arrogant than the others and seems to attempt to discredit anyone else. He is quick to inform Nave that the work they do is hard, long, and most don't make it.

He also is very inquisitive asking Nave how he even got the job. "So who do you know? Not too many people just get hired randomly off the street," the guy says in an almost demanding fashion. Nave assures him he doesn't know anyone, and that he must have just interviewed well.

The assistant foreman is a bigger guy, a farm boy type, who has a helpful and positive demeanor; he tells the arrogant one, "Dude, you always want to have drama. You are like a little bitch. Goddamn, my daughter is in junior high and has less drama than you try to stir. Listen bro, you will do just fine. All we ask is that you pull your weight. Guy, you are replacing was a lazy fuck. We work. Plain and simple. Sometimes we bust ass, sometimes we have it easy. Take the good with the bad."

As promised, the work is nothing easy. They have to dig through railroad ballast, pull cable, and push cable into signal cabins. Nave is very aware that a good part of the day is a tryout. Would he be able to keep up, not give up, and not complain about doing some real labor?

Robert knew there would be a few weeks of inactivity as Nave settled in and got things in order. The work schedule of this crew will work very well with Nave's private work with the unit. The railroad contractors work a week, then have a week off. During that week off, they are not obligated to do any rail work. After a few cycles, Nave is ready to get back to tracking targets.

After a few months of working the Salt Lake area, the crew is notified they will have some work near Southern Utah. On the start of the next shift, all the guys travel to Southern Utah. Nave checks in, and talks to the hotel manager. He is very stern about no one being permitted in his room at any time. The manager assures him this is a normal policy, yet does enquire as to why. The manager tells Nave that no one has ever been so adamant in a request. Nave makes it lighter in nature, and explains that these guys are all practical jokers, and like to mess with each other any way they can. He explains some of the pranks from taking each other's' clothes, filling boots up with salsa, and many other inconveniences he does not wish to participate in. The rest of the crew often spend their nights in the bar, or finds places to party, golf, and burn off steam after the workday. Occasionally Nave will join them, yet usually he likes to go to the gym, and do his real work. He is older than all but the foreman, and that works well to divert the pressure to go out and party.

The next evening Nave returns from work, goes to the gym, and then gets his briefcase out to review a few cases. His case is secure and with the technology built into the case, no one but Nave can enter the code and open it with the fingerprint feature. He opens his computer, and looks closely at targets in St. George and Las Vegas. Both targets are chipped and there are difficulties with each person.

The next day after work, Nave gets his briefcase and walks down to his car. His foreman, Gary, is also leaving and sees Nave. The foreman is an old-timer who has a carefree, old-school, happy personality. He seems to laugh more than talk. Always in Harley Davidson clothing, and a beard to match. He is not a trendy "biker," yet he is a guy who sincerely has a love for being on his bike. He often gives Nave crap about being a well-dressed yuppie.

All in fun and equally expressive of how glad he is to have Nave working with them, he asks, "Is that your car?" Nave tells him he brought it down to see how it does on the road and in the mountains. "Yeah, I love the mountains around here, and figured I would go check out some places after work," Nave tells him.

Gary starts up his bike and while it runs, he has to look over the Camero. He first laughs as he usually does and then makes a claim. "Whew, I bet you get all kinds of puss in this thing. Let me sniff that passenger seat. Bet there is still some fresh residue right now." Ending his banter with another expressive laugh, he asks if it is all looks or if it actually has some balls and tells Nave, "Bro, fire that thing up. Let's hear what's doing."

The key turns, the center of the grill has a single thin, high intensity light and the headlight covers slide up. The heart of the car begins to pump, and the throaty exhaust assures there is a battle between the looks and the power of this impressive beast.

Gary jokes, "Goddamn, sounds like its tummy is growly for more petro. How fast have you had it?"

Nave half smiles and tells him, "Going across the Salt Flats at Bonneville, I pushed it to one hundred and seventy. Suspension is tight, but the tires seem to be a little loose at that point. Hell, one-seventy is plenty fast I think." Gary lets him go and they each head off.

About an hour away, Nave roams the St. George area. He is rolling slowly down a main road. He thinks he sees something on the way in, but it can't be absolutely verified. He turns down a road which he thought would take him closer, yet he loses sight of what it was that had his interest so drawn. He is determined, and continues to search. Somehow he is stopped in a parking lot, and looking in his rear view mirror. He quickly spins the car around, crosses the parking lot, and he has arrived. He parks his car away from any other vehicles, and slowly walks directly to the doors. There is a young girl at the counter, and she does not even have to ask Nave anything. He knew exactly what he was there for. "I want a number one, no onion, mustard and catsup instead of the spread, and do a chocolate shake instead of the drink."

"She smiles and repeats, "Okay, so that is a double-double, mustard, catsup instead of the sauce, no onion, and chocolate shake no drink. To stay or to go?"

Nave sits outside on the white round table with a red umbrella, and has his burger and fries in a red tray just like from his childhood. He was told of an In-N-Out Burger in St. George, and this quick dinner was reminiscent of his party days growing up in Southern California.

The short break is over, and he drives up the ridge along some very impressive homes, one of which is supposed to be that of his target. He drives past the home, and there is no signal indicating a target to be nearby. The properties in the area are very open, and provide several entry opportunities. Easy to access, and just as easy to be seen. Nave wants to get inside yet cannot risk the rush, and continues down the street. Surveillance and recon from the past indicate he lives alone. There were also data that told of frequent parties at the location. As he drives the neighborhood, he finds a home for sale that is above and to the right by four houses. It still offers a line of sight to the backyard. He leaves the neighborhood, and drives through Hurricane where the man's sister lives.

Hurricane is a quiet, dark town, and Nave pulls into a small tavern. The jukebox has Jonny Cash playing, and one bartender singing along. "Jesse, you best get ya ass off my pool table, or I'm shovin' that pool stick up your ass!" the short, blond-haired bartender hollers.

Jesse replies, "Hell, maybe then you might have at least one straight cue in this rundown shithole!"

She wipes off her hands, smiles at Nave, and asks what he wants to drink. "You ain't one of my locals. How did you wander on in here," she asks?

Nave explains he is just heading back to the hotel—says he has been looking at houses all day. "My work is relocating me to St. George, and I have a few days to check out a few places," he tells her.

They talk more about the area, the activities, and she offers advice on the good and bad.

"What areas are you lookin' in?" she asks. He names a few and one of the middle-named areas causes her to respond. "My brother has a house up there. Nice area, but lord you better have some coin saved up. My dumbass brother has a nice place in there and is hardly in it."

Nave laughs and says, "Dumbass brother, you have so much love for him." She is a straight shooter, and explains that she doesn't have anything to do with her brother.

She openly offers more information. "Hey, I don't usually judge others but when someone is dirty . . . well brother, family or not . . . person is dirty. I can't really say what he does in Vegas and Mesquite to get the money he gets, but if you ask me it is shady. Last year, he ran into trouble. Sure he says he didn't do anything, but had it not been for some rookie wet behind the ears, sloppy, donut-eating cop messin' up, I think my brother might have been sent up the river."

Nave loosely plays with the woman who seems to be very flirtatious, perhaps for tips—maybe because of a fondness for Nave.

Whichever, she catches the attention of other patrons in the bar. "Damn girl, that man don't want to hear your drama. You just trying to replace that deadbeat boyfriend you got at home," one guy says in a truthful, joking manner. She takes care of a few others and makes her way back over to Nave.

She leans her tight jeans against the bar, folds her tattooed arms, and offers some advice. "If you do buy in there, just be sure you don't let your kids roam the neighborhood or the pool, and don't let them undress in there. I was told my brother was taking pervy pics of the kids, and doing some internet stuff with it. Sorta sad, but the investigator who came out here one day said he didn't have total proof, but he thinks Leonard, that's my brother's name, thinks he has something to do with young, foreign kids in Vegas." She goes on some more about how her brother was always weird growing up, and even would try to pull the shower curtain open when she showered. She then tells Nave that her brother stays in Summerlin during the week. He usually only comes home every other weekend.

Nave dismisses the conversation, and agrees how absurd the legal system is. He finishes his drink, and heads back to the hotel. He rolls into the hotel just a little after midnight.

Each morning, the crew meets in the foreman's room to go over the plan for the day. As they gather, Gary, the foreman, calls out Nave on coming in late. "So, where were you out whorein' around until after midnight? Bro, don't act like you weren't—goddam car of yours probably woke the whole hotel up." He laughs, and encourages others to join in on the fray.

Collin, another guy who works on the crew, turns the jokes toward Gary. "Oh hell, you are one to talk. You seem to have a skank road wife in every town we stay at. What about Elko, when the one barely left your room and then you were off to have dinner with the other one that came up from Winnemucca?"

Gary responds, "Oh come one now, I didn't set it up like that. The one just surprised me and came over. See, was all horned up and I just got out of the shower."

Collin says, "Yeah, man whore! You were taking a shower to go meet the Winnemucca woman. This filthy had to text Winnemucca and say he was running late."

"HaaaaHaaa, shit bro, had to buy time to let the little blue pill kick in for round two. I'm gettin' older. That shit don't just spring back up after round one."

There is more laughing, and a volley of barbs at each other. Nave dismisses his time as going to the gym late.

Briefing finishes up, and they head out to the desert to work. The Southern Utah sky is a deep blue over and behind the multiple colors of mountain formations. Their drive takes them to areas many normal people will never access. Often a careful navigator is needed to keep the trucks from slamming into holes, ruts, and road edges that can send a truck several hundreds of feet down. The brilliance and admiration of how men over a hundred years in the past, lay these tracks and constructed this vast pattern of American history, brings conversation. The men proudly tell Nave he will see many areas that will be much more impressive than even this area. There is also humorous conversation about how brutal the industry was in those early years—how many men died, gave up home lives to make a little money, and several beliefs are expressed of how the Chinese were almost like slaves and killed. None of the men have knowledgeable intellect to support the conversation, yet history channels abundantly note the many railroads. Each man is grateful for the regulations of government that make their daily tasks safer and much easier.

The arrogant one is driving the boom truck and spouts off, "Yeah, nowadays everyone is a bunch of pansy-ass pussies. I would have done just fine back then. Hell if you ask me, we ought to go back to those days and weed out some of these fucks who whine if they have to work too hard."

Collin is quick to reply, "Well, I think today you should let someone else run the mini, and you can pull cable and dig by hand . . . mister, we should do it like the old days!" The mini is a smaller excavator used to dig and grade the ground. Nick, the arrogant one, often places himself on the mini, and that is just a seniority privilege.

Nick looks to the mirror in Nave's direction and questions, "What do you think? You just sit there quiet, and don't add much."

Nave replies, "I'm just glad to work outside, see these places, and actually get paid for it. Besides, I was always told, if the toilet is already backed up, not much sense to add more crap to it." The guys in the truck laugh as they continue along the long, dirt road. The rest of the crew is in the other truck with Gary, and eventually they come to the site. After a few hours working, the trench is dug several hundred feet from a signal to a control cabin. Now that the work with the mini is done, Nick quickly goes to the controls of the boom crane where he will perch himself while the others pull cable. Nave climbs into the mini, and positions the digging buckets near the suspended cable.

Nick is quick to climb down and question Nave. "Hey buddy, what the fuck? Why are you swinging the mini right in the goddam way?"

Nave half ignores him, and takes the end of the cable. He slides the end into a cleaves, and tells Nick, "You have a smooth path all the way down to the house. Someone can use the mini to run the cable out, one of us can man the spool, and you can relax up there on the platform." The others stand by as Nave tries to reason with Nick, and Gary is walking toward them from the house. Nick insists they do it by hand and gets agitated at Nave.

He gets close to his face and says, "You might want to realize your place around here, and you best know who is over you, comprende?"

Nave stands his ground and quietly, yet boldly replies, "To have a piece of equipment sit, and three of us guys pull this heavy-ass cable five hundred feet is ignorant. And for someone to orchestrate from his throne, and command ignorance is ludicrous. If that was too many big words for you I can simplify it, as, your way is stupid." As Nick starts to tell the other guys they need to get the cable and start pulling, Gary is in the mini and begins to run the cable out using the equipment. Gary calls Collin over and has him take Nave to the house, and start driving in ground rods. The workday rolls on, and as the sun turns the horizon a dirty orange, the trucks stir up powder dust that hovers through the sage brush. It's fun for the guys in the truck as Gary goes faster chasing down the random rabbits that dart out in front of them.

The streetlights have been on for about thirty minutes once they finally arrive at the hotel. They shuffle in and a few ask if everyone is going to get some dinner. Nave declines stating he is feeling sluggish, and wants to go to the gym again. He goes to the gym, and some nights he will hurry down to the bar in Hurricane. The week passes, and the last night he goes to the bar, the bartender talks more about her brother. There were random guests throughout the night; however, the flow is light. After nine thirty, he looks up, and it is just him, the bartender, and a stocky man who always hangs out to be a presence so the bartender isn't there by herself. This night, she opens up a little more to Nave. At one point, she is shows him pictures of her two kids. Current pics would put them around sixteen and eighteen. The woman sits next to Nave, as she shows the photos. Then the photos drift back into time and like a view master in reverse, the two teens are now toddlers. She stops at a photo of the two on a rock. All look very happy in the photo, and as she looks, a quiet ball of translucent tears covers one of the kid's faces. She first wipes the screen, and then grabs a napkin to dab her eyes.

She looks behind her to reassure herself no others are around, and then explains her emotion. "He took this picture, my brother. We all went over to Zion, and spent the night. He has a nice trailer, and the kids loved to go camping. We would just sit in the river on our lawn chairs, and those two would catch frogs, spy on deer, and do kid stuff. My brother never had kids, *thank god,* and then it seemed like he was just a good uncle. I guess when you have that sickness, it is just in you. No one is safe. All that shit I told you about him taking pics of kids and stuff, well when my oldest found out he came to me one night. I still can't tell you how I didn't go shoot that sick bastard that night. One side knew I had to be here for them. They never really knew their dad. He died when they were young. Was a good guy, worked up in the Dakotas on oil rigs. Snow and trucks and speed through the Rock Springs area took him off the road. So when he passed, it was nice to have Leonard around. You have no idea the guilt you experience knowing you brought a monster into your own home. I felt that was the missing piece–a father, uncle figure. Hell, the kids have everything. My family owns most of this area, the life insurance was hefty, and my bars do very well. I just keep hope that my oldest told me everything. He did say it was only pictures and nothing more. Sad, because he also told me there were other kids that Leo made do some really rank stuff to each other while Leo took pictures and video. I mean, what sick bastards get off on that stuff? Hey, I am not a saint and have done some crazy, sexy stuff. Some may even make you blush, but who gets excited over kids? I have so many times wished that one of the parents would have just taken Leo out to some far-off place and ended it all. I know it's wrong to think that of someone, even a family member, but I just can't see him as family any longer." It seems her venting and anger sopped up the tears, and she slides her phone between her tank top and breast.

Nave tells her as she spins her seat toward him, "Well, for all you know, if he has been publicly recognized for all this, one of those parents is probably just waiting for the right time. Maybe he will go camping in that trailer, and have a sudden fall off Angels Landing." She laughs, and comments on the irony of such a demonic guy falling from Angles Landing. Nave gets up to get on his way, when she stands and hugs him. A quiet thank you in his ear, and she slightly pulls back and then a warm connection of her lips against his. She backs away, and tells him he is welcome to come in more than a few times a week.

The work week is done, and Nave spends the off-time showing Amanda around the canyons, mountains, and enjoying a good family bar be que in the park. She is still adjusting to the new way school is and the phrases that get her objectionable looks. One phrase she has said for so long is, "Oh My God."

Apparently, this is a phrase that brings a judgmental scorn and ridicule upon any who speak or think the phrase. The part which Amanda finds ridiculously hypocritical is from the same person's lips which scowl at her when she says it, comes the over-exaggerated abbreviation, "OMG!" She is quick to smirk, and tell them that everyone knows they don't mean, "Oh My Goodness." Nave and Amanda discuss the cultural differences as well as the observation of how much cleaner and safer it appears to be compared to Florida. Nave adds that she should feel lucky she is not living where he grew up in Southern California.

Amanda enjoys the time she gets to stay with her aunt when Nave is away. She tries to convince him she could stay at home by herself. This is a proposition she knew would not go her way. As any of us who work because we have to as opposed to because we want to, the days off move more swiftly than when we are at work. The days go quickly, and Sunday night Nave is leaving for Southern Utah again.

He is climbing the grade up Scipio when his radio silences; behind the flat glass of his dash, it turns neon, dark blue and there is the woman's voice in his ear.

He advises, "NES 10-40 southbound Interstate 15 Scipio, Utah." His dash slides, and a monitor comes on. There are photos and text information on Leonard. The information informs him that an ES was traveling south out of the Virgin River Gorge when the alert beacon went off. By approximation, it was determined the target was traveling north through the gorge. Reported by the ES, his signal increased in strength, and as a Chevy Duramax with a fifth wheel on the back, black and white, came directly across, the signal went solid. There are no turnarounds until you reach the exit of the gorge, and the ES could not catch the signal once he turned back north into the canyon. The ES reported the truck was not at the last known-address, which Nave had scouted out on his last trip. The woman advises all information is ready, and will be available on his computer as well.

Nave acknowledges the transmission and the woman in his ear simply signs off, "10-01."

There is no change in his travel; he is calm, and the paused CD of Ice Cube resumes. Perhaps Nave uses the bass of this rap music to muffle the growl of the exhaust. It is known by those who grew up with him that the culture of the Southern California rap scene was very present in his high school years. A close set of friends he played basketball and football with were transplants from the harsh streets of L.A. As Nave listens, he can recall the times he and Halsey, or John Gallow would cruise Normandy. His girlfriend in high school asked these two once why he could go to the hood and be okay, and they would laugh and say, he wasn't okay; he was just a crazy white boy who keeps it real. This fact didn't detract from the realty that a few times Nave was shot at, chased, and even cut once in a fight as he struggled to get out of a bad area of town. This seemed to be morbidly entertaining to him. He had a connection to the reality of eighties and nineties rap. The tracks of the CD thump on, and he glides the Camero around the turns of the road.

The second night after work, Nave has already reviewed all the information sent to him. He plans to head down to Hurricane, and snoop around for the truck. He does as usual, and throws his gym clothes on. He grabs his towel, a bottle of water, and walks out his hotel door. Collin had just walked out as well. Collin asks if Nave could take him to the State Store to get some whiskey. He doesn't want to refuse, yet he is anxious to get down to Hurricane and check the home in St. George. Collin gets in and admires the custom work in the car. They head down the freeway, as the State Store to buy liquor is two exits down.

Collin asks, "Aren't you coming in? You gotta get some alcohol don't you?" Nave declines and says he really doesn't drink much.

Collin laughs and says, "Hell, out on the road I drink my ass off. The wife doesn't like me to drink at home so I make up for lost time at work." He returns with his brown bags clutched better than most people carry their newborns. They leave out of the parking lot, and back on the highway. No sooner than clearing the off-ramp, the radio goes silent, the dash illuminates blue, and the woman in Nave's ear asks him to advise.

Nave responds, "10-2; 10-5." This allows her to know that Nave is with someone and unable to clear. She can transmit info to Nave with this technology, and no one around can hear. It is so vital to this operation, and this is a key moment. This target has been on the list for several years and a delayed investigation, time he spent in jail, and his frequent moves have made him difficult to track.

Now the blue light slowly flashes, and increases its speed.

She advises, "NES 1912 is 10-19 of target FLASH." Nave motions to Collin to stay quiet. The blue flash in his dash is almost steady, and Nave's demeanor is serious and deliberate. He looks ahead and sees a black Chevy on I-15 in the opposite lanes. There isn't a trailer attached, yet the signal is indicating the target is near. He increases his speed and as the two vehicles exchange directions; the solid blue light and tone assures that this is the confirmed target.

He hammers the gas and Collin lips can be seen to say, "Holy Shit!"

Nave takes the next off-ramp; Collin's feet press hard to the floor as he seemingly doesn't believe Nave is going to stop. Nave slides sideways through the intersection; the rear tires paint a black half circle from under the overpass until he is straight again going the opposite direction on I-15. By the end of the off-ramp, the Camero is back to one hundred and five mph. Focused yet very relaxed, Nave has changed the song to Mötley Crüe's, "Kick Start My Heart." Collin is still stunned, and Nave quietly reminds him to stay quiet. The highway is dark; the lines are reflecting almost solid at one hundred and thirty mph, and in the dark distance well ahead, the red and blue lights of a Utah Highway Patrol unit flash back and forth. Nave slows, and when he reaches the spot where the patrol car is, he notices the truck pulled over is that which Leonard is driving. Nave pulls behind the patrol car and waits at the door of the Camero.

Nave advises in a way that the Control Operator who is the woman who contacts the ESs can hear him. "I'm going to stop out with this UHP officer to see if he has any information on the missing person." He is stopped with a black Chevy. The truck is a "FLASHER." Collin is a little confused, yet thinks Nave is just talking to him.

The CO broadcasts, "NES 1912; 10-19X local law enforcement activity. 1912 cannot engage target." Nave waits at his door, and the officer comes cautiously to him. Outside of the car, Nave informs the officer that he was a cop in Florida. They are more comfortable, and Nave asks about the guy in the truck.

As many officers do, he has the driver's license of the driver just under a writing pen clasp over his pocket. Just before the officer approached, Nave activated a feature that takes video continuously. Sometimes, luck is a virtue. The officer had that driver's license facing outward so the photo and information could be seen. Collin is confused, looking at the dash, looking at Nave talk to the officer, and peering over to the driver's side to see if there was anything to make sense of what just happened.

Nave returns, and tells Collin, "Oh well, we can head back now."

Collin sort of shakes his head and asks, "What the hell just happened? I get in your car and all the sudden you are talking to thin air, and poof we are road rallying down the freeway. And let me tell you, I think I may have shit myself with the stunt under the overpass and back
onto the freeway back there. What the hell Nave?"

Nave looks over and shortly laughs asking, "You weren't really scared, were you?" Nave continues to explain he wasn't talking to think air. He convinces Collin that he was a medic for a time in Florida, and did search and rescue. He tells of how his car has a computer linked to missing or stranded alerts by the search and rescue in the area. Nave also says that Collin just didn't see him turn his phone on, and responding as he did was just done through his phone. Collin then wonders what happened to the missing or stranded person. Nave simply says that is why he stopped out with the officer. He tells Collin that the officer had more access to the notification, and it was cancelled. They pull into the hotel, and Collin steps out.

He looks through the window, and thanking Nave for the ride says, "I don't know if I need a drink after the adrenalin rush. I think I might have to decompress for a bit."

Nave finds his way to a secluded spot on a turnout. He presses the codes, and places his thumb on the case. He inputs his passcode and soon is looking over the video recording at the stop. Robert joins in over the link and they discuss their thoughts on where he may be going.

Robert has access to talk through the earpiece and asks Nave, "Okay, so this guy was going north a few days ago, and now where you are, he was going south on the same route. Do you think he is heading back to Vegas or those ties in the Hurricane/St. George area have him sticking around?" Nave looks over the video with Robert and they see he still shows the address where Nave first went. Robert asks about the camper. Robert also recalls there to be little room to store the big fifth wheel at the home. "Do you think he dropped the trailer at his grandmother's old property or over in Hurricane near his sister's?" Robert asks.

Nave tells him, "I am quite sure he isn't going around his sister's. I am not sure what ties are left with the rest of the family. Hell Robert, he may be living out of that trailer to lie low from a lot of people that may be after him." Nave pauses as he looks over the footage at the stop. Nothing light in his voice and in an eerie deep tone, Nave tells Robert, "Robert, I am going to the hotel. I assure you, the target 'FLASH' will be eliminated by the end of the week, if I am seeing this right." Robert asks more, but Nave says he has to get some sleep and has a lot to plan. He also tells Robert that this may not be very easy.

A last inquiry by Robert, "Nave, what do you mean not that easy, what's wrong? Don't rush this and risk your safety."

Nave tells him, "Nothing about this is easy or safe, ever. There is one way this has to be done if I am to do it. You will understand after the notification later this week. Oh, and Robert, advise the CO I will be unavailable for anything else until this is delivered." Nave closes the case.

Clusters of stars are bright beyond the passing clouds. Pitch black surrounds the only light that comes from his headlights. In the distance, are the few rays of lighter darkness that indicate the city is still up. After a stop for a fried chicken salad, he is back in his hotel. Where most would be wound up, nervous, or struggle to sleep, Nave is now somber. Whatever he noticed in that video, made him instantly float like a bright yellow maple leaf that will land softly on the ground. No fear of crashing, or being blown away. He has his direction, and now comes the part where he is the precise eliminator that is respected.

Over the next few days, it is work as usual. There are long days, and even a Friday night where they all go to dinner, and many to get drunk. Gary cuts loose at the country bar, and has a quest to dance with every lady in the place. Easy for him, as the personality he projects gives these women a secure and happy vibe. It may not hurt that he keeps the alcohol in front of these ladies as well. Nave serves as a good designated driver; however, Collin warns everyone to take another vehicle and stay out of the "DMONRYD."

Sunday is a beautiful day–still brisk, yet the afternoon temperature makes it very comfortable. It has been clear the entire week, and a few of the guys want to go golfing. They try to get Nave to go, and he tells them he was never a golfer. Says it was something he was told to never take up as it will cause great frustration, loss of funds, and has the potential for addiction.

They take off early to golf, and Nave heads to St. George. He first goes through the neighborhood where Leonard has his house. The house now has a For Sale sign in the yard. The truck isn't around, and Nave continues out of the subdivision.

Back at Robert's office, Robert sits with the Judge Grace; they have looked over the video many times.

Suddenly, Judge Grace smiles, leans back in his chair, and tells Robert, "Nave is going hiking." In the video, the judge points out what he thinks Nave noticed. Through the flashes of red and blue lights, as Nave pulled past the truck, the video very quickly shows a reflection on the glass of the truck. It is an entry pass to the campground in Zion National Park.

Nave drives in, and stops at a fort well before the entrance to the park. He grabs a water, and buys a few carrots to feed the donkeys and lamas that live behind the replica Old Town buildings. He continues his drive inward, and parks in the parking lot of a nearby hotel. He decides to walk over the bridge to the entry booth. The park ranger advises there isn't much time, but he could still have several hours to see a few areas. Just over the bridge, he looks over the models of the entire park; he has a park map, and laughs at a few kids who try to chase down a lizard. The tram is frequent, and he is among the many who look up, forward, back, and from each side; each possess a questionable gaze doubting that this can even be real. How is a place so unimaginably astonishing? Cameras continually click picture after picture. Even sitting in the same tram, many have to nudge others and point out the view. Nave exits the tram, and finds the campground. This particular task has to be precise in the way Nave can't carry much on him. He comes to a black truck; it is parked in front of a black and white fifth wheel, and by the matching of the license plate, and the one dent on the left bumper he noticed at the stop, he knows it is Leonard walking along the dirt path. There is absolute certainty he has his target.

He approaches Leonard and asks, "Do you know the park well?"

Leonard assures him, "I probably know this park better than most of the guides. Been crawlin' these rocks all my life." He extends his hand and introduces himself. He notes that most visitors are best to just stick to the simple stuff, and not wander too far off.

Nave explains, "See, I am what many would call an extreme photographer. Sure, anyone can take a photo where and when they are supposed to be. I seek that one picture not many can grasp. Tonight is a chance to capture a perfect shot from Angels Landing. I just need someone who can guide me up there in the dark."

Leonard laughs and says, "Good luck buddy. As soon as they see your lights, they are sending someone to stop you." Nave agrees and says it has to be done totally in the dark. He asks if the park allows special passes to climb at night.

Leonard is doubtful and enquires, "You are serious aren't you?"

Nave shows him a roll of money and says, "When the moon shines on the river below and the glow comes off each side of these mountains, I will have a series of photos that will bring in a fortune. My work has many waiting to have the first shot at the original prints." He holds the cash, and tells Leonard it could be worth $5,000 if he takes him up there.

Still doubtful, yet now greed has a hook, Leonard asks another interesting question. "If you are willing to pay so much, why not just arrange with the park to have a guide take you?"

Nave holds a dark blue pack and says, "I have approached them. See, I may have left out the part where these photos will be taken as I glide down the night sky once I base jump off the peak."

He shakes his head after listening to him, and curiously ponders, "Five grand just to guide you up? When do I get the cash?" Nave tells him he will get the money when they reach the last vertical climb to the top. He agrees if they are stopped, he will still get half. Leonard assures Nave he knows their schedules, and that there is not much likelihood they will be stopped once they get to the climb. It will be the trek to the area that the rangers usually patrol. He advises Nave to meet him back at his camper around eleven this night.

A helmet, the glider pack is on, and there is just the quiet chirps of the many bugs watching from the bushes. The air is perfectly still; the stars are not as bright once the moon is high and almost full. They look up, and know it has to be a careful yet prompt hike to the top. No time to stop and gaze. Leonard requests half the money before they even start. A smile, a nod, and a comment, "You extreme thrill junkies will pay for anything that makes your blood pump faster, won't you?" Midway up, Nave pauses to drink a little water. He has a second bottle, and offers it to Leonard. He replies that he has done this climb so many times, he hardly needs water in the day, much less at night. They continue on. Leonard maneuvers over a rock, and slips against another portion protruding from the wall. Leonard makes light of how different it is at night. He mentions how he can feel the blood running down his knee. Nave pulls a bandana from his pack, and the water again.

"Here man, we have a second to splash some water on that, and you can have this bandana to wrap it." He steps up, and has his right leg up on a rock. He throws a little water on the cut, and then drinks some after he wraps his knee. The moon is directly above when they reach the chained section. Leonard has been slowing down, and even claims to be a little light-headed.

He tells Nave, "I am not sure if the knee bleeding is getting me, or just because I didn't eat much tonight, and now climbing my skinny ass up this mountain." He sits down and leans back.

Nave sits across from him and opens up the conversation. "Sorry you are not feeling so great. I do appreciate you trekking me up this far. See, I love video and photography. Have you ever been into photography? I mean being here all the time, you must have a collection of great pictures. What sort of photos are you in to?"

Leonard looks dizzy, and speaks very slowly. "I have several cameras. I like more of the people stuff. Oh man, I am so light-headed. I guess I see this so much I don't take as many pictures as one would think."

Nave moves closer and tells him, "Oh that is too bad. See, there is a spot down there just as you walk over the bridge to Emerald Pools. A nice little spot that is great for a family photo."

Now Leonard springs his head up, looking very concerned and confused. He asks, "You have a family? Kids?"

Nave is now standing as Leonard's head is balanced against the rock behind him as his limp neck no longer has the strength to hold it up. Nave looks down as he explains, "Well yes, I have an older daughter. I also have a friend who has two great kids. Years ago, they came here and at the very spot I told you about. You know that spot. There as you get ready to turn to go up the path to the pools. It is a good picture. She is standing, her daughter is just above her on the rock, and so is her son. They are older now. Turned out to be good kids, as she tells me. Good thing they had an uncle around to take that picture. See, their dad died in an accident as he drove back from South Dakota during the winter."

Leonard has a lazy fright in his eyes. Nave leans down and quietly dictates, "Do you remember that day Leo? Do you remember how happy those kids were here? I'm sure you know why they never want to go camping again too, don't you Leo? You still like taking pictures of people? You still like lurking around Vegas, and shuffling foreign children to the clubs and private parties for the wealthy?"

Leonard's eyes water and if he had not drank the water, he would have the strength to actually exert the effort to cry. He feels internal pain, yet cannot move his body. Leonard begs Nave to help him back down. Nave tells him, "Leo, you will make it down." Nave assures him he will forever be in Zion.

At four thirty, Gary is out filling up the ice chest with water, and having his coffee. At six a.m., everyone meets in his room. He is busy checking through the updates and material list on his computer and without looking over, just starts talking, "You know, funny how all the cars out there have a little dew on them. Nave's, nope. His is clear, and hell the hood still seems a little warm." He makes a funny face, and subjectively throws his thumb toward Nave and says, "I am not mentioning any names, but I think someone might have slept . . . wait, wait . . . been in another bed other than his own last night!" Quickly Gary, with his mouth wide open, expresses his contagious laugh. They give Nave a lot of crap over being out all night.

Nick adds, "I guess while we were golfing, someone was getting a hole in one!" More laughs, and then it was off to work.

As they drove into the work site, Nave sits quietly; he is very tired. He looks out the window at the morning of sunlight; there are a few black ravens picking at a carcass, a farmer's horses sifting through the hay, and it all feels so peaceful at this moment.

Just then, Robert can be heard in his earpiece, "Amazing, just amazing."

They end out the week, and have the following week off. When he stops by his sister's house to meet up with Amanda, his sister, Cherie, asks if he was still thinking of going hiking in Zion and Moab. He tells her he wants to wait another few weeks when it is warmer. She scolds him, and tells him be very careful. She goes on to tell him how just this morning they found a guy whom they think was hiking at night and fell off a huge cliff. He asks if the guy lived and she says, "Umm, let's see. He fell almost four hundred feet before landing on a rock. Not even *your* hard head is going to survive that; brat!" He makes a weak attempt to bring her comfort by telling her that he would not hike around Zion at night. She tries to make him promise he won't hike up steep cliffs, period.

After his week home, he returns to work. Sunday nights he usually gets in, unpacks, and then goes to the grocery store for things he will need for lunch and in the room. While walking back into the hotel, he grabs a paper. Inside the local section is coverage of the man who fell from Angels Landing in Zion. The local news received notice over the week that Leonard Lightfoot apparently took his own life. The report indicated a note was found in his trailer, he had just put his house up for sale, and there was evidence which the department was investigating further in regard to what was found on his computer. The next day, Nave goes to the gym then down to Hurricane. He sits at the bar, and thinks Tammy may have taken time off. He sits there having a tea and snacking on the peanuts.

The door to the freezer opens, and she looks over. "Well, you found your way back," she hollers over to Nave. He tells her he had been home, and work had been crazy. She asks if he has decided on a house and even sarcastically jokes that she knew of another house in the neighborhood that was for sale. She walks over, sits down, and asks, "Have you seen the news about my brother?" He shakes his head as to answer he had not. "I guess the guilt got to him. Oh my God, oh my God! I totally forgot you said something about one of those parents pushing him off Angles Landing. FaReekee! That was him. My brother hiked up Angels last Sunday night, and took one last dive. The sheriff's office found a note and other stuff. They gave me a note he wrote that I hope makes things better for my kids. Do you want to hear it?" Little did she know that Nave could have read the same note to her.

"Tammy, let those two know I am sorry for what I did. As I will not ever change, I can stop myself. I will stop all this tonight. No pity do I seek, I only wish to take my dark clouds away so you all can see the brilliant skies once again. No person

should deny you the full enjoyment of life. Included in that is the natural beauty of so many places. I know these places harbor visions of disgust and guilt. You two are old enough now to know, you were victims–not the ones to be ever faulted. Seek happiness and believe that the truth is, most are good. Many are kind and few are disturbed. In this you will always know it is hard to see the disturbed among the sane. Never drop your guard, and always be aware. As I have taken my dark cloud away, there are others. Believe in the good, and trust only your mother. Regretfully, Uncle Leo."

She folds the paper, and asks Nave what he thinks. Nave tells her he believes many get to a point where they know there is no changing, and they either continue until they are caught or they do what her brother did. She wants to know how he feels about the difference between those who are caught versus those who take their own lives.

He is unwavering when he says, "It is best if they dissolve their existence as they just cannot ever be rehabilitated or trusted. It is a sickness that becomes an addiction. These head doctors will claim they can help them with the right medication and therapy. In all the years, have you seen one case where the person didn't revert back to his old ways?" They sit and talk more, and soon Nave has to get back.

He would not return as his task was done. He would remember Tammy, her tattoos, her sharp, shaky, spiked hair, and the toned CrossFit body. Tammy likely would see the door open at times, and wonder if he would break the threshold of her pub door.

Chapter 15
Morrow Digs

Agent Calvin Morrow has a link on his computer that tracks every single death, homicide, suicide, or suspicious deaths. He does it as a hobby even when he is off duty. Some people play video games, watch TV, go to the movies, etc. Not Morrow. When he gets home, he tinkers with his death chart.

Mike Holcomb walks into his office, and notices that Morrow has the death chart up, and starts teasing him again about it. "Morrow, brother, you have issues. You really should just go be a mortician—all the time working on that weird shit about how people die. One day this department is going to start investigating your sick ass." Morrow dismisses Holcomb, who walks out; Morrow continues to drop and drag several dead profiles from page to page. He presses his phone to call Holcomb back into his office. When Holcomb walks in he tells him to sit down. "Morrow, is this more about the dead people? Let me guess, you are still not settled with how some of these people died."

Morrow lays out a few printed charts for Holcomb to look over as he tells him, "Okay, may sound completely loony at first, but just stay with me on this. Over the last ten years, I have run these charts. I have tweaked, adjusted, reorganized, and investigated many of these over and over. Okay just look at these few":

"Miami, suicide by unknown concoction of chemicals":

"Boston, suicide by jumping off a bridge, yet no fingerprints anywhere on the bridge";

"New York, suicide by electrocution, but coroner surprised he was stuck in an awkward position";

"Key West, guy is tangled up in his boat ropes."

"Colorado, now Zion, Utah, and so many others. What do you notice about all these? I mean, there are over seventy-five of these in the last ten years in this category alone. What category is this Morrow?"

Holcomb looks carefully, and tells Morrow, "They were all pedophiles in some way. And a bad way. These all were serious offenders."

Morrow slams his hands down, and is excited when he feels he has made a huge discovery. "Now, Mike, what else is unique about every single one of these dead fucks? Every single, goddam one of them?"

Holcomb can't see much in what he is getting at. Then Morrow pulls out a stack of cases he had copied. He hands them to Holcomb, one by one. Holcomb opens each, and after about twenty cases he looks at Morrow very concerned and strangely.

The door of their lieutenant swings open, and Morrow and Holcomb roll in a message cart. It has stacks of files. The lieutenant cautiously looks up and asks, "Do I need to immediately deny whatever the hell you two are about to present to me?"

Holcomb tells the lieutenant that he wanted to call Calvin nuts and just walk out; however, there is something to what he has found. Calvin runs the lieutenant through step by step, and then the lieutenant asks, "So what you are wanting me to take upstairs and present for an investigatory case, is that all these high-profile child molesters who found a way to slip through the cracks are suddenly put on a hit list? I am not sure if you are implying the families are behind it, if there is some vigilante exercising his good will, or whatever the hell, really. Here is my hesitation, guys. These are proven cases that these people did these acts, yet somehow someway there were errors in the cases and they walked. Not many people really want to see justice in this. Hell, most will see the justice in how someone erased these perverts from existence."

Holcomb interjects, "Lieutenant, in what I looked at closely, it does seem legit. It almost seems like there are remarkable professionals who are highly skilled at taking people out, and leaving very little to trace. It isn't going to be easy to track this down and who knows, maybe we do find it all to be coincidence and karma that found its way to right these wrongs. But if it is the other then we have **two wrongs.**"

The lieutenant looks up and hesitantly states, "Is it wrong? I am not so sure, really. And that stays here in this room. I have to tell you, and you think of this yourself, if it were your kids, if the prick got off, what would your mindset be?" They both look to each other and agree. Yet in the scope of their duty, they want to at least seek the truth.

Calvin sits down and politely asks, "Let us follow this out and as it develops; we will have everything across this desk as it happens. If it is as I think, well once we have solid findings, then YOU, Lieutenant can make that call. I simply have to know. It burns inside of me, and too much is left unknown." The lieutenant picks up the office phone. He asks for his captain, and tells the two he will meet with them later this same day.

The lieutenant calls Morrow, "Calvin, where are you two?" He tells him, he and Holcomb are having lunch and then working on flights to go chase that internet scam he wanted them to look into.

"You need to go the other direction. The captain and our special crimes division looked over all that crap Morrow has been playing with for ten years, and wants you two in Florida to meet with the medical examiner this week."

The plane nears the runway of Miami International Airport, and Holcomb is commenting on how it appears the entire state is covered with small patches of water everywhere. He makes a point to hit Morrow, and shows him a medium-sized gator on the bank just feet away from the road.

When they get off the plane, he says, "I can't believe there was a gator right by the road." Morrow tells him one of the tactical guys lived down in Florida and said anywhere there is water, you should guess there could be a gator. He added the one who lived down there also told him the gators are no problem. It is the damn water moccasins you have to watch out for. Given the fact these animals are intimidating, they soon find out the worst aggressors in Florida are the mosquitoes. As they wait for a local agent to pick them up, they each fed a few of the annoying pests.

They make a quick dash over to the M.E.'s office where a very happy, upbeat woman in her early forties, silky smooth Puerto Rican skin, and a seductive accent guided by her big, dark brown eyes, greet them and escort the men to her office. She is very proficient, and has prepared for their visit. She has more documents than they had expected. After their stop at her office, they decide to take a look around the town where a few of the suicides had taken place. As they stand in the parking lot in Del Ray, Holcomb holds the file and comments about the fresh contusion on the victim's jaw. He points out that the M.E. noted it was indicative of firm pressure, and even questioned some light impressions on the forehead.

Morrow asks, "Why here, why not just do it at home? And let me ask this: Why was there caking of the poison around his throat, and rear of his tongue?"

They go over to the park where one of the victims had died on the park bench.

"It says here this wasn't likely a suicide, and that someone laced this pervert's cigarette. Here is what has me perplexed; the substance the M.E. found isn't even a known chemical. No one has been able to tell what it is," Morrow says to Holcomb. They spend a few days traveling the areas of interest in Florida. They skip Key West, as everything pertaining to that death looks like an accident. Even though they both looked over the file, and how it did relate to another child molester. They decide to travel up the Eastern Seaboard, and make stops along the way.

One stop in Charlotte is tense. A nice horse pasture, cobblestone road, and thick clusters of trees hide the enormous colonial-style home. As they stop in the circular drive, a very large black man comes out. He wears a tailored suit, and hair finely trimmed; his strong chin is covered by the precise lines of his beard. He has no smile to express as he exclaims, "I have not requested any visitors, I am certain I don't know you, and being that you are parked in my drive, I am guessing you know me. Whatever your business here, you may consider my right to protect my property and use any force I see fit to escort you back to the road where you can continue on to harass someone else. And should you feel there to be any common ground or special treatment based on the fact you are as black as myself, you now know that is not of my will."

Mike and Calvin look to each other as to flip the imaginary coin regarding who will talk to this man . "Calvin Morrow. I am an agent with the FBI; I was hopeful we could talk."

The man on the porch still clear and firm says, "I am sure this is in regard to that deplorable, waste of human life that was found tied up and left to smother in a slow, and if you ask me, deserving painful expiration of his life."

A tall, black woman comes to the porch on her horse, dismounts, hands the man on the porch her helmet, and proceeds to where Mike and Calvin are standing. She seems pleasant, and even shakes the hands of each. When she introduces herself it is more of a warning than a greeting. "Gentlemen, for over twenty years I have been handling the most difficult cases to include government harassment. My husband is more likely to use force, and given his size and abusive punishment he so misses from playing professional football, I would say he might enjoy tossing a few people around. Now myself, on the other hand, I get my thrill in the legal aspect of publicly humiliating those who attempt to open up more anguish upon my family. Now if you are from the FBI, or any other branch of the government, I would assume you know I have a right to request identification upon your appearance. I'm sure you both have a card handy and ID to validate that information. I will be contacting your office, and advise that you or any other member of your organization will not be welcome to breach the boundaries of our property, and if I feel you are anywhere near us in public, inquire any associates of ours, or contact any member of our family, I will be swift to take action." She smiles as she looks over their names, and advises the way out of town.

Calvin and Mike say nothing, get in their car, and it isn't until they reach the road when Mike says, "You realize there isn't going to be one person who has any relation to the affected families that will offer us any help. I must say, I don't see how they would either."

The activity of the agents is swift to reach Judge Grace. Nave is with Amanda having dinner at Texas Roadhouse when his earpiece tones. The CO advises, "NES 1912, review new information via secured portal 10-17."

Amanda Dean has no clue he just received information, and they go on with cracking peanuts and allowing cinnamon butter to melt upon fresh rolls. Nave isn't one to eat out a lot, but he is easily recognized with Amanda in his local Texas Roadhouse. When he gets home, he goes to check the updated information. As he reads, he learns of the information that FBI agents Calvin Morrow and Mike Holcomb have been canvasing the areas where targets have been eliminated. The update also shows detailed information of the diversions and inside assistance to the operation. There are not names or positions listed; yet it does show a proficient outline and working action in keeping each ES protected. It warns each ES must exercise skills and make judgments to protect the anonymity of the operation as a whole.

After reading the information, Nave closes his case, finds Amanda, and hands her a page he printed out. "This is what I had to go print in my office. If it seems boring, I can still cancel." She looks at it and hugs him. On the paper, is a roundtrip ticket to Florida for two weeks in the coming summer. He had already spoken with Lynn, and is allowing Amanda to go visit her friends. She is still shocked and even comments that she is excited, but will wait to see if he really lets her get on the plane. She has worries that her over cautious dad will back out, and tell her he changed his mind because he is scared.

Amanda is online chatting with Lynn, and planning all the things they will try to do when she gets there. Lynn enquires about Nave. She asks how his new job is going, if he seems to like Utah, and presents a subtle question asking if he is dating anyone. Amanda keys in on the enquiry, and writes back, asking why Lynn wants to know. Amanda has at times tried to play matchmaker not realizing the deeper working knowledge Lynn Grace has of her father's real line of work. Lynn writes, asking if there is any chance Nave is coming with her. Amanda tells Lynn that his work travel may not give him enough time to come, and honestly Amanda wants the grown-up freedom to be out of her dad's shadow of protection. They close the email conversation, and Amanda spends the rest of the night emailing her friends back in Florida.

As Nave prepares his clothes for the next week, Amanda Dean comes in with a full line of questions and thoughts generated from her emails between her friends. It is evident she and her friends are very expeditious in planning the future, all of which have regular monetary deductions coming from her dad. She sits in his leather chair as she lays out her projected itinerary for the summer trip. He assures her he will give her what she needs to survive for a few days. He also advises she may think about saving money until then.

She rolls her eyes, spins in the chair, and debates, "Padre, I am not a flashy, pretentious, snob. I don't require much, just some board shorts, food, and entertainment money. I think . . . let's see . . . a grand ought to do it."

He folds his shirt, calculates in his mind as he mumbles to himself, and answers,
"Yeah, you might be right. I didn't account for all the stuff you would need, I mean REALLY need when you go out there. Here, you sure a thousand bucks is even enough?"

She squints her eyes as she knows his facetious expressions.

He continues, "Yeah, Dean, I wasn't even thinking of all that. We might want to wait until you can save up about $900.00 to go with the hundred I was going to give you. After all, you did all the number crunching, and I trust your numbers. You probably do need a grand."

She stops her spin, eases out of the black leather chair, and puts her hands on his shoulders and says, "Oh, I will so enjoy seeing Florida on a budget. Beg of my old friends for mere crumbs, sneak into Islands of Adventure, and fight the homeless for forty-nine cents so I can get a single taco. Yet, I will be among the sun and sea. Love you Padre." She laughs, and heads to her room.

Now back in Charlotte, Morrow and Holcomb piece together more information. Holcomb reviews financials of several families when he notices one out of Spokane, Washington is quite questionable. He has Morrow validate what he is calculating. He shows how a prominent family had gone through a rough court battle trying to convict a woman who had been accused of unspeakable assault, sodomy, and abuse of one of her students. It was noted the boy felt ashamed, and there were indications he may have been threatened by a third party, likely the woman's drug-addicted boyfriend. The boy, who was fourteen at the time, refused to cooperate after the threat, and changed his story. The prosecution had so little solid evidence, the judge dismissed the case. Eight months after the dismissed case, the victim's father sold several stock holdings in his company, and auctioned off a rare Grand National. Holcomb notes that there is no indication that they needed the money; nor are there any deposits that align with the $100,000 in stocks. There is no trace of how much he received for the car as the transaction seemed to be barter for a collector in Florida.

Holcomb lays out the papers, articles, and reports what they have to this point. He walks Morrow through his thoughts. "Okay, follow me . . . follow me sir!"

"One: Naughty teacher does some really bad shit to a nerdy boy. The court case said he was a nerdy outsider and unsocial"

"Two: Boy's mom notices strange behavior, mood swings, and some messy shorts. The poor kid had to even go to the hospital on two occasions"

"Three: School is notified; report filed and into court they go";

"Four: Boy is threatened, feels like the news is going to show and tell all that this woman made him do, and thinks he will be labeled gay. He backs off"

"Five: Case dismissed";

"Six: Eight months later, this high-end car dealer decides to pull a hundred Gs from stocks, and practically gives his collectible Grand National to some guy in Florida?"

Now wait. Check this shit out. Six months after this guy pulls cash and gives away a car, (Holcomb opens a page on his computer to show the news story of the woman being found, dead), naughty teacher is found floating in Coeur d' Alene, and ruled she drowned and no suspicious circumstances. Side note of coroner . . . unknown trace of a chemical unidentified. Ya think there might be some coincidence here? I say we take a trip to Spokane, and see what we might uncover."

Morrow slaps Holcomb on the head and says, "I knew I trusted you to back me on this shit. Son of a bitch, you smart bastard. I told you. I told you there is something here. Let's find this shit out!" Morrow holds up the computer with one hand and the stack of papers with the other. Open his wing span and looks to the ceiling. Surely looking beyond the ceiling as he asks, "Dear lord, be it right, wrong, or just peace of mind, bring thy truth to my heart so I may sleep sound knowing I did my due." Holcomb leans back in the hotel chair, and tells him to stop with all the religious crap, and if there is a God, he likely has rejected the applications of all the victims they are searching for.

Three days have past and the two are in Airway Heights, just outside of Spokane, Washington. They deliberately stay at the indian casino, and view the classic Chevrolet Bel Air that is on display. Many wanting players funnel money into the machines with the hope they may press the button that will produce the winning jackpot that may include this restored Chevy. Now if the agents were really good, they might find proof for those who frequent these casinos all over that they never see anyone actually win the cars placed as an enticement. Many believe it is as elusive as finding the tooth fairy when you are a kid. Somehow someone wins, has their photo taken, yet has anyone ever really been next to that old lady in a walker who wins a brand new Corvette or classic car? Near the bottom of the platform where the car sits waiting to be driven off, is authenticity paperwork to show everything about the car, including what collector the car came from. Morrow writes down what he needs, and the two head to see more antique cars.

The two drive down Sprague, and Morrow whips his head back, turns the car around and Holcomb asks what the hell did he just see. Morrow smiles and says, "I don't want some coffee, my ass needs to stop for coffee!" He pulls into a dive-type motel, which has a small coffee hut out front. He tells Holcomb, "Maybe it's the thin air here but I know when we drove by here, I saw some hot, dark-haired lovely with nothing on in the window serving coffee."

Covered only by a very tiny see-through bra, a thread of panties which proves she has not a single hair anywhere below her eyebrows, and several colorful tattoos, the woman smiles, flirts and seductively asks "Is there something nice and hot you would like to order?" She knows her talent is in the flirt. The men recess to their high school mentalities as they gaze in disbelief.

Morrow is polite, yet tells the woman, "You know, I did not believe my eyes when I drove by. And now I am right here and hell, I still don't believe my eyes." She laughs and acknowledges her assumptions that they are not from the area. Had there not been a line of work trucks behind them, it is likely they would have delayed as long as possible.

Now with a shot of caffeine and testosterone, they find their way to a glass-front building with shining chrome and candy-painted cars just past the glass. The two try to convince the other of which car is better, faster, or more collectible. One thing they can agree on is most are well out of their wallet depth. A thin man, silver-haired, with black stylish glasses, and a polo shirt with the name of the business greets them. He is appreciative of anyone coming in to look or to actually buy. When he discovers the two are merely window shopping, he assures them they are welcome to spend as much time as they wish. He tells them he sees his place as more of a museum as 95 percent of the guests are doing just the same. He walks with them, and explains how he and his dad have restored most of the cars themselves. He has a transparent joy when pointing out the rarity and perfection of each car that has been transformed from rust to a jewel. The two are taken back by just how pleasant and happy the man is.

He tells Morrow and Holcomb, "The best part of these cars is taking them to the schools—showing the kids history, perfection, and the true Americana of what I believe built this country. The kids see these cars, and you can see them just dream of being back in time." On the walls, are numerous pictures of the cars in the grass at shows, football games, fundraisers, and all have a flock of kids around them. There is an absence of any mention of money. He has a full love of the cars. Easy to look at several millions of dollars in metal, chrome, and rubber sitting in this building, yet the man has a joy that surpasses the greed. He hands each of them a calendar, and says, "You two take your time and enjoy the cars. Any questions, just holler for me. The calendars are yours because eventually I do go home and close the doors. Sorry big guy (talking to Morrow, who is holding a cup from the coffee stop), this year we didn't put any hotties next to the cars, but I see you found the bikini coffee on your way here." He laughs, as he looks over to Holcomb.

They leave and even talk of how this guy is just a real cool, old car guy. Two days later, they walk into the lounge at the hotel. They have given the bartender a heavy tip to know when Frank will be in. There are comfortable seats near a fireplace and beaded curtains that are somewhat private. Frank has come in to check on the car, and sits down to have a drink. Morrow and Holcomb walk over, and are easily recognized. Happy as when they had seen him last, he stands and says hello. Marrow leans back, one arm across the back of his seat, and he rests his foot on his knee. When the man asks if they had changed their mind about actually buying one of the cars, Morrow tells him they are actually more interested in finding the Grand National. A slight stall in response, and he advises that is a difficult find. Holcomb informs him they are aware he had one not too long ago, and perhaps they might locate who he sold it to. Frank says that was a charity auction item, and usually there isn't any info he would have after it was gone.

Holcomb leans in and tells him, "Hey listen, you're a damn good guy, and we can see that. I am not a car collector, and I don't know much about Grand National. I am Agent Holcomb, and this is Agent Morrow. That Grand National is part of an FBI investigation, and you may understand we need you to cooperate in any way you can." The man now flush, looks to Morrow, then back to Holcomb. He expresses he doesn't know where the car is, and wants to know if he needs a lawyer as he feels this is more about questions than just car talk.

Holcomb is compassionate in his words as he advises, "Look, you are a decent guy. You have a family, business, and for all we can see, you're a stand-up guy. That car may have been part of something we are trying to get to the bottom of long after you auctioned, gave away, or donated. We just need to see anything you have that may help us find it."

He stammers to convince them he may not have that paperwork and Morrow swiftly interjects, "Come on man, you don't donate a $150,000 car, and there not be no paper work, trade of title, who picked it up, NOTHING. Look, we are going to meet you at your shop tomorrow. You think about it a while, and we can talk more then. We simply want to find who has the car now." They stand, hand him a card, and leave the man to think.

The next morning, they sit having breakfast and bouncing ideas back and forth. Morrow wonders if someone just drove the car away, and there was no transport company to find.

Holcomb assures him, "That time of year, a rear-wheel, high-powered, heavy car is not likely going to be driven anywhere far. Look at the report. When that car left, there was packed snow any way out of here. So it is either still right in this town, or it was taken in an enclosed hauler. Now tell me this, how the hell is it I can't find this damn car on any records check. It is as if the damn thing never existed." Morrow stops eating and tells Holcomb they need to find Frank before he gets even more spooked. They pull into the parking lot of the collectors shop. They walk inside, and find Frank. They are polite, and ask to sit in private. They all head back to his office to talk. Morrow sits on a tuck-and-roll, rear backseat of a Lemans Pontiac.

He comes clean with the guy. "Hey, I'm a straight forward guy. You gave that car away, and somehow have no paper trail for it. It is very suspicious to us that a guy like you who loves his cars would not know where a prize like that would go. We will find it; we will know then how it got to where it is, and why you gave it away. See Frank, you are not the only one who has had some really bad shit go down with a young person in your family. Yeah that! I know all about that."

Frank looks sad, yet sits tall and tells Morrow, "You know about that, sure. Do you know, do you really know the depth of sorrow? Do you know what the law is, or what life will really be like for a kid? We are talking about a kid for god sake. Tell me, does the FBI have a program to allow you to feel the unimaginable? At the time I was restoring that worthless piece of shit pile of metal, as my son needed me. So yeah, I got rid of the damn thing. Didn't care about it. It helped me heal. Not him! I couldn't bear to even have it in my shop. Never claimed the loss on my taxes, never worried any more about it." As he reaches to open a drawer, his wife walks in. She says there is a call he needs to answer, NOW. He listens, looks to Holcomb who was closer to him, and hands him the phone.

Holcomb listens, says "yes sir," and hands the phone back to Frank. Frank listens, and calmly expresses his acceptance of the apology being offered by the caller. Holcomb stands, tells Morrow they have to leave, and tells Frank they will not be any bother again.

In the car Morrow asks, "What the hell was that!"

Holcomb looks out the window, takes a heavy hand over his head and says, "That was our boss. He wanted to know why he was on the phone with a federal attorney, who was asking why two of his agents were harassing a man in Spokane, and requesting files or paperwork that we had not a single Court Order to request." Morrow pounds the steering wheel, and after several words that would not make any Disney movie, asks if they are being ordered back.

Holcomb smiles and says, "He was pissed. He did not like having to answer that question when he had no idea where we were. The last thing he said was, 'You have to pan a ton of mud to find an ounce of gold.'" They both laugh;

Morrow turns up the radio and says, "Looks like we have a free day to play some poker my friend."

Chapter 16
Vegas

The air is thick; everyone's skin is clammy. A Chinese lady sits on a suitcase fanning herself only to move the humid air against her wrinkled face. Her mouth agape shows the few teeth that remain; they look to be fragile enough for mashed potatoes to crack. Another woman stands waiting with designer bags, one child in hand, whose hair was likely styled just for the plane trip. She looks to her mom, and asks why her mom continues to huff. A group of men gather, Anyone can hear their strong New Joysey accents. Then the groups of families with pale skin soon to be blistered by the Florida sun stand eager, happy, and excited by the many pamphlets of tourist attractions.

Amanda Dean just smiles and says to herself how she loves the diversity of the guests who flock to Florida. She realizes she is officially a guest, yet will never abdicate her roots of being a true Floridian. About the time she passes the herd of sweating guests, she sees Lynn waiving to her. Amanda slides into the rich black leather seats, dark-tinted windows, and absolute luxury, as she asks Lynn why she is driving this car and not the Charger. Lynn explains she has a few cars, and the Charger is just an around-town fun car.

Amanda asks, "What is this? I love it! I see it's a BMW, but it doesn't look like most I see."

Lynn is excited to tell her, "Oh I love, love this thing! Okay Dean, you know I have to have my speed no matter what, right? This thing is a monster! It's an X6 M. OMG watch this." Lynn gets out of the main airport area and a straight-away offers her a tarmac playground. She holds the wheel, sits back, and a huge smile erupts likely lasting from the previous time she found the ending point of her accelerator; she again buries her right foot. The all-wheel drive powerhouse propels smoothly forward at high- performance car speed. There is a low growl behind them, as the X6 M literally floats to a high rate of speed before she has to ease up. "Don't you dare tell you father I did that," Lynn says over a happy out cry of exhilaration.

Amanda has never been to where Lynn lives. Which is a guest house off of her father's home in Tuskawilla. It is a sprawling home, several driveways, and Lynn follows one to the back of the property. There is a separate guest home just to one side of a massive garage. They go in, and she shows Amanda to her room. Amanda just smiles, shakes her head, and tells Lynn how this place is totally what she would picture her in. Out the window is a natural herb garden, a well-manicured Koi pond, sand and stone walkways, vines, a comfortable fire pit, and a place Amanda will surely enjoy with a nice big hammock. The interior is artistic, and has an array of contemporary and abstract art. On the countertop is fresh veggies and fruit. As they look over things and visit in the kitchen, Lynn assures her that she can still have pizza and those other un-natural foods she is used to. She tells Lynn she wants to actually see what all this healthy stuff is like for a change.

The mixer comes out and Amanda has a precautionary statement: "Lynn, you do know people do not have four stomachs like cows. We are not biologically made to eat grass. You just put grass in that mixer and tried to disguise it with some berries, pom, and what is that, apple vinegar? Oh I am not sure about that one." She tries it and as her face began to invert, she shivers and sets the glass down.

Lynn laughs and says, "Okay, not a good one to start you off with. Next time, we will just do an all-fruit and beet. Much sweeter and you will like it." "Amanda assures her she may just stick with teen food. They spend the rest of the evening talking about Utah. Amanda must have told Lynn twenty times how much she wants her to come and visit. The strange reality of missing someone often comes when we see that person again. There is a chemical reaction that we have no control over. The very senses that nourish our love for life, give us that emotion we can't control. Something many can verbally exercise their dishonesty of, yet internally they will only know the falsehood of that expression. Amanda is reunited with the oils Lynn would put on at night, the fragrance she would burn in a ceramic bowl, and the CD of natural music to sleep to. There is a particular calm she notices returning when Lynn is around. Amanda sleeps soundly, and feels peace in Lynn's home.

The new assignment with Nave's work has them in Henderson, Nevada. The group is excited, and the conversation is mostly about how much partying will be done. The first few days go by quickly, and late work hours don't leave much time for the guys to go out. It is typical to find a few drinking their dinner by the pool, or in the bar. The fourth night Nave gets back from the gym and joins up with a few at the small bar in the hotel. By this time, the other guys have made very good friends with the attractive bartender, and even the cool guys who work the bar as well. The bartender looks to be in her mid-thirties, and has bright, whitened teeth that are often exposed with her wide-open smile. Her nose is bold, like a Jewish girl. Her hair is tied up, and a long black ponytail falls free to the middle of her back. Once Nave sits at the high-top with the guys, she comes up and asks what he will have. When he asks for a water, he first asks if it is tap or filtered.

Jill, the bartender, tosses a round paper coaster his way, laughs and says, "What the fuck, water . . . and filtered. Is this a water bar? Gary, who is this guy?" In her raspy voice, she laughs and assures Nave she is just being a smart-ass.

She asks why he hasn't been in with the others, and Gary answers for him. "He can't hang with the degenerates, he is too high-class. Always dresses nice, does healthy shit all the time, hell this guy has cocktail shrimp for lunch half the time." He backhands Nave, and bugles his unique laugh. Nave knows this is all in fun. Jill plays along, and even asks if Dasani water would suffice for the picky one. The rest of the night the beer keeps flowing, and everyone challenges the audible levels allowed by the hotel staff. After several encouraging warnings to settle the lounge down, Jill cuts everyone off.

The next morning there is not much ambition to go full speed in the heat of Vegas. The work day wraps up, and Nave is on his way to the gym.

As he enters the parking lot of the gym the CO announces, "NES 1912, advise status."

He replies, "NES 1912; 10-10."

"NES 1912, level 4 target last detected in the Las Vegas area. Possible vehicles: One: 2005 Porsche Cayenne Black, left taillight cracked. Two: 2001 Acura NSX red, plate out of New Mexico M Y N S X. End vehicle data. Target vehicles have been spotted with other drivers in the Las Vegas area, New Mexico, and Arizona. Target known to paint, detail, and deliver vehicles in many states. Target does have a beacon locator in which we have detected faults. Verification and history ready on your computer. Level four status for thirty-eight months. Elimination by any means. Review information and accept target via secured computer. 10-17."

He continues with his trip to the gym, has dinner, and that night reviews the information. The target has eluded the team for several years. Joe Allen was one of many trafficking children from El Paso to New Mexico. While several others were captured and stood trial, Allen fled and was known to be protected by a very wealthy drug lord who has a disturbing desire for young Mexican boys he would often dress to look like girls. A high-level access indicates there is possibly funding by the Mexican government to see Allen eliminated. All NESs, GESs, and ESs are open to eliminate this target. Nave receives information to acquire a vehicle near the raceway to use during his stay in the Las Vegas area. The vehicle is known to be equipped with all necessary intelligence, and has no traceable identification. Later Nave talks to the tech, Jason about the car. Jason is his usual excited, mind-jittered self. He tells Nave all about the car, but will not tell him what car it is. He assures him this is a car they don't get very often.

The next day after work, Nave heads hastily to the raceway to find the hangar and agent he will get the car from. He pulls past the Shelby garages, and hopes he will be sitting in a Shelby Cobra. However, his navigation soon shows he is passing the Shelby building. He comes upon a small garage with a single door, and his navigation system advises he has arrived at the correct location. The door and building are heavily secured, and as he approaches, the intercom gives instructions to hold the door handle, and place his right thumb on the pad to his right. A quick scan, and an unlock is granted. He passes the desk, and being lowered from a rafter is a 1999 Lamborghini Diablo. The black is like looking through a perfect glass marble. The five holed rims have been powder-coated black with a hint of blood red accents. The interior has been hand-stitched. A walk around the back shows a license plate out of Oregon which reads, "SI666DE."

He is educated on the vehicle by the specialist, and Jason has shown up to offer any help needed. Jason and the specialist finish bringing Nave up to speed with this vehicle and then Jason tells Nave, "Now we have to drive up the street to the track, and get you really up to speed." He laughs and tells Nave that this is the real reason he made the trip. The two take the beast around the course until the track lights are about to be cut off. That night, Nave pulls into the hotel, and quietly covers the car. He isn't seen by anyone, and is able to float back to reality as he lies in bed contemplating the urge to just keep driving the car.

The next morning there isn't any question of the car as the work trucks are parked in an opposite lot. Everyone loads up, and head over to the gas station for fuel, coffee, energy drinks, and to see what sort of women may be on their way to work as well. A typical work group of men, it usually takes very little to stimulate the salivation of the mouths that mutter the words that are unlikely to ever be acted out. As predicted, a convertible Audi TT pulls in, the top is down, and the bare, tan shoulders can be seen just past the high-dollar hair job of the woman. The imagination will portray a person to be as stunning as one can wish until the validation is set forth when actually seen. The door of the Audi opens; a thin, dark leg extends long and precise to land the ball of her high heel on the concrete. An anklet glimmers of grace and fortune. Still, with three-quarters of her leg out the door, there is still no evidence of clothing. Her thigh is of quadriceps defined with lean muscle. Her left hand now holds the door, and her glossy French manicure hints to complete the suited decoration of a well-attended woman. Finally, the men will see if the woman has been also gifted with stunning beauty, or is the exterior of this package the expensive attempt to overcome what has shamed her. There is no fail as she stands tall, built, and aware–very aware that the trucks she passed coming in are the usual array of attention she will deal with. She pauses at her door, and looks directly at the group. She has a quick twitch of her eyebrow, and asks if the men are doing anything fun after work.

Gary is more realistic and says, "I know what I would like to do, but something tells me it might hit my pocketbook." Then of course his wide, happy smile and an eruption of laughter. She has a small Coach purse, and walks to the truck. She pulls out a few cards, and hands each guy one. This only after she presses her dark lips to the blank white back of each card. She tells them if they take that card to the club she dances at, they can get in free. Nave is coming out of the store and to the back of the truck to put a few drinks in the cooler.

She stands at the front of the truck and tells him, "You almost missed out. Why don't you come here and get your card too?"

Nave shuffles the ice around as he tells her, "I didn't ask for your card, and I am not going to come to you. I surely don't have a desire to have some . . . what are you, maybe twenty-four at best? Play pretend until the money runs out. Plus, it seems you already have a good group of horned-up guys recruited here."

One of the guys is on the other side of the truck, and tells her to forget him and that he will make sure he comes in to see her tonight. She acts playful, still polite, and walks back to her car. She gets in and drives off.

Gary smacks Collin and tells him to save his money. "Bro, did you see that? She had us pegged. Two work trucks, she knows it's some horned-up fucks, so she swoops in for some business. That bimbo didn't even need gas. Ha, ha, ha, she probably just drives around the gas stations early and at lunchtime. Ha, ha, ha, bet she doesn't even dance at the club."

After work, Collin runs into Nave heading out the door. Collin is going to walk to the shuttle pickup to head into Vegas. He likes going over to the strip to people-watch and play Texas Hold'em. Collin is finishing a beer as the warm wind gently escorts a square piece of cardboard across the parking lot. His cologne is also noticed downwind, as Nave makes a comment about him being splashed up to lure in some honeys. He persuades Nave to skip the gym, and hit the table for a few hours.

Collin says, "Hey, but you have to drive. I already started drinking and hey, free drinks at the table. That right there is winning as long as that one slow bitch isn't working. I sat there for two big blinds, and finally she came around. About dehydrated." Nave agrees, and is a bit eager to show off the car he has. He already plans to tell him he rented it for a few days. Collin realizes he didn't grab his player's card and wants to run up and get it. Nave says he will just meet him by the front doors.

Collin is looking down at his phone as the double sliding glass doors open. He walks out just past the rock pillars, and glances to see the Diablo. He looks the car over in boyhood fanatical awe then goes back to his phone. He awaits Nave still not knowing Nave is sitting behind the wheel. A few seconds pass, and the driver door rises gracefully upward. Collin now has to look to see who would be getting out of such a unique super car.

Nave breaches the low hood and tells Collin, "First you want a ride, and what now? You want me to open your door too?" Collin stuffs his phone away, and squats to the level of the car's roof. The Diablo is wider than many trucks, yet the roof may not even hide Gary Colman.

"What the hell are you doing with this? This is a freakin' Lambo. You are driving a Lambo? Screw the questions, let's roll this sexy bitch!" Just a few streets away from the hotel is a long, separated highway. There's not much traffic, and sight distance is at least five miles. There is a steady baritone hum only interrupted occasionally by the louder billow of mild power, as Nave plays with the persuasive throttle. They approach the intersection, and Nave slows well below the speed limit. Collin asks no questions, still looking over all the gadgets and even makes a comment about the clock, which costs more than many cars. Nave coasts to the yellow light and for this time, is happy to have the red completely stop him. The sky has turned a slight purple, and that wind from before now dances with a line of palms that line the center median. In the distance, is the first warmth of busy city lights that lure people easier than a bass to a good spinner.

Collin says to Nave, "I feel like I am in a rocket, and the countdown is at five, and I have no option other than being launched beyond my own control, and it is freakin' awesome!" This declaration is likely from the rpms being held steady at 4,500. A Ford Aerostar van stops next to them. A middle-aged woman appears far less impressed than the four kids, who now stretch their necks to see the car. Many taps, waves, and one boy gives two thumbs up then motions his pointer fingers in a rotation as a plea to have Nave burn out. The boy is too young to know this car isn't a burn out exhibitor, yet crafted to grip, and go. The momentary car show is quick to end, yet will live on for each one of those boys and the repetitive recounting to each buddy in school the next day. The red light squeezes shut its illumination, and there is a drift of anticipation between the fraction of ohms law that drops one light, and soon opens the green road of acceleration. There is a burst of noise, thrust, and diminishing space between the dashed road of painted lines as Nave takes the Diablo from being admired to being a fading dream. As he reaches one hundred and sixty-five miles per hour, he still has open asphalt to find more speed. He slows, and calms the devil that wants to escort him and Collin to judgment day. Collin can't help but smile. He asks, "Did it have more or did you have to slow down?" Nave tells him there is a sensor on the driver's side that indicates if cops are around. The truth is Nave was advised by the CO that there were two patrol cars two miles in the opposite lanes approaching them. She talks to him, and Collin has no idea.

Nave says, "I didn't know this car had that."

Collin adds, "I bet this car has a lot of shit."

CO says, "NES 1912, I hear you have company."

Nave replies, "Yeah, it's pretty amazing how advanced this thing is."

CO says, "NES 1912, we are always here to protect and help you. We take care of our people."

Collin finally asks "You have to tell me, how did you end up with a car like this?"

CO jokes, "I hope you don't tell him the truth!"

Nave says, "See, you guys party, drink, gamble, and frequent strip clubs, and all that. I love badass cars. This was for rent so I figured I could have more fun renting this than blowing it other places."

CO interjects, "Good cover."

Collin states unequivocally, "Damn, I have to say, that was a much better tease than the chick this morning."

The three-way conversation is typical with Nave and the CO. Many times Nave's daughter has been with him when he had to speak with the CO. It has become a normal thing; he is used to now.

They take a few gratuitous passes up and down the strip, and then go to play some poker. Collin has a few drinks, and is buzzing happy. The Diablo becomes his fun as a few cocktail waitresses have come for drinks. Collin tells the girls, "This guy can't drink tonight. He is driving his Diablo and can't wreck it." He continues to be funny, and enjoys the banter while playing cards. He will poke fun, and urge others to bet higher. Nave is quieter, and plays more safely. They figure they should wrap it up, and Collin wants to see the strip from the passenger seat of the Diablo at night. There are obvious looks, photos, and the annoying cars that only spent money on a tin can exhaust wanting to race. They decide to grab something to eat at The Ale House, just off the mall. Nave parks off to the side of the Whole Foods. Clear of other cars, they walk over. Just before cutting past the bushes, a woman parks in a space. She and her friends get out of a black Bentley. They offer polite hellos; they are just behind Nave and Collin. Nave opens and holds the door. The women are also going to The Ale House. As the host approaches, one woman motions that Nave and Collin were first. Both men are well-mannered, and advise they will step back and allow the women to be served first. As it is, they all end up outside on the patio. Close enough to joke back and forth, the conversations are pleasant, and as Collin is very happily intoxicated, the conversations are bawdy in a respectful playfulness. The woman who was driving is casual, and of a simple yet tailored manner. Her wide-legged, cream pants are likely from the newest collection out of Nordstrom's. Her nails are a perfect pink. The jewelry adorning her thin, exposed neckline defines class and her selective taste. A blouse falls tightly off her shoulders, and there is no question of her fitness. Collin, and one of the girls decide to play darts; the other girl knows a friend at the bar and sits to talk there.

"Lucy, my name is Lucy," she tells him. He introduces himself, and she respectfully enquires his name.

They talk a while, and she looks at him inquisitively. "Okay, so I take it you are not religious. Or does the personal plate you have, have some meaning? Or maybe it's just for fun? I did take a minute to figure it out, "She confidently says.

Collin and the other girl sit back down, and Collin brusquely asks, "What did you figure out?"

She smiles as she says,"SI666DE—his license plate. Devil in SIDE."

He assures her it just goes with the car. She asks why the devil, and he passes it off as it is a Diablo.

Collin jokes with her and says, "Oh here we go, just like the gas station girl, chasing money. Hey when did you see us in anyway?" The other girl tells them they were turning behind Whole Foods when Nave passed.

Lucy then offers, "Sweetie, I am not chasing any money. I am one of the busiest divorce attorneys here in Vegas and in San Diego. I just thought it was fun and edgy." Collin asks what the other girls do, and is impressed that the girl who had become increasingly closer to him was not only fun, but educated. She tells him she is a dentist, and presents a business card to him. No lipstick kiss on the back, yet there is a smear under his lip that the attorney can easily place at the scene of "the crime."

The time goes quickly, and as Nave is ready to head back to Henderson. Lucy asks if they want to go have a nightcap, and talk some more. Nave can see Collin is committed to staying connected to the woman he was with. The group walks out to a now bare parking lot. The third woman stays to spend more time with the bartender she knows, as the other two are safely walked to Lucy's car. They are told of the late night piano bar, and know the location. Still, Nave says he will just follow them. They both pull out onto Las Vegas Boulevard, and head back toward town. When they stop at Flamingo, the dash of the Diablo illuminates that deep blue. A screen rises near the center of the dash, and a mapping window opens.

There is the pulsing target light, and in Nave's ear is the CO. "NES 1912; 10-19,.Las Vegas. NES advise status."

Nave drives smoothly and answers, "10-39; 10-5."

Collin is drunk, and almost oblivious to Nave's random code talk. Collin is intoxicated by the lights and map. He believes it to be a GPS to lead them to the piano bar. They pull up, and Lucy has already parked. Nave pulls to the door, and the gull wing doors open. He explains to Lucy he has to go pick up another friend who is at a club drunk, and will make it quick. She asks if they should all go, and he urges them to hang out; he will try to be fast. Lucy's friend is armed-locked with Collin, and Lucy walks closer to Nave. She is elegant and soft-spoken when she tells him to be sure to come back. Right as he hugs her, a red Acura NSX drives up the street. He can hear his dash computer beeping, and has to hastily part. He drops both doors, and rallies out of the parking lot. Around the building, he violently takes the Diablo around the corner.

He advises, "NES 10-40, reacquire target locate."

The weeknight is lighter on traffic, yet still a few cars remain. He heads south on Interstate 15, as the computer leads him to the target that is also moving south.

As he approaches Tropicana the CO advises, "NES 1912; 10-19 (within ten miles of target). The ping on the target alerts that the moving target now is headed on the belt loop toward the Red Rock/ Summerlin area. He has a smooth passing of the few cars as his Diablo is solid at one hundred and forty-five mph. Opposite northbound traffic, there is an unwelcome vehicle that just illuminated flashing red and blue lights. He can see the NHP cruiser take the off-ramp which predicts more to come. The car isn't exactly the most common, and would be hard to blend in, especially at twelve thirty in the morning. Soon, Nave is allowing the powerful super car to enjoy caressing the long sweeping curve to head onto the belt route. The wall next to him is a smooth smear of grey in the night from his lights, and the taillights ahead of him luckily favor the right lanes.

Nave enquires, "CO, how am I doing with my local guests?"

CO reports,"NES 1912, you are clear. Tech support has all units to kill their pursuit."
The ping on his map shows the tracking excited, and has now lost signal.

It is advised to all ESs, NESs GESs, "Level 4 target is now dark. Last known track, Summerlin."

Nave passes the Carrabbas Restaurant, and scans the area. He turns onto the main road, and decides to head back on the belt route; just past the light, he is greeted with red and blue lights. He pulls into a gas station, and the officer comes to his open door.

"I guess you think the belt route is your personal raceway. And don't go and act like you are not the one. Let's see, Black Lamborghini traveling at speeds in excess of one hundred and forty mph last seen taking ramp onto 295. And wouldn't you know it, poof! A black Lamborghini here just off of the belt route. Oh wait; maybe it was another one, right?"

The officer steps back, holds his earpiece snug to his ear, and looks disgusted. He approaches Nave and says, "I am not sure who the hell you are, but I was just advised to not hold you up any longer. You might want to get your toy here back home before I step out of my orders and just haul your ass in anyway." He walks backward and stands at his car until Nave pulls away. Nave is stopped just before the onramp to travel back to get Collin. He starts down the Interstate, and the ping of his target locator reactivates. He looks ahead, and headlights approach quickly. Passing the opposite way is a red Acura NSX. The pedal finds its place on the bottom of the floorboard once again, and he races toward the nearest ramp. Off the ramp, a swift drift under the overpass, and he is soon to see the needle terminate it's path to the end of the gage, as he has an open, early-morning highway. No taillights in sight, and he approaches Interstate 15 again.

CO advises, "Target southbound Interstate 15 near Blue Diamond." It is presumed the NSX is also bending the relative rule at this time of the morning. Leaving the glow of Vegas behind him, he can see the thin, low-profile taillights ahead. His ping becomes stronger, and there is no hesitation in the Diablo's attack. Unaware of the intent within the car behind him, Joe Allen likely believes this to be a challenge to test his car's performance. His car and he will soon fail as any equal. The NSX attempts to accelerate, yet, like a great white hunting its prey, the gap is quickly closed. The NSX stays to the right as Nave has to slow his Diablo to pace next to Allen. The cameras onboard capture images that are quickly transmitted to intelligence.

CO advises, "NES 1912, you are 10-19X. Elimination by any means."

The two race down the Interstate, and Nave then passes. He gets in front, and taps his brakes quickly. Allen flips his brights on, and leaves them on. Nave moves to the left, and slows. The NSX passes, and gives a harassing swerve into his lane. Nave then tails in behind, and turns all his lights off. The NSX makes an honorable effort to push the speedometer to over one hundred and forty-five mph as the Diablo cruises comfortably behind. As they approach Sloan, Allen takes the exit. Nave blasts past him, and reaching the end of the off-ramp, he stops. In the distance the faint chime of sirens can be heard between the sweeping winds. The warm air of the desert pushes against Nave's back as he exits the car. The NSX is stopped nearly against the bumper of the Diablo. Allen steps out, and moments later the silhouette of Allen's shadow falls. His car runs next to him; the only motion now is the slow crawl of warm blood following the grooves of the pavement ,and the taillights of the Diablo fade in the distance. Nave makes a short dash into a rail yard where he knows of an ideal cool off-location for the car. Red and blue lights pass Sloan, and abruptly take the opposing on- ramp. Soon a barrage of patrol cars, a helicopter, and EMS flood the area.

Nave's only communication is via the earpiece. The CO inquires of his status and he coldly answers, "Las Vegas has been eliminated."

CO sends advisement. "NES 1912 confirming level 4 target Las Vegas has been eliminated."

Hours later, Nave drives in the direction of the lights and investigation near the highway. He is stopped as the officers check the large Ford utility truck he is now driving. After advising he has been working back in the canyon on powerlines, the way is cleared and he now takes the on-ramp north on Interstate 15. Hours later, a Peterbuilt semi truck will find its way into the back of this yard, and quietly exit several days later with one Lamborghini Diablo secured in the enclosed trailer.

No worries about Collin as he has sent a message to Nave advising the girls had taken him back to the hotel. There is also the message of one very unhappy Lucy who had expected Nave to return.

The next morning brings new conversation of the car, the girls, and enquiries about whether or not he still has the car for them to go hunt down more hotties tonight. Nave lets Collin down easy, telling him he took the car back last night. Nick shrugs the excitement off, and even implies one would have to be an idiot to rent a car like that.

When he asks if it was worth it, Nave looked to Collin and says, "I don't know Collin, don't you have a few photos to remember the night?" Collin pans his phone over to Gary, who dramatizes himself by nearly falling backward out of his chair.

Gary holds the phone as he looks it over and assures, "Bro, those are perfect! I bet those cost a pretty penny. Did you tap that?"

Collin smiles and says, "Last night and this morning. Matter fact, might again tonight." The envious disgust can be seen in that same smug expression of Nick, who attempts to claim Collin is either lying or he paid for the night. All the while, Nave sits quietly, and is glad there is little questioning regarding his departure last night.

After work, Nave is contacted by Robert. He asks Nave to meet him at Brand for dinner, and to meet someone. The hostess walks him to the back, where Robert is seated. Next to Robert, is a man with a dark, receding, thick hairline—very curly with strands of grey. His eyebrows are thick and show more grey, as does his bushy mustache. Dressed in many glistens of brown, the Mexican man stands to offer respect to Nave. They sit, and the man looks remorseful and drawn.

The hurt in his emotion can be felt through his inability to even raise an eyebrow or smile. He speaks in Spanish as he will not remove his focus from Nave.
Robert translates:

"He says, my family is for many lifetimes in debt to you. I have only to bear three sons and one daughter. My family now lives our struggles with only my daughter and one son. Two sons I will never to be near again. Young, they were young, and last went to school. El Paso our family cannot go as that is where Jason Allen took my boys. I have only one son to pass our family business who will have many longer years to remorse his brothers having left our lives. My daughter fears the wind, the shadows, the world. She believed our new world in Texas was a dream. Now she has a life of nightmare. Señor Nave, when I show her the news, my girl, she go to the window and for the first time, opened and breathed in the life outside. You Señor Nave, YOU! Take the monster from our nightmare. Our family will not stop hurt, but now we can step forward. My family say our thank you to you forever."

The small, Mexican man stands and three bodyguards come to the table. He walks away, and Robert motions to the waiter. They enjoy their dinner and just before they leave, he asks if he and the guys like MMA. He slides front-row tickets for each guy in his work crew. He tells him this is a little stress relief for the flawless work he has done.

Nave leans back into his seat and jokes, "That wasn't any stress. Now having my daughter in Florida and not being there . . . well that is stress."

Robert dips his head and tells Nave, "Who you kidding, you think your girl isn't being tailed every second? Hell, we know what time she goes to sleep and wakes up. Our team watches out for you and your girl. Always will."

While there is comfort at this table, there is a very different excitement at a meeting desk for Morrow and Holcomb. Morrow is called late at night by his lieutenant. He asks if he and

Holcomb are available, and can meet in the legal room at the headquarters. When Morrow insists to know what this was about, the lieutenant rejects his plea and simply advises to be in the meeting room at eleven p.m.

"Yo, Holcomb, boss man insisting on us meeting him, in legal meeting room at eleven tonight. I am just about to your crib so just throw some shit on and let's see what this dude has going on now," Morrow says over his cell phone. Morrow waits in the driveway, and politely has his lights off. Polite and scared to awaken the wife who has already expressed her dislike for Holcomb not being home enough as it is. The night is very still. There is no porch light, nor any streetlights. He waits reclined listening to Teddy Pendergrass. His eyes are dry; his left arm is stretched behind his head, and over the headrest. He lifts up then reaches for the lever to upright the seat when a dark, pouncing blur attacks his windshield. He jolts back, and unlike the smooth, deep voice on his radio, Morrow shrills. He can only be glad that no others see his fear of Holcomb's neighborly cat. The cat is brushed away as Holcomb comes by the front of the car. Along the drive, they try to compare the possible reasons they would be called in so late and it not being able to wait until the morning. The two settle that at most, they will be called off the special assignment, and even worry they might have ruffled the wrong feathers by their past visit.

The office is quiet, very dim lighting leads to the closed door of the legal office. The two walk in, and sitting across from the lieutenant is a man they have never seen. He appears to be in his mid-fifties; he has a slightly open silk shirt, and a thick, gold rope chain is around his dark, brown neck.

The lieutenant orders the door shut and says, "Gentlemen, this is Dominic Lopez. You might want to sit down and be ready to listen for a little while. Morrow, Mr. Lopez was quite impressed with your, let's say, hobby." As they sit down, Lopez slides a light brown folder to each of them.

As the folders are opened, examined, and create curious expressions, Lopez proceeds to fill them in on who he is and what it is he has been doing for the past five years. He stands and paces the parameter of the long, cherry table at which they sit.

He tells them, "For five years my team, I say team as we have four dedicated agents on this task, five years we have made every effort to track the very suspicion of your hobby, Morrow. Five years ago there was a child predator that, like some, slipped through the judicial fractures that allowed him to walk free. He came to our division one day, and claimed some crazy shit. Oh he was being tracked, he was being hunted; he would see some guy frequently trying to follow him. One day, he came in and said after he blacked out in jail, he always had headaches and a twitch in the back of his head. Sure we all thought he was crazy, and some even told him, 'Hey you might have a lot of people after you,' and he clearly understood why. A week later, the guy was found to have overdosed in his home. The medical examiner concurred with the overdose, and it was ruled a suicide. Something just didn't sit right, and I went to the examiner; he spoke to me off the record. (Dominic holds a small Ziplock baggie, and tosses it to Holcomb who is near him.) The examiner gave me this, and said it resembled a monitor as a pet would have, yet it is made of the highest grade medical components and composites."

Morrow swipes his hands over his face, rolls back over his head, and as he cradles the back of his neck says, "This motha fuck was, HE WAS being tracked! Goddamn, I knew I was right!"

Dominic continues, "This was where we started. For the first three years, nothing added up. Mostly dead ends. Hell, still have more dead ends, well and dead sex offenders. Now, about a year and a half ago, a new girl joined our team. This woman is B.A.D. I have to tell you, I have never come across a woman who is this smart. Now I have to tell you now, you will never meet her. She has her quirks and she demands that she work secluded, and only with our team. Look at page fourteen. (He pauses to allow them to review the page). On the page is seven predator/victim names. Next in a graph is the assaulted victims of these deceased predators. To the far right, is the net worth of six of the juveniles' families."

Holcomb looks to Morrow, and Morrow stands. He is quiet as he enquires, "Okay, you are telling me you tracked this, and have found a link that these are targets are related to wealthy families who hiring hitmen? Is it random? What about, let's see here, number four on here. The family here is on welfare. How does that flow?"

The lieutenant adds his thoughts, "Guys, Dominic has produced to me some very precise data. This shit has just given your happy asses more funding to continue. And let me say this right now: You two better really listen to this part, or you are going to be abruptly done for good. You two now work under the supervision of Mr. Lopez."

Dominic sits as he opens his computer near them. "Guys, our data tell us a few very important things we, you as well, need in order to more efficiently use our resources and efforts."

"First, you have been on wild goose chases until now. And no offense meant, yet you have just been collecting a scrapbook to this point. Our team has predicted five targets in the last three years. Three this year alone. Oh by the way, if you ask me, Key West wasn't a freak accident in a storm. Look at who his victim was. The family is worth over 2.3 billion."

"Second, we have recently seen activity globally. There is a huge focus on families in Canada, Tokyo, Chili, and Mexico."

"Third, and this should be the scariest part for all of us, this is believed to be very skilled person or persons. That crap in Colorado was no fluke. There is an unimaginable perplexity to the operation."

Morrow is excited and sounds a bit mad, "Operation? What the fuck operation? You mean to tell me this shit is organized to a level that the FBI can't track?"
Holcomb sentiments are that they are in fact all predators who harm kids. He sheds light on the fact that most are not looking to defend this guys.

Dominic closes his computer, closes his briefcase, and tells Morrow and Holcomb, "I will be straight with you; this is a rollercoaster ride. Just when we think we have a good lead, poof, all our work is just too late or we have trailed a dead-end case. Gentlemen, in your folders are a list of ten families who have had bad shit happen to them. They are wealthy, you will see powerful, and you will see two who have walked the red carpet. You stick with the shit bags who got off on these cases, and I think you may have a better shot at what you seek. Now the one family who was on welfare, the smart chick also found that it is likely there are a few who just hit the heart strings, and this operation does it *pro bono*. She noted that the way the killing was carried out was so precise that it was characteristically with the skill set of the others."

The lieutenant lays his forearms on the dark cherry table, and looks to the guys as he projects his way of encouragement, "What I believe Mr. Lopez is saying is that those ghost hunters on TV probably have it easier than you will at catching whoever is behind these executions."

Dominic's phone chimes; he looks at it, looks up, and slides his phone to Morrow. "Read it Morrow," he says.

Morrow holds it in front of him and reads, "Lopez, just to let you know, last night on a dark Vegas off-ramp, Allen was found with one single 45cal shot precisely between his eyebrows as he died next to his running car."

Dominic sways his head side to side as he says, "That was Mexico. Global as I said. We had two agents, have two agents practically living in Vegas, and have tailed Allen for over three months. You see this shit, no sign, no witness, nothing and now Mexico lay bled out in Vegas. Damn these fucks are amazing. Fucking amazing! Damn, I love a challenge." Holcomb opens his folder and blacks out the info on Mexico. Dominic smiles and asks, "Why?"

Holcomb stands, folds up his folder, and tells the room, "No mas worry of Mexico; dude is dead. Unless we are going back to building a scrapbook, looks like Calvin and I have nine others to get ahead of now."

Dominic has a greedy smile, bounces both index fingers, one toward Morrow and the other toward Holcomb and says,

"Oh this is good, so fuckin' good. These two are going to fit well. I can't fuckin' wait to see how deep this operation goes."

The men leave quiet and shocked, as they get back into the car and neither can find the ability to settle their minds to sleep.

Two days later, the two arrive in Las Vegas. Even though they don't want to trail behind, there is a benefit to sniffing a hot trail. They scour every place Allen was known to live or visit; they spend several hours reviewing the traffic cameras from that night. A very robust, happy, and flirtatious woman has the two in the video room. Morrow looks over to Holcomb to alert with a head nod. He is trying to get his attention to have him see what she is doing. She has her right hand on Morrow's shoulder; she is standing.

As he sits, given there is plenty of room, her right breast still finds closeness to brush his arm. She makes several comments such as, "Oh, you aren't from Vegas? Well, you know our motto here? What happens in Vegas stays in Vegas. You just gotta make it happen, right?" As she laughs it off, she can't see Holcomb who is using sign language to illustrate the obvious effect of her flirting, and that he thinks she is crazy.

"THERE, whoa, whoa back it up! There is Allen's car!" Morrow exclaims. This is footage as he sped down the beltway. They continue to watch film, and later run it to see a black Lamborghini in a blistering rage against the night.

"Holy shit, that car is flying!" Holcomb says. He adds that is well after the NSX passed, and probably just another rich jackass playing in his expensive toy.

Then Morrow calculates on a scratch paper and says, "It's a long shot, but let's say the Lambo was trying to catch

Allen. Look here, Allen found on the off-ramp, last seen here on the beltway, and could the other car catch him? He would have had to be doing close to one-fifty, maybe more like one-eighty."

The woman then recalls, "Hey, I remember the dispatch talking about a super-exotic car that night. They said it was odd because they got a call to break pursuit because several units were trying to catch him."

Morrow rolls back saying, "Wait a second, who? Just who made the call to have dispatch send a message to the road guys to back off?" She says she doesn't have that info. They will have to reach dispatch.

A visit to the captain's office and he walks the men to dispatch. "I will tell you guys, probably the weirdest interruption we have had in a while. Lannie was working that night, and she claims ATF sergeant called direct into dispatch, and advised they had a high- profile case, and had several units tracking this car, and could not risk him being stopped. They wanted to continue their track, so our dispatch released our units and advised ATF we would stage for help if needed." Lannie sits listening to the men, and Morrow asks if any of the units got close enough to see. She says one unit reported the driver seemed to be a pro as he was able to sling the car through traffic, and they could never get anywhere near it.

She laughs and says, "That was until our very special officer, Officer 'Special Ed,' decided he was going to pull the car over anyhow." She rolls her eyes as she informs the men she is not convinced it is even the same car. She continues to give her opinion on why she believes is was different, stating how the car seen racing was closer to downtown area, and the one pulled over was way up in Summerlin.

Holcomb asks about the car pulled over and she advises, "When 'Special Ed' pulled him over once he read the plate, we received another call to release the driver and advise on direction only."

Holcomb asks, "Advise to who?" She advises it was ATF again and that they will call to update.

The captain looking disgusted asks the men to return to his office. In the office, he offers his humble apologies. "Our dispatch has been training some new staff. They were mostly new, and this call seemed legit to them, and was so sudden they believed it to be ATF. Our supervisor quickly called ATF, and was advised that the call was valid. They did their checks, and all panned out. Someone hacked our phone communication, and for security and public safety we are not ready to release any information on this. We checked the plate, oh get this plate, SI666DE, out of Oregon, and there has never been a plate issued for that number or car. OMG Devil In Side. Hell would be proud." Morrow says he will need to speak with the officer who stopped the car. When the captain asks why the FBI is so interested in the car or driver, they tell him they are tracking a string of stolen, high-end sports cars. The captain inquires as how this correlates with the death of Allen, and Morrow dismisses the connection as simply two racing on the beltway, and he doesn't think the Lamborghini even continued on the 15 southbound.

"My guess is the Diablo is on a cargo carrier leaving Long Beach by now," Morrow says.

The next day, Calvin and Mike have the delighted treat of meeting with Officer Ed Eddie, also known by dispatch, as "Special Ed."

He has a fresh layer of "Just for Men" to color his thick, coarse mustache, razor sharp buzz-cut hair, and gold-rimmed aviator glasses (still remaining on indoors of course). His belt was likely shined along with his shoes. The pants nearly meet the pockets of his triple-starched shirt, and between the four-inch gap between his pant cuff and dress shoes are gold socks— perhaps his attempt to match the socks in some way with the brown uniform shirt. No one has asked. The two men advised Ed he could relax and have a seat.

Ed replies, "All the better, prefer to stand." He bends only at the hip forward toward the sitting Morrow and Holcomb and creases his lip, which pushes the heavy bush upward until his cheek touches the low rim of those purposeful aviator glasses.

Calvin asks, "You stopped a black Lamborghini a few nights back."

Even though Calvin has more to ask, he is immediately answered by Ed. "Ya, damn correct on that fact sir FBI agent Mawrow. See, that neighborhood is my beat! The FBI wanna know why Summerlin streets are safe? Well, do ya?" still bent he asks.

The awkward pause soon turns to an uncomfortable staring contest until Morrow finally breaks and answers cautiously, "I am guessing because you don't let no crap slide?"

"FBI, CIA, military, and ATF can try to swagga on in and play like they are some special shit, but guess what? Well let me say now, Summerlin is my house part na! Ya'll got some sneaky shit happnin', covert operations, X CET ER A! Well, I guess you fellas may want to send an interoffice memo tellin' the rest, tell them this one . . . when breaching the confines of Summerlin, Nevada, pay due respect to Deputy Eddie, who will afford a preliminary task operation briefing. Now I will stand down and allow those the respect to conduct their investigations; however I best be in the loop prior to my beat being encroached on," says Ed in a rehearsed manner.

Holcomb takes a deep breath and plays to Ed's personality. "Deputy Eddie sir, it is apparent you hold your duties at an elevated level which the others do not. I am sure fortunate that my partner and I have the opportunity to speak with you in private as you shouldn't be interrupted. I am most grateful to your attention to detail, and predict that your thorough work can likely be a benefit to our investigation. I can even see a possible lean toward a recommendation for advancement in your future. Being said that you were the only one who took the appropriate action to stop this jackass who, well in our eyes completely insulted your position and furthermore the respect for Summerlin, Nevada, I want to ask you what information you have on the driver, and any passengers."

Ed bobs his head, and folds his arms in a manner as a woman would who is trying to cover her chest. His hip snaps out to the right, and he ever so slowly rotates only his upper body to face the office window looking toward the open commons of the rest of the department. He is quiet and calm in his answer, "They, out there, are robots. Just day-to-day. Not like us in here. Oh can see ya'll get it. Wouldn't be in here askin' ol' Eddie the reals if you didn't feel the passion. Gots to have it to make a difference out there. Mr, Steve McQueen the other night didn't say a word. It's all political bullshit if you askin' Eddie. These rich, I'm-above-the-law bastards feel they can just flaunt their toys, race around a different car for different days of the week, and don't even let me tell you about the Botox and whiskey party girls who are catered to. All superficial nonsense, I say. Hey, I didn't see the guy speeding. When he come down the road, he was rolling scared. He ought to know he was about to meet me. Think he felt it. I was on him. See, I listened to the other units call it in. Knew the direction, and said to myself, liken' to just play it right and let the bee come to the nectar. Sho nuff, I hear the purr. See the cat and it's Christmas time for that son of a bitch. Ol' Eddie has him dead to rights. I no sooner get ready to ask for his info, and our head-in-her-ass dispatcher is calling me off. Goddamned ATF stepping on toes. What am I to do? Can't be insubordinate. So there he goes. Free to insult the law once more."

Morrow appears half exhausted just listening to Ed, yet asks, "What can you tell us about the guy? Looks, size, anything."

Ed stands quietly until he replies, "What's it matter? Maybe ATF can show you a nice picture. Obvious I don't matter so why now. But for what it's worth, he was alone, close-cut hair, white guy. Seemed to be a little big for that car. Like I said he never even spoke."

The two can see this was all Ed could offer, and politely allow him to be excused.

The helpful information is the location where he stopped the car. A visit to the store reveals they operate external cameras. Would Morrow and Holcomb get an image?

Chapter 17
Unexpected Guest

Nave pulls up his street after a long week. He is eager to unpack, and yet has his mind set on retiring to the backyard as the last few hours of a picture perfect late summer day slowly rolls into well-lit evening hours. Nave passes through the garage door and he stands at the kitchen window overlooking the shaded domain he will claim after retrieving a drink from the fridge. Like a fictional likeness to The Three Bears, somebody has been sleeping in Nave's hammock and still is. There in the hammock, a black, loose sundress drapes the thin body of a woman. Familiar tan legs are crossed at her delicate ankles. One painted big toe dances up and down against the brown braided tethers. The woman's left hand grips a glass half-filled with tea swimming in ice. Bright yellow lemon quarters float among the ice and tea in unison with the sway of the hammock. Spaghetti straps over defined shoulders and whisking hair like upside down wheat fields allow the subtle breezes to enchant Nave to admire the natural wonder of a woman. As man will never understand or capture the meaning of chemistry, the simplicity is our gift, as we only need to appreciate what the mere sight, sound, and smell of a woman does for us. He opens the back door so quietly. Bare feet make no sound across the short concrete walk to be comforted by tall, cool grass. He only knows the eyes behind the closed lids are a brilliant blue. The shade, the calming hum of leaves above, and the surprise of Lynn Grace in his hammock has made his return home better than usual.

"You can either make room, or get out. Because today is my day in my hammock Ma'am!" he boldly orders. Lemons, ice, and a half glass of tea have just landed on the grass. The support chains of the hammock clank against the metal frame. A jolted woman dramatizes her right hand over her chest as she tells him she may have suffered a mild heart attack. Being that she is truly fine, she hops up and greets him with a huge hug. They lay back into the hammock, and she blames her unannounced appearance on Amanda.

"Dean did not want to travel home alone, and she would not stop talking about how beautiful the mountains are here. So mister, I agreed to get a flight with her and check it out. We just got in last night and, wow it is so pretty here!" It has been a while since they have been close and in person. The looks, the closeness and excitement are only cooled by the shade they enjoy as the sun is blocked by the hill. At the window, unknown to them, is a girl and her friend.

Amanda tells her friend, "Don't they just fit? I'm such a wonderful little Chuck Woolery." The two dip cocktail shrimp into cocktail sauce, and ad-lib the words as Lynn and Nave talk. This leads to the two girls holding the tails of their shrimp as they puppeteer the acts of the two in the hammock.

The next morning, Nave and Lynn are gone before Amanda has even had her first of usual three wake-up calls. The tall peak is turning bluer, and as they pull into a dirt parking area, the headlights become less luminous. The sun shows promise as the stars have become faint, and morning colors highlight the mountain rim. Nave wears a small pack; Lynn comes around the back of the truck, closes her eyes, tilts her head slightly back, and opens her nostrils as she expands her chest allowing the Utah air into her soul. The two start up the first level of sandy switchbacks. Nave is ahead to lead, yet his mind is wishing he was behind Lynn. Unintentionally, she has an allure of a natural magnificent. She wears tan and blue hiking shoes, and her sun-soaked skin leads to small, fitted shorts. A thin, fitted tee shirt tapers to her small waistline, and her hair is pulled through the back of a ball cap. Often he looks back; in the wider areas, they hike side by side, and her playfulness has her often pouncing on rocks, and balancing on downed trees. They reach a spot nearly three-fourths into the hike, and she admires the rushing water over and though the enormous rocks.

"Oh my god Nave, we just don't have this in Florida. I feel like I want to hike every trail and mountain you know of," she tells him.

They sit on a rock ledge and he replies, "Oh Lynn, there is no end to the trails and hikes. It would take years if not forever to see all of this. Here, the places like Zion, Moab, then north into Logan and Bear Lake—you might have to extend your return flight a few years out." He slightly laughs.

Lynn doesn't laugh in return. She steps off the ledge, walks a few steps from where they sat, turns and walks in front of him. With her body lightly resting against his knees, she takes his hand and almost in a stated question says, "If I had a personal tour guide, I would extend my flight until he found the last sunset to show me." He knew what he heard, his voice cannot respond. His pulse speeds, and his brain cannot find a way to even speak. The silence is appropriate to her as she knows her words sank deep in the area which no others have been allowed in many years. For the first time, his hand does not let go. For three-fourths of this hike he enjoys his guest, his admiration of her, and now during the last climb to the waterfall, he will have so much more to think about. Not until the trail narrows, will he and Lynn loosen their fingers. The crevasse opens, and an amplified sound of a shower is steady. Around the corners, mist moistens the path. The two carefully step through the shallow waters, and Lynn's head rests back into his chest while she looks up to Adams Falls—forty feet of rolling, rushing waters. The early weekday morning has few other hikers, and the sun poses now like a radiant lamp directly atop the natural pool. Daring and adventurous, she lures Nave near the falls. She takes one hand to test the cold mountain flow.

A splash and she says, "Oh I dare you to stand in the waterfall." He reaches for her, and she tries to escape. He clenches around her waist as she laughs. A half spin, and he has Lynn firmly closer than ever before. Her feet no longer touch the river-washed rocks. Her eyes lock into his, and she pleas for him to not step back into the falls; yet her plea will not ask to be let go. Months prior to this day, dark skies brought days of snow that stayed blanketed over the surrounding hills. To some, the miserable scorching sun was the same heat that would melt each fallen flake that seems to have waited for this very moment. It is said that opposites attract. Here under the drop of these falls, the cold waters plummet to land across the heated bodies, locked in passion. A first kiss should mean something—should be remembered. The woman in the distance standing next to her husband as she envies the moment, looks into the waterfall, and can see the adolescent act; yet she does not know that she along with the few others cheering Nave and Lynn, have stood witness to this first kiss.

Amanda walks in with her friend, hears jazz playing, the sound of a knife striking a cutting board, and then sees the two in the kitchen. Lynn is sitting at the counter across from Nave who is cooking.

"Hey girls, is Shannon going to eat with us tonight?" Nave asks.

Shannon does not hesitate to reply, "Mr. Nave, you know this girl loves your food. Wouldn't matter if I just ate, which I haven't, I would hang here just to get some of your cooking."

Lynn suggests to the girls that they get the patio table ready, and the three of them head out back. He watches the trio and in a life that has its unrest, this moment is solitude for him. He can see the gestures, the smiles, and yet cannot hear the trading of suggestions from Lynn and Dean.

"So . . . , where did you two go so early?" Amanda asks through a set of accusatory eyes.

"We went on a morning hike up, is it called Adams Waterfall?" Lynn tells her. Amanda agrees the hike is so nice. The girls have the table ready and sit talking.

"It is absolutely so beautiful here. Dean, you are crazy to miss Florida. Yeah, the beach is a big deal I guess. But I was looking at that Explore Utah book you guys have and oh my God! So much to see. Your dad said we are heading up to Park City tomorrow, and then coming back around Weber canyon."

Amanda grips both hands on the table and she and Shannon look to each other, "Raspberry shake at Chris's."

Amanda is blunt. She folds her arms, as she dictates her thoughts.
"Okay I am just going to speak my speak! See, I am seeing some Chem-AH-stray happening here. I know my padre, and when you are around, he is so happy. Sorta too happy, but better than the usual Mr. Serious."

Lynn can't help to chuckle a little.

Amanda continues, "And Lynn, I think I am noticing a little romanticals sneaking away from your aura as well. So was your hike just 'a hike,' or did the mountain get you two all Bambi?" Shannon and Amanda laugh.

Lynn is smiling, blushing, and tries her best to distract and enquires, "Wait, Bambi. What is that? I don't speak code here. You have to tell me what craziness you are coming out with."

Shannon gets up and mimics her best Disney vocals, and dances around the table as she explains the term Bambi. "Think Thumper, Bambi movie, springtime? Twitterpeeted?"

Lynn has a smile that she likely is unaware has erupted so noticeably. She looks toward the window and back to a fixated stare of Amanda. "Oh Dean, I shouldn't say this. Okay, maybe I can. Dean, that was the best hike I have ever been on." She looks again to the window and says, "I guess part of me is still on the hike."

Over the next few days, the two scamper from Bear Lake, to Park City to Timpanogos Cave. They spend a night in the bed of his truck at the drive-in movie, as well as nights on the hammock. The day comes when he has to return to Vegas for work. Lynn also has work back in Florida, and they part with less struggle than one may expect. The power of their connection has nourished a part of them, which had been absent. To have elevated their desire for each other in a mutual energy, has given them a new hope for what may develop.

After his week at work, Nave returns and makes plans to spend the days off with Amanda for a Jeep tour of Moab. That night they find their night on the hammock as the fire pit burns to their side. He senses there are contemplative uncertainties this night when his Dean struggles to focus on her conversation.

"Dean, you have something either on your mind that you are not sure how to express, or you have done something which you are unsure how to tell me. This is the zone of the hammock. All can be told and you know that." He tries to give her an open door to let him know what she is thinking.

She is quiet and in her trust of what they have built together, she says in her calm, somber way, "I am so looking forward to the whole Jeep thing, mountain biking, and just seeing Moab. It's just . . . well, I am not sure the whole emotion behind it all, but after Lynn being here, I like seeing you alive like that. I guess I may have some sort of trapped guilt for you being such a kick-butt dad, and not having someone for you–you know adult-type stuff."

His left foot pushes them slowly and he knows exactly what she is feeling. There would be no value to blow her emotions away with the night air. He tries to give her his view and the honesty that she will have to process in what may be good or bad.

"Oh Dean, you are past the years I can use mental barricades to distract my own unreadiness to address these things only a maturing, young woman can feel and see. See, when you were younger and your mom played her tricks, and used the unbalance of the legal system to take you away from me, well the dictionaries, I think intentionally, do not have a way to give the deeper meaning of *empty*. It will say empty is having nothing left, void, and to capture EMPTY you have to know, there has to be something within first to then acquire *empty*. Your room was empty. My little girl who once played, as she didn't know I stood at her door listening. Every night I would hold her, rocking her as I sang 'Rockabye Baby.' The carpet that we would lay on looking to the ceiling at your night lights. The animals, your clothes, every fiber, material, and odor was painful. This is what the courts don't see. The system is so brutally ignorant that there are many fathers who for the first time, obtain the hidden last line of the dictionary for the meaning of *empty*. I immediately understood that the room that was once so full of my love for you, was now *empty*. I learned when you lose that love, it empties your entire soul. I was *empty*. So every day I would prepare for each court appearance to have you back, very motion, anything . . . I would go to your room and sit on your bed. And here is something you can now understand and are mature enough to cope with—the carpet next to your bed had absorbed every tear I was capable to drop. One very late night, I realized all the struggle, the fight to get you, and my effort to battle the system was not what you would see. I had a moment when it was as if you looked at me through that photo. Yes! That old black and white photo you wonder why I have always had on my dresser. Those eyes looked through the pain and I knew no matter the court outcome, what lies your mom may have laced in your young mind, nothing would keep me from loving you. I would refill that *emptiness* that nearly collapsed me, and fill it full of every memory of you I had. Two years after that was when you were with me for the summer, and had realized all the lies, and what was more important, you finally were old enough to know the love you got here with me was genuine. You had not been happy at your mom's. I guess this is a long way of telling you, once I saw you in your room for good again, I would give you all that love I had saved for many years. It was as if each day I would remember a time, a place, a teardrop that came from the littlest thought of you. Dean, you remember this: When judging the character of a man; *a real man, a real FATHER does not pretend.*"

She tries to respond, yet her throat is obstructed with emotion and a loving gratitude for his open expression to illustrate how she is the one person he truly loves. She has thoughts of how fortunate she is to not only have a father, but to know she is and will always be in his front row. Her face is streaking as warm, salty tears roll from the corner of her eyes and pool in her ear.

She can only hug her dad and lowly say, "I love you padre. Dad, Thank you."

Chapter 18
Close Call

Only a week of summer left, and Nave and Amanda are in the Kimball Junction outlet malls looking for school clothes. As she and a few friends shop just beyond the watchful protection of Nave, he gets a call from Robert. Robert says the judge wants him to come to Florida as soon as possible and have a meeting. He explains it has to do with heavy action regarding the level 5 target that flew off when Nave was in South Florida. Robert advises there was also a very high-profile client who will only speak directly to Nave. The judge is a long-time friend of the family, and has assured this client that Nave would be the very best specialist to trust.

Two days go by, and Nave tells Amanda, "Hey Dean, if we were to escape for a few days, what would you take with you? You couldn't pack, you just had one hour to throw what you would want in a small bag. What would it be?"

She looks curious, sits at the counter, her elbows outward, her long hair covers the counter top, and she asks, "Are we going somewhere that we have to hide? Witness protection? OMG I knew it. You are a spy, and we have to skip out!"

"Oh your crazy mind, Dean. Okay, well if you want to go on a fun last week get-out-of -town, I am leaving in one hour."

She seems stressed, but excited. She begs him to tell her, and he is having far too much fun knowing once they check in at the airport, she will know then.

They park, and on the tram she only knows they are flying somewhere. He has one large bag; she has a carryon size, and they reach the ticket counter to check in. The airlines famous heart is behind the woman dressed in blue who smiles and says, "Oh I wish I was going to Orlando."

"Padre!" she says surprisingly. He tells her he has some meetings to go to, and she is going to spend a few days with Lynn. They discuss that the end of the week will be Islands of Adventure and the beach. She immediately hammers questions about Lynn. She has no hidden feelings on her quest to match her dad with Lynn. If she only knew of the waterfall kiss!

They arrive later that day at the judge's house, and Amanda Dean quickly vanishes with Lynn. Nave, Robert, and Judge Grace secure themselves in the judge's private meeting room.

"Let's talk about this Ghost we cannot seem to nail down," Robert says.

Robert sits in a corner chair, holding a drink in one hand and an audio/visual remote for a PowerPoint presentation. Screen after screen are photos, GPS pings, acquaintances, and several locations of the plane Nave reported. Robert then shows a data sheet of the tracking dates of the plane.

Robert stands, goes to the screen, and talks in detail of the elusiveness. "Each location the plane is re-crewed. The routes are always on time, they fly Key West to Miami to the small, corporate airstrip Nave saw it at, then over to a secured government hangar. This is not a weekend joyride fellas. This damn plane has high connections, and here is an even more difficult task. This plane, the one Nave spotted which we believe Ghost was on, this plane is owned by The Mexican Government!" Robert says before looking to the judge.

The judge then informs Nave of more news that has been discovered. "I have connections which are vital to this operation, and are on a level which the Secretary of State has even offered us assistance. When I attempted to inquire on this plane, well let's just say it was made very clear that no further intel or anyone from this operation shall attempt ascertaining so much as what tires this plane uses. The contact on Ghost was created at the highest level, and the target allowance last week was just increased to five million."

After the judge provides this information, Robert then walks near Nave. He sits across from Nave and if admiration, concern, and a plea can be of one, he tells Nave, "You are here alone for a reason. Yes, the target price and normal percentage including bonus will be available to all ES agents; however, this stays here in this room. You have a way, a gift, and a scary procedure to just find people. You also either take risks others won't, or you are simply that good. The client has urged the elimination of this target as quickly as our operation can make it happen. If this Ghost is eliminated, and you are the Specialist to eliminate, your percentage will be 75 percent of that five million. Whatever tech support, vehicles, toys— anything you ask—will be made immediately available. There is one particular the client asks. They demand video proof." Robert has his forearms on his legs, dangles the glass of whiskey, takes the last swig, stands and tells Nave, "This will likely be the biggest risk you will ever be involved in based on the whole connection with the Mexican Cartel. We don't even know what that is bringing to the game." He turns and looks confidently and says, "Somehow I will not be a bit surprised when you come back in here, and have that missing link we can't seem to nail down."

Nave holds a printout of the spreadsheet, looks it over quietly, and places it in his case. He asks Robert if that is all they have, which Robert acknowledges. Nave sits comfortably back, and asks what the next order of their visit is.

Judge Grace is across the room, dips his head, and inquires, "Nave, no questions or comment on the Ghost situation?"

Nave is quiet, sits still, takes a silver metal pen between his fingers, and slowly rolls it back and forth. He looks to the pen as he speaks—almost in a trance or as if the pen mellows his demons. "Your operation can only do so much. Yes, you know a lot about me. There is more you don't know." He looks in the judge's eyes and assures him, "More nobody wants to know!"

He sets the pen on the arm of the chair, and asks to now move on to the other order of business. Robert sort of twitches his eyebrow, and lightens the mood as he reaches for the remote again.

Robert has audio with this file. Powerful, deep base rumbles in the private room, Robert has a swagger and slight hip hop dance as the gangster rap plays. The music stops, and the rap icon's family photo is on the first page. Robert shows a little bio of the star, and then tells Nave, "I could go through the entire thing; however, the file is already loaded in your computer. The audio feature and GPS have been pre-programed in the car you will be using, and you are set to meet him tomorrow morning. After we are done here, I will take you over to pick up your ride. Hey, but I am telling you now, I am thumpin' this shit just to get you in the rhythm of this case."

Nave waits near the garages, and he hears Robert before seeing him. The windows are down, and the driver's seat is laid back as he is in full rapper mode. They head off, and a few miles down the road, he lowers the volume, looks to Nave and says,

"Now this is as real as it gets man. I'll bet you never even heard this shit, man. In a hommie's soul, you can hear the street in this shit. Damn, I miss being young and reckless. Bet you can't name one rapper can you?"

Nave laughs and enlightens Robert with a little history of his own. "I grew up in diversity no one can imagine. You think you know this rap stuff? When have you ever been in the garage of the underground buying cassettes that still have seeds and buds on them? Yeah, I played football but after the games me and Hershey would roll back to the tracks, and hang with guys who really scratched. Not this computer shit. Back when I grew up, these guys had raw in them. They had anger, hate, and ironically a joyful pride in their struggle. Few white guys have seen Watts, Normandy, and Crenshaw like I did. Hell, my dad, he hung on Sunset in the days of Jimmy Hendricks. So let me tell you Mr. Rap man, I probably bought these spits when they were recorded on a D-cell battery boom box. See, more your intel didn't gather." He laughs at Robert.

Soon, they arrive in Bay Hill at a home just off of the golf course. Robert pulls around back, and presses the button; one of the many doors rolls up. Stuffed inside, is a beast of a SUV/ assault vehicle. The 2002 four-door H-l Hummer sits wide, bold, dark, and ominous. Lifted over thirty-eight-inch tires and a body of military bulletproof steel, solid chassis not built for comfort, and a fuel guzzling habit that makes Nave very glad he isn't paying the diesel bill, Nave gazes appreciatively. Robert jokes about how it might be just a little nicer than the ones he had driven back in the day. Nave climbs inside, and head south.

Amanda and Lynn catching up. Oh sure there is plenty of seriousness, questions, strategies, and planning going on—at least by Amanda. She is quick to tell Lynn how her dad was so happy when she came, how he was so alive, and then starts asking Lynn if she will always be in Florida.

Lynn drives across the Beeline, and is more open to the conversation than ever. "Dean, you know your dad works a lot, and when he is home, well he spends every second with you. You know as well as I do, he wants no interruption of your time."

Amanda looks sassy, and with both hands dramatizes pointing at herself as she says, "This is no longer a helpless girl. I have my life, my friends, well a few, and I have stuff to do that doesn't involve 'daddy.'"

They laugh and Lynn says, "I wouldn't over-stress anything involving booooys to your 'daddy.' OMG if he thought some little brat was making moves on his DEAN—poor kid may not ever be found."

"He has dated once in a while and stuff, but nothing like when you were around. I miss seeing that side of him, really. I do love my Padre and know he is the one person that will always be true with me. But, I feel like I am holding him back from having that someone–having that, *Lynn* in his life." She smiles sarcastically in Lynn's direction.

Lynn quiets a little, and reaches for the volume knob. She looks to Amanda and asks, "You know your dad better than anyone. Do you think he . . . I mean, do you believe he would ever settle down and want a family life again?"

Amanda just stares in Lynn's direction, with her mouth wide, her right outstretched hand gripping the dash, her left hand on the center console, and her body stiff, but lifting out of her seat. She finds her voice to say, "Lynn Grace . . . you like my dad. Like for real! OH . . . MY . . . GOD! This might just be the best news of the year! And oh, don't worry about him. I will just let Mr. Have Everything-Set and-Structured know that you are now his woomaan. Oh wait, home? Where is home in all this?"

Lynn is not able to bring her smile under control, yet she is able to still rationalize. "Now, you are getting way ahead of yourself Dean. And you don't go playing matchmaker. Your dad has more on his plate than you realize. If it is right, and it is to be, then it will." (There is a pause as two girls just keep smiling at each other.) Lynn blurts out, "He kissed me under a waterfall!"

Amanda puts her hands together as to pray; she looks to the headliner yet metaphorically to the heavens and lips, "Yes, yes, yes, done deal."

They crank up the music, windows down, and hair and smiles continue to the beach.

The next morning, a scatter of landscapers stand on riding mowers as they tailor the grounds of the park, golf courses, and lawns of homeowners. Steam evaporates as the sun awakens the dew, and early squirrels dart from tree to tree. Overlooking the many boats just past the nets of a driving range, Nave stands at a park walking path. So many live a pampered life, and the servants who enable the rich are so often criticized by those who rely on their efforts. He stands and talks with an older woman, who has been a resident of the area all her life. The woman is dressed in modest, comfortable jogging attire; her hair is fresh, and there is a slight painting of her face. As false as they are, her teeth sparkle of a smile brought from within.

He asks her, "Just what do all these people do that affords so many this lifestyle? I mean, I look, and all I see are million-dollar boats, 100,000 dollar cars, and I don't want to even imagine what some of those homes cost."

She has a sweet demeanor and graceful smile as she reaches for his hand. Her nails are glossy pink, several fragile fingers hold heavy gold rings, and she speaks with elegance. "Let me tell you, many are simply products of false wealth. They come and go; they use the system to betray and swindle. It is like a breeding pond for them to take advantage of the elderly, the less educated, and the corrupt. Oh and drugs . . . legal and illegal. It is so prevalent, and there seems to be no comprehensive structure to mitigate any of it. You look and see what they have, and so few are even happy. So much anger and self-righteousness. Let me tell you, when you don't have to work for it, you don't . . . you can't respect what you have. Take me. I am eighty-four years old. I had a very wealthy family. A few bad investments, and my father was broke. Hey, so life is that way. Our family stayed strong and many, many years gave us new gifts. Our once useless land became this desired location for vacationers and the privileged. I can say every day I am still here; I am grateful for my father, my mother, and the value of life. Listen to me, I am eighty-four. Have had it all, lost it, and now . . . well let me say this, I am not hurting. Through it all, our family was humble and we loved life. I still love life. Each sunrise I see new life even though I have few sunrises left. Don't just see the sun, close your eyes, and soak it in young man." She looks to him from her much shorter stature; the sun she has captured glistens from her blue eyes, and he thanks her for being the best part of his day. She returns to her walk, and he leaves to meet his client.

An elderly couple wearing pruning gloves, wide-rimmed sunhats, sandals over knee-high white tube socks, and the famous, large, dark sunglasses stand up, and look in disgust as Nave drives the H-l beast up the affluent neighborhood street.

The woman shakes her head in a twitch as she tells her husband, "I just don't know if we should stay here. You saw Vern, these cars, the type of people going to the end of the street. Drugs, Vern, drugs. Has to be drugs. Like Scarface, Vern. I hate to say it, but we used to just have our kind on this street. Once the coloreds moved in that beautiful home, well UGHH all I see is their kind in those ridiculous cars. I just know there are going to be shootings and a major bust soon. I hope we are not out here, Vern. When that happens, I hope we are not minding our own business and get shot by the coloreds. They do that, Vern. I read about it. Maybe we should just move." She tosses her gloves on the flowerbed, and walks back into the house.

Nave pulls up to a very unique gate—the replica of a European castle gate. Before him is a long driveway, and just past the paved drive is a twelve-foot wide moat. The gate is lowered by a heavy chain until it rests to span the moat. A green light comes on, and Nave drives over the gate. The decorated concrete drive leads to a covered drive near the front entrance to the home. He parks, and as he walks around the H-l he is greeted by the rap artist/producer/actor. He looks serious, almost stand-offish, and gives Nave a hard look over. Nave holds his case that is always used to check for recorders, cameras, and bugs. The rap icon is immediately inquisitive and more, suspects a weapon.

He says to Nave in a negative tone, "Ain't no one said anything about bringin' cases of shit into my crib. You gonna have to pop open that case before we even go to steppin' inside."

Nave looks at him with no expression and answers "Think about why you have me here. If I were not on your side . . . well you wouldn't need to worry about the case."

The rap icon's head tilts back, and he half-smiles as he says, "You almost creepin' me, and I like that. Let's take this shit inside, and chat about this shit." Once Nave clears the room they use to talk, the mood is lightened.

Along the walls are framed records, posters, and many photos of famous friends. A window overlooks the inlet and the tailored property of a successful owner. The rap icon stands at the window, opens a tin container, and pulls out a joint. He offers it to Nave, who declines.

As he casually smokes his joint he tells Nave, "Twenty years makes a big difference. Look at this shit, man. Boat, boat house! Pool, mutha fuckin' pool house! Look, big-ass shit in my yard, bad-ass Doby dog, and no shit . . . a big-ass dog house! Car for every day of the week, and look . . . a nigga got his own Hispanas cuttin' my goddamn grass. Hell, back in the day I wooda just been poppin' shots at these muthas. Nigga think it's all good until his niece comes home and can't talk. Here the shit man; part of me want to just be the old me. Do work on a dude. Tech Nine, and shit is done. But here the thing, Big Baller, YUP big mutha fuckin' house! Big cameras, big press, and big po-po always watchin'.''

"I tell you this is messed up shit, man. After that deal with my niece, Po-po come here acting like I'm the bad guy. Askin', 'you and your boys going to handle things? We are watching you.' Saying shit like, 'This ain't Compton; we have laws here.' Mutha fuckin' boot fuck, should have popped his cracka ass on my door that day. Oh well, so here we are. This why you in the picture. Shit is gettin' handled, but I still not sure you cool like that."

He takes a slow, drawn hit of the joint, sits in a brown leather chair, and says to Nave, "I guess I need comfort knowing you ain't just taking care of shit, but you down. Almost like, well, like you one of us."

Nave reaches in his case. He pulls out a paper. On the paper is symbols and markings. He hands the paper, which is old and faded, to the rap icon. He also takes a pen and writes a number just below the symbols. Nave looks to him and says, "You know exactly what this says. Maybe you are a little rusty, but I am seeing by the look on your face you are a little shocked that some rogue white guy you never met has these words. See, I grew up just forty miles from your hood. That number I wrote, you call it, and I will sit here and wait a second. I think you will get a lot out of that call." Nave steps back, and finishes rolling wire and packing his case. Nave walks over, hands him a cell phone, and assures him that it was coded so it cannot be tapped into.

He calls the number. After a short conversation, he looks shocked, humbled, and now very comfortable to do business with Nave. "You connected mutha fucker. How you know Smoke? Not many people know Smoke to just call up and be like, Yeah white dude cool! I tell you man, that some sick-ass history on a high level. Damn, that shit take me back. Shit dude, you were able to creep in the hood back in the day?"

Nave smiles and tells him, "I was real. No phony shit. I took care of the boys in the so-called white neighborhoods, and they knew they could count on me and a few of my friends. I was not pro crip, blood, nothing. Liked the culture you had in the

South Cali way, and harvested the education I knew would come from that. I don't think it hurt that I could sell those cassettes to those kids in school who could never get out to South Central." Nave explains that one night his friend started showing him the secret writing of gang symbols, and he learned the entire gang dictionary.

"Here is the focus. I have your target, I reviewed all the information and all the possible victims he has had contact with. Your niece isn't the only one. You are the only to come forward, and the only who has the means to contract the elimination of this guy. After this meeting, you will never hear from me. I will vanish and more importantly, the one you want to vanish will do so. The people you know . . . well they will advise details once it is terminated. I can say this: My ETA on elimination is quick on this one. I will leave here, and you can expect less than a week. Once I accept this in our coded process, it is done. I understand you have already met your obligation, and I will assure that you will have a closing to your family's cavity that has created this pain. If you are comfortable and are sure I am the specialist you want isolated on this case, I need you to confirm once I leave here. I do it this way so there is no pressure face to face."

The rap icon takes his last hit of the joint, and stands up. He looks to Nave and says, "You a scary white dude; I can see why you were cool in the hood. I feel you, I feel you. Damn, I got the right mutha fucka on this shit, I will tell you! Let's get out of this room, and let me show you some real shit."

They wrap up; Nave truly enjoys spending a few hours looking over some memorabilia and listening to old cuts that never hit records. Just before he leaves, a few more music artists stop in.

As soon as they walk in one asks, "What the fuck, who this dude?"

Then the rap icon speaks up almost in admiration, "Hold up, hold the fuck up. Look at this shit niggas." He spins his computer around, and during that call earlier, Smoke had shot over an old picture of Nave, Smoke, Hershey, and a few others back in 1987 on Smoke's aunt's porch. The group all offer handshakes and a full welcome to the home.

As they are about to part, a chime alerts the rap icon that someone else is at the gate. "Shit, it those damn FBI fucks," the icon says.

Nave, a bit concerned, enquires, "Should I know anything about them? What are they poking around here for?"

He tells Nave, "Like I said, fuckin' po-po been creepin' ever since that shit happened." The rap artist and Nave dismiss themselves from the rest, and he tells Nave that the two guys had been there once before asking a bunch of question regarding retaliation. "Dudes be like, you hire anyone, you call someone to do anything to this Morrice dude? Told them two puppets, 'dude, you know where I from, you know my past.' Shit I wanna a nigga to taste dirt, I tap that nigga out, click back . . ."

"POP. Nigga out,
face down, like a clown,
cold heat, meet the street
nigga raw, like a dog
take a bite, make the shit right,
Tell that mutha fucka
POW gun shot, YO mutha fuckin LAST NIGHT!!"

He hits a quick, angry rap note.

The rap icon asks Nave if he wants him to blow the guys off and hold up so Nave can leave unnoticed.

Nave looks, and contemplates. "You know what? Remember how it was back in the day when you had someone trying to sniff around your work? What would you do then?"

The icon smiles, his eyes now heavy and red, as he says, "My man, I likes your style. I hear dat. Show out!! Face to Face that mutha fuck! Face to face."

Always prepared, Nave hands the icon a writer's contract and the icon is amazed how well calculated he is. This contract makes it look as if Nave is hiring the icon for a New Year's Eve concert. So he lowers the gate, and lets the agents in. These agents are in fact Morrow and Holcomb!

The Crown Victoria pulls aside the H-1 under the covered parking. The agents come to the door, and ask to speak with the icon again. The icon steps out, and assures Morrow and Holcomb that there is no need to even take the time to come in. He tells them he doesn't have the time to keep talking to them. The icon puts it to them, "Look fellas, you come trippin' about retaliation, and who I am having hit this dirty fuck who messed with my niece. You see we ain't exactly in Compton anymore. I mean, look through the glass and you can see the fuckin' water Jack! Do you see what I say? You don't hear rounds being rapped off, or cop sirens, po-po in the damn copter above us. Homeboys, this be South Florida, not L.A."

Holcomb seems casual, hands in his pockets, sort of pacing on the breezeway, and looks off to the distance as he says, "No, sure isn't where you came from. No doubt. You still pretty hardcore on your cuts. You still the truest, rawest rapper who keeps it real. You can't change that. You don't lose that my brotha."

Morrow breaks in and in more of an asking tone says, "Look man, we are not saying you are even looking to get at this piece of shit that hurt your niece. I am not even saying you would. Hell, we all would have the thoughts, no god damn doubt. Hey, what I do know . . . you have a shitload of cash. And I will hit you straight. There just happens to be a strange coincidence that some really wealthy people, who are in your same situation, seem to find out the person who did the shit they did, will come up missing or dead. Now don't you think that is odd? See, all I ask is, I think whoever it is that happens to, let's say assist these wealthy families with their issues, may end up coming to you about your niece. When they do, I hope you give us a call."

The icon laughs at the men, and tells them he hopes someone does whack this dude and anyone else who does the same thing. He is deliberate in saying the guy should be dropped out of a plane with no chute.

Nave walks out as Morrow tells the icon, "You are aware we are watching this close. You slip up and something happens, you might be sending your raps via jail mail. We will find out who is involved, and you are next in line to take a ride."

Nave steps in front of Morrow and very quietly says, "I have recorded this entire conversation. You two are on some chase with little to validate. You have only incriminated my firm's client based on what you feel you know of him and his past. I remind you his past is of entertainment, words on paper, and then to song—a talent to emulate the young struggles of urban life. Now I have seen many white actors murder, hire for murder, and act out gruesome acts of violence; however, you are not on any of their doorsteps, now are you? Perhaps when the press sees--yes you are on camera here, and hears this interrogation of a successful black artist, you can then be the ones answering the questions. This man has no history of violence. Sure, he was arrested. Arrested for rapping in a venue which middle-class white parents struggled with. Their white children were shocked by this new music. Yet you have him as an aggressor, who actively hunts down any and all who cross him. I will tell you now, and if you want to get your cuffs ready get them out. I will say this,he may return to his roots, and take care of this his way. He may spit out some really damning rhymes about what this piece of shit did, and produce it. After all, as you said, he and his crew are the rawest truest, and you can't change that. That is all you can come up with . . . my brotha!"

They look deflated, and the icon looks deep into them, and with an angry scowl requests, "I guess you might take that as your departure note you phony black fucks, and if I see you near my gate I will have a restraining order slapped on your asses."

The icon is happily stoned about this time, and can't stop laughing inside as he tells the other guys how Nave set the po-po straight. The group also only knows Nave is an old friend of Smoke, and met with the icon to have a few things signed. They all head to the studio as Nave leaves.

A few miles down the street, Nave expects a visit from Morrow and Holcomb. There is a marina with an outside seating area and a snack bar. Nave sees the Crown Vic following, so he pulls into the marina. He orders at the window then finds a table near a wood railing. The table has two chairs so he takes another from a nearby table. He is seated at the table when Morrow and Holcomb approach. He expects them, and has a seat ready. A high school-aged boy comes out with three fresh-squeezed lemonades. He sets a glass in front of each man, who only focuses their attention on Nave. The men are on one side, Nave on the other. The wood is hot; the air is still. The men are in suits, and the Florida humidity has set in to challenge their tolerance. Nave has deliberately positioned his seat to be under the umbrella, and he is dressed much lighter. A few minutes pass as the two men stare at Nave; Nave has a calm demeanor while he is relaxed. Each side is trained in body language and the art of allowing the other side to speak. See, often interrogators simply want the other side to start speaking as this usually paves a lane for error. Nave remains quiet and enjoys his lemonade. The eyes of three men remain in a trance in their desire to read the other. Nave has the advantage as he knows their motive. Morrow and Holcomb struggle to associate Nave with the icon. Nave sits peacefully, slowly twirling his straw between the ice; he takes an occasional sip. He never breaks eye contact from either man. He trades glances to see if either will break their silence. The men are now sweating; the ice on the sunny side of the table is nearly melted. Holcomb sets his cup down, and folds his arms. Morrow removes his jacket, and drapes it over the wood rail. Nave smiles as to console the mistake the two made to dress like the typical agents. Still—no word spoken. Until the boy comes. The boy stands at the table, and asks if any of them would care to order lunch or a snack. The humid air holds the tension as the men coldly stare at each other. The boy looks each way then looks down, and as if he were backing out of a gunfight to not be noticed, he takes a few concentrated steps back before turning and getting back in the snack bar. From Nave's view, he can see in the distance a bicycle cop coming their way. Nave stands, keeps his cup, and leaves the two sitting at the table. As he pulls away, the bicycle cop approaches the table. He explains to Morrow and Holcomb that the snack bar boy called because he thought it may be a drug deal or hit going down with three strange men just staring and refusing to talk. They show their badges, and advise why they are there. As they are about to leave, the boy comes out.

He tells the cop, "The drinks are not paid for. The other guy said the guy in the blue jacket was paying for them. I need $9.75."

Morrow laughs, and tells Holcomb, "Goddamn that guy is good. You got the blue jacket, pay the kid. And being he didn't pay, he took his cup, and I am sure he used a paper towel to move the chairs . . . we are not getting any fingerprints to see who he is. " The cop asks about what he was driving, and Morrow tells him the Hummer had military plates which came back as being assigned to the army.

That night, Morrow and Holcomb try to find leads to Morrice, which only yield one dead end after another.

Nave drives south as he converses with the tactical team. He advises he needs a pick-up ready in Homestead. When he arrives in the desolate area of Homestead, there is a helicopter waiting in an unused baseball field. The neighbor kids gathered as it is unusual to see a flat black helicopter land in the old field. Nave drives straight to the jet copter, and a woman exits. She takes the H-1 away, and Nave is gone. Forty minutes later, a commercial jet departs St. Thomas as it flies to California.

Among the passengers is Nave. Once in California, he enters the parking garage of the airport. He is advised of a particular space in which a car would be waiting. As he exits the garage, the sun provides the light needed to see the faint graphics of dark, thick stripes down each side of the hood, which continue over the roof and drip onto the deck lid of the trunk. The flat black-on-black with deep blue highlights make the 1969 Chevelle SS turn heads as he drives up the California coast. By night, he arrives in Napa Valley.

The next day, he visits a gallery and takes a wine tour. The sun is shared by the many tan shoulders of happy women on ladies-only getaways. There are couples on honeymoons traveling in either direction through the valleys of vines. Some lifers, who cater to the increasing populous of wine collectors, seem to live the dreams of those visiting. The beautiful landscape of vineyards has been collected by the many dreams and cameras to then take to those who may not make their way to the California wine country. One particular guest is accompanied by a small Chinese girl. They are on a less populated tour, and want to keep to themselves. Perhaps it is due to her foreign heritage and no command of the English language. The man appears to clench to her either in admiration or control. Her expression tells a story that she is to resist eye contact, obey, as well as stay in his clutch. There are a few other age-varied couples, which is not uncommon in a land where wealthy men acquire younger women in an exhibition of status. Dismiss the awkward, forced affection and indulgent rubbing of her buttocks, one would have more likely seen this as a daughter or foreign exchange student. The day passes, and the crowds disburse. Stars flicker, winds massage the leaves of each plant absent the moon, and dark is deeper in the fields. Nave sits in his car just on the isolated side of the room where the man and young girl are staying. Hours pass, and then the man exits the room. He goes to smoke near the end of the building.

Nave exits his car, and starts past the guy. "Hey, are you going to be right here for like two minutes?" Nave asks.

The guy is hesitant and asks, "Yeah, but why are you hanging out here?" Nave explains he has to use the computer, and can't get any signal in his room. He says if he were in his car, and on this side of the building it was much better.

Nave goes to his room and returns. "Thanks man. My name is Jake. I just had to go piss real quick. Hey aren't you the guy who had the hot, young oriental earlier?" Nave leads into him.

The guy seems to be sparked by the attention. "Yeah, picked her up in L.A. on my way up here. Dude, not a word of Enguish, and hell I can't say she is even legal here in the country."

Nave acts to look around, extends his cigarette pack out to offer the guy, and says, "Hey between you and me, she doesn't look like she is even eighteen. Damn, how did you manage that?" He leans against the wall, rolls the round metal against the flint as he lights his gifted cigarette, and tells Nave it is all in who you know.

Nave confides, "Well, matter of fact, I do know a few people. Take a look at what I was doing on the computer. I actually help set things up for guys I know and trust." The guy sits in the passenger seat, and is pornographically hypnotized by the material. It is a fake ad to arrange encounters for older men with young Asian girls. The guy spends a few minutes reading and looking at photos. All the photos are clothed, yet he can see the pictures of whom he believes are girls for sale.

His eyes start to get heavy, and Nave tells the guy, "You like what you see? You can't help yourself. You are tired; you don't feel so good right, now do you, Morrice? Yeah, I know your name. You don't have to worry about going back to Florida. You are staying here now. You will be here a while. Morrice, do you have your Epipen?" He can't open his eyes any longer, and falls asleep.

In that deep, dark night the four-wheeler heads far into the outer border of the fields. Just beyond the hillside, are rows of bee boxes. The four-wheeler stops along the boxes. Morrice is limp over the back rack as a deer would be after a hunt. Nave slips on a white bee suit, and lifts Morrice's lethargic body off the back. He takes Morrice's hand, and grabs a generous lump of raw honeycomb. He puts his hand down his pants to coat his genitals with honey. The man's body is tired and leaning against the bee boxes. Nave removes several bees, and places them under the man's shirt and also many in the man's pants then buttons him up. The bees are aggravated and one sting releases a stress pheromone that engages the other bees into a frenzy. The trapped bees sting, and sting, and sting. Nave parks the four-wheeler near the man, and walks back. When he returns to his car, the surrounding area is quiet. The mild pulsing exhaust of the Chevelle becomes faint as he leaves Napa Valley.

Mid-after noon comes, and Nave lands in Orlando. Further south, a group of rappers are fixated on the news. The local reporter comes in with breaking news out of Napa Valley. Reporter:

"A local man, Morrice Dunaway, was found in a bizarre accident just outside of trendy Napa Valley wine country. Dunaway, if viewers recall, was still under investigation for sexual battery, including that of a minor. Notably, the case is pending in relation to a famous rapper's niece here locally. Local reports are minimal at this time, yet say Dunaway was reported to be staying at a trendy inn where an underage Asian girl was being held inside, cuffed to the bed. She was found when housekeeping came in, surely shocked to find her. Dunaway was not in the room, authorities claim. This lead to a search for him at the time hotel staff reported the girl restrained in the room. A dog found Dunaway four miles away in a field leaning against beehives. They say the hives are vital to the pollination, and key to the area, and not closely watched. Dunaway was said to have likely been using the sticky honey to . . . um . . . let's see . . . how to tell our viewers this . . . it was reported he placed his hand with honey in the crotch area which likely stirred up the bees. Whoo, this is a really disturbing account of events. The medical examiner's initial report claims he was stung in excess of five hundred times, mostly in the genital area. Any person would struggle to combat the effects given immediate attention; however, Dunaway who was prescribed and had an Epipen, was known to be severely allergic to bees. The local departments report the girl is unknown and working with translators. They also say there are no signs of foul play. We will report further details as we receive them, and at this point we can say that Morrice Dunaway, resident of nearby Fort Lauderdale, has died from what the medical examiner says was anaphylactic shock."

Sitting in amazed appreciation, the icon is speechless. His close friends are ecstatic and one makes note, "That sick fuck.

Had some girl cuffed to the fuckin' bed. And still roams out at night in the middle of fuckin' wine country to find honey to jerk off with. Got his junk stung up."

Another member of the group adds, "See here, pervert wanted to swell up. I have heard of that shit, but damn hommies, thought it was just jokes. Dudes be swelling they shit to be bigger I guess. Hey, I ain't got to get stung, My shit swole enough, aaahh know, what I say hommies?"

Two other men are just getting details as well. "You got to be shitting me right now. You have to be absolutely shitting me right now. How the hell is it we can't find this bastard, and he ends up dead in Napa Valley?" Morrow says frustrated.

Holcomb simply shakes his head and says, "Either fate is really that good, or there is someone out there that is even better than fate." The two discuss going out; however, they know the scene has been grossly contaminated by this time as not a soul out there would know the connection. They also are puzzled by the encounter with Nave. They try to match the times; the puzzle just doesn't fit.

On the plane ride home, Nave pulls out a thick manila envelope and hands it to Amanda. "Here my Dean, I figured you may like this. Just promise me if you don't want it anymore, you will give it back to me." She opens it, and there are several signed pieces from this rap icon, who is now incredibly popular with the teens. She will enjoy showing these off to the friends and telling of how her "Padre" is a friend of this rapper.

"Padre, I spent the entire time with Lynn. You know what I learned?" Amanda seriously asks her dad.

He is attentive, and listens over the noise of the plane. He surprises her as he says, "Dean, I would be very interested in what you learned about Lynn. I should tell you, I care a lot for her."

Amanda smiles and tells him, "She is hurting. She so badly wants something. She has a career, stability, some sort of fame in the news, but she is sinking dad. She doesn't by any means need a guy, but I can tell her time with us, gave her something she didn't realize was missing. I know I am still just a kid in a way but let me tell you dad, you like her. You are such a match, and with your work, well let's face it, not many women will be cool with that. On top of it, I need her. I like having what she adds to the time when she is with us. So I said my mind piece. Just wanted you to be open and listen." He holds her hand, and tells her he has thought about it often and is just not sure if she would come to Utah, and if she really could be who she is away from her family.

Amanda naps, and Nave as usual pays attention to any passenger who goes to the restroom, stands too long etc. The plane lands, they walk out, grab bags, and when they reach the sliding doors, Nave tells Amanda, "Your aunt will be here any second to pick you up." Amanda looks sleepy and is so confused. She enquires as to what he means—pick her up?

" "I left something in Florida that I have to go back and get," he tells her.

Amanda looks disgusted. "Padre, really? Just call Lynn, and have her overnight it."

He gazes at Amanda, and he looks so happy. "Dean, this is something you have to ask a woman in person. I already looked, and there is a red-eye in just over an hour. If I get on that plane I won't back out."

Amanda is frozen, as she stalls. Her emotional elation is stuck. Her smile and eyes say she is excited, and finally she breaks. Her eyes tear up, and she pushes her dad and says, "Padre, don't you freakin' miss that flight!"

CHAPTER 19
The Bench

Lynn Grace sits in a hammock hanging from a beam on the back porch of her father's home. She has a few pieces of mail she needs to read and one letter from Nave. He had returned, and took a few days to plan things out. She opens a large envelope, and inside, it instructs her to take the small package enclosed to Lake Eola; it further instructs her exactly what bench to sit on when she opens it. She is excited, as the curious anticipation is almost too much for someone like her to handle. She rocks in the hammock looking at the small brown box. There is a little weight to it, and she knows there is something more than a picture or jewelry. The night comes, and she sets the box on the kitchen island. The judge is passing through and inquires about the box at which she is staring. She explains it is from Nave, and she has to wait to open it. He laughs, and as he walks away from the kitchen, he tells her that if it came from Nave and has specific instructions, you can be sure it is precise and to not mess up his plans.

It is 10:00 a.m. The sun seeps through the branches. Swans, ducks, and birds follow the small hands of children, who have come to toss pieces of bread. A few older couples are finishing morning walks. Younger crowds ride bikes, run, and some are on in line skates. Lynn finds her way to the bench that he requested. As she sits, she looks around. In her mind, there is hope in the panning of the park that she will see him walking to her. After a few minutes and no sight of her fairytale, she takes the box and places it on her lap. From her small bag, she retrieves a knife— just in a side pocket next to a small handgun. She whips the blade open, and carefully severs the tape. She returns the knife, and then opens the box. A plain white envelope with the words, "Lynn Grace, No man has seen a true woman as I have in you."

 She lifts the envelope; under are a pair of binoculars. Her eyes squint, her lips tighten, and a tilt of her head as she ponders with a very inquisitive gaze. She holds the envelope a second then proceeds to open. This woman sits on the bench, her long hair flows behind her, her hands holding a letter by each side. Her black, crochet-style sundress caresses her tan legs and soft, pink paint is fresh on the toes that clinch to her sandals. Those who pass will see the smile, yet not ever know of the words which soak her heart and flood her eyes:

 "In my time, I have not felt love hold me so loosely, yet felt so firmly. I had not dreamt of such love, nor known it to be true. In her presence, I am full. I parted and emptied. Each moment forward, it will be my desire to show her the lustful temptation with which she captures me—. My hands to learn her body, my faith to be her solidarity, the journey of each tomorrow to be shared in her eyes. Sunrises will come and be blocked by her kiss. Seas will challenge to squeeze between our feet as we embrace the sunset. Laughter will echo the solid white hills as we share one sled. Photos . . . will no longer be absent the other side. Times to come will show two who were destined to be together; they had no intent to join. These two sought no lasting time in each other. Perhaps those seeking the answer to what love is, will look to us and realize Love is as elusive as the fairytales written. Love becomes. Love saturates two souls until it takes over. It is often said, (you can't find love). Has anyone realized that which cannot be found cannot be discarded? When Love has welded two souls, it is then forged. I have no power to

resist you, Lynn Grace. You are within me. My thoughts are of you, they are of my hope. Each day, I want to wake to your scent on my pillow—each night feel your hand covering my heart. I scribe this, and ask this to be my last day alone. In the box, you can see a way to find me. You will look straight forward, and find a man alone on a bench. Please, now look directly across the lake. You will have to answer this one question."

Lynn has to first dab her eyes. She takes the binoculars and over her quivering smile, she brings them to her eyes. The rubber eye piece is now wet, and she finds Nave alone on the bench holding a small chalkboard with a question.

"Lynn Grace. . . will you sit next to me. . . *forever?"*

Her right hand lowers still holding the binoculars. Her left hand tries to catch each tear. He stands and walks around the lake to her side. She holds the letter in her lap spotted by an occasional teardrop. She watches him come to her. When he is a few steps away, she stands, goes to the center of the path, and awaits him like a first place ribbon. Less than a foot apart, he stops. She looks at him.

He holds the sign up and says, "You never shook your head and I couldn't hear you from over there. So I still am not sure if I will be sitting on benches by myself."

She steps forward; her hands grasp his neck and head. She nears him and says, "You will never be alone!" She kisses him there as people are passing.

An older man slowly walks by. The two are oblivious to the world. He can be heard imparting wisdom to Nave," Today you hold her like a treasure. Tomorrow reassure her of today. Forever, hold her just as tight and you will never lose life's only true fortune. Today. Tomorrow. Forever. Remember that young man."

A few days later, Amanda and a few friends stop in. Amanda was not sure when her dad would return. Even though she had frequently harassed him on details.

A girl goes to the kitchen to get water out of the refrigerator. She looks out the back glass door, and asks, "Dean, who is the chick laying in your hammock?"

Amanda slams the side of the kitchen island as she vaults toward the door. In the hammock, Lynn is asleep. She sways with her bare feet dangling off one end. Peacefully, in a late summer trance, until Amanda slides open the door and yells, " Lynn. Oh my god, what in the world? When did you come?"

Amanda hugs her, and sits in a patio chair next to her. The other girls grab drinks, and come out. Like a dorm of silly girls, they huddle around as they listen to Lynn tell Amanda how the day at the lake went.

Amanda smirks and makes comments of how she is so surprised her dad could have any romantic bone in him at all. She says how he is so firm, so harsh.

Amanda has a somber moment. She lies back in her chair and asks, "Lynn, I don't want to be out of place, but how long are you staying? You just came to visit a little longer or what?" She seemed to have a sad preparation for the departure that would come.

Lynn sits more upright, and tells Amanda, "Dean, I am here. I'm not going back. Your father is my life now. Our energy is to build something incredible. Now, if it is awkward at first, I can buy a place nearby, and not just blast into your guys' world."

Amanda jumps in and assures Lynn that she would not want her to be anywhere but in that house.

One girl asks if there is a wedding to be had soon because she wants to be invited to the party.

Lynn laughs, and tells the girls that she and Nave both feel marriage is a legal process that doesn't have a place in their desire for what they want. Lynn expresses how they will spend their time enjoying life and a ceremony doesn't make two people anymore connected.

After the excitement settles, Amanda finally realizes she hadn't asked where her dad is. Lynn lets her know that her dad was just getting groceries for the night. The girls have to head home, and Amanda wants to stay and catch up with Lynn. They didn't get much time in before Nave returned.

The summer ended after a few good trips to Bear Lake, Zion, Lake Powell, and many hikes throughout the Wasatch Range. In between Nave's work schedule, Lynn and Amanda had time to see Park City, and some outdoor, live concerts that Lynn liked. The two spent a day up at Snow Basin's summer event where Lynn fell in love with the Huntsville / Eden area.

She tells Amanda, This is like a pocket of heaven. So many places have an appeal, and this is a place that has that true life energy. People are happy, and the views are ridiculously abundant." Amanda was not so sure about the horse ride Lynn made her take but she got through it.

As the air cools with summer fading, Lynn sits out back embracing the freshness of a change of season—something not well offered in Florida. An unusual event for her to go buy a new wardrobe that included something warm and layered, and even warm boots. This is all to her liking, as she has explored a realm of clothing never to hang in her closest.

The time has only brought the three closer, and into the winter, Lynn reminds Nave of the promise to go sledding. The first fluffy snowfall, and she can't take herself away from the window. Hot tea in hand, she sits next to the fire. She is now placed in her new life. Nave has had regular work that has taken him away for his shifts and now a future to return to.

Christmas comes, and Amanda works quite hard with the help of her aunt, old friends in Florida, and even a few of her dad's old police family. The three open presents, and then go to Nave's sister's home as they always had. This is the first year for Lynn to join. Cherie, Nave's sister, always does a full layout for dinner, and the family sits around and exchanges presents. All the presents have been opened, and Amanda stands and says she has one more to give her dad and Lynn. Nave and Lynn have to cover their eyes as Cherie and Amanda brought the gift in. A large item sits in the living room. It is wrapped and neither of the two can begin to guess what it was. They are told to stand behind the present, and both open it together. One tear each, and it is revealed. It is a bench. They finish removing the paper, and then notice it was the bench Lynn sat on. On the wood slates Amanda had a guy wood burn and engrave,

" *TODAY, TOMORROW, FOREVER*
you will never sit alone"

The cameras click, and the two are speechless. His sister smacks him as she says they better sit their butts down so everyone can take a picture.

As they sit, Lynn asks Amanda how she pulled this off.

Amanda laughs and explains, "First, I have the most awesome aunt ever. Then I sorta borrowed your note to get the words right. Then, I had to get the bench. At first, I was going to just get a bench, but knowing the romance in this, well I had to have THE BENCH. So Padre, Oly, Kaybark, and Tack kind of said it needed to be removed from the park. You know they love me. So when it got here we had it done. This story I want to be a part of our home forever. It belongs here"

The room is quiet, and the one dry eye soon glasses up when Amanda sits between Lynn and Nave as Nave holds his daughter tight. This Christmas made life brilliantly shine for the entire family. How could they not but only adore Lynn and how they came together?

Chapter 20
<u>Wyoming</u>

It is said you cannot see wind. This is true. You can, however, see what the wind blows. There is a steady display of this as the snow, ice, and trash cans make their way across the open road just outside Kemmerer, Wyoming. A Peterbuilt rests along the highway, still running. Truckers leave them to run as the bitter cold may leave the diesel motor stranded if it gets too cold. Inside, a man rests in the back of his sleeper as he combs the internet. One site after another. Saved photo files of pictures he has taken as he has driven across the Northwest. He enlarges one photo. It was obviously taken earlier in the year as the park is green, trees full, and people are in shorts. One photo after another, of children playing, and each one closer to the children. Parks, fast food places, shopping malls, grocery stores—each focuses on children. The man spends his rest time hunched over, sweating, and grossly manipulating himself as he looks over his photos. Meanwhile, a few people in their cars pass the amber marker lights unaware of the horrid activity inside the idle rig in the early morning hours.

Nave is working closer to home in Logan, Utah. His shift has just started, and he is unloading his bags for the week. The air instantly tingles against his face as he walks outside. Crisp, clear skies brought the thermometer in a direction Nave is not so keen to. He still has to go get food for the week, and at nine p.m. his dash advises it is a wintery ten degrees. After he returns, he heats some tea and prepares to review some files. He goes through his routine of opening his case, and enabling security blocks so the hotel and surrounding intrusion threats cannot intercept his communications. There are a few cases he has on his cue, and one in particular has been more active. A few ES agents reported to the database of pings and mobile tracking of a level 3 target that has been moving back and forth from Chicago to areas of the Northwest. Along with these cases, there has been more focus on Ghost level 5. It was reported he was last picked up in The Columbia Gorge near Multnomah Falls. The track diminished, and there was nothing more for several days. He finally closes things down and lies in bed. His mind grinds over the cases and this Ghost. After seeing the clock hit two thirty a.m. he next wakes to see it at five a.m.

The crew meets in Gary's room as normal and no one is at all energetic to start a new week in this bitter cold. They finish the planning for the day, and go to breakfast. As they walk in, the warmth is an instant welcome. They peel their jackets off, and stand at the hostess station. From the back comes an attractive, yet young girl to seat them. She has a little hint of a country accent; her hair is in a hat and ponytail, and she wears boots that look like they have kicked a few rocks. Nave tells the girl that by the looks of her boots, she must actually ride horses and not just shop at the country store. She smiles and says she has had horses all her life, and her daddy owns a boarding farm. She asks Nave if he rides, and he just laughs.

He explains to her, "Oh I have a daughter, who isn't much younger than you and she tried to get me to ride a horse one time. It wasn't a good day." She laughs, and asks why. He gives her a brief synopsis of how he was not ready for the horse to go fast; however, the horse decided to do what it wanted anyhow. He elaborates, "See, my daughter rode before. Her mother rode, and I grew up in the city. We drove cars, dirt bikes, and things with brakes. After all, isn't that the whole idea of vehicles? So we don't have to ride animals any longer." The guys are laughing and the girl giggles as she says it is for fun and that the horses like to be ridden. He adamantly disagrees, "Okay, a horse. You have to break it, right? Why? Because the animal doesn't want some 200 pound man on its back."

She answers, "Oh stop. They love the companionship."

He continues his original story. "Anyhow, we start riding and I am thinking, hey this isn't bad. I like horses, the ride is nice, and being out is beautiful. Well, then my daughter decides she wants to go faster. Fine with me, go ahead. My horse and I, we can just cruise here and enjoy, right? Not so much, as no one bothered to tell me horses are naturally competitive. So there she goes. Then my horse decides, hey oh I want to run too. NO! NO! NO, I say. Then I remember. It is supposed to be, 'whoa horse.' Well, whoever says that, 'whoa' stops a horse is full of shit! My horse didn't stop. This little riding lesson also failed to advise of this rock in the saddle crap. That saddle beat me up in places a man doesn't like to be beaten up. So there you have it. I gave up the riding this animals thing." The girl laughing, says he should try it again. Nave looks to the guys and says he isn't ever trying to ride a horse again.

No sun will be seen this day, and the cold fails to leave the air. Their work does not allow for cold off-days, so the crew pushes on. On the way back to the hotel, Nave looks out the window and notices that every house, store, barn and anything with an overhang has thick, solid and varied-shaped icicles. Some nearly reach the ground. Some hang high, and as the drip of day gives way to the shadows of the freeze, the points rest in a sharp needle-like shape. The trucks pull into the hotel, and the crew waste no time to head to warm showers. Once partially thawed, Nave decides he will spend a little time at the gym.

The truck enters the parking lot for the gym just as Nave's earpiece announces, "NES 1912; 10-10?" Nave parks and replies that he is alone, and is able to copy transmission by the CO. The Control Operator advises the target now known as Park-and-Ride has been detected in Wyoming, and tracking indicates this target will likely travel west. This would put Nave in proximity to track and possibly eliminate the Level 3 target. The Control Operator advises that the file and information have been updated to every ES file. The CO advises the target is often traveling with hitchhikers and random riders, and that the last ES has to abort elimination due to a passenger/witness threat. Nave has previously validated the information he needed to accept the target case, and was anxious to learn what had been updated.

Moments after his communication of what could likely be his next target, he graciously opens the gym door for an older man. The man is fragile and his slow shuffle stops. The man looks to take effort to turn his head toward Nave.

He smiles and acknowledges the politeness, "Son, it is nice to see kindness in some. You look like you could take down a house by yourself, but I bet you wouldn't harm a soul. Thank you for holding the door." The older man heads toward the therapy room, and Nave continues toward the gym. The gym is crowded, and there is a particular click of fashion-chased women who are on the treadmills just behind Nave. Typical in the early evening hours of this gym, are the ones there for social time and attention. Most of the improvements in their appearance has been paid for and created by a knife. Nave never wears headphones or anything that would distract him from hearing everything around him.

Behind him the conversation is between three women judging each person passing. One is heard saying, "Really, really, if you have rolls, why would you wear that? And why not come like during a time when there aren't so many people here?"

The middle princess replies, "I think they should just try doing it at home or some low-budget gym until they dropped the lb's."

The last pampered woman doesn't ridicule as the other two had, yet she is more focused on herself. She explains how she and her husband battle over her workout clothes. She tells the other two, "He is such a pain in my ass. He sure wants me to look good, but then wonders why I have to buy new shit every week. Plus, not like his old ass is doing much about it anyway. Hell, my purpose is to make him look good. So glad he agreed to let me fuck the guy I met online."

The middle asks, "Oh my god, I forgot about that. How is that guy? Will you share?"

The other answers, "Oh honey, I am not sharing this one. He is a little young, but hell he can just go and go. He is only twenty-seven, but he knows I am married and he doesn't care as long as he is getting to hit it a few times during the week." The middle woman asks the other woman on the end if she is still thinking of leaving her husband.

The end woman explains, "I want to; he is a good dad and all, but I want something different. I met one guy who has old money, but he already said there is no way he would get married again. I have been with him a few times, and he knows my situation and it sucks because the jackass I am with now was smart and had me sign that fucking prenup." The other two laugh, and tell her she is stuck.

Nave is beyond nauseated by this point, and heads to the weight-lifting area. He finishes after a while, and heads out the door. As he nears the door, a few younger kids are coming in and Nave holds the door for them. Each kid says thank you. Nave walks back in. The boys are likely junior high school age. Nave tells them he appreciates how polite they were, and hands each one a five-dollar bill. He tells them to go over to the smoothie bar and get a smoothie.

Nave walks out to the parking lot and on his way to his truck, the woman who was in the middle stands in a jacket next to her car. The front tire has completely deflated.

She sees Nave and asks, "Hey, do you know how to change a tire?"

Nave replies, "Yeah, don't you?"

She grips her arms into herself with her gloved hands near her bulging cleavage, and with a sway and delicate voice says, "I have no idea, and you look like a real man. Can you help me? I tried to call a tire place but everyone is closed."

Nave looks at the tire from the edge of the curb and tells her, "Well, princess, between your husband, your boyfriend, your friends' boyfriends, or some other sucker that may come out in a minute, you might have a chance getting this fixed. Might want to run the heater as you wait for help; I hear cold-blooded animals don't last very long in this weather." He walks two spaces over and climbs into his truck. He pulls past her; she stands looking with her arms slightly open as if she was still thinking he would stop and help.

Back at the hotel, Nave is eager to get the information on this park-and-ride target. He opens the case and notices is some disturbing activity. The family who contracted the elimination had recently filed a new complaint with the court. It was revealed a second child had come to them. The second child became terrified until the court case was in place. Once Bob Lee, now listed as park-and-ride target, was set free, the second child came to the parents and advised she too knew the neighbor. The new information shows copies of the complaint which mirror the first child. Bob Lee is a self-employed over-the-road truck driver. He had owned and operated a very busy trucking company. He lives in the open property neighborhood, and often has a few trucks parked at his house. The neighbor kids like to play on and in the trucks as they pretend to be truckers. The densely populated neighborhood allows kids to roam and explore. This opportunity presents a perverted disaster for this family. To increase the tension and heartache, Bob Lee refuses to move. The attorneys for Lee have made it where he can be free to work while awaiting the continued legal actions. The recent court documents suggest a warrant to seize all electronic devices from the home, yet must wait for his return to obtain his phone and personal laptop. There is emphasis to eliminate the target before his return.

Nave closes the file, and reviews all possible traveled directions the target may go. For hours, Nave calculates the last known ping of this target—the possible fueling stops, road conditions, routes he may take in to avoid the scales, and where he may find his best possible striking location. Nave must account for any evidence that may stay frozen, tracks, terrain, and how to enter and exit. Nave looks at a highway over and over. He keeps going back to this highway as it has several directions in and out. The truck Lee drives could travel through this area if conditions were clear and roads had been plowed. It would also allow Lee to avoid checkpoint scales. Nave believes with the new information, Lee's attorneys have likely contacted him and advised of the new warrant. As Nave studies the map, he calls tech support. Jason is alarmingly always awake and must have a Redbull IV permanently stabbed into his veins.

Jason is excited to get the call and asks, "Hey, so what the hell do you know? What am I going to get for you?"

Nave asks, "Jason, why am I not seeing anything on the truck? No bill of laden, no shipping pick-up, drop-off, nothing. That is easy shit we should have. Can't you dip into what he is hauling and for whom? If I can get that, I may have a good idea where his next stop will be, and what direction he is going to be traveling." Jason tells Nave that he dropped a load in Butte, Montana, but did not pick anything up. He explains he has been trying to find what Lee would be hauling next, and does have a dead head chart to try and trace. He let's Nave know they received a ping coming into Kemmerer, Wyoming, and the signal faded.

Nave asks, "Jason, Lee is hauling a refer unit correct? Can we check everything within one hundred to two hundred miles that will need a refer? Also, can you tap into the cameras at any truck stops?"

Over the phone something can be heard falling as Jason replies, "Oh, oh, oh, I am on that! I have gone through several, and the ones we have satellite feeds on have not come up with anything. Give me a few hours, and I will call you back."

Nave says, "No, No, No, Jason, I am going to sleep. I have to be up in four hours to go to work. If it is urgent let me know during work, otherwise I will call you tomorrow."

Nave is about an hour from being done the next day at work when his phone starts chiming over and over.

Gary asks, "Bro, who the hell is blowing up your phone?" Nave dismisses it as Lynn asking a ton of questions. The phone keeps chiming, and Nave finds a second to look. There are eight messages from Jason that simply say, "check mail." Once Nave gets into the room, he immediately opens the file.

The file opens, and immediately Jason calls. "Hey, are you seeing what I found? Can you believe how scary good I am? Oh, and what about the toys I have? See Nave, you ask and POW there you go. Okay yes, took almost a day, but there it is. You have anything else you want? Have you thought of more? What else can I find or do? No stopping me here."

Nave breaks in, "Jason, slow down. Let me have a second to study this."

Jason relaxes and tells Nave, "Okay, what I updated to the file is this: Lee last dropped in Butte, Montana. He dead-headed to Rock Springs, Wyoming and grabbed a load. See, that load didn't need a refer so that threw me off. That ping in Kemmerer was just a rest stop. Now earlier today, my genius skills downloaded the images you can see there. He was at that truck stop just near the Idaho border. So I checked into anything that would require a refer for a load in that travel route and found a place near the Idaho/Utah border just off HWY 91. He is scheduled to pick up the load between eight and eleven a.m. tomorrow. He has to take that load to Montpelier, Idaho and then back to Kemmerer. After Kemmerer, it is unclear what will happen." Nave's room is only lighted by the computer screen. He sits in his work clothes, looking at the information. Jason wonders if he dropped the call. Jason asks, "Hey, are you there? I can't hear you."

Quietly Nave replies, "Jason, park-and-ride won't be available after Kemmerer." Nave hangs up, and Jason asks for him a few times before realizing Nave is gone.

Nave studies each detail of the route. He pulls geo-map pictures of the locations, and sends a request to have a car waiting in Ogden.

Morning is dark and clear. The trucks warm up as the frost on the windows slowly melts from the heaters. Like tiny diamonds floating in the air, crystals dance before the streetlights. The sun will soon rise and bring only light. The temperature is promised to stay behind a negative sign, and dip further into freezing as the night returns. There are a few hours of light before darkness returns. Gary is in Nick's room when they hear Nave leave. They comment on why he would even think of leaving when it is negative ten degrees outside. Nave quickly heads toward Ogden. They finish work at four o'clock which makes his departure even better.

The blue screen illuminates on his dash and calls for the CO."NES 1912; 10-51. park- and-ride," (10-51 indicates a request for updated information on a target.)

The CO replies, "NES 19-12; park-and- ride stationary. Location - Kemmerer, Wyoming.1912, be advised no 10-12 available." (The 10-12 would be a diversion group, but it is unavailable at this location on short notice.) Nave will be on his own, and the long open stretches will be risky if anything goes wrong. Then CO advises that the car request is in place, and sends a locator to his dash computer. The car is moved to Morgan, Utah and soon Nave reached the location. He pulls back onto the highway now in a black Range Rover. He activates the computer, and has contact with the CO and Jason. He slides a CD in. The base is deep, the vocals clear, and each chord of the hard and heavy sound of Godsmack pumps through the sound system. He passes Devils Slide, cruises past the 84/80 exchange and soon rips through Evanston, Wyoming. Eventually, the Range Rover nears HYW 30.

The CO comes on and advises, "NES 19-12; 10-19." As such, his alert activates and the map shows a tracking. Nave reaches the town of Diamondville, and silences the music. He wants to hear the town, sense the atmosphere, and feel the energy of the small, quiet place. If it were warmer, he could listen for the refer unit running; however, in the brutal cold, the refer likely isn't needed. He slowly passes a fossil and rock shop, and sees a red Peterbilt parked behind a convenience store. The store is still open, and one car sits idle just in front of the door. Nave parks down the street, and aims the camera at the truck.

Jason advises, "Negative. Negative. DOT numbers do not match target." Nave leaves and drives further into town. His tracker on his map is hitting precisely on a direction just west of his path. He comes up to a grocery store and pulls around the back side street. It is dark. The store has closed. The town is quiet, and as he sits across the road, he pans the camera toward the front of a red and black Peterbilt. The rig is still running. Jason advises, "NES 19-12, tractor confirmed registered to target." Nave has no idea if Bob Lee is in the truck, or has anyone in the truck. To spend any amount of time outside would be challenging. The Range Rover dash has bad news. The temperature outside is minus seventeen degrees. Nave moves his Rover inside the back of the store near the dumpsters. He is near the back of the trailer yet out of view. He takes a rock and throws it to hit the rear section of the trailer. Seconds later, the rig lights come on. From the passenger side of the rig, Nave can see the shadows of someone exiting the truck on the driver's side. One person's boots can be seen walking down the driver's side, all the way to the rear. The person comes around the back, which is pulled about ten feet away from the dock. It is too dark for the camera to capture the image. Nave is not in the Rover. Nave is positioned near the dock, out of sight. A man comes around the side. He stands nearly six four. His dark, long hair is pulled back into a loose ponytail that reaches the middle of his back. His left hand is covered with a thick, florescent orange glove. His right hand is ungloved, and grips tightly to a black hand gun. As he nears the side of the trailer, Nave can see the thick eyebrows, a large

knot-hooked nose, and long grey beard. There is no question that this is in fact Bob Lee. Lee tucks the gun into his jacket, and walks the side of the trailer. Slowly, he dips to look under the trailer. He stops, and pauses. He doesn't move for a second as he faces to the front away from the rear which he just passes. He then slowly turns, and just stares in the direction of the dock. His thick brow comes closer together as his cold eyes squint. He takes a step toward the rear again. He looks closer. He slowly walks back to the rear of his trailer. He looks around the dock. Nave stands motionless in between a cardboard compactor and bread racks. Nave is nearly impossible to see at a glance. He has a flat black, bullet, and puncture-proof tactical suit; his face is covered with a thin thermal wear, and tactical night glasses. The pitch black night and Nave's black tactical wear work well as Lee stands less than twenty feet away; he turns to return to his truck. The optic tracer glasses Nave wears allow Jason to see what Nave sees.

The confirmation is made and the CO advises, "NES 19-12 is 10-19x." Jason can see that Lee is just twenty feet away.

Back in his lab, Jason is going nuts. In the lab he loudly chants to himself,
"What! He was right there. Why is he waiting? Jump out, do your thing, and be out of there. Nave, Nave, you have the glasses on, and for once I was going to see how you do what you do!" Jason flops into his seat, and scans the computer. Jason has to track police traffic, any EMS calls, cameras, and routes for Nave to depart; he also has a link to track vitals on Nave.

Twenty minutes pass, and there is complete silence. The rig idles; the Rover sits out of sight. The night blackens even further, and the stars look like Christmas glitter in the sky. The sleeper of the rig has dark back windows yet with the inside light, there is a faint purple hue. Nave notices periodic shifting in the cab. Inside the sleeper, there is an ironic drip of hot sweat as the cab heater blows. Lee sits with only socks on. His eyes are dilated; there are several empty glass beer bottles, and a tipped-over prescription bottle with one less erectile dysfunction tablet inside. Since his return to his truck, he quickly engrosses himself into the photos and porn that has occupied his life. He looks, he touches, he attempts to chat; he goes from window to window, fixated on each new page . . .

SLAM!
SLAM!
SLAM!

The computer drops, and he spills part of his beer. He scrambles to find his pants, jacket, boots, and gun. He tries to look through the windows first, yet they are well-fogged from the inside heat. He opens the rig door and looks back. The rear trailer door is open and slams the side of the trailer. He is sure someone is in his trailer as this night there is no wind to swing the heavy doors, and he is sure he had them clasped shut. Quietly, he stays close to the side of his trailer as he walks closer to the rear. He gets to the open door and waits. He tries to listen yet hears nothing. He comes around the door, and to the back open portion of the trailer. He looks inside, and sticks his head slightly in to see if anything is missing. He pulls his head out and turns. A bright light flashes.

Fifteen minutes pass and Nave announces, "NES 19-12 advises target park-and-ride confirmed 10-07."

The Control Operator validates Nave's transmission. "NES 19-12, you are confirming target park-and-ride 10-07?"

Nave repeats, "NES 19-12; 10-04, target is 10-07. 19-12 is en route to drop origin, 10-17."

Jason is stunned. He wanted Nave to keep the glasses on, yet Nave has advises he will never wear the glasses during the elimination process. Nave drops off the Range Rover, and early in the morning returns to the hotel.

Morning chill glazes the dock of a grocery store. The doors roll up, and a woman stands looking at the back of Lee's trailer. She rolls the doors down, and goes to her store manager.

It is unclear if she is always spicy, or if the cold has made her that way, she says, "Listen! It is too damn cold for my ass to run off the truckers. That fool was supposed to have that piece of shit gone by five a.m. I didn't like that weirdo anyhow. Ask me, he seemed creepy. Big Lurch-like guy. You gonna go tell him to move that truck? We got the bread guy waiting and he has to use that dock!"

The store manager rolls his chair back, looks disgusted at the woman, and grabs his big coat. He makes his way to the truck's door and knocks. He notices the door is slightly open, and thinks the guy must be up and around. The manager climbs up the first step and calls into the guy, "Hey buddy, you awake? We gotta have this truck moved." There is no answer. He calls again and then climbs further in. He looks inside and notices the open beers and the laptop, yet there is no driver. He walks back into the store, and asks a few workers if anyone has come in to use the restroom or if they have seen the driver of the truck. The woman and an older local driver sit at the back shipping desk talking. The manager approaches and asks if they have seen him.

She replies, "Well, no we ain't seen his ass. If I see him, I am gonna give him a load of shit. He is screwing up the whole damn process. He ain't in his cab?" The manager shakes his head and goes back to the cab. After waiting an hour, the manager calls a tow truck.

The tow truck driver asks about the truck, and the manager of the store tells him, "Judging by the empty beers, he got drunk, wandered to a bar, and found some honey to go home with or he is in jail to sleep it off. All I know, it is getting out of my dock space." The truck is hooked and towed to a lot. Part of the lot policy is to inventory and check the cargo to assure there is no hazmat on the property. The driver pulls in and they check the cab. Then they open the back doors.

A lot supervisor calls local police. "Hey, we just towed this truck out of the grocery store. As you know, we have to check cargo. Well, you might want to send your guys down here and to the store. The driver they couldn't find, well we found him."

One patrol unit pulls to the rear of the store and one to the front of the store. Outside agencies send investigators to the tow lot. The investigator at the tow lot meets with the tow driver. The investigator asks, "What can you tell me?"

The driver says, "Opened the door and there he is, frozen. Pretty simple."

The investigator replies, "Simple? Really? Let me ask you, you drive a big truck right? Have you ever driven one with a trailer van?"

The driver curiously answers, "Yeah, plenty. Why?"

The investigator looks at the lot supervisor, and back to the driver. Then he asks, "Have you ever known any refer unit or van to latch and close from the inside? And you say frozen. Did you not notice the red frozen blanket the frozen guy is lying on? Okay for starters we need your information, and you will be fingerprinted and I will tell you now, you may be listed as a suspect. Why would you take this away from the scene without checking the cargo before?" The investigator calls the units at the store, and advises they need to secure that entire store and preserve the scene as they do have a homicide. The sergeant at the store asks the investigator what they are looking for. The investigator replies; "has to be a large knife or more likely a round axe pick. This guy has a huge hole in his chest."

At the store the police advise the manager they will be closing the store for a while to conduct an investigation. The manager announces on the intercom, "Attention customers, we have to ask that you leave you carts where they are and please safely exit the store. You are safe, and this is just a request of law enforcement as they have overnight police activity to investigate. Sorry for the inconvenience, and staff will be helping you to the door." Once the store is cleared of all three of the customers, staff are taken into the manager's office where an officer awaits. They learn of the situation, minus any details. All of the staff are quickly cleared for now, and exit the store. In the back, investigators now search for any object that could have been used. The sergeant advises what the investigator told him and they look in the dumpster, the racks, the surrounding area, and find nothing.

Back at the lot the cab is cleared out, the computer is turned on, and the beer bottles collected. The pills confirm the identity of the driver found in the back.

Investigators working the computer notify the lead investigator, "Hey, you may want to take a look at this." There, they show him the evidence found on the computer and realize the case is a bit more complex. The investigator calls the sergeant and advises of the new child porn found, and asks if there are any locals who may have a history. The investigator goes to the store, and meets with the sergeant. They are at the back of the store now bordered with yellow tape. The first news van appears.

The investigator looks toward the van and comments, "We are in the middle of nowhere. How in the hell do these guys find us, and just how god-damned fast can a big, dopey news van go?" The investigator, the sergeant, and one new rookie stand in the rear. They are over where they believed a car or truck sat, but they are unsure if it is even connected. It is the very location that Nave parked the Rover.

The sergeant states, "A few impressions, but of a pretty common tire. No irregularities I can see."

The rookie looks toward the dock. He asks the investigator, "You think the person used a large knife or pick-like object?"

The investigator answers, "I do. The guy's chest was impaled with something sharp, went through his jacket, and out his back. Not sure until autopsy has a better look. But whatever it was, it was pretty big. If it were here, we would have seen it by now."

The young boot inquisitively suggests, "What if the weapon could never be found? What if the weapon was sure to vanish and leave no trace?" The investigator looks curiously puzzled. He asks the rookie to elaborate. The rookie tells the investigator and his sergeant to look over to the dock.

The rookie asks the investigator, "May be a long shot, however, you have one dead frozen guy, a huge hole in his chest, no weapon, and there is a row of solid, sharp icicles with one missing." There along the row of icicles, like a carnival game where you throw the ball to knock out a clown's wooden tooth, is just the upper section of a broken-off icicle. They walk over and see there is nothing on the ground to show where it may have fallen.

The investigator looks to the rookie, "Hey, kid, you just found our murder weapon. Son of a bitch, that is smart. Ram the thing through the chest, the body heat melts the ice, yet there is still a fatal puncture through the heart. Brilliant, really!"

On the last day Nave works, the crew returns to the hotel. As the trucks pulled in, next to Nave's personal truck is a small

SUV with the lights on and running. As Nave walks over to his truck, he is greeted by Holcomb and Morrow.

Gary asks, "Who are the guys in the suits? You got a fancy dinner party to go to Nave?"

Nave replies, "I am not sure who they are, and I am sure they are lost." Nave says this as he looks at both Holcomb and Morrow. He assures Gary all is fine, and the guys take off.

Morrow begins to ask, "Can you tell me where you were when some pervert was having a chunk of ice rammed through his chest not very far from here?"

Nave takes his phone out and dials a number. As the line answers Nave can be heard by Morrow and Holcomb: "Yes, I am at the back parking lot of the hotel here on Main Street. I need a unit sent over in regard to harassment by a federal agent. I will request an informational report. I will stand by. Not sure if the agents will be here or not." Nave hangs up, and takes their photos and a photo of the car they are driving.

Nave reaches for his wallet. He opens it and pulls out a scan key for the local gym. He also retrieves a receipt. He shows the scan key, and the receipt to the two. He walks near. He looks at both of them. He hands the scan key to Holcomb. He gives the receipt to Morrow. He looks over to the end of the parking lot where a patrol car pulls in. Before the car reaches them, he tells the men, "I know your moves before you make them. I knew you would be here. I am not someone you should pressure. It doesn't end well." He quietly turns and greets the officer. He explains to the officer that the two agents have been following him, and demands a simple IR. After the quick meeting with local law enforcement, Nave heads home and Holcomb and Morrow head to the gym. They ask to see the log of when Nave scanned. The worker at the gym tells them it was at four forty-five. Then they go to the place where Nave got gas for his truck. The clerk says the receipt is from the store, and Nave's last four numbers match his card. The receipt time shows Nave fueled his truck at 10:37 p.m.

Morrow sits in the car. "I just don't get it. There is no way he could have gotten gas at 10:37, raced to Kemmerer, and made it back to work. Even if the guys covered for him, he couldn't make it there, set up the plan, ice-stick the dude, and be clear before store staff come in." Holcomb sits quietly then steps out of the SUV. Morrow steps out, and asks what he is thinking.

Holcomb says, "We have a receipt. Just a receipt, nothing more. What if one of his homeboys just took his card and got gas and covered for him? I don't think he was even here. I'm going to check the tape. Bet your ass he isn't on the tape." They walk back into the store, and ask if there is any way they can look at the tape for that night.

The store clerk laughs, as she says, "Tape? Oh honey, you don't know who runs this store do you? He ain't spending any money on a camera. Lucky we have a new cash register. For years we still had to count change like it was in 1960. Camera? Tapes? Oh dear, I think we are the last store that doesn't have one." They look at each other and simply sigh.

Chapter 21
Search Warrant

Morrow and Holcomb meet with Special Agent Lopez. A large table is covered in paper, folders, and pictures; on the wall, is a United States map on which are pin tacks of locations they are interested in. Lopez stands at the map, his hands clasped tightly behind his neck.

He talks to the men yet looks at the map. "Guys, we can keep chasing, but whoever these guys are, well they are damn good. This is a group I honestly wish worked on our side. How they do the shit they do is beyond me."

Morrow sits at the table looking over the charts, the maps, and the information and asks,
"Sir, I want a search warrant. I want to ask a judge for a search warrant for this Nave guy's phone and computer."

Lopez looks concerned, sits down, and is calm in his reply. "Calvin, you want a phone tap? A tap on the computer? Or do you want to seize the shit?"

Morrow answers, "I want the computer in our possession. Hell, a phone tap would be awesome. I think if we can show a judge the evidence we have, it is slim, but just maybe with your backing and the lieutenant's, we just might get lucky."

Holcomb adds, "Dominic, look at what we have to bring to the table. In the last three years alone, we have seven dead pedophiles, and in the last eight years, we have twenty-three missing persons, who are all on the child predator wanted list. No one can ever find these guys, yet randomly bones are found, and records of some turn up here and there. A judge can see the same thing we can. I know we will at least get a warrant to tap a few phones."

Morrow exclaims, "I want that Nave fucker's laptop!"

Lopez looks at the table, looks at the guys, and looks at the map. He says, "It may be a long shot, but let's put something together, and I will take it to a judge."

There is a dark room with a single, dying plant in one corner. There are books neatly placed in order in several rows along the walls of the room. An old desk sits near a window, and there is an elderly man looking out the window. He is sharply dressed with his hair perfectly in place. His left hand rests on the desk as he taps his old, modest gold band on the wood. His door echoes the beat of Lopez's knock.

His low order calls, "Come in." Lopez walks in, and greets the judge. Judge Halk has been on the federal bench for thirteen years. He has a solid reputation for being fair, being pro-law enforcement, and perhaps the most likely to grant a warrant to the FBI for most causes. It is no mistake that Lopez chose to approach Judge Halk in this matter.

Judge Halk speaks, "Agent Lopez, you come to seek a warrant I believe. I will say I have not reviewed any portion of the request, I will not yet listen to your request, yet I do ask you leave the warrant request on my desk. I want to see what you and your team have put together and I tell you this, I do hope it is properly formed. You know my intent is to support the agency. I do ask you have the same intent to make my work easier."

Lopez sets the file on the old desk as he says, "Your Honor, all the information is included, and we do look forward to your decision at your convenience. Thank you, sir." Lopez slowly backs out and closes the door. Down the hall, Morrow and Holcomb wait. When they see Lopez, they ask if they have the warrant. Lopez explains there is a process, and they may not know for a few days.

Just as the file is left for Judge Halk to review, Nave is called by Robert. "Nave, we have been advised those clowns at the FBI have submitted a request to tap your phone, and submitted a request for a warrant to seize and investigate your laptop. Here is the first thing. Jason has so much tech shit linked to your phone, no one will be able to crack that thing. No worries there. The laptop you know can't be obtained unless you use your code to open the case. You know the process of entering the ditch code. That will open the case, and completely crash the entire system. There is no hard drive to retrieve. Oh, that is the beauty of our operation. The backup is in a secured location that no one can access. As far as your personal laptop, well is there any worry there?" Nave assures that the personal laptop contains family pictures, work-related emails, and everyday, happy home life apple pie family stuff. Robert also tells Nave that the only requests are for the laptop and a phone tap. There is no indication for the vehicle.

Robert laughs as he says, "Our technology is so far beyond what they can even dream, that they would never even think your truck has what it does. If they are granted the phone tap, we should know by the time the paper is processed. However, if they do get it, they can send the tap immediately. If they tap your phone, you will hear a pong tone every ten seconds. That is simply letting you know they are trying to intercept your conversation, and trying to download any text messages. Jason assures me if they download messages, it will come to them as a scripted message. If their tech group is sharp, they will decode the scripted message. At that point it will read, 'you did a good job last week' over and over." Nave informs his intent to file a restraining order, and Robert laughs. Robert says he is not sure it will fly, but might be a fun idea.

The next few days, Nave takes Lynn up snowboarding. There is a fresh layer of white clean powder. With a new jacket, new pants, nice gloves, snowboard boots, goggles, and a helmet, the woman is ready to learn all about snowboarding. She walks funny and even comments on how they should really make the boots more flexible and comfy. Nave shows her how to click her straps, and how to get out of them. He stands with her as he illustrates how to fall.

She asks, "Okay, shouldn't you be showing me how not to fall?" He explains to her that falling or not falling isn't an option.

He laughs and says, "You are going to fall, a lot. And I am going to laugh, a lot!" They spend a while just near the bottom of the mountain getting her used to the way the board feels. Then they finally go up the easy lift, and she can ease out of the chair. She sits near the top of this first hill, and just looks out over the valley. He sits next to her and tells her, "Many times I have been on this hill and sat in this spot. It never gets old. I honestly didn't know it could get better, yet today it has."

She looks to him and says, "Oh, if I wasn't strapped to this board, I would climb right on you and give you the best kiss ever."

All day they work to get her down the mountain, each time a little better than before. The afternoon is spent with hot cocoa, and her red nose being dabbed every so often by a tissue.

Later that night, Nave finds her on the back porch. The propane heater is going, and her hands are wrapped around a cup of tea.

He asks what she is doing and she replies, "Oh I was trying to decide if the hot tub should go near the house, or if we will build a nice path and have a gazebo, maybe we should put it under that."

Nave smiles as he enquires, "Hot tub? Tell me more about this hot tub." As he wraps his arms around her, she tells him she really liked going up the mountain and playing in the snow. She says that the thing is, if she is going to do that, she wants to have a hot tub to recover in. Amanda walks to the door, peaks out, and asks what they are doing.

Lynn tells her, "We are figuring out where the hot tub will go."

"Hot tub? We are getting a hot tub, like with jets and the lounge type?" Amanda excitedly asks. Nave and Lynn walk in, and Nave says they are just thinking about it. Nave walks to his office, and Lynn spins her computer around in Amanda's direction.

She takes a sip of her tea and tells Amanda, "Dean, I just bought one. Done! We will be soaking in that thing when your dad heads off to work next week."

Judge Halk calls Dominic Lopez. He tells Dominic to bring Morrow and Holcomb in. Lopez has wondered about the warrant, as it was taking a little longer to get a reply. Lopez, Holcomb, and Morrow meet in the judge's chambers. When they walk in, the lieutenant is waiting. He advises that the judge called, and wanted to have a group meeting to go over the parameters of their request. Lopez tells the two that this is typically a good sign.

He says, "He will likely have stipulations, and go over his expectations regarding how we conduct our business because he is the one issuing the warrant." The judge walks in, and sits at his chair.

The judge looks to the lieutenant. "Lieutenant, Calvin Morrow, and Michael Holcomb are under your authority if I understand this, right? They are also somewhat lent out or working in correlation with Dominic Lopez. Do I understand this as fact?" The lieutenant acknowledges the statement of the judge. Judge Halk has two files before him. He sets one aside. He tells the group, "We have two matters to cover here today. Let's start with the search warrant request. Agent Lopez, do you possibly have any grasp of the legal guidelines as to what it takes to obtain a legal and warranted phone tap? And I am asking the question; however, you all are to sit and simply listen. I will answer your question, my questions, and all of the questions. You remain quiet until I am finished, and specifically ask you to answer me." Morrow's eyes close and Lopez bows his head as he continues to listen. Judge Halk continues, "You requested a phone tap of this Valerio Nave—some guy who works for a company that helps build railroads. In your statement, you elaborate on how you have reasonable suspicion that this guy may in fact be linked to the murders of several known sex offenders. The document you filed with me states over the course of many years, there is evidence that some agency, let me see here, some agency that yet has to be identified has these special highly trained assassins whom no one can find. That this individual is a person of interest and you now must tap his phones, and you also seek to remove his laptop from his personal possession. As I reviewed the request you submitted, I became disgusted with the lack of content which is absolutely necessary to even consider granting a warrant. Over the years, you have taken it upon yourselves to create this theory that an elite group is being hired to knock off these sex offenders, these child predators. Agent Calvin Morrow and Michael Holcomb predicted, with just a hunch, that a rap star might hire this unknown hit man group; so you two head down to Florida and just happen to run into this Nave guy. I tell you, I am disturbed at how not only did you casually bump into this guy, but some guy gets offed in Wyoming several hundred miles away, and you are on the next flight to pay this guy a visit. You, by my account already, violated the law to obtain his work history and seek him out. What part of this am I not catching onto here? You want a goddamn phone tap for what? You have not a thing to show me that tells me this guy is remotely connected to your far-fetched theory. Next, you want a warrant to take his laptop. You state you believe there could be evidence that may be on his laptop to support your theory once again. Yet, you have no basis as to why you believe this, or supportive evidence to show me that this contract worker somehow is secretively the mastermind, and his computer has all your answers. Okay, so I took some time and looked into what it takes to do this person of interest's job. These guys go out at six or seven a.m. It's freezing, and they still have to work. They work all day, and it isn't easy work. They typically work ten to twelve hours a day. So am I to believe this guy works in shitty conditions for ten to twelve hours a day, gets back to his hotel, and then throws on a superhero, vigilante-type suit and hunts down child sex offenders across the country? Lieutenant, you authorized this investigation?"

"So now I am asking a question for any of you to answer. Is this request for a warrant complete, or are there any missing pages of supportive content that I would need in order to even consider granting a warrant?"

Lopez stands. "Judge Halk, Your Honor, we respectfully resend our request for this warrant, and will only resubmit once we obtain the needed facts to present."

The judge then looks at the men, and reaches for the other file. "Do you have any idea what this file is? Oh you guys have barked up the wrong tree, I am afraid. Here is a document filed this week. This is a request for a restraining order against FBI Agents Calvin Morrow, and Michael Holcomb. Now, unlike your unsubstantiated request for a warrant, this guy has statutes listed, documentary evidence of when you made contact with him, witnesses from Florida and Utah, photos, a police report, and dash cam video of you taking his gym card, and a receipt, WITHOUT A GODDAMNED WARRANT! Followed up with the fact you went to the gym and the gas station the very same day. In addition to the restraining order, he has inquired about filing harassment charges against the agency, and once you leave my office, you likely will have a call in the near and very bleak future from Internal Affairs. Lieutenant, please escort this mess out of my chambers. And Lieutenant, I strongly advise you on overseeing the conduct of your subordinates."

The group exits with no words spoken. Lopez leaves the parking lot and the lieutenant, Holcomb, and Morrow ride together back to their office.

A week passes, and Michael Holcomb calls Morrow and his lieutenant in for a meeting.

Holcomb is at his desk and as the two come in he tells them, "Morrow, I understand the interest you have in this case. And I will say is I didn't see it at first, and there are definitely some real questions that we have. Even with all that, it isn't a fight I am looking to chase. I am accepting a position in Georgia. I enjoy tracking down money. That is my thing. This child predator hunt is draining me. All the same, it is hard because honestly, just in this room, I can say to you two, I would rather be on their side. Do you know how much any of us have felt to work one of those cases and know in the moment . . . I would rather just squeeze the trigger and not ever lose a wink of sleep? So I am going in a different direction."

Morrow walks near him; his hand swings out with an open palm, and the two smack hands as their thumbs lock. Morrow says, "Homeboy, you go do you. You gotta do what Mike gotta do. You always my partna. Beside, I keep fuckin' up; I may need to head down to Georgia and be your sidekick."

The lieutenant tells him, "Mike, you know money. You have a bloodhound nose for crooked white-collar crap. Go knock that shit out."

Holcomb looks over the room; he makes his way to the window, and peers down to the street below. He has both hands in his pockets, and his head eases forward.

The lieutenant and Morrow watch while Holcomb dictates his thoughts. "Statistically, we are failing. We chase, we create new techniques, new equipment, and technology, yet there is one ironic twist in this. We will never be out of work. This will never end. We have an unattainable goal. Those old farts see it. Their goal has changed to simply make it to their retirement, and walk away. Right now, it is happening out there, and we will wait until the call comes in. Another call, and then another. Calvin, my brother, if you end up having leads down my way, well you call me first. I will show you around, and give you a hand." Holcomb turns to the men, walks over and shakes their hands. Goodbye has a different quiet, as if the person leaving takes the sound with them. Their presence departing and the unforetold future leave a mystery. How can a door can be so heavy, and the footprints fade so fast when a friend's steps move forward in the distance? Two men sit quietly, one determined to find motivation to press on, the other knowing his support is vital at this time. No words need to be spoken. Emotions are thick, and each knows the day is best left to memory. They will follow the path their friend took, and admire his direction.

Chapter 22
Portland

Nave is sitting next to the fire with his feet up, and resting back into the couch with a big blanket covering him. In the waving glow of the fire's light, are Lynn's toes swaying, slow, side to side. They touch against his, and her smooth legs crawl under the blanket as she enjoys being close. A bronze illumination filters through her glass of wine. A cool drop leaves her lips, flows over her chin, and falls gracefully between her breasts. Wine would not be his first choice of drink; however, the opportunity to taste the sweet wine from her skin is too tempting to pass up. She turns her back to the fire; her right knee comes over his hip. Her left knee is now on his other side. She looks down to him; he looks up to her. She dips her finger into her wine glass and removes it slowly. Her finger is brought to her lips, yet her eyes never stray the sultry attention given to him. She takes her finger into her tightened lips. Her brow raises, and she returns her finger to the glass. Her finger slowly massages the rim of the glass. Her smile is seductive, and she plunges her finger deeper into the wine. She whispers to him that the wine is so silky and wet. She holds the glass with her left hand near her breasts directly in front of his wanting eyes. Her right hand swirls her finger in the wine. Slowly, her finger rises up. She moves the glass, and allows her finger to drip the wine over her breast. A slow, rolling bead of passion red, moves down her skin until it is met by the warmth of his breath. Drop after drop, side to side, and eventually the droplets of wine puddle in her belly button. Lustfully drunk on her passion, he lays her before the fire. There is a moment of admiration as he soaks in every inch of her body, her womanly curves, the blanket of hair on the floor, and the face of a woman who has more heat that the fire she lies beside. No further need for wine to direct his lips, he explores her body. She speaks only sighs, shortened breaths, and progressively the intense moan of pleasure. The wine-stained fingers now graze his head to assure him she enjoys his attention. She rolls her head back slightly, her bottom lip tucked under her teeth, and her heels land firmly on his back. The fire is fueled and burns hot, crackling, popping, and changing direction. In time, he finds himself lying on his back, looking up and seeing her in control. The fire has shifted, and now the flame is crawling up a rigid, hot timber. Her skin beads with heat. She rocks back and forth. She arches back, and her hair drops behind her. One hand braced on the floor, the other covers her breast not covered in modesty, yet more in pleasure. The painted nails rotate across her nipples as she increases her glide back and forth. She jolts forward as she grabs his hands. With tight gripping tension in her body, their hands are locked. That strong gripping glide stutters into a jittery, twitching until she lies flat against his chest. The fire is still warm, and burns steady beside them. It no longer climbs or pops with heat, yet now smolders in a soothing, warm comfort. The night darkens, the fires diminish, and they lie still though the night.

The new day comes, but the sun has yet to creep any light onto the two restful bodies which lie under a heavy blanket. Her eyes closed. His eyes closed. The fingernails of her left hand gently caress back and forth over his shoulder and neck. His left hand is over the back of her head. This is the dream in which he feels a new life, which had been absent for many years. In his reluctance to wake, is a reward to embrace a woman he cherishes each day. She eases her leg over his, and then encourages his legs to slightly part. Now her firm, smooth leg slowly slides upward.

Her bare torso covers his body and Lynn whispers into Nave's ear, "Good morning. Please lie still, keep those gorgeous blue eyes closed, and don't move. There is something I need to do. Something I crave at this moment, and you have just what I need to satisfy that hunger!"

She takes his ear, and gives him a mild bite before she moves each kiss down his neck, across his collarbone until she reaches the center of his chest. She momentarily rises and quietly reminds him he is to remain still, and do nothing. A warm suckle of his upper lip and then she begins to descend. She takes great care to lustfully grip him. She tenderly yet deliberately concentrates the erotic pressure of her tongue and lips, and strategically blows warm against him. It may be a challenge to tell if he enjoys it more, or if she has a deeper craving; perhaps he has simply become her tool for fulfillment of a fetish-like need. Both know that each benefits from ample amounts of endorphins being generated. She exhibits knowledge of when to relax, and allow the moment to prolong. She brings him to the edge of release, and then calms him–this seemingly to provide her with more time to indulge herself in what she desires. Now focused on him, she knows he must climax in order to achieve the full pleasure of this sexual hangover. No longer will she lightly dance her tongue and lips. She becomes vigorously loud, wet, and generously accommodates him fully until she has taken the power away from him. Impressively, she comforts him as he relaxes. She touches with ease and care to bring him to rest once again. She kisses him up his body, brings her lips to his ear and says, "Thank you so much, I needed that."

Some days start out in a way that makes us happy to be alive. This day for Nave would only have a good beginning, as near noon his phone would ring. Robert advises he needs to check his computer as soon as he can. Nave is home, and on his regular days off so he immediately goes to his office. His briefcase is on the desk; he enters his code, scans his thumbprint, and the case opens. He reviews the information. He learns the Level 5 target, Ghost, is likely in the Colombia River Gorge, Portland, and Clackamas area. Tech support has tried to figure out how Ghost is interrupting the signal and eliminating detection, yet they still get random pings that alert proximities. Tech strongly believes it is faults in the tracking device, and advises there is no way to rectify that issue. He reads the itinerary which indicates a private plane will be waiting tonight. It will fly out of Ogden Airport at 10:10 p.m. Nave studies the little details he can view, and looks over static mappings of the area. He has worked in the area at times, and will utilize what he can for his few days in Portland.

Lynn sees him walk out of the office, and greets him. He says nothing and she tells him, "You go and keep your mind clear. I am here to take care of the house, and you have no need to worry."

That night, dim yellow lights glow behind the steady white flurries falling. The cold air softly blows the hint of jet fuel through the air. Opposite of where he parked, he can hear the distinct sound of a private jet fired up. He walks into the hangar, and a small man stands near a door. Looking out the glass, he opens the door as Nave approaches. He has a pleasant demeanor, yet it is also serious.

He addresses Nave, "I guess you may want a little verification before we fly?" Nave opens his case, and uses a scanner that the pilot places in his palm.

In Nave's earpiece, he is advised by the CO. "NES 19-12, verification, pilot is known GES, Poung. Proceed with travel."

Alone in a dark cabin, he looks out to see the lights below fade once they break the cloud level. A short quiet flight, and soon the wheels of the plane bark as they reach a private airstrip just east of Portland. The wind sock can be seen out of his window as the plane makes its way to the hangar. The sock lay still and dripping from the Oregon rain. The plane comes to a stop in a well-lit hangar. Large doors automatically roll back down, and they are secured. Poung comes through, opens the door, and asks Nave to follow him to the office. In this office there are no windows, one old, faded wooden desk, a new leather office chair, and a smart board. The pilot closes the door, and offers the one chair to Nave.

Nave tells him, "I just sat all the way here, I think I will just stand." The pilot uses a pointer and remote as he activates the smart board. On the board is a split screen. One side are four different photos of the target, Ghost. The other side is a map ranging from the Dalles, Oregon to Eugene, Oregon area— scattered markings of where the intermittent detections have come up.

Poung tells him, "Okay see here, this is a remote location just across The Bridge of The Gods. It is a small park area just on the Washington side. There are five separate pings, and yet at all random times. Then here, look. All the way down to Eugene, a few days later a ping over in Clackamas. Never for very long. This guy doesn't camp out for too long, as we suspected. Seems about the time an ES is near, we have already lost the signal. Hell, we went for five months without a signal. Then all the sudden, he is flying over you in Florida. This guy gets around." He depresses the remote, and the right side changes to a screen with location details that are at the precise GPS ping locations. He converses with Nave. "Maybe you can piece this together. One place here in Portland, we checked it out, and it is a house that has been abandon for seven years. Not a bad area, just never put on the market. Then up in the gorge, another empty house. Tillamook, yes, empty house. Several of these locations are empty houses. All different owners, and the owners don't have any negative record and some are just regular people."

Nave folds his arm, and with a deliberate gaze says, "My neighbors think I am just a regular dad with an average job."

Poung shakes his head up and down and says, "Yeah, I guess you have a valid point there. Now some places are common, Home Depot, grocery stores, and several late nights at porn shops. Here is a place he has been often. It is an underground swingers' sex club. The ping shows he is only there for a short time. Our speculation . . . he is shuffling to clients. This is our biggest fear. We have had surveillance on this location and come up dead." He laughs and tells how they have seen many high-ranking members of sports teams, government staff, and plenty of law enforcement in and out of there. But he notes that all seems to be legal from their perspective. The pilot makes note of the many different looks this Ghost will range in time. He continues, "He will change his look often, and these are the few shots we have from random cameras tech support has been able to capture. What we do know is in the last month we have received more pings in the gorge than anywhere. Short times, and one steady signal showed a short stop in the Multnomah Falls attraction then continued to Cascade Locks. Was there for hours then the signal dropped. The next ping tech received was in Southern Arizona. Now where did I come into this? Being a GES, I am not normally here in the States. I live in Thailand. Believe me, I have my hands full over there. However, this son of a bitch popped up three blocks from my business there." He flips to a new screen that now has a global map. On the map, there is a clutter of red dots. The ping dots show particular clusters. The most prominent are in Southern Florida, Portland, San Francisco, Thailand, Costa Rica, Panama, Chili, and Mexico.

Nave walks closer and says, "He isn't alone. This is a huge operation. This guy isn't shuffling a few kids here and there. He is herding them in quantities. This bastard is likely one of the main players in a global enterprise."

Nave calls Robert. When Robert picks up, he says, "Nave, I guess you are going to fill me in on some new ideas?" Nave has Robert link into the secured smart board. In one corner, is Robert's ID icon to show he is logged in and the system is secured. Nave has the pilot return to the page that shows the Multnomah Falls location.

Nave begins to tell the men what he feels is happening. "Look here, I have been to the falls several times. Now look at the area of San Fran, and then Mexico, Costa Rica, and Panama, and you can see each place has something perfect for this sick fuck. Every place has tour buses and sightseeing. These buses aren't school tours; they don't have a login and logout to make sure everyone is there. If someone gets on the bus at the pickup location, goes to the tourist location, and decides they are going to stay, well the bus leaves. It is an ideal cover for this guy."

Robert asks, "Okay so our target, is he taking them to these places or picking them up?"

Nave replies, "I would say he has to be the pickup guy. He can wait until the group has scattered, people are distracted, and now, I also think there must be an escort to show the victims where to go. Remember, some of these kids don't even speak English. They have never been here. These poor kids think they are coming to work, live, and be free in the land of prosperity. The escort likely rides the bus, shows them the tourist sights, and then quietly ushers them off to this bastard's waiting car. He isn't dumb, and we can only hope the greed has compromised his judgment. That will be our best chance."

Poung looks over a few more slides and comes to a slide he talks to the two about. "We may not be alone in this thought. I looked at this before, and now it makes more logical sense. See this graph? In the last year, several agencies have developed multi- agency task forces to watch cargo ships. Look at the key focus . . . to document crew, and account for any questionable passengers. A year ago, they found eight children in a small room. When interpreters questioned the Chinese passengers, they were told they were paid to come here and work, yet the name they had to contact did not exist. When the task force tracked the location they were to meet, a cab driver stated he was called to pick up three tourists and take them to the Rose Center. He had already been paid in cash. No recollection of who paid him."

Robert takes a deep breath and tells Nave, "Nave, you might have stumbled into one of our biggest contracts. You will know what to do, I trust. We will be in your ear, and diversion teams are already in place."

Poung closes the screen out, and tells Nave he has a car in the other garage. He tells Nave he has a nice Corvette, yet the weather is likely to be rainy during the week. He walks Nave through the hangar then through a side door.

Nave quietly expresses to the pilot, "You might not get this one back." Slate grey, black windows, brush guard up front, and sitting easily on top of thirty-eight inch Toyos, is a new Toyota Tundra 4 x 4. The pilot explains how it has been modified for power, and also shrugs his shoulders and says how he might be lucky to get nine miles per gallon.

The back garage door goes up, and Nave looks out. It is a straight down pouring of rain. He mutters to himself, "I hate this rainy state!"

He leaves there and checks into a hotel in Gresham. This will put him close to the gorge, and provide him with easy access to Portland. Once in and settled, he can't stop looking over the information on this case. He particularly looks over the path, and the connection with The Bridge of The Gods.

Nave is not sure if the sun hasn't come up, or if there are just too many thick clouds as the rain continues to fall. He sits at a diner looking out at the locals who dismiss the fluid dumping upon themselves, as they ride their bikes along the street. In this part of the country, rain is just an occurrence and has to be dealt with. Locals are accustomed to it, and it seems to have little effect.

A bouncy, cheerful woman comes over to make sure he is okay on his drink, and asks, "You are not from here I take it. What brings you into town?"

He looks to her and answers, "I work for an extermination company, and we have meetings this week. We specialize in getting rid of problematic pests."

She tells him how she has had issues with ants in her basement, and can't find anything to get rid of them. "Do ya'll handle ants? What sort of bugs do you kill?"

He takes a quick drink as he stands to leave. He tells her, "We don't mess with ants; there seems to be a problem particularly in the gorge, and the company is looking to attack it before it spreads any further. So they sent our group up to dig around and see what we can do."

She takes his money and wishes him luck. "I hope you find what ya'll are lookin' for, and get rid of it for good."

The road is still wet, yet the rain has stopped as he travels past a sign indicating the beginning of this picturesque carve of asphalt through one of the most enchanting places on earth. There are walls of high cliffs to his right as he drives east. Decorated by dark, sturdy tree trunks with glowing green moss, the trees are abundantly dressed with thick coats of leaves. The many waterfalls drop free and graciously into hidden landscapes. As he looks to his left, the grand span of the Colombia River yawns before him. The road can be mesmerizing allowing a driver easily to drift away in awe at the grandeur of such a place. This is no place to err behind the wheel. This pass can be unforgiving with standing water, dark shadows, and narrow lanes. It is, however, a journey each person will not forget once humbled beneath its natural power. He leaves the highway to take a more scenic byway. Nave must absorb the surroundings in a way to etch himself into his task. Just as a dog can't resist stopping at a willing hand for a pet, Nave will not make the drive past Multnomah Falls without his hesitation to be humbled by nature's power. Many times, he has walked across the concrete span near the lower falls. Still, he takes the walk near the railing to pay respect to that which is so naturally commanding. A quick stretch and he continues a few miles east to the small town of Cascade Locks. The Locks and dam are heavily guarded. It will be very unlikely that the target will risk a place with cameras and guards. There is not much to this little fishing community—a couple of hotels, some tourist stops, and a place at which he usually has lunch. The one side of the restaurant is generously lined with big windows. He sits looking out at the massive, steel Bridge of the Gods. As vehicles pass over, the distinct sound of steel grating echoes throughout the river canyon. There is a brilliant white, red, and black river paddle boat making its way slowly downstream. Lined on the top deck are riders covered in ponchos, as they brave the damp air to capture picture after picture. He can see them point, nudge, and encourage those nearby to see what they already likely saw. Strange how when people see something so magnificent, they dismiss the fact that those right next to them can see the same thing. Yet, we still have to assure that we are in the company of others to witness the magnificence. After lunch, Nave crosses over and drives past the toll. His Toyota's 38-inch tires hum across the steel span of this bridge, and he reaches the Washington side. His information indicates a range to which the target has been tracked. He discovers there is a small turnout on a muddy road. It only leads to a long, weathered dock descending to the river below. He takes a few photos, and decides to make his way back to Portland. He knows he has limited time on this trip, and must work fast to cover the leads he has available. During his drive, he calls Jason. It seems that Jason has a rapid answer as whenever Nave calls, Jason seems to answer before the first ring stops.

Jason picks up, "Yo, what do you know, did you find him already? I haven't heard anything, what can I do for you Nave?"

"No sign of him yet. I did find that location near Washington. It has heavy traffic. I need to see if you can check boat records for the area. Also, have any of the satellite photos shown a dually-type truck or even a shuttle van?"

"Oh let me scan this file. Scanning . . . hold on, it's coming up, okay. See here, the frames . . . and. Nave, Nave, I can't be 100 percent, yet there is, holy shit, hold on. One, two, (he mumbles) six, seven, (he mumbles again) yes, seven. Hey, I will send this out ASAP, but let me tell you this now. Two satellite images show a black Dodge Mega-cab dually parked off the road at that exact location. The other five show what looks to be the same truck either on the bridge, or at a small hotel there in that small town. It looks to be a brand new truck, and doesn't have a plate. I tried to zoom in on the paper tag in the window, but it is behind the glass. The angle or perhaps tent isn't letting me see anything. Fuck!"

"This is good. Very good Jason. Okay, I am heading to Portland to poke around some dirty areas. Thanks. See about the boat records."

Nave travels back down the highway en route to Portland. The weather has cleared slightly and off to his right, he notices a pair of sea lions breaching the water. They have increased in their numbers searching for fish up the river. He is close to passing the falls, and looks over to the parking lot. He sees an uncrowded tour bus on the outer parking area. Looking back to the falls, he notices a black dually. Just as he looks back, the passenger door opens. From a distance that is uncertain, he notices a man helping two small people in to a truck. The two he sees have long, straight, black hair, and their heads come just below the man's chest. The westbound lanes are light; there is a left-sided onramp from the parking area of the falls. Meant for highway entrance only, Nave takes the Toyota down the wrong way. As he passes the tour bus, the driver's hand extends out of the window. The driver jolts a point of his left finger, retracts his hand, and then thrusts a vigorous middle finger in Nave's direction. The black Dodge is pulling out, and Nave whips through the parking lot to close the distance. The narrow road winds closely and tightly against the mountain. The truck is not racing away, yet a red and black Mini Cooper, in between them is surely sightseeing. It is slowing, and bobbing heads attempt to look out the window. There are few areas to pass, and the entire road in this area is double-yellowed. Finally a short stretch where he can see ahead. The throttle opens in the beast of the Toyota; he thunders past the Mini which cowers to a complete stop as the tires of the Toyota are equal to the Mini driver's roof height. The Dodge travels past the highway entrance, and near a grass-lined private driveway.

As Nave has the truck approximately a mile and half ahead, he notifies the CO. "NES 19-12; request 10-19 attempt."

CO answers in his earpiece, "NES 19-12 at Ainsworth, signal not detecting. 10-19, advise information."

"Black new dually Dodge, no plate, seen at suspected location, two small individuals assisted into the truck by one male, short, dark, thick hair. Info on satellite imaging should be uploaded relative to target investigation."

CO answers, "Upload from tech support verified, advise if 10-12 is needed."

Nave catches up to the Dodge. The driver slowly eases the truck to the grassy patch just off the road. Nave also slows and as he nears the stopped truck, a man steps out of the truck. He is an older man with thick, dark hair. There is concern in his light brown eyes as he walks to the rear of his Dodge. He looks in Nave's direction, looks at the rear of his truck, and then stands at his tailgate. Nave comes to rest in the soft, damp soil.

He approaches the man, who is standing fifteen feet apart from Nave. Nave directs, "You have one chance to explain why you were at the falls, and who you picked up." As the man begins to answer, the driver's side rear window drops, and a dark-haired child with long hair peaks her head out.

Simultaneously, the CO advises, "NES 19-12, photo recognition scan is negative. Repeat, XRAY, negative target match, XRAY."

The man looks back and says, "Sweat Pea, roll the winda up. Papa will be back in a second." He looks back to Nave and asks, "Hey buddy, noticed you were looking like you wanted to catch up to me, and I was wondering what the hell was wrong with my truck. Now you carry on asking strange questions, and frankly none ya biness what I may be doing."

Nave politely answers, "I didn't mean to alarm you— unintended. We had a report of a truck matching yours that is suspected to be following young girls. Our task force was dispatched as someone alerted of the match. I saw you help the two in your truck, and here we are."

The man leans back to his truck, folds his arms and shakes his head until his eyes look to his boots. He raises and extends his right hand.

He tells Nave, "Those two girls are my only granddaughters. I live two houses up, and I never let them out of my sight when they come and visit Papa. My daughter lives down in Salem. We just had lunch in the cafe, there at the falls. She had to head back today. I tell ya now, it sickens me that guys like you have to be out here watching over the decay of these perverts. I am just grateful you are doing what you do." He shakes Nave's hand, and Nave tells him to go enjoy the time with his girls. Nave turns and goes his way, and the older man stops to make a funny face in the window at his granddaughters, likely to comfort them in the erratic situation.

Far away, a similar black Dodge is parked in long driveway of a home in an elite, gated community. Inside the sprawling home, two men sit in a billiard room discussing the flavor of the imported cigars they hold. They puff their cigars, and then gaze at them. The older of the two men does the majority of the talking. He is average height, wiry, has rows of hair plugs, stretched facial skin darkened by UV lamps, and an open collar of his trendy shirt struggles to cover his girth. His faded jeans likely cost a few hundred dollars. The other man has thick, dark hair, a simple tee shirt, and black pants. His goatee is sharp-edged, and he holds a pool stick in one hand and his cigar in the other.

The heavier man puffs another drag and through the expelled smoke he asks, "Tell me, do we need to switch up the process, or are we still okay? I see this shit on TV how these task operations are poking around more and more."

The Dodge dually with no license plate is Kaleb Pond's. Kaleb walks over to a bar chair.

He sits, pours a drink, and asks the man, "Alex, can you follow through on your end? After all, you are the one who has the inside connections. You know when these fucks are requesting your department's police support. See, how I figure, you are at the top. As long as you can be sure your guys stay in the dark and you keep my doors open, well you will continue to have first pick. Top pick, just like what is waiting in your room now."

The heavy man, Alex, chuckles; his brows furrow demonically inward, and in his perverted tone exclaims, "Ah, me do likie the Ching Chongs from da Hong Kong. They know how to lovie me so long long, and play with daddy's dingy dong."

Kaleb laughs as he says, "You crooked, sick fuck; I love doing business with you! Listen, I have been thinking to actually give Multnomah a rest, and look into the outlet malls down I-5, especially since we are doing more business with Orientals. Ha, everyone knows all they do is shop and take fuckin' pictures. Hell, I see them slant-eyed bastards taking pictures of shopping. So anyhow, I figure we can play that side safe when we know our stock is coming in I will have them on a shopping shuttle. The location is ideal—either a smooth jaunt down I-5, or the many routes through Portland."

Alex asks if there have been any more developments on the underground strip club in the Hollywood District. Kaleb advises they are only dealing with the tight parking, and how they will keep it low-key for the neighborhood. Then the man advises, "KP (Kaleb Ponds), for twelve years I have known two of my best. They started as lousy pedal bike cops along the steel bridge. There was some shit that happened with a homeless bitch, and they were all but going down. I stepped in and, well let's say she decided her story wasn't actually so accurate. Since then, those two have been in my back pocket." Alex stands up, walks over to the bar, and from behind the bar leans over and tells Kaleb, "Hell, don't take this the wrong way, but Fabian was a little skittish. I worried about him, and in my office I laid it out. I told that foreign pecker for me to trust him and know he wasn't going to turn, he would have to, let's say, bow and prove himself."

Kaleb looks shocked, and states, "No way that guy did not suck your dick!"

Alex leans back, says, "Damned if he didn't. Finished it off too. Don't believe me? For my assurance, got it on tape."

Kaleb taps the pool cue toward him saying, "Homo fuck, you better not be checking out my ass."

Alex replies, "KP, why would I want your old ass? If I want ass, it's going to be one of those tight Hispanic boys you bring form Mexico."

The men continue discussing how his two guys will be assigned to the Hollywood patrol. Alex encourages Kaleb to put things in place for the underground private strip club. The talk about the surrounding area will accommodate good cover housing for some of the girls and boys. They note that the clientele in this area have an increasing appetite for young boys. The closeted gay community is a huge profit for their operation. The two continue to drink and smoke. The day passes, and eventually Kaleb tells Alex, he has to hurry down to Redding, California.

Alex asks how Redding is working and Kaleb explains, "Redding is working really good. Hell, San Fran is so cluttered with people and the Asian presence is ridiculous. No question with them being shuttled to Redding. I just make sure the right people are in Redding, and at the right time. Then follow the bus back to here. I think we are pretty low-key. Shit, we are only doing maybe four a month out of there. Then the two or three from Mexico and South America."

Alex looks serious and says, "KP, that is our golden ticket there. Do you realize it costs me and my partners quite a bit to house, feed, and dress these girls? The boys you get from down there are simple turnover. The last one brought forty Gs. And we are free and clear. Out of our hands. Now, I know you stress on those because you have to escort them most of the way. But look, we have you covered. Inside track, baby. There are too many, let's say special clients, who have a lot of clout. Good to be dirty, and I have the bucket of dirt on most of them."

Nave reaches the downtown area of Portland. Nothing he seeks will be found from the dry comfort of his truck. He parks the truck off the main road before taking to the streets. A wet, uneven, and cracked sidewalk has discarded coffee cups, empty cigarette packages, very small Ziploc-type baggies with white residue, and multiple heaps of wet blankets which cover the sleeping bodies. Those who are coherent enough are quick to beg for change, cigarettes, or drugs from the walking. The effect of addiction has turned the begging to a lethargic lifting of a cardboard sign—many not even able or willing to voice a plea for the handouts they seek. Vacant buildings rest where hope once welcomed new customers. Some perhaps moved as the homeless and drugs took over. With limited resources and tied hands, law enforcement along with regulatory government has little control over the homeless. Across the street is a bright new sign, all in a neon glow of red. Unlike the dark, dirty path of this walk, the business there has clear, cleaned glass. There is fresh paint and artistic window art that invite customers in. Although the glass is clean and clear, all one will see four feet past the glass is a wall. More decor stapled to the wall shows why that new, glowing neon sign doesn't have to say anything in detail. It is as easily recognized as a child looking at a golden yellow arch of the letter M. This simplistic, bright XXX illustrates a much different play place. Upon the door is a small plaque with the etched warning that no person under the age of eighteen will be permitted beyond the first counter, and that proper identification must be given before entry. Unfortunately, this is a starting point for which Nave may find a path toward Ghost. The steel door opens, and the cowbells clang against the glass and steel doorframe. Behind an elevated counter, is a young person. If it were not for the fact that this person is wearing a bra, and only a bra up top, one might have difficulty accurately deciding a gender. The voice supports the assumption she is female much better than what the bra supports. Ink crawls across the girl's chest, arms, neck, and belly. Steel gages the size of a half dollars was ribboned of her earlobe. Tiny, dark steel studs line her bottom lip. Her eyes are intentionally lined and painted a dark black, and false contact lenses look like vertical goat eyes definitely procuring her any attention she may seek. She sets her phone down and with a smile asks, "Hey sugar, can I see ID?"

Nave hands her an ID with his photo, yet it states his name as John Pardy.

The girl is very polite and happy as she smiles and asks, "Well Mr. Pardy, I kinda wish I had that name. Cause, well I like to party. So have you been to this shop before?" Nave just shakes his head in a side to side indicating he has not.

She tells him how the shop works. "See, this is the normal gift shop area. No cost to shop. Buy all the fun stuff you wanna play with Pardy man. Now if you want to use the glory hole area, it is four dollars to enter. We don't guarantee anyone will be there, and if you go in, there aren't any refunds. The back is the theater. That is six dollars for two hours, or you can pay twelve dollars for a twenty-four-hour period. You don't look homeless but we always tell people, there isn't any sleeping in any section of this shop. Rules for the glory holes are posted, and any questions you can always come to me." Nave asks if the theater is open or if it is private stalls. He also enquires if there are any private, live shows. She tells him, "No private shows, Mr. Pardy. I know those are fun, hell I used to do some, but it has gotten crazy. So we went strictly to an open theater and glory holes. And let me tell you, absolutely no solicitation or underage stuff. We are more than willing to call authorities if we suspect anyone is underage. Not our thing here. That crap is down the road. Well, as long as they last before getting busted."

Nave assures her he is not seeking anything such as what she mentioned. He says he was looking more for clothes that you don't really find in a regular department store. Off her perch, she steps down. Now seeing the rest of her, he notices she either was running very late for work, or the comfort of a bra and panties is her preferred work uniform. After a few minutes looking over clothes, he has zero intent to purchase; he excuses himself, and continues down the sidewalk. Live, alternative music is heard coming from a club a few doors down. He stops to listen and sees a collage of young partiers enjoying friends, drinks, and their local talent. Several clubs he passes are busy with people meeting, dancing, and drinking, and many have a live band to bring that unique energy vibe that sparks people's happiness. Along one club's rear patio is a swinging back door. He opens it, and sees a dark stairwell that drops to a single door. The door is hard to see, yet near the bottom of the door is a thin, straight line of light. The crowd of locals pays little attention to him, and he closes the swinging back door. The band's riffs continue on from inside and Nave steps down to the single door. Unseen from the top of the stairs, is a symbol. It looks like a triangle, or perhaps a pie or pizza shape. The point is up yet the bottom of the shape is slightly curved and thicker, almost like a crust shape. The symbol is directly in the center of the door. He tries the handle, and it is locked. The music of the band above is faint, which allows him to listen to the room behind the door. He struggles to hear the voices that seem to be moving around. He does hear a short part of a woman's voice. Nave believes it to have said, "Take this card to room six." Nave then hears what sounds like a chair being pushed in or pulled out. He hears the woman again, "Take this card." After that, a door up the steps opens, and more live music carries down the stairs. He walks up the steps, and notices two men standing at the top. One closes the swinging gate, while the other stands with his arms folded over the tight black shirt he intentionally bought one size too small. Three steps before the top, Nave hears the closer one tell the other to make sure the door stays closed, and to watch for anyone coming out. He positions himself to block the top of these steps as he looks down to Nave.

He snidely states, "My friend, you went down the wrong steps. I know you don't belong there because those are my steps. And your happy ass didn't come to me to receive my authority to be down there. Now you are going to take a walk with me to the office because I need to know what the hell you were doing on my steps. Those steps. My steps. My fucking steps and your fucking ass I don't know."

The guy looks over his right shoulder and tells the other guy, "Ain't had to work someone over in a long-ass time. How bout you? You think we might need a little practice? This guy might give us some fight."

He looks back down at Nave and in a cocky dance of his head he says, "So whatcha think my friend? You want the easy route, or want to give me and my partner some exercise tonight?" The landing at the top of the steps is only about a five-foot by four-foot pad. Both men are close, and with the swinging door closed there is not room to get around the men. The steps behind Nave are about twelve feet down. The closer of the men, who blocks the top step, turns to say something to his partner. Nave's eye level is in line with the guy's crotch. Before turning back, Nave's open right hand delivers a solid, cupped, blow to his crotch. Then his left hand grabs the guy's belt area. He slams the guy to the left wall, as he picks him up from his suffering scrotum. Nave launches the man headfirst to where he lands at the base of the steps below.

The second guys moves forward and as he tells Nave, "I'm gonna fuck . . ." Nave clenches the man's lower pant legs, and pulls them quickly forward causing the man to hit hard on the concrete landing. Nave takes one leg to pull the guy's body near him. With the hard part of his outer fist, Nave strikes the second guy's neck. The guy's arm drops limp, and he is unconscious. Nave takes a card out of the guy's wallet, and presses the man's fingers one by one onto the smooth face of the card. He uses a separate card to do the same with the man at the bottom of HIS steps! After sliding the limp body to the side, Nave leaves the small bar. Wanting to discover these guys' identities, Nave quickly makes his way back to his truck and leaves the area.

In the hotel, Nave places the cards on an image scanner that is in his briefcase. In minutes, tech support gives Nave illustrated information:

Identified Subject Number 1	Marcus Escobar. 33 years of age
	Registered felony sex offender
	Active federal warrant
	Deportation once captured
Identified Subject Number 2	Paul Port. 30 years of age
	Hate crimes
	Lude Act on a Child
	Prior prison term of 5 years

The file includes additional information and a photo file. What Nave seeks most is any known address. Paul Port is currently checking in with a parole officer, and Nave has a current location to visit.

Two nights later, Nave eases down a dark street with his lights out. He walks past the quiet, modest homes in the middle-class neighborhood. Finally, he sees a silver Ford Mark VIII in the driveway of the home of Paul Port. In the subject information, Nave learned this was the car registered to Port. He approaches the house on the darker side. Nave stands in the dark as he listens to what he can from the house inside. He hears Port talking, yet there is no answering voice. Nave believes Port must be on the phone. Nave maneuvers to suction an audio amplifier on a window. He hears Port advising he cannot run the private club right now.

Port speaks to whoever is on the other end of the phone. "Look, I am sorry. I know you need me at the basement club and I want to keep our guys happy, but I simply cannot not get out of bed. Fuck me, I am lucky to be alive."

(Phone pause).

"Yes, I know; we have three new girls."

(Phone pause).

"Ugh, I'm sorry, I told you that. Can't we set these guys up in a VIP at Casa? I know the girls there will at least blow them."

(Phone pause).

"Yes, Yes, Oriental, and petite. All these pedophile pricks want young Asian girls. What about having Escobar watch the door for a few days?"

(Phone pause).

"Damn, well hey let me make a few calls and I will call you back. I will make it happen one way or another." Port presses the end call button, yet still grasps the phone as he looks to the blank screen.

Port lies on his back in bed as he tries to figure out what he can do in order to meet the clients' demands at the private club. Meanwhile, Nave has found the rear door to be open. His handheld scanner shows the home to not have any alarm. He creaks the door open, and listens for Port. In a rear bedroom, Port lies in pain as the Vicodin has started to wear off. Nave no longer feels a need to be cautious and walks into the room where Port lies bandaged on his bed.

"What the fuck are you doing MOTHER fucker? You crazy fuck, bastard! Okay look, the trip down the stairs did the job. I am not looking for a fuck bit of trouble from you. Who the hell are you anyway?" Port begs. Nave is silent and walks to the foot of the bed. That cold, piercing look is directly focused on Port. Port still has his phone clenched, and fumbles to swipe his unlock.

Nave stands still and says, "Paul, if you dial 911, I will take your phone and force it through your eye socket." Port opens his hand very slowly, and allows it to fall onto the floor below.

"Damn guy, what is the deal? Hey if we took your girls or clients, I am sorry. Didn't know. You just tell me what you want. We can work this shit out. The main guys have the cash. Name it. We can talk to him, and squash this." Nave finds a chair and sits next to Paul Port.

Sitting relaxed, both feet flat on the floor, his back resting into the chair, and his arms folded, Nave tells Port, "What I want are names. I want the names of who you work for, who are bringing you the girls, where they are from, and how you get them."

Ports rolls his head back on a pillow and explains, "Man, I don't know that shit. I work the club. I am a worker. I simply check IDs. I don't know the clients. I never talk to the main guy. I don't even have his number. I go to the club and work."

Nave unfolds his arms, leans forward, rests his elbows on his legs, and tells Port, "You are going to be in a lot of pain real soon. See, for many years in special operations, I was extensively trained in how to inflict some of the worst pain to a person. Have you ever known someone to remove one eye from a person's socket, and then show them their own eye looking back at them? Now we can skip the prolonged pain, and end all this much quicker. That is your part to decide." Port begins to sweat. He can't move very easily, yet squirms in the bed. He pleads with Nave, and tells him that he doesn't know anything; he sniffles his case as to why Nave should not hurt him. Nave explains; "I am not sure yet how long you have been involved with this operation. I am guessing ever since you paroled out. What I do know is, you are completely aware of what it is you are doing."

Port, now weeping says, "I never touched any of those girls. Fuck dude, I just work for the guy. I never even see the girls really."

Nave continues, "Paul, you have an illness and there just is no way to trust you will stop. You know when I leave here, you won't see another day. That is just what needs to be done. You know everyone, all the kids, will be safer if we just terminate this life for you."

A blinkless, sweating gaze of disbelief is the only expression the man can show. He can't speak. His mouth is plaster-like dry. Nave gives him water and tells him, "I want to know who. You have this last moment in your life to do something right. Look back. Look at each time you opened a door and saw the frightened look of a child's face, yet only saw a dollar. Know your perverted and sick tendencies will finally rest. Most of all, think of how your departure will rid you of the guilt you suffer each day; yet you can't stop what you do. I am here to help. I am going to do what you have so many times wished you could do yourself. I will not fail as you have. Paul. Many times you wished you could go to sleep, and not return. Now you will."

Port has that look of a defeated opponent gazing at the game clock, as the reality sets in, knowing time will soon expire and the game will end.

With a stream of tears and a guilty resistance to look at Nave, Port quietly confesses, "You are right. I should end it. Should have before prison. Before the ones I abused. I'm sick. Fuck man, I am fucking sick. I can't help it. I wanted to, but it comes back. And comes back and fuckin' comes creeping back into my head." Port asks for a pen. He writes three, double-digit numbers down on a piece of paper. "That's the combination. The safe is in the closet. In there is a thumb drive. Page thirteen. Thirteen is what you wanna pay attention to. He is not the top, but he is who is making a lot of this possible. You won't touch him though. He is connected, and he is pretty high up in the police department.

Nave leaves the home. Port will lie still for a few hours as his pain eases. He will eventually feel heavy-eyed, and the eternity of sleep will begin.

Slow turning of a knob, and each notch makes a distinctive sound of a safe combination. He rotates the knob first to the right. Tick, tick, tick, tick, tick . . . tick, tick, tick, tick . . . tick . . . tick . . . tick.. Then the ticking of the rotation to the left, until he then turns it back to the right. A small, shiny silver handle to the right of the knob is turned, and the small safe opens. Two gold watches lay flat, a black velvet sack is cinched by a braid, a neatly bundled stack of one-hundred-dollar bills, and one thumb drive are safely kept inside. Nave removes the contents, and departs the home. He quickly returns to his hotel, and uses a separate computer for the foreign thumb drive. The file takes time to load as the percentage bar slowly progresses from the left side to the right. It reaches the end, and Nave clicks, OPEN. Several pages of client information, underground locations, suppliers, drivers, guards, and government officials linked to this human trafficking operation are on the drive. A few pages in, there is a spreadsheet. In a tier-level and dropdown graph; it shows a chain of command. The top name is, "The Man." A drop-direction graph lists several names as financial supporters. Another line off of "The Man" is a list, "protective service." The last line list is for safe host locations. In the box for "The Man," is an icon that can be clicked to open for further detail. Nave rolls the mouse over the icon and opens the additional window.

There to the left of the page, is a man in a suit and tie. The dark suit opens up to expose a crisp white shirt, and a dark tie which is slightly covered by a lanyard-attached badge. Behind the man in the photo, is the traditional United States flag to one side and the State flag to the other. The top right of the page is headed by, "THE MAN." Under this, it lists his level as Captain of the sex crimes division. It continues in line by line listing his name, Alex Loftski, his address, secondary residence, known numbers, vehicles, associates, memberships, and presumed weapons. Nave can see this is information which Port kept as security, and is not likely known by any others. He closes this window, and reviews the others listed in the protective service. There, he discovers many different members of government, investigations, and law enforcement which all are in the loop on this operation. It can be assumed many may be lured in my money, then once exposed, unable to depart for fear of deadly consequences. This verified as two listed names were in a grey shadowed box. Nave clicks to open these boxes. Both names are officers who had been killed in the line of duty. One was responding to a domestic dispute, and both the officer and subject were found with gunshot wounds. The other was shot while conducting a traffic stop on a dark road off his normal patrol territory. He spends the evening reviewing each detail. He looks over the members, the locations, and the routes. He duplicates the thumb drive on a secured device, and calls Robert.

Robert immediately answers, "Nave, I'm here with the judge. We just received the download. You just uncovered a den of rattlesnakes it appears."

Nave says, "I don't believe Ghost will be departing any time soon. This operation has become very comfortable and as you can see by the file, they are expecting a new safe house to open very soon. Here is something you may think is crazy."

The judge speaks up, "Nave, is anything you do not a little crazy?"

Nave continues to tell them, "Judge, Robert, I want you to put a bug in Morrow's ear. There is a direction this has to play out. You trust my judgment, and you will have the outcome on Ghost. Your client wants this bastard eliminated by any means, and the gap is getting much narrower."

"Nave! You don't want any more attention around you than what is already there. This Morrow guy wants your ass," Robert states.

Nave is calm. He is deliberate and tells the men, "Morrow wants answers, he wants to know, and most of all he wants recognition for what he has been chasing. Morrow is quite easy to figure; just make sure he has a reason to be in Portland."

FBI Agent Dominic Lopez is looking over an anonymous email, as he sits at his desk the first thing in the morning. He mumbles to himself, "Portland . . . task force . . . underground houses, yada, yada, yada . . . high-level child sex offender says being followed . . . . holy crap. Shit! Morrow, Morrow, I have to call Morrow!"

Morrow is in his office looking over an unrelated case file when his cell phone vibrates in his deep grey slacks pocket. He leans back, and stretches his leg so he can reach easily in to retrieve the phone. Still vibrating, he sees it is Lopez.

He answers to barely say hey, when Lopez starts right in, "Portland, fuckin' Oregon, bro! I need you to get your happy black ass on a plane ASAP, and go check out what the hell is going down."

Morrow is confused and asks, "Whoa man, what the hell? You have to give me some 411 on what the hell you spittin'. What the hell got you all jumpin'?"

Lopez tells him, "I just got this email. Inside shit with some legit info on a child sex offender that is in the Portland area. Whoever sent the email is internal because it came coded and protected. There is a task force working several leads, and they have already been notified you will be visiting yet not interfering with their deal. This task force is after the offenders, and fully aware you are mirroring them as you are investigating the other end."

Morrow expresses concern about his sergeant who wasn't so happy. Lopez advises he has already approved the trip, and Morrow can review the memo on his Lotus Notes.

The day in Portland is cool. After visiting a few jewelers, Nave walks along an empty boardwalk looking out at the echoing trains to one side, and the city skyline to the other. There is a unique collection of people in this state as the homeless don't look much different than many locals who are ragged and casual. Accustom to the every dripping precipitation, many no longer bother with umbrellas or rain gear. A way of life has taught them that the rain will always dampen the cloth, and the cloth will always dry. To defeat either is futile, and effort should not be wasted. The water of the inlet has demanded this to be a city connected by many bridges. Some are towering and others are mechanical built to rise when the ships request passage. Below him on this river, he pauses to watch an activity he realizes he has never done, yet always had an interest in. Four long, narrow boats skim swiftly along the water. One team member sits barking encouraging orders to the others rowing. Sequential slaps of paddles and smooth motion of bodies take a craft, which has been meticulously built to offer the least friction and brilliant speed. The boats glide away, and he continues his meditational walk before he must visit the shadows once more in the humid night just outside the city.

The architectural canopy spans high above the passenger pickup as Morrow awaits a member of the Portland task force. A white plain Crown Victoria pulls near, and Morrow slides his small travel bag in the rear seat. A woman in cutoff shorts with a loose, low, and very thin blouse that hides little, sits behind the wheel.

She immediately excuses her appearance, "No comments on my fancy outfit, mister. I had to come grab you on last-minute notice, and in the middle of a street walk sting. I didn't grab my coat, and so here I am. Besides, my shit looks hot anyway, right? I am Layna" She laughs and Morrow just shakes his head. The woman is approximately five three, and may easily hit one hundred and ninety-five pounds. One may think it would be impossible for her to be a decoy in a prostitution sting, yet the desperate men trolling for women along the curb often seek the easily obtainable. High-end escorts are far to cunning, and will dedicate their time to a hotel bar. The clientele they seek have available funds to demand a classy facade.

The car drives away, and on the radio is the local news. After advising the obvious of the weather, the evening reporter leads in with an opening story. "Tonight we are just learning of an anonymous donation made to the local children's center here in the inner city. This foundation is most respectively known for the help it offers for abused children, and the center, being a non-profit charity, often relies on donations such as this one. The spokesperson for the center advised the donation was in cash, and there is no mention of who gave this nearly . . . wow get this . . . nearly $75,000 to be used for the children. The spokesperson did advise that a note had one request—that the center have a huge chalk-and-dry erase board to encourage the children to do art."

Another co-reporter offers her insight. "I guess we might believe the donation may have come from a local artist; whoever gave so generously, it is good to have this story to show our community."

Layna talks about the donation, and expresses how their team often does visits and fundraisers for the same center. She tells Morrow how the investigation they are involved in now just sickens her, and she isn't sure how much longer she can remain in the task force. The emotional drain of such a crime has worn on her, and she expresses being a mother makes it even harder. Layna tightly grips the steering wheel as she tells Morrow, "The hardest part is when we find one of these sick bastards, we have to treat them with professional courtesy, we have to follow the rules, we have to bite our tongue and let me tell you . . . not one of us would like anything more than to just cut those fuckers' dicks right off."

Morrow looks to her and says, "Well you and I know, we took an oath to be righteous. See, a tiny part of our brain is what some refer to as our 'gut' feeling. We react and want to punish immediately and that 'gut' feeling tells us it's right—that in some way we are making it better for the victims. However, we are the law. We represent what the legal system has put in place for reasons of justice."

Layna looks to him and says, "Our system is a fucking joke. Too many get off and we keep having to pick up the same trash over and over while the innocent suffer. I just hope we find the link. Shut it down completely."

On the other side of town, the gated community is secured from unknown vehicles passing through the entrance, as well as the rear exit of the upscale neighborhood. A premium each homeowner takes pride to brag for their elitist persona. Lush landscapes of natural trees and hillsides border each home in their unique lots. Trickling waterfalls, walking trails, and equestrian grounds offer this area a prestigious appeal. It also offers Nave an easy way to scale the grounds, and remain elusive. Cameras and detection devices are to be expected. Having calculated the grounds in several different formats gained by his GPS views and research, he has optional ways to comb the neighborhood where the captain lives. Down a slick hill, he reaches the edge of this neighborhood not long before the first bark of a nearby dog that runs free on a screened porch. Nave in the tree line, and remains still as the rear lights come on. Typical of a homeowner to reluctantly peek and when nothing jumps directly in his path, he dismisses the bark and returns as he has no intent to wander the shadows, which the light does not reach. Careful steps and patient, Nave soon sits watching the home of the captain. Few lights illuminate inside. The backyard patio is decoratively lined with running lights. An enclosed Jacuzzi gazebo hums of the jetted tub and heater. The stone walk leads perfectly to the side, rear door. Wet footprints remain, yet it is unclear if they have returned to the tub. One corner of this property is secluded, and has no view of any other home. Against the night, he is unseen.

The sound of a door opens and then shuts. The robust man covered in a black heavy robe walks toward the gazebo. Happy and slightly drunk, he sings to himself. He shuffles, side steps, swirls his drink, and after a sip he performs a full twirl as his jingle continues. The gazebo is an octagon shape, and every other panel is of decorated slat wood. The open areas are tinted glass. He opens the door and can be heard saying, "DADA back my baby chicks, chirpy, chirpy." The door closes, and no more is heard.

The captain's girth rumbles with the jets of the tub. The two foreign children sit across scared and ignorant of English. Forced to drink the whiskey, the two quickly cough. The captain laughs, and encourages another drink. The over-tanned, naked, shaved body of the man leans toward the children. Though the tinted panes of glass, the yard lights glow. The jets of the Jacuzzi stop. The lights in the yard are now dark. The heater motor stops running, and the few lights in the house are extinguished.

His drunken humor continues, "Hold on to DADA drink. Damn breaker must have tripped." One of the children holds the glass as the man exits and puts his robe back on. Through the dark house, the light of a phone is all he has to find his way. Out the front window, he looks and sees the streetlights are well-illuminated; the neighbor's drive is welcoming, as in the iron lampposts three hanging lamps shine brightly. He cautiously follows the light of his phone, and reaches the garage. The door opens, and he steps down three steps to reach the painted, concrete garage floor. There, just before lifting the light toward the box, he pauses. The large body stays still, as his head slowly turns to the left. His ears have that hazing, rapid thumping pulse of fear. Light-headed and faint, he begins to feel flush. In the dark of the garage, his mind is delayed in what his eyes try to send; that there by the garage steps is an object not previously known to have ever stood there before. The carotid artery in his neck is heavy and rapid. His head finishes the turn, and his right hand is lowered holding the phone which had timed-out the light. His eyes, nervously wide, get as much light from the thin garage door crack as they can. The phone still at his side, his shaking hand finds a way to press the button that will turn the screen back on for light. A dim, obscured light gives just enough for the man to see Nave wearing a black tight, full-face, tactical hood. Glasses block his eyes. Nave wears a form-fitted black suit tucked tightly into his boots that have been covered. The heel of Nave's right hand strikes against the captain's neck. A flash later and Nave strikes the other side of his neck. The phone lies dark on the garage floor as the man goes limp.

On the other side of town, Morrow is walking into an unscheduled briefing. The task force unit he came to meet was just contacted by a parole officer about a known sex offender, who had not checked in. Morrow and the female officer sit in the back. She excuses herself to find a coat, at the request of all others in the room.

She walks out saying, "Screw all you. Just cause you can't handle all this love, don't have to get rude, plus I'm taken anyway so none ya get this anyway."

The parole officer addresses the unit, "Today at approximately 16:45 hours, myself and a deputy arrived at Mr. Paul Port's home. This, after receiving information from the hospital that he had sustained some major injuries. Mr. Port, I am sure, is a familiar name around here as he is on your watch list. He had not been out of prison but two years after the incident at the daycare his crackhead girlfriend was running over in Oregon City. The ER staff stated he claimed he had slipped and fallen down the stairs, yet medical records show impact to his head, a broken clavicle, and one hand with a compound fracture. Staff believes, and I agree, he was dropped or tossed on the ground. He was released in fair condition and while badly injured, nothing was life-threatening. My son works the ER room, and notified me of the situation. When I arrived with the deputy for a well-being check, Mr. Port was found in his bed no longer living.

Not too heartbroken will any of us be. What is the reason for this briefing? Port had a cell phone that was not divulged to our agency. We found this phone, and as we processed the scene; there were numerous blocked texts asking if he had the club covered. One particular incoming text indicated, and I quote, 'You son of a bitch pussy bastard. We have three high-rollers, and they want new girls. You better not fuck this up.' That was the last text. We don't think the same person offed Port just due to the fact that the texts were incoming as we were there. Port was recently deceased. Our tech guys are trying to trace and locate the origin of the text, but so far they have been scrambled. We did discover one address that has been listed for sale. The owner has yet to be found. Your packets have the information, and the lieutenant is already organizing a plan. A search warrant is being carried to the judge now, and as soon as everything is in place, we are going to converge on the location. Let me be clear, NO ACTIVITY near the location until we obtain the warrant. We have even notified dispatch to keep all units clear."

Morrow is soaking all this in, and at the same time texting Holcomb. He isn't trying to get Holcomb to come—just sharing the event. Holcomb sends encouraging words to support Morrow in his work.

In a dark garage, a steering wheel is gripped tightly, and unwillingly by the open mouth of the captain. His feet are tied and taped to the brake pedal. The man's hands are bound behind his naked body. Unable to move his head, directly before his weeping eyes are the photos he collected of the foreign children he once photographed. Nave sits behind him. Captain Alex Loftski gags, and tries to jerk away from having his mouth pressed over the steering wheel.

Nave tells him, "You know by now, I am not here to arrest you. I am not calling anyone to take you in. I want to know where I can find Kaleb Ponds. Alex, you know where he is, and that is who I want. I am not a man who is going to sit in your garage all night. There is one, just one chance for you to tell me how to find Kaleb Ponds. If you do tell me what I need and I feel you are being honest, well you will simply fall asleep like Paul did."

Just then the captain's phone begins to buzz. Nave looks and sees the incoming text is simple, ***911*** ***ORCA*** Again it shows, ***911*** ***ORCA***

Nave looks and tells the captain, "Look there, 911 ORCA. See, on that thumb drive, that is your emergency code to dispatch your guys because there is a call or someone getting ready to raid one of your outfits. Doesn't look like you are going to make the call for this one."

Alex Loftski jolts back and forth, grunting, as he rocks the car with his teeth grinding deeper into the leather, double-stitched wheel of his Cadillac. Nave convinces him to calm down, and Nave slices one side of the tape away.

Loftski asks, Who are you? Do you realize who the fuck I am? Buddy, you really fucked up!"

Nave replies, "I know everything about you. Paul had a very helpful download, and it was very informative of how well you trusted him. I have also researched all your guys on the inside. It is all over, but I still need Ponds. Or KP as you know him, right Alex?"

Alex Loftski demands to have the tape off his eyes so he can see the man who is doing this to him. Nave advises that he saw enough when he turned around. Nave directs, "Now you realize, I know who you are, I know who you work for, I know you are in no position to demand anything. Where is Kaleb Ponds?"

The captain says, "I am not tellin' you a fuc . . ."

Before he finishes, Nave presses his head forward, and tapes the captain's head back to the wheel. He pleads to be released, and then feels a needle pierce his neck.

"You had the option to tell me, and you did not. I do not give second chances. Now you will feel an incredible amount of pain. In testing, it was advised that this is just a little more potent than the venom of an inland taipan snake. As the exhaust will fill the tight seal of this Caddi, you can be assured you will eventually fail to the poison of carbon monoxide. Before that moment, your nervous system is going to take you through a brief preview of the hell you will finally reach. Your body will tighten to a point where you may even fracture your own bones. The jaw that should have told me what I asked for, will press so vigorously into that nice steering wheel, you will easily crush your bleached teeth. As you profusely sweat, your heart will nearly explode. Hell it might, given the poor health you are in and the erectile pills you already swallowed earlier. One of the first things that will likely happen is you are going to erupt in a fecal mess, which you cannot avoid. The good part is, you will not have to wonder why. See there on your dash? Just look there and you will know."

The injection is rapid, and Nave advises he has to depart before it gets messy. The captain has already started clenching the wheel with his teeth. His muscles twitch and tighten. Nave closes the car door, and in the dark garage the motor runs smoothly. He steps through the house, and brings a blanket to the girls still sitting in the calm, warm Jacuzzi. He places them in a room, and motions for them to stay put. A quick departure over the hill, and he is soon in his truck and on his way back to his hotel.

Back in the police briefing, the unit puts a plan in place and unknowingly has one officer who is in with Alex Loftski. He remains quiet as the rest of the unit preps local units, child services, translators, medical, and foreign affairs. The chief has been called in, and will address the press if needed. This is a big step for this task force, yet there is only one underground operation that will likely yield a few arrests and victims. Still, it is an encouraging direction after months of leads turned up empty. This, as they have no clue the operations are being tipped from within. The officer steps out, and texts the other, who is inside the operation. Neither has any idea where the captain is, and why he hasn't answered. They are sure he is aware, and likely cleared the club.

The chief pulls the lieutenant aside and asks, "We are keeping this quiet, but where the hell is Loftski? Not a word, not returning calls. I know he advised he was taking off tonight and not to call, but he knows goddamned well when this sort of crap goes down, you get your ass in. That worthless piece of shit better be passed out, drunk, or dead."

The lieutenant assures they can handle it better without him and confesses, "To be forthright Chief, he hasn't been involved much anyhow. He says he is trusting we are taking care of it and if you ask me, well . . . he may have some issues you may want to check into."

The chief looks irritated and angered. He assures the lieutenant this matter will be handled, and the captain may be taking a little break very soon. As they discuss the captain, the unit is notified that they have the search warrant.

The dark, narrow street has the usual local crowd mingling and playing music. One UC car drives unnoticed to see how the address appears. The task force unit is aware that this is known to be an abandoned building, yet power service advised regular readings at the location. This is indicative of some type of activity or residence. The support vans are in place, and the team meets a few blocks down. Each person has precise tasks to perform, and orders on how to proceed. There is one officer who still believes that they will arrive and as usual, find the place to be empty. It has been the norm for the captain to have inside knowledge, and clear out well before anyone discovers him.

Lead cars are dark, and roll down the street. Swiftly, each unit follows and soon eight officers blast through the small bar, through the back, and Escobar makes a weak attempt to block the path. Escobar is immediately escorted aggressively to the ground, and placed in cuffs. Four other officers secure the private ally entrance used primarily by the underground club members. The slim stairs end at the door with the pie-shaped logo. There is one rear exit that was previously noticed to be blocked off. Still, two officers stand watch. A pounding on the door and an announcement, "Search warrant is in effect! All occupants remain in the building and comply. Search warrant is in effect. All occupants remain in the building and comply with law enforcement immediately."

The steel door opens out, and officers stand clear. They can hear people inside asking where the back door is. The unit lead uses an extraction tool, and breaks the door lock. The door is opened, and the interior of this makeshift sex club is exposed.

As expected, the neighboring club has built a crowd looking on. The club is dimly lit; there is a common area where two men sit casually with their legs crossed over their knees as they drink and smoke. Officers instruct the men to stand against the wall, yet the one advises he is an attorney and knows his rights. This man is then removed from his place of comfort, placed face down on the tile floor, and handcuffed. The second man agrees to stand and turn around. While this takes place, other officers quickly cover the club. Past the common lounge is one dedicated hall with bare cream walls, and four red doors. As the officers breach the doors, each room exposes a middle-aged man scrambling to collect his belongings and clothes. The men are all gathered in the common lounge, and yet there is no sign of anyone in charge. The girls are gathered safely in a separate room, and the unit clears the club. The men are removed and then victim advocates accompanied by translators are allowed in. The lead officer is puzzled as there is not a sign of who runs the place. She believes they likely arrange it with Escobar, and it is all paid prior to entry. Escobar is adamant that he only watches the door. He says he doesn't know anything about the guys or girls. He attempts to get the detectives to believe he was hired only to make sure no one from the bar goes down the steps.

In a back room, a translator talks to the girls one at a time. After the translator assures them they are safe, one girl tells the translator that a bald white man is always in charge and in the club. This does not match Escobar. They are stunned as to how this man could have been tipped off and slipped out. In the common lounge, detectives take pictures and collect evidence. The girls are escorted through the hall, out the door, and just as they reach the top of the steps, one girl pushes her way back down the steps. The translator calls out to her, yet she keeps going. A detective grabs her, and she fights. She kicks, and points to the inside. The language barrier makes the chaos difficult.

The translator reaches the girl who is repetitively saying, "Bald man in the floor, bald man in floor!" Looking surprised, the detective loosens her and the girl stands near the lounge pointing to an area just behind the bar. The detectives draw guns, and order the man out. Noting happens and they repeat the order. Still the floor lay flat. They are unsure of what the girl says; the floor seems to be level, and no sign of how to lift the floor. They call for the dog. A handler is tugged behind a thick black and tan German Shepard. Once across the floor, the teeth of this remarkable dog snarl at the floor. Scratching and pouncing, the dog has no doubt there is something under the floor. The lead female officer believes it could be a push-type latch that releases. She walks over bravely, and steps on one side. The floor sinks and pops up. The dog goes in after the man. Screaming, he now wishes to comply and begs for the dog to be called off.

As he is being walked to a medic, the first news van has arrived. The chief has prepared for this and offers a preliminary release.

"First; I want to advise our department, with the assistance of several agencies, we are still conducting an investigation of illegal activity involving a private, unregistered club. It should be noted at this time that the neighboring bars and businesses are not in question and should be treated with respect. Now, earlier today we received a credible tip that this location was possibly being used illegally in the trafficking and harboring of underage individuals. Our department obtained a warrant which our task force team executed. This did expose what we believe will be discovered as an accurate tip. Protective services safely removed occupants from this location and none of the victims were harmed. We have detained several individuals found to be willfully inside the club, and they are being questioned at the department. That is all we have available at this time, and more will be released as this unfolds. I do want to give a tremendous amount of credit to the officers involved. They are responsible for bringing this criminally run club to an end. We fear there may be more, and we ask the community to be aware and report any suspicious situation immediately."

The chief meets with the lieutenant at his car, and advises if Loftski is not heard from by morning, then the lieutenant is to personally go drag him in to the station. Morrow is with the lieutenant and inquires more about Paul Port. Morrow is determined to know exactly how Port died, and the lieutenant says they will have to wait for the coroner to do a full autopsy before knowing 100 percent.

The lieutenant looks to Morrow and asks, "Tell me, you seem to have a bigger concern for how this Port douchebag died than anything. What exactly is your business here? Why is the FBI poking around on this case?" Morrow tells him that he has a strong feeling when the autopsy comes back that Port will have an unknown trace of a foreign chemical in his blood.

He tells the lieutenant, "Port was no accident, and let me tell you now, there is more to come. Someone is in town, and he has a very unique way of eliminating his targets. Believe me, we have watched this for years. It is actually pretty goddamned amazing how good this guy is. Get ready lieutenant, you are about to see some very creative work in your city."

The lieutenant looks to Morrow and says, "Agent Morrow, don't think for a second that the FBI is going to waltz in here and take over this operation. Furthermore, you guys best not get in the way. Besides, if some lunatic is running around knocking off these sick fucks, well I may see if I can put him on the payroll. God knows we aren't doing very well at stopping them!"

It's nine a.m. the next morning; Morrow is waiting in the lieutenant's office. As the lieutenant comes in Morrow has coffee waiting, and offers a new start. "Lieutenant, I am in no way wanting to interfere with what you guys have going on here. Listen, for years our own team has accumulated a solid amount of evidence that there is either a team, or one very talented person hunting down these types of sex offenders."

The lieutenant interrupts, "Okay, you are saying the FBI believes someone is tracking down sex offenders and killing them?"

Morrow explains, "Not just any sex offenders. Our data show most, not all, but most are ones who are high-profile victims, and the perp has either gotten off on a technicality, or possibly awaiting trial. I'm only here to poke around, shadow your unit, and see if anything strange pops up. In a few days, I will be gone. Just like your guy on the cold steel table. That is very similar to how precise this operation is. He is here, count on it."

The lieutenant sits down, and his office phone rings. He only listens and acknowledges with a, "Yes Sir." He stands back up and says, "Well if you want to get more answers, you can come with me. I have to go figure out why the captain isn't answering his phone, and escort his worthless ass back in here to have a nice, private conversation with the chief."

They drive down a crowded one-way street dodging delivery trucks parked in the right and left lanes, and bicyclists as they frequently tap their brakes and weave in and out of traffic.

Morrow finally asks, "It's winter. What the hell is with all the damned bikes? These peddling fools don't even watch where they are going."

The lieutenant just shakes his head and says, "You know, I have been here for over fifteen years. It's only gotten worse. Hell, some have gotten so fed up with it lately, on the news I saw a guy take one of those orange traffic cones, and as one of the bikes whipped down, he hauled off and smacked the dude right in the mouth. Guy on the bike lost some teeth. I tell you, in some areas it is hard to even drive."

They finally reach the gated community and as the lieutenant punches in the code to get in. Morrow comments, "Looks like captains here in Portland do pretty good for themselves."

The lieutenant looks and replies, "Wait until you see this guy's house. He says it was a gift from his family. One hell of a gift if you ask me."

The car reaches the captain's drive. The house sits up at the end of the long, decorated driveway. There is a fountain lined with manicured shrubs and plants, and a wide single-level home with a four-car garage. As the lieutenant shuts off the car and steps out, he tells Morrow, "I wouldn't be surprised to find this fat bastard laying fried to death in his personal tanning bed."

Morrow is on the side closer to the garage door. He stops, walks closer to the garage door, and looks over to the lieutenant.

He says, "Sounds like the car is running." They try to look in a side garage door, but everything is dark inside. They knock on the front door. They walk around back, and knock on the back door. Several times the lieutenant tries his phone. Morrow turns the rear-side doorknob. He lets the lieutenant know it is open.

The lieutenant says, "Just remember this is a cop, and he has guns. I don't want to startle the guy and get shot." He opens the door and calls in for the captain, "Captain, bro . . . Captain, you in here? It's Lieutenant Bask. Alex, wake up. I have one person with me, don't shoot our asses." It is almost 10:30 AM, yet the inside is still a little dark. He tries the light switch and discovers it to not turn any lights on. The kitchen is the first room, and across from that is the living room. The two step into the kitchen still calling for the captain. The kitchen has a wall that separates the living room, which has openings on each side. The lieutenant walks through the kitchen, and exits the other side. Morrow continues along the hall walking across the imported stone floor. Morrow stops.

The lieutenant is passed him when Morrow says, "Lieutenant, is your captain Asian and does he have kids?"

Now standing near Morrow, the lieutenant quietly whispers, "Oh shit!" The two girls sit cuddled together in a blanket on the couch scared and only looking directly at the two men. They say nothing as their obedience has been vigorously trained into their roles in this house. Bask asks Morrow to stay with the girls as he checks the rest of the home.

Morrow stands in the hall; he clasps the back of his neck with his interlaced fingers as he tells Bask, "I would start with the garage."

Bask looks at him. Bask looks at the girls. Bask slowly rotates his head toward the hall in the direction of the garage door. He says, "You said you heard the car running." The lieutenant slowly walks to the end of the hall. He opens the door, and moments later Morrow's nostrils expand. His eyes close, and his head motions slowly side to side.

The lieutenant walks slowly back in Morrow's direction. Morrow asks, "Hose from the tailpipe?"

The lieutenant stands next to Morrow, looks at the girls and says, "I think your guy may have been here."

The lieutenant and Morrow check the rest of the house, and bring the girls to the car. Outside, the lieutenant calls CSI and advises what he has.

Morrow stands against the car and when Bask hangs up he says, "If this, in fact, was my guy, you can be pretty sure you are only going to get the evidence he wants you to have." A few minutes pass, and the two still await CSI and a patrol unit. As they do, a black Dodge races up the street. The truck nears the end of the captain's drive, and with no hesitation whips in. Bask and Morrow leave the edge of the car, and stand in the middle of the drive near the fountain. Their eyes meet Ponds's eyes. The truck stops. Silence over the low chatter of the diesel motor. Ponds studies them. They study Ponds. Morrow's right foot begins to rise and step forward, and the truck immediately retreats. Morrow runs toward the truck, which quickly reaches the street and races off. The lieutenant calmly walks over to his car. He grabs his radio, and advises units to secure the only two exits. The rear exit has a patrol unit and an unmarked Explorer SUV. The iron power-gate is closed, and the truck stops short of the gate. Officers outside of their units, and two shot guns are aimed in Ponds's direction. As he contemplates reverse once again, two patrol units arrive tightly behind his truck.

"120 to Lieutenant Bask, one white male detained, advise."

The lieutenant has the patrol unit stop at the end of the drive where he awaits. The car stops and the lieutenant leans toward the open window. Ponds does not look. Bask says, "You are going to take a ride, and have time to think about our conversation when I see you again. You better have your story straight because you are in some deep shit."

After the unit drives away with Ponds, the CSI crew fill the driveway. Yellow tape is tied by a sorrowed-looking officer. Pictures of every inch show an undisturbed home leading to a horrific scene within the garage. The breaker is turned back on to provide power and make photos technically easier; yet it is difficult in the eyes of those who once worked with and for the man bound in the car. First, the photos click one after another from outside. Through the windshield, a picture will show a tanned face in distress, sweat-soaked disheveled, fake hair, and the split gums from the bleached teeth that embedded the wheel as they pushed into the tender tissue of his mouth. The door is then opened, and one officer covers her mouth. The enclosed stench of excrement and urine escape with the heavy exhaust-filled air of the passenger compartment. One by one, the photos taped to the dash are removed and placed in an evidence baggie.

Captain Loftski is removed and cautiously placed in the van. The door is opened, and the car is covered in evidence tape and loaded on a flatbed. Passing the confused faces lined in the street, the van departs and then awaits an escort through the waiting news crews just outside the gates. Less than an hour later, Captain Loftski lies lifeless in a morgue cold storage. Two boxes down, Port lies in kind.

A steel door opens and Ponds sits calmly looking as the lieutenant walks in. "Kaleb Ponds. You are no stranger to showing up where little girls and boys are. Wow, and now you show up at my crime scene unannounced and leave the party. So tell me Kaleb, just how do you know the owner of that house?"

Kaleb stretches his arms out like he is preparing for a nap. He raises them over his head, cracks his neck each way, and leans back in his chair. He rests the back of his head onto his hands, and looks up to the ceiling as he says, "Hmmm, let me see, I pulled into a
driveway, realized I was at the wrong house, and left. You guys come chasing after me, and haul me off to this shitty place. You now come in asking me questions about shit I have no clue about, yet I don't know if I am arrested or what. I do know I have not been read any rights. I also know I do not have my attorney here. And I won't be needing your worthless, just-out-of-school public pretender defenders. So you tell me, just what am I being arrested for, and when do I get my phone call?"

Bask replies, "We can play it that way if you wish. See, I am pretty sure we will find your prints on the inside of that house, and probably a hair or two. Once we do, well you better have a damn good attorney, buddy."

The lieutenant leaves and Morrow comes in the office. He wants to speak with Ponds, and Bask asks if he thinks Ponds is his guy he has been looking for. Morrow assures him the person he is looking for was nowhere near the location. He has an interest in talking to Ponds, and getting any information on the operation and where it may go. All this, so he can try and find

Nave. The lieutenant agrees, yet warns that Ponds isn't under oath and they intentionally have not read him any rights.

Morrow walks in the room. Immediately, Ponds laughs and says, "Are you the bad cop or good cop? Is this where you offer me a cigarette and drink, play nice, and see if your skills are better than that other dipshit?"

Morrow holds a briefcase. He doesn't say anything. He opens the case, and removes several pictures attached to pages of case information. The pictures are laid on the table side by side. Morrow then sets the briefcase out of the way, and looks at Ponds. He tells him, "Look at each one of these."

Ponds casually glances and says, "Yeah, dead guys. Like I said, I ain't saying shit and you can't force me to. Anything I say right now will be thrown out and you know it." Morrow takes the first file, and holds the picture up to show Ponds. Then Morrow reads each name one by one:

"Arrested, sexual child abuse, got off on a technicality . . . later found dead."

"Arrested, aggravated sexual battery to an underage person . . . awaiting trial . . . dead."

"Arrested, sexual battery on a child . . . off on technicality . . . Yes, later found dead."

"All these are the same, and these are only a few. This doesn't even include the number of registered sex offenders who have come up missing all across the country." Morrow takes the files away. All but one. One has no photo attached. Morrow slides the file directly in front of Ponds.

Ponds looks with inquisition upon his face. Morrow looks back to him.

"Kaleb, read it," Morrow requests quietly. Kaleb shrugs, yet does ponder the heading. He looks back up to Morrow, who says, "Yes, Kaleb that is your file. Not anything to be proud of, and I'm sure you need not read it as you know what would be included in that file. Kaleb Ponds, you are being hunted and I will tell you now, this is one special individual. *He will find you* and when he does, you will wish you could claw your way back into this room. Now depending on what turns up at the house today, well only one person in this room knows how that will go. If you are 110 percent% sure you don't know the guy in that house and you have never been there, well I guess you have no need to work with me at all. However, however, Kaleb . . . you know everything that has gone on in that house. I am sure of that."

The door opens, and the lieutenant asks Morrow to come out. In the hall is an older man, standing less than average at five foot, five. He appears to be very fit in his older years, and offers no ill words. He smiles and shakes Morrows hand. Bask advises that Ponds's attorney was promptly notified, and wishes to have his client released immediately. The attorney is allowed to enter and speak with Ponds. Outside the door, they discuss the matter of having to hurry and process in order to prolong the detention of Ponds.

The attorney exits and politely says, "I have spoken to my client, and he wishes to leave now. Unless you have evidence to hold my client, you are unjustified in detaining him any further as he has cooperated to the extent he wishes. This, of course, if you have not charged him with anything. Are you ready to officially charge my client?" The attorney and Kaleb Ponds walk out of the department.

Outside, Morrow approaches Kaleb and gives him a card. Morrow tells Kaleb, "I guarantee you will wish you kept this when he comes. He will come."

The attorney takes Kaleb and they leave. In the car, the attorney questions Ponds. He advises, "Okay look, Loftski is dead. You are just damn lucky you didn't show up twenty minutes earlier, or your ass would have been up shit creek. Don't get tied up on this crap. Captain Loftski was a huge benefit to your operation, and yes we all know this is your gig. Why do you think we watch over you so well?" Ponds types on a laptop, and is looking for flights. He tells the attorney how he has to get out of Portland today! The attorney advises that Ponds should think about driving because the task force is already looking to set guys at the airport. He advises the few guys on the inside are trying to stay as close to the information as possible. Ponds and the attorney pull into a home just outside Vancouver, Washington.

Ponds tells the attorney, "It's done, I have a flight set in three hours. There is no way they will have anything to hold me on by then, and by tonight I will be in Mexico."

Quietly, the attorney goes to Ponds and says, "Kaleb, Kaleb, if they so much as find a fingerprint of yours anywhere on that car, in the house, anything, they are going to hold you. And we can't risk that." Ponds is cocky, and holds his arms out like a child pretending to fly. He says to the attorney that in three hours he will be in the clouds on his way to Mexico.

At the captain's house, the team receives frequent calls on the progress and also notification if anything has been pulled. The team advises they have pulled several prints, and ran into one issue. The mobile scanner they use has stopped working, and anything—prints or evidence—will have to be returned to the lab for crosschecks. The lieutenant is understanding yet stressed needing to gain the information to hold Ponds. The task force has sent two members to the address they obtained off of Ponds driver's license. The units pull into a back ally of a rundown drug area. The address listed is a few apartments up. They walk over the bodies, the needles, and the clouds of cannabis though the halls. The two come to a door that is listed as Ponds's address. On the door is a landlord lock and a notice of eviction. The officers go to the property manager. There, in a smoky room, is a woman. She has thick pink cotton sweatpants stretched mercilessly over the enlarged belly drooped between her legs. Resting upon the waistband of her pink sweats are two very heavy breasts and no bra. The straps of the tank top show signs of little time left before the fibers can no longer hold the load. She has stained purple hair cut short, and dark lips hold a burning cigarette. Before she answers the request of the officers, she removes the cigarette, billows a hacking cough, wipes her mouth, and with her right hand scratches the heavy growth of hair on her lip. She asks for a badge, and then hands the officers a key.

She advises, "You can take a look, but he never moved in; the place been empty the entire time. Weird guy, he rented the place, paid for six months up front, and then never heard anything more. Guess we may have been too low-class for him."

After their time at the slum house, they let the lieutenant know the situation. Morrow is still with the lieutenant and says, "He is gone. You let him walk out and I tell you now, the next time you see him he will be like the rest. Or he will just vanish." Bask looks at Morrow as he uses his phone. He tells someone to check the airport. He tells Morrow that he just has a feeling the guy is going to try and make a quick departure. Morrow laughs and says, "Okay so you find him there, you let him go. What are you going to do without a reason to hold him? He will probably have his cool-talking attorney with him."

The lieutenant smiles and says, "There are ways."

Ponds sits in the passenger side of the attorney's Escalade. He swirls his drink; he has his sunglasses on, and speaks ridiculous Spanish. As they cross over the water into Oregon, he tells the attorney how he will need to get a new identification and may even just stay in Mexico. He laughs regarding his situation of having to bounce all over the U.S. The SUV pulls up, passes airport police, and Ponds comments on how they are all idiots. He departs the SUV, and walks high and proud rolling a single carryon bag behind him. He made sure to time his arrival with just enough time to pass through security and spend little time waiting. As often in PDX, there is a line of people and one TSA qualified to scan IDs. Ponds stops at a shop before going through security. He gets a tee shirt that says, "Keep Portland Weird."

A small line forms behind him, and he rudely comments to one behind him, "Look lady, I just need to pay for my shit and I will be out. You don't need to be right up on me."

She looks at him and says, "You're a dick. Take your cheesy shirt and lame glasses, and just go." He turns to pay and she squats down briefly then stands before he turns to leave. He leaves and finds his way to the maze, which all passengers must go through for security. He waits in the line and finally reaches the ID check desk.

He shows his ID, smiles, and says, "Viva La Mexico Amigos." There is the usual routine of removing his shoes, belt, and tossing the bag on the conveyor. He holds his hands up, spreads his legs, and the white bar rotates past him. He is told to wait. The TSA employee looks at the screen, looks at Ponds, and then back at the screen. Green light, Ponds is waved through security. He stands at the rollers just past the enclosed section of the scanner. His shoes come out with his belt and wallet. He waits.

The man sitting looking at the imaging screen calls another agent over, and radios for another. "Sir, is this your bag? The blue Nautical bag?" Ponds looks and smiles. He says it is his bag, and airport police are swiftly in place behind him. As he is detained and expletives flow easily, he instructs the airport police to immediately release him. The woman, who was behind him in the gift shop, now passes by. She stops, winks, brings her right hand near her chest and from her loosely closed fist, her middle finger extends upward.

She smiles and tells him, "Guess you might not be having a Corona anytime soon, will you, Amigo?"

Morrow and the lieutenant are in his office when the call is made. Bask hangs up the phone and advises, "That sucks, Mr. Ponds is going to miss his flight to Mexico. He should know you can't bring a bag of dope and a metal pipe in your carryon. Dumb ass." Morrow's eyes raise, and he tells Bask he is impressed.

Ponds is detained, and taken to central booking on contraband and illegal possession of marijuana. Lieutenant Bask pulls into booking. He meets with jail staff member, who has him leave his gun in a lockbox as no weapons are allowed anywhere in a jail.

He walks through the rows of chairs and then over to Ponds. He tells Ponds, "Look, I know you have that high-dollar, slick, and probably just-as-sick-as-you-are attorney. I am not here to ask you questions. I am not here to try to get you to talk to me. I am here to simply impart some wisdom your way. Your luck in this whole twisted crap is diminishing, Ponds. You have to see what is happening. It is all going to eventually crumble. And, AND I will say this, you are not going to be able to hold the weight of the stones which will fall upon you. You were all set to vacate town once the heat came on. Now where are you? You know where you are; Ha, ha, and you know where you are not. Your narrow ass is not in the first-class seat. See, I had you pegged. Oh and then you slipped up, didn't you? Damn, thought you were a smart guy. Crooked as hell, but still smart. But you go and try to take a pipe and a little Oregon green with you? Makes me think of that football guy who has that bit, 'Com-ON Man.'"

Ponds looks over to him with a smug smile, crosses his legs at the ankles, and folds his arms. He tells the lieutenant, "This is a pit stop. See for cop pigs like you, well a first-class ticket would probably break your ass. Me? I will just go buy another." He leans over to the lieutenant as he whispers, "And I just might use some of the captain's cash to pay for it. By the way, where are the captain's friends? I could use some company in Mexico." He bounces his eyebrows up and down quickly, and the lieutenant stands. The attorney for Ponds has been very expeditious to post bail, and have Ponds ready for release. As Ponds is being processed and in high spirits knowing he is about to quickly leave the holding cell, Lieutenant Bask is in the control booth of the booking office. Bask particularly went to the holding cell as he was made aware the prints taken from Captain Loftski's home had several positive matches for Ponds. Bask had his team submit an arrest warrant for Ponds, and was awaiting word. Ponds is called to the release window. Bask stands at the booking office computer and fax machine awaiting the word as he watches Ponds walk closer. Ponds stands and walks through the chairs, and reaches the window. Bask watches the screen, and calls his guy pushing the warrant. The releasing deputy turns to Bask and silently asks if the warrant has come in. The deputy advises he can't deny the release if Bask doesn't have the warrant. The deputy turns to Ponds and has Ponds sign a few documents. The deputy is organizing all the papers as Ponds stands at the window. Bask's officer doesn't answer.

The deputy acts like he has to look for a paper clip, and mumbles to Bask, "Dude, he is about outta here." The deputy checks the documents, and then asks Ponds if anyone has fingerprinted him. Ponds is less than cooperative, and claims he has been fingerprinted before, so he shouldn't need any additional prints today. The deputy advises it is protocol and before he can finalize the release, Ponds has to be fully processed, which includes being fingerprinted. The deputy tells Ponds to return to the seating area. When he is fingerprinted, he will able to leave. Ponds stands at the window, looks at the deputy, and then to Bask

He shakes his head and says, "You lousy fucks are just stallin' to buy time. Bullshit! You better just sign my shit, and let me be on my way."

The deputy advises, "Go ahead, get combative and you will buy more time in here. Now, take a seat, we will quickly do your prints on the pad, and you will be done. Or you can stand here and find more trouble." Ponds sits.

The deputy tells Bask, "You have maybe fifteen, twenty minutes tops before this guy's attorney is going to get involved. Sorry bro, can't just hold this shithead all night." The control room phone rings, and it is for Bask.

He leaps over the room as he says, "Yes! That bastard isn't going anywhere!" The on-call State Attorney's office is on the phone. Bask sits half on and half off the end of the desk. His demeanor shows frustration.

The advisor tells Bask, "Sorry to be the bearer of bad news, but we have to look at the totality of the case and the likelihood is a warrant is not going to hold up in court. What we have is this, Ponds knows the deceased, and has likely been to the home many times judging by the report from forensics. He has no motive to murder the captain. And the huge factor here— there was zero foreign evidence found in the general area of the very gruesome

crime scene. Honestly, your own CSI and forensic specialist are dumfounded as to how there is no evidence of another person being in that garage with the captain. We do know this. There is not anything to link Ponds to being in that garage with the captain. If we were to file charges on Ponds, we would be compelled by the same evidence to file charges on four other officers, a city council member, and quite a few very high-ranking public officials. The captain has some very powerful friends. I'm sorry Lieutenant, the judge looking at this called us. He actually was the one who advised I should call you. Look, don't rush this. Let's put the puzzle together and develop a solid case. Too loose right now."

Bask simply hangs up with no words. He looks at the deputy and shakes his head. He walks out, and Ponds is called over to have his prints done. Ponds would step out once again, and slip into the seat of his attorney's SUV.

Two days pass, and the afternoon is dreary. Thick, low clouds hover between the quiet streets. Damp air collects on Nave's light jacket, as he walks up the sidewalk of a unique screen door restaurant community. The aromas are like nasal-infused advertising to lure one in. Drifts of fog seem to change the scents with each block. Modest decor and simplicity is the draw for this tourist diversion from the tighter and more crowded downtown areas. He waits at a street, and is approached by a woman. Her hemp twill hat covers the coarse brown dreadlocks that reach below her shoulders. She wears layers of frumpy clothing; metal studs line her eyebrows, and the pale white face is offset by black lipstick.

She holds a remnant of a cigarette out toward Nave's direction when she says, "Light," and nods her head back.

Nave looks to her in that expressionless, cold look and answers, "Yes, if you decide to finish that, you will need a light."

She lifts the cigarette over her head and says, "Dude, duh . . . do you have a light? Fuck!" He tells her he doesn't smoke, and this brings more confused frustration.

She then says, "Cool, but still dude, do you like have a lighter I can use?"

"If I do not smoke, why would I have a lighter?" he says without looking at her. She has the cigarette between her fingers on her right hand.

She brings both hands to her forehead, and with a very concentrated gaze, she seems to impart her theory to him. "One may have that what one does not need. Thus, held for one who needs. See that is life, man. That is aura. You could have been my light. But damn dude, you were my extinguisher. I am now left to seek a brighter light and thus when I do, I will take a drag. I will ponder you my man, and when I exhale, well I will pray that the smoke drifts through the world to touch those who are lost. Like you. Do you catch what I am sayin'?"

Nave looks to her and says, "Yeah, where I come from, we call it pollution." He walks on, and she stands at the curb. Her hands rest near her sides, and she just watches him walk.

After her absorption time she lifts her cigarette hand and says, "Dude, pollution. The smoke, the air, others, whoa . . . pollution. That is deep shit, dude." She looks at the partial cigarette, and talks to it. She tells the small white paper filled with tobacco how it is the start of pollution, and vows she will this day stop, starting the pollution. She carries the now symbolic token of pollution around to impart her new wisdom of why she will not light the cigarette.

A small trailer sits steaming under a makeshift awning. Near the sizzling flat grill, is an old retro school bus. Local, painted murals adorn the outside. Nave orders, and waits in the bus. Inside, is plenty of memorabilia to read, enjoy, and get an idea of the culture. Most often the term, "rich" is equated with money. Until it is seen in the eyes of culture. This street is abundantly rich with culture. Within the bus, status holds no special row. You can sit in the back, the middle, or the front. Just depends on if there is an available seat. You will not find a reservationist, valet, nor will you see an upturned nose should a homeless person sit to eat a sandwich, which the cook generously handed him. This day, Nave sits in the last row. One other couple is seated, and the time of day is light for guests. Nave's hot, fresh-grilled sandwich is brought in by a familiar face, and the man places it on the table. The man sits down, and slides his chair near the bus window.

He tells Nave, "You know, I hate to admit this, but I can recall the early days of my school life being spent twice a day in a bus just like this. Oh, guess that shows my age." He looks around the bus a little and then says, "You know, I had a feeling the information I got wasn't just random. I have to say, I would have not predicted I would be sitting in a damp, old bus on some outskirt street of Portland across from you."

Nave opens his sandwich to be sure there are no onions or peppers. He lays the warm top piece of bread back, and looks to the man. He tells him, "Agent Calvin Morrow, you are correct in your query that I am indeed the reason you had to be here. After today, you are going to return to your home office, and begin to connect the dots of a very complex picture. Once the last line reaches the final dot, you will stand back and see a picture which will frighten you, disgust you, and then anger you. You must first understand, your energy cannot sustain the endeavor you have, to seek answers you will not discover. I am giving you something I trust will direct you to the right focus. Sure Calvin, for sport, you can try to chase me. I will know when you are, where you are, and how you are trying. However, note this: this file you must realize is what will catapult your career, and you will expose an operation that has ties so deep, it will take months if not years to calm the ripple effect."

Morrow asks, "Okay, so we get a tip to get out here. You tellin' me, you want me to believe, you wanted me here? How do I know you are not just realizing that I am just getting closer to your every move?"

Nave slides his plate to one side. He tells Morrow, "Calvin, you were on your way to Boston. You booked flights; you were going to look over a case where a guy was found in a construction excavation site, and the body was over seven years decayed. Dental records indicated the body was a guy who had come up missing after his conviction. The previous owner of the property was the same guy whose kids were the victims. Now, you must admit that doesn't quite match up to very professional work, now does it? Calvin, if you had not been lured here, you would have had no clue about Portland."

Morrow sits comfortably, his hands on his lap and he inquires, "Then I must ask, what are we doing here? Why me? And I just don't see what you gain on your end and when."

Nave reaches into his inside jacket pocket. He holds a small thumb drive. He places the black plastic device on the table just past his plate. He comments on how so much evil can be held by such a small contraption. He slides it in Morrow's direction. Nave is quiet in saying, "Let me be very direct here. You don't open this on any state or federal device. I am sure you have a scan device at home, and can review it there. And Calvin, do NOT mistake me when I say, you do not want any trace of this where any state or federal level will first see it. DON'T chance it. These people are deep, and you will not make it."

Morrow's concentration turns to a look of disbelief and intrigue. He questions, "What people? Just what the hell have you unearthed?"

Nave tells him, "Calvin, you asked why you. Why you, because for years I have watched your moves. I have seen your eagerness. I have seen your integrity. Calvin, it is no joke when I tell you, I have spent years studying many of the ones you have close to you. I have faith that you will take this file, and do what is right. You have two close people who I have dug deep into. They are solid. Holcomb and your captain."

Morrow asks, "Lopez?" Nave just gives that cold stare and a slow side to side of his head. Morrow holds the file and asks, "Portland, this file, this trip, the shit with the captain, Ponds, all of it. This file is the answer, isn't it?"

Morrow turns the conversation to his own questions. "So you, do you have a name? Why do you do what you do? What makes you feel right about any of what you do? Yeah, yeah, I mean I get why, I guess, but how is it right? I stand on the morals of two wrongs don't make a right."

Nave sits a table-width apart from the man who has tried for years to find him, and now asks the very question he has only speculated any form of answers. Nave quietly tells him, "No-one will ever know my true name. I have been wired not to feel. And, I don't make anything right . . . I make it end."

Nave has to return to Utah, and a few days later Morrow walks into his office at home. One dim lamp on his desk, and he holds the small thumb drive. He looks at it then looks at his computer. There he looks at a screensaver with his two children —a girl who looks to be approximately twelve. Her big smile shines with colored braces. She has tight cornrow braids pulled back, sunglasses, and the beach behind her. The other girl is younger, looking up toward the older sister, and expresses a sassy yet playful grin. There is a joyful power of a photo to return our mind to a happy moment. His happiness is challenged by the virtue of why there was not a mother in the photo. He closes his eyes and each time he looks at this screen. As his eyes shut, it is the day he and his daughters said goodbye to a mother and wife. Illness cares not who loves you, or how long you want to stay on earth. It will come and take those with no prejudice.

He opens his eyes, and looks at the thumb drive as he taps it on the desk. A deep inhale, and as he exhales, he inserts it into the port on his computer. The customary window comes up asking if the user wishes to copy, save, or open the file. His right hand navigates the mouse and the white slanted arrow on the screen nears the OPEN tab. His index finger gives a tap and CLICK a new window pops up. It states, *This is a protected document intended only for whom was personally handed this device. Enter the user's return confirmation flight, middle 2 numbers of users SSN, and zip code of location user first obtained this file.* The first two requests were quick to enter, yet the zip code took Morrow a few minutes to research. He eventually enters the numbers carefully, and just as he depressed the last digit of the zip, the file opens. The first page is a briefing for him. It advises, *"The information contained in this file will illustrate the intricate workings of a large, and very active human trafficking operation.*

Operatives include Judicial Magistrates, Attorneys, Government officials, Foreign officials, law enforcement personnel, medical professionals, business owners, and local mules and street-level contacts."

"Strategic Layouts include: Entry routes, decoys, shuttles, drivers, workforces, housing, medical, doctors, and a family/abortion specialist."

"Photo and Video files include: holding locations, drivers, underground clubs, patrons, driver's licenses on video downloads of buyers, and renters (Buyers purchase child for personal use or private operation. Renters are what the operation calls the men and women who attend the underground clubs where they are able to rent a person and a room.)"

"And photo and video of actual footage of several clubs and transactions."

Morrow opens page after page. He has to stop several times to get up and collect his thoughts. He studies a pyramid page that shows a leader out of Portland. The branches below have two district judges, and several attorneys. It continues to include names and photographic verification of each person on each level. Above the local law enforcement officers, is a photo and the name, "Captain Alex Loftski." Above the named attorneys, is the State Attorney who advised she would not proceed with the case against Ponds. Morrow reads the names and levels of authority in disbelief. Just below the one holding the top position, is Kaleb Ponds. Morrow realizes Ponds has a team of very high-ranking members, who keep him well-protected and in the dark.

His pen has worked through a barrel of ink with notes when Morrow reaches for a new pen. He moves to the start of who supports the delivery of these children, and how the process flows. As he watches a PowerPoint created by Paul Port, his phone rings. Holcomb has called to check in on his old partner. Morrow advises he is deep into something and as Holcomb asks to know what it is, Morrow stalls and then advises he can't risk saying anything over the phone. Holcomb knows Morrow, and realizes his old partner has breached a new level in this operation. He tells Morrow he will come if he really needs him. Morrow is quiet. He holds the phone with his left hand to his ear. His right hand is bent behind his head, and he rocks in his chair before he answers. He looks up to his ceiling and his right hand slides over his weary eyes.

He asks in a very concerning, somber tone, "Bro, you have no idea what I have in front of my eyes right this second. If you have a few days, I can come down to you, and I will show you some shit you won't believe. This shit is beyond reality, bro. Can you lend a couch, and let your ol' pawtna come on down?" Holcomb assures him he is always welcome.

Holcomb tells him, "Hey, get some rest man. Wrap it up, and come down. Let's look this shit over together. I'm your man, you know this."

A few days later, and Morrow is sitting on the edge of a desk in Holcomb's house. Morrow could not sleep the night he talked to Holcomb. Before flying down to Georgia, Morrow looked over every detail, every video, and each strategic map of how this all worked. Morrow leans against the desk as he watches the expressions on Holcomb's face. Morrow knows every squint, shock, and fury is a mirror of what he felt a few nights before. Each of them has held a position in which they know the career they elected to excel in would present visual challenges. At times, they would question if what they must witness could allow them to stay on the side of the law and righteousness. No person will likely ever be prepared to see their family in the path of the sick and demented.

As Holcomb reviews a page that is labeled, "Leverage Strategies," he reads through how the operation will stop at no cost to protect itself. It shows bribes, murder, blackmail, and potential targets of interest. The operation is precise, and knows who might be a threat and concern. Holcomb is stone-faced and frozen when he sees Dominic Lopez listed as an operation positive contact. Next to Lopez, is a tab that has many of the other names. The tab is used to open a new window of potential threats, and those not listed as positive to the operation.

Holcomb looks to Morrow and questions in an accusatory manner, "What the fuck, Lopez? Lopez be in with this shit? How we know it isn't his in, his way of following the trail?"

Morrow has his arms folded, looks up, and Holcomb now sees Morrow is disturbed. Morrow's nose tightens, and his lip crinkles up as he sniffs. His eyes begin to get glassy and he tells Holcomb, "Bro, you are going to have to really be my rock on this. Bro, I am having some bad desires and I tell you true, I feel like a hypocrite, but what I been trying to stop . . . I try to stop, what all this time I been saying isn't right, well hasn't hit home. My home. All is off the table, bro."

Holcomb asks, "Cal, can I open this tab? Do I want to open this tab?" Morrow simply gestures with his head nod, and Holcomb opens the tab.

Among several members of Lopez's team is Morrow. Each member of Lopez's team is listed. Names, family, addresses, and how the operation can abduct the children if needed. Yes, pictures of the two precious girls left only with their dad appear in several photos as they are at dance, cheer, and school.

Morrow angrily stands and tells Holcomb, "I will put a fuckin' bullet in every one of them myself. Here I am, for years trying to stop this guy from doing exactly what I now wish I could do. Mike, and you know what? I would feel just fine with seeing that fucker drop. That fuckin' Lopez might just come up missing!"

Holcomb is still in disbelief. He then asks, "Okay, Cal, so you see all this and yet you trust me. I mean, I know I am not any part of this sick shit, but tell me, why trust anyone, and I just ask to get in your head a little. I have to say, if all this went down, I don't think I could trust anyone."

Morrow calms and tells Holcomb, "Get this, our guy in Florida, the one with no words, the one in Utah, well he arranged to have me sent to Portland. I sat less than a foot away in a shitty bus as this scary fuck handed me this device. You don't know, hell I don't know, what this meticulous engineer of his craft is capable of. He gives us this, and tells me I am the one to handle this. WTF? How?"

Holcomb clinches his lips, looks through the upper portion of his eyelids, and tells Morrow that he is smart, and he must have the insight that Morrow will do what needs to be done. Morrow then tells Holcomb that in a separate attached file, there was detailed information showing the captain and Holcomb are clear. They can be trusted; include their help in this exposition though the FBI.

"What about the girls, Cal?" Holcomb asks. Morrow tells him he has them in the federal building with the captain. He advises he did go to the captain, and so far just advised there is a safety concern. Holcomb tells Morrow, "Bro, set it aside. I'm your man, you know this. It's time to do work. That is your way. That is my way. We work. We taking this shit to da house!"

The day of light can be seen to pass shadows through the windows as the two dissect each file, each page, every video, and soon only the lamps of the room offer light as they cannot seem to peel themselves away from the information Nave handed them. The long hours of night turn to days of research, validating the accused, and formulating a difficult plan to take down this entire operation in the midst of doubt–that doubt of not knowing who, other than the captain, to include in the action. How should they hit each level of Portland and yet remain covert?

The two men walk into the federal building early in the morning, and sit exhaustedly anxious in their captain's office. The clock shows it to be shortly after 4 a.m., and the eyes of Morrow and Holcomb show the previous days to have worn heavy on their minds. A black cup of coffee enters the door held by the captain.

He does not bother to sit, and with respectful inquisition asks, "Men, why are we here? I know you both very well. This is big, isn't it? I have that gut feeling you are going to be asking me to give you more than I may be able to, so don't stall. Lay this shit on me."

Morrow and Holcomb give a brief rundown as to what the last four days and nights have been about. Morrow hands the captain a laptop, and the captain takes a seat. Morrow had carefully placed all the information into a much more condensed format for the sake of time. The clock turns, as does the captain's mind. There are brief glances of disbelief as he looks periodically up from the computer.

The captain eventually slides the computer away. He reaches for a pen, and writes on a piece of paper. He extends the paper to Holcomb, who is now leaning near the edge of the desk.

He tells them, "Shit, look it is damn near noon. I know what I just read, yet my mind is still going to process this for a while. On this paper is a number. You call this number, and the person you speak to will advise where to meet. I will be there. This is the only number you call. This is the only person you speak to. You do exactly as the man says. I will be where you are told to go. Morrow, you did it. You fucking hound dog mutha fucka, you did it!" The captain leaves, and the two men depart the office as well.

Morrow and Holcomb return to Morrow's house and call the number. The phone rings and a man answers. He does not say hello, he does not ask who it may be. He only instructs the two to an address and notes a time to meet. Five days later, at nine a.m., they enter the private room of an FBI office. There sits the most senior federal judge. Also in the room is seven other men including the captain. The judge has aged lines of character, and solid brown eyes of confidence. His presence is centered and focused, and he begins to speak in a low, clear commanding voice, as when he speaks the only thing others will do is listen.

Holding a one thick file, and more to each side, he tells the men, "For many years, I have had requests land upon my desk. Each missing something. Many missing too much. None so complex as what the captain, my longtime friend, has brought me almost what, a week ago? I don't have to advise that this was difficult, and I had to once-over the entire file. Perhaps my disgust slowed my progress. However, Agent Morrow and Agent Holcomb, you two might have brought my first and probably only file of perfection, and I can only see to it that I assign my most trusted team to provide you all the necessary support you deem appropriate. Gentlemen, the rest of you are here, as you have been carefully chosen by myself, my trusted colleagues, and the captain. Each of you have a particular skill set that will aid Agents Morrow and Holcomb in what will likely be your most intricate operation in your career. I trust a full briefing will be orchestrated and submitted to me personally in three days' time, at which point I will grant all warrants needed to briskly sweep each level of the Portland operation. No person in this room will speak of this case outside the supervision of Morrow. No person will stray from the directive of Morrow, and should any person compromise any portion of this operation, you will be in direct violation of a federal case, and immediately placed in custody for such obstruction. I have a room secluded for this use, and this room is the only place to be used for the planning of taking down Portland. With that, Agent Morrow . . . you are in control. Get it done. Three days, I want a full presentation and each arrest warrant request ready in three days." No one speaks; the judge stands and walks out.

The judge returns to his private chambers, and picks up the phone. He dials, and when the caller answers he says, "Well my old friend, looks like your guy is better than ever imagined."

Judge Grace sits in a Florida home smiling as he listens to the federal judge, a man he shared a dorm with, many beers, and some wild stories of spring break in their years through law school. Judge Grace replies, "Oh, Mr. Nave is unique in many ways. He has given you an incredible amount of information, I see. Yes, Judge Clark, Nave made a trip here and we reviewed the entire file. I am beyond amazed at what he discovered, and now your team better hit each level just right."

Judge Clark can be heard laughing slightly as he assures Judge Grace, "You might want to keep your national news on next week. I have a feeling it will be quite a show."

Morrow, now in full control, first gathers the specialties of the men in the room. Once each person details what they specialize in and how they will dedicate their time, Morrow stands in the center of the strategy room. The buzz of anxiousness calms, and the voices terminate one by one. Soon, all open eyes look and await his order. He acknowledges the group as powerful integrity.

He then says, "The judge gave us three days. We have two weeks of work to compile. The judge gave us three days, and we have weeks of coordinating a tactical plan. Three! Three days, men! Now, we have to do some soul-searching. Are you here?. Is your mind here in this room? Do you believe that what we are about to do can be done? Does each one of us know our craft? If you are in doubt, well you can hold your head up and dismiss yourself now."

No foot so much as lifts off the floor. Each man and woman appears more solid than when they walked into the unknown. Morrow rotates to connect firmly with each individual, eye to eye. He asks each person by name for a solid confirmation to isolate their focus on this one task. One by one, pride is infectiously passed onto the next.

He then tells them, "Okay, okay. Looks like we have already started. For the next two days, no one leaves this room. Judge Clark will have my detailed report by midnight on the second day. The third day folks, that day, Judge Clark can see how goddamn good we are, and we will sleep then."

Over the next two days, the power of determination can practically be seen, heard, felt, even the odor of smoldering brilliance lies heavy like fog. The walls are covered in straight lines, photos, routes, takedown times, personnel, numbers, weather, and equipment. Each specialist is cordoned off to perfect his or her piece of the puzzle.

One specialist walks to Morrow, who is seated behind a desk covered in many brown file boxes. She sits a box down and advises, "There are no holes. Each person on the legal side of Portland has been verified, identified, checked in every aspect available, and then some. There will be no gaps in my team, and we are ready for submission. Morrow stands. He looks over the men and women who have just put their lives on hold in order to complete their task. Some practically sleeping through open-glassed eyes.

He walks to the front of the desk and quietly says, "You, all of you did it." He reaches for his phone and looks. He slides his phone back into his pocket and says, "It is 1:20 in the morning. Two days. Two long-ass days and like I asked, we can submit to the judge. Go home. Go to sleep."

Holcomb appears to be asleep on a couch yet speaks up, "Cal, you out your damn mind? We just kicked the shit out of two weeks' work in two days, and you just say go to sleep? Now ya'll can go home, go to sleep whatever ya'll want. But Calvin, you taking my tired ass down to the bar, and you buyin' my ass a few shots, calling me a cab, and then my drunk, tired, overworked ass will go to sleep." Many laugh, and back Holcomb. Drink names are called out, Tom Collins- Long Island for me- Crown and Coke, and Morrow is literally dragged out of the room.

Accomplishment celebrations have a different relief that others can sense. The known bartender asks what they just won, who they arrested, or why they look like a group who just defeated death. They could not speak of why, yet each gloated pridefully and deservingly of their contributions.

At six a.m., Judge Clark listens to his messages. There is a message left at one forty-five a.m. advising him he could retrieve the requests in the private room on his arrival. He sits listening, and smiles. Like a father in the stands who does not have to say anything, he just smiles and admiration unfolds.

Days later, Judge Grace and Robert sit in the study watching the national news. Judge Clark is in his chambers as Fox News is breaking. A full coffeehouse of people on a busy Portland street gather around a wall mounted flay screen. Portland area radio stations begin to discuss and talk to the drivers on the commute. Fox News, CNN, MSN, and every major news channel all focus in on the split screen, aerial shots, close-up camera feeds, and preliminary reports out of Portland.

A local news anchor reports, "Thank you for joining us, and what a morning we have so far. Details are not clear, but what we are being told is the FBI, you can see the shirts and jackets there, along with local agencies, and several other government task forces have, well basically swept through and uncovered a major human trafficking operation here in the Portland area. We will do our best to show the different shots around the city, and I understand this spans Portland, Clackamas, Eugene, all the way up the gorge, and into Vancouver. We have Mark in front of the police station where it almost looks as if a few officers are being escorted out in cuffs."

Mark, the reporter at the stations replies, "Yes, now here we have witnessed FBI agents removing actual officers, and they are not giving us any information here on the ground. We did try to speak to one of the officers as he was being walked in the clutch of two FBI agents, and as you can see, he held his head down and declined any comment."

The studio anchor continues, "This all breaking in the last hour, and we have not yet heard from the FBI or local police. We break to the aerial footage, and you can see as the chopper cam zooms in, it appears agents are around a small club and what looks like children. Some adults are being taken from that location. All of our reports are telling us over seven different locations have this same event happening. Callers advise a swift attack, as one caller tells us, the FBI and SWAT teams just converged and announced search warrants."

Another anchor breaks in, and looks shocked. She states, "Well, we are just now getting a report that more agents are at the home of a member of the State Attorney's office. A caller advised the house is surrounded, one person was taken, and now the house is filled with what the caller states, detectives searching the home."

Judge Grace and Robert watch Fox news, and now the aerial footage is on a constant loop. After hours of video, breaking shots on the ground, and all the major news channels updating reports, all stations break into a live shot. The stations advise they are being told there will be a press conference in moments.

Near the courthouse, a podium has been placed. Quickly, every news station fights for position and the nearby street is lined with vans with telescopic antennas raised high. Out of the doors, Agents Calvin Morrow and Mike Holcomb walk. Morrow first approaches the microphones.

He stands with his hands rested on the podium as begins to address the press. "Thank you all for being here; I am FBI Agent Calvin Morrow. To my left, is FBI Agent Mike Holcomb. This morning you now know our agency moved in and effected a sweep of the Portland area. After the events several weeks ago with Captain Alex Loftski, our agency discovered details of a major, very intricate human trafficking and prostitution operation being primarily run out of the Portland area. While I will not elaborate on certain members or those being detained, I can inform you all that our investigation has been very precise, and this operation is unlike anything ever seen before. So far we have seen involvement from the street level, all the way to the federal level, and many levels of government activity to aid and support this activity. This is obviously a very sensitive matter, and for the integrity of protecting any accused or detained, we cannot elaborate on any individual at this time. The persons detained and those arrested will be dealt with on an individual basis, and most likely on the federal level. Under my investigation, the FBI orchestrated one of the largest interruptions of human trafficking to date. Over the next few weeks, more discoveries will be made. Agent Holcomb will take your questions; however, know we have very limited information we can offer."

Holcomb approaches as the barrage of questions are nearly unintelligible. The press calms and one asks, "We are getting reports that several officers and a local judge have been arrested. This operation, was it being run by members of the police department?"

Holcomb answers, "We have solid evidence that certain law enforcement members and government officials were involved; however, to what extent is still to be investigated. To say it was being run by law enforcement would be inaccurate. The Portland area law enforcement is largely comprised of good, honest individuals who are a positive asset to this city and our efforts. The operation was not being run or known by the City of Portland."

Another reporter asks, "We have seen your agents at the shipyards in a few locations, and we know that buildings are being searched. What do you know of these locations?"

Holcomb states, "While I know precisely the involvement of each location under a search warrant, I cannot advise to the extent of each. The shipyards are of interest, as our investigation leads us to information that these locations are associated with illegal trafficking.".

The reporter forces a second question. "The many locations being targeted by your agency seem to have a unique symbol. Is there a connection to this, and is it particular to the Portland area, or have you seen this in other cities?"

Morrow interjects momentarily. "The symbol, which we still know little of, has been observed in other cities. The pie-shaped, almost triangular figure has appeared on only some locations, and we will continue to investigate if there is any correlation to this operation."

A third reporter stands and says, "Your agency is utilizing a search warrant at the home of a member of the State Attorney's office. That person was seen escorted away in handcuffs. Can you tell us what her involvement is, and how deep this really is going?"

Holcomb takes a breath and looks over the crowd. Beyond the reporters' pit are crowds. Bikes are stopped as riders look on. The early morning runners stand still. The quiet of a normally busy area is unusually present. The city has a feeling of being violated, and unknowingly betrayed by those assigned to protect and care for it. Holcomb may have answered, yet his response was more from the heart and not so matter-of-fact.

He tells the reporter, "For years this city has been infected. We have an incredible amount of intelligence that allows us to know this infection began to spread over ten years ago. You ask if there was involvement at a higher level, and I will put my neck on the line and say yes! It is a sad day when we must take our own into custody. I am not a judge. I cannot sit upon the jury. I can only reply to what we believe to be true today. Over the next few days, the public will gain more knowledge of what has been taking place. Agent Morrow led this team and this investigation. I have faith that those detained will face dire consequences as this unravels."

The revelation of a high-ranking official being arrested causes unrest and excitement for the press. They obviously salivate over such dirt. The excitement is extinguished by the next question. The question comes from beyond the reporters' pit. A young, Asian woman stands near the right edge of the reporters. Her voice cracks; her speech is not clear English.

Everyone is silent as Morrow stands and asks her to repeat herself. "Ma'am, come closer. Repeat what you he said. She is shy or scared, and likely both as she looks to the reporters who make way for her to approach closer. One reporter puts her arm around the small, Asian woman, holds a microphone to her, and with a smile and comfort, tells the woman it's okay, and tells her to ask her question again. The woman looks to the reporters and then to Morrow.

She asks, "What going happen to girls? What we have to do now? Are we no more have home here? We no more make money? I scared not know where I able to go now."

Calm is when not one person can breathe. Eyelids fail to close, and a pulse can be heard and felt as everyone's heart beats deeply and heavily. Morrow is paused in his remorseful compassion for the woman. He steps toward her, and takes her hand. He walks her past the press and toward the building door as a woman comes to meet him. The woman takes the Asian lady, and Morrow returns to the podium next to Holcomb.

He then answers her question that supports the many in her absence. "The City of Portland, our agency, and the Department of Human Services were well-placed once we knew we would have many displaced women, girls, and boys. Each affected person will be taken in, and given proper attention. This is, in fact, the largest effort of this entire operation. Our team was adamant we would first take care of those, such as this young woman, involved in this. That, I believe, is about all we need to discuss for now. We have a lot of work ahead, and this will unfold as the days go on. What I will leave you with is that several agencies worked very hard to stop the trade and cruelty of many young individuals here in this part of the Northwest. We want nothing less than to see each person associated with these crimes punished and held accountable. Thank you."

Over the following week, the news continues with footage and reports as the case unfolds. People are exposed, businesses shut down, and the confiscations of cars, money, boats, and businesses are the hot topic of morning and evening news.

Two weeks pass, and Morrow walks into a hole-in the-wall BBQ place just outside of his hometown. He sits down; his usual waitress sits down, and puts a tall glass of iced tea for him. She knows what he has come for, and a menu hasn't been needed for over ten years. She walks off, and in a few minutes the seat is filled again.

Morrow sits back, takes a drink and says, "You know you are not really my type, but after Florida it is your turn to pay my friend." Nave shows slight acceptance of his humor with a light lifting of his eyes.

Nave tells him, "Yes, I guess I do owe you. Agent Morrow, I knew you would take care of Portland. I trusted you, and you came through. Now it is time to pay." Morrow is still very uncomfortable with Nave, and has a concerned, guarded look as he asks what he means by time to pay. Nave tells him, "Ponds, while he lost his contacts with Portland, he still has a way to disappear. See, he was supposed to go to Mexico and then he had that delay. Then he was allowed to leave again. But something happened, didn't it Agent Morrow?"

A skinny black woman walks up to the table. She will never reach five feet, and her smile appears to be permanently shining before her. She stands and looks to Morrow, and then to Nave. She holds a wet cloth in one hand, and the other lands on her hip.

She asks, "Oh dear, who is you? Now I ain't be one to cast no ill words, but you done stumbled on a side of town most pale folk avoid. Now Cal, you going to tell who putting the butter on the bread?"

Morrow assures her it is okay, and asks her to bring another glass of that real southern sweat tea. Morrow rests into the torn red vinyl seat. The silver rim around the table is broken in a few places, and an old glass jar can be lifted up to expose a selection of straws. On the kitchen counter, is an old radio playing R & B. The grease and grime on the radio show clear evidence that the station will not be changed. A signed poster and record by Fats Domino hang near the front door just past the curious eyes of a few black guys at the counter.

Morrow shares, "You know not many people can grow up, live, go to school, and eventually work in the same town all their life. But I did. This joint always been here. My Granddad would bring me here every Friday when he got the lousy cash from doing odd jobs. My dad was hard. He worked and kicked my ass. He laughs and looks around at the place. Yeah, the man only had those two jobs. Go to work and come home, and kick my ass. Loved him for that. I stayed straight. My ol' man never took a thing from anyone. Grew me right. I never had shit as a boy. Young and even though I wanted stuff, I never questioned the man. We fished. We built my first truck. Ha ha, hell never did run right but it rolled down the road. Let me tell you, when I walked off the stage after graduation my dad was quiet. He met me man to man and shook my hand. Told me, 'Son, I'm proud of you.' In the other hand, he handed me a roll of hundred dollar bills. See all the stuff, I wanted, I didn't need. There was enough money for me to pay for the extras I needed for school. Yeah, college funds were available and I took that, but the cash he gave me took care of the extras. The stuff I needed. It was that what made me a man. Gave me the faith. That little pat on the back to say I would always do the right thing. See, I knew you had Ponds nailed after Portland. I couldn't allow another wrong in my mind. We took Ponds. He never made it out of the Mexico terminal. Wasn't until I saw the file and my girls that I felt that hair stand up. When I saw the photos, the information, the sick feeling of my baby girls being victims of this sick fuck, is when I myself wish I had your number. What you do isn't right. Never will be. And sure as we sit here, I have to uphold my oath to bring justice to all. That's my job, my right. That is who I am."

Morrow takes a drink. He has a small briefcase next to him. He sits it on the table. He tells Nave, "I always have to make sure Macy get my ribs going right. I'll be a few minutes. Now you watch over this case for me."

Morrow stands and tells Nave, "What I don't know, what I don't help with, well that isn't on me. I know I will not be seeing you after tonight, but I'm sure I will know where you been."

Morrow walks to the kitchen and in a far-back booth Nave stays only for a few minutes. Morrow returns, sits, and puts the small case back near his side. He looks down to a piece of paper. His BBQ tacky fingers pick the paper up that reads, "Your girls will always be safe."

Chapter 23
Mexico

An exhausted flight attendant still finds the energy to say goodbye to each passing guest. A slim, young captain stands drinking from a bronze cup that is adorned with photos likely to be his kids, symbolic perhaps to remind him why he should be as safe as possible, and to always return home to those smiling around his cup.

Nave passes and continues through the terminal. One more set of sliding doors, and he finds a spot near the passenger pickup area. Behind a clear window only skewed by the lights reflecting from above, is Lynn. Her hair is tied back under a ball cap; she wears a loose, thin jersey shirt, and as he sits down, he sees she once again didn't bother with a bra.

He comments, "Do you do that on purpose just to immediately excite me?" She asks if he is referring to the ball cap and he reaches over, takes his left index finger, and brushes the noticeable, erect protruding nipple of her right breast. She laughs, slaps his hand, and rotates her torso away as her left eyebrow rises.

The bright white smile pinches her light pink tongue, and she tells him, "You behave. Well, behave now. Until I get your sexy butt home. Then Mr. Cause-Chaos-in-Portland, you are all mine." The rear window is clean and clear, which allows a perfect view of the red and blue lights pulsating directly behind her.

"Nice car Ma'am. 69 Charger right?" the highway patrol officer asks. Lynn tells him that it is, and she didn't realize she was going too fast.

The officer asks another question. "So, what agency do you work for? As I stopped you, I entered your tag out of Florida, and it's flagged. That tells me you might have your info blocked." Lynn says her dad is a judge, and that she works in the legal field as well.

The officer smiles, and asks, "Well, Ms. Grace, can you promise you won't drive 101 miles per hour on I-80 again? A little fast, don't you think?" He walks back, and she slowly departs. Nave just shakes his head while telling her she is lucky to not get a ticket a week. He even jokes that there is a raceway not far from there, and she ought to spend a few hours a week getting the speed out of her system.

That night after dinner, he secludes himself in his office. He is on the phone with Robert, and links in to a mutual video feed. The two now include Jason the tech.

Robert asks, "Nave, show us what you have and what we need to get this done."

Nave details, "Jason, here is the GPS; I want you to zoom, and run a constant mono-feed. Just like a cat watching a gopher hole, the rodent will poke his head out soon enough. I want stats on every person going in and out of every building connected to the gift shop. If you see return customers, delivery, anyone coming more than once or twice, we need to know who they are. Robert, all connections to the gift shop . . . I have a strong idea that four Federales who are heavily armed are not there to protect keychains and shells. A car, solid identity, and a tour package to the resort will provide low profile for my stay. Include a companion female from the agency as well. Time is tight. I will do my regular work away, and when I return, we have to be in place. The information I sent you will show that

Morrow advised that the Mexican government and Ghost are not communicating well."

Robert interjects, "Nave, this looks to me like Ghost may be shuttled by the Mexican Cartel to Moscow. But your report shows a Russian interest is attempting to move him soon. I mean, do we even have the week and a half to move in?"

Nave assures them, "Yes, the Mexican government is negotiating with the Cartel. We well know there are many palms being lined through this, and with Portland compromised the Cartel is eager to get movement through Boston now. The government was burned by Ponds/Ghost after he released tapes showing many officials on video making deals with the links in Portland, San Diego, Long Beach, and El Paso. The way those involved with the Mexican Government feel, they would just as soon hang Ponds and see him dead. The Cartel knows the connections Ponds has and his strong Russian ties, will bring a monetary strength to the eastern traffic, and as you see on page twelve. The Cartel is almost done with an all-inclusive, adult-only-based resort in a remote mountain area. I wouldn't be at all surprised if there are private jets taking reservations from all over the world as we speak—thus, why it has been so difficult to track him. He has ties to Mexican Cartel, Russia, China, and a lot of greedy help here in the U.S. I predict his being so closely monitored will make my access very difficult.
Now we can see why the urgency to eliminate Ghost is so strong."

Robert and Jason assure Nave that when he returns from work, they will have everything in place.

A slight opening of a hotel curtain exposes a parking lot light indicating Nave has awakened early, and will soon start a regular work day. He looks out to gage the real weather before being advised by the news. Between the light and his window, tiny sparkles pass and disappear into the dark asphalt parking lot. Coming from low clouds, they look like glitter as each drop passes the light; they regain their presence in sound as they join in an audible termination against the ground. He heats water for his spiced tea, and carefully places food in baggies. Sitting near the door, he laces his work boots. With Nave's door open, Gary walks by and comments on how it seems like Utah is as wet as Portland. Gary makes a comment on how he is glad he is not in Portland, though. They chat a little about the stuff they did over their days off, and Gary moves on to his room.

The work week is mild. Each night, Nave returns to his room and vigorously plans for Mexico. The crew has no idea that each night Nave stays up until 1 a.m. reviewing each new detail from Jason. Friday night Nave returns, looks over information, and chats with Jason. Jason is his usual, excited self once he has broken the walls of information.

Jason updates Nave, "Oh man, I am seeing some interesting shit here. Okay first, see the woman in the right box? Okay, she is a cab driver. She always parks to the north back corner, and never brings anyone to the shop. Just hold that thought. We will return to her in a minute. The armed Federales are always posted . . . one inside, three outside. Never by the north back corner. The photo under the driver, he owns the gift shop. American guy, Harper Guy. Strange I know, but Harper is the eldest stepson of the captain who tried to eat a steering wheel in Portland. Oh Nave that was crazy, good shit! Damn, this is lacing together like those goofy boots the goons guarding this place wear. The last photo is Gutierrez. Not the top, but he is old Cartel roots. Gutierrez always has that briefcase, and always arrives on Wednesday. Times are not consistent, however."

Nave sends a message asking, "Ponds? Have you seen Ponds?"

"Not really. I say not really, as here we go back to the chica driving the cab. See, the cab parks near an old gas pump. The pumps haven't worked as records tell me for ten years. Yet she always pulls in, and hangs out. Sure, it's easy to say she is just chilling, but look at what I am putting up now." Nave looks over a historic page of an old building that used to be where the gift shop is now. In the document, there is a view of how the old building had a leach field and a concrete channel that led to the building, likely for waste from the building. The channel ends precisely where the old pumps are now.

Jason then announces, "Nave, Nave, Nave, you are aware I am amazing right? You just never knew how amazing I really am. Ha, I even surpassed my own pure excellence here. Okay, opening now is the circle of scumbags. Start, gift shop is built on the old foundation. Old foundation had a basement. New shop and even building records show a single level, no basement. Long ago, the pumps were added over the channel that to this day still lay under the ground connecting the shop and the old pumps. Little Ms. Cab Driver happens to always pull out, and drive west away from the shop. I may have a little Mexican friend I know who took a trip down for a night. The cab had a person assumed to be a male, wearing a hoodie in the back seat. I believe Ponds is in that cab, and is being driven to a home about thirty miles outside of Cabo. Then at around 4 a.m., a small Ford

Ranger is seen pulling in to the pumps. Lights never go out, truck stays running, and leaves. So Nave, ask me if that is all I know? You are right, it is not. Satellite track of the cab to the house, and research of the house . . . yeah I find a home listed as a vacation home owned by the ex-girlfriend of Mr. Kaleb Ponds."

Nave sends a message, "Have me in Mexico next Thursday."

Nave closes his computer, and heads to dinner. The guys he works with are true practical jokers, and are always looking for an opportunity to play a prank. Gary saw Nave leave, and was already past drunk. He is with the other guys, and they decide they will break into Nave's room and see what they can do. Nick knows the girl at the desk very well, and she gives him a room key. One stands watch as the other proceed to stack furniture on the bed, crank the AC on high, fill the tub with his clothes, and dispense shaving cream to fill his work boots. Before they hurry out, Nick wants to put a silly message on Nave's screen saver of his personal computer. He sees the other case, and tries to open it. He turns the case, examines the handle, attempts to figure out the lock, and then decides to just mess with the laptop on the desk. Nave has a separate laptop that is not linked to his secure laptop in the case. He still has it highly protected at the agency's request. Nick lifts the top screen, and depresses the power button. A black screen with a grey middle bar opens which reads, "Enter access code." Nick laughs and comments how it is so like Nave to have an access code," and not normal password.

He is hurried and says, "Shit, what would he have as a password, ha, ha no wait . . . ACCESS code!" He begins to type, and once he presses, "Enter," the screen flashes red, and then a warning is in text and announced by the computer, "Warning, you are attempting to access a federally protected communications outlet. Your photo has been uploaded from this device, and you are now being investigated in conjunction with the unauthorized attempt to gain government documentation. You are instructed to terminate all attempts, and leave the device in the location immediately. The authorized user will determine appropriate civil and criminal penalties upon discovery!"

Nick looks at Gary. "What a load of crap. That is a pretty cool password lockout feature, though. I might ask him where he got that."

They hurry off to avoid being caught by Nave, even though they are well aware he will know who trashed his room in fun. The rain has stopped, yet still a trail of drops follow behind Nave as he carries clothes to the hotel laundry. Waiting for them to dry, he opens his computer and laughs at the video of Nick and Gary. His computer message is accurate, and Nave had been contacted even before returning to his room. Morning comes, and he walks into Gary's room for the day's briefing. He sits down and hands Nick a paper. It is a color print of when he tried to open his computer.

Gary swings back and laughs as he makes light of the prank. "HAAAA, see Nick, bro, it did take your ugly-ass picture. Hey Nave, don't get pissed and kill anyone, we just had to have fun with you. Listen, take a few hours off, and get your room straight and clothes dry."

Nave laughs and says, "Oh my room is fine. Clothes, well as you see, they are dry. And I'm not upset at all. I just hope you guys don't get upset when it comes back around."

The next few days go quickly, and they are soon at the end of their workweek. They are out working, and wrap it up. The trucks pull into the parking lot, and each of them heads to their personal trucks and cars to travel home. Nave pulls out, and knows he will have one night home; he has to be on a plane to Mexico in the morning. Nick drives away, and keeps getting a hint of a strange odor. A few miles into his drive, he can't help but pull into a gas station to see if he can figure out what the smell is. What Nick doesn't know is that tuna mixed with vinegar strategically placed in a vehicle will permeate into the fibers, the vents, and only gets worse with the heat of the engine. Gary drives the other direction. He stops at a light, and looks over to his floorboard. He thinks he has seen something, but quickly dismisses it. He continues on, and adjusts his seatbelt that keeps rubbing his neck. Then from under his seat, he again sees something move. It is then from over his right shoulder, a white mouse crawls over him and down his squirming body. Everyone on the crew knows Gary can't stand mice and rats. There, on the side of the busy interstate, is a grown man with all his doors open, trying to fling mice out of his truck. He will not drive in comfort unsure if all twelve mice were ejected or not. Collin is not off the hook. He learns quickly that he will not be using a turn signal on the way home unless he wants to give visual and audible warning. The turn indicator is wired to the horn and with each flash, a clear honk blares out.

Gary texts Nick and Collin, "Did he get you?"

Humid air causes a clammy texture to Nave's hands as he and Lynn carry their bags to the shuttle that will take them from the airport to the resort where they will spend the next six nights. The shuttle driver is thin, and exhibits a shiny gratitude for each tip handed to him as the guests step onto the bus. The driver walks delicately while often resting his hands inward, palms out on his narrow hips.

He speaks perfect English, and welcomes everyone in his own delightful words "Heeey, well I want to welcome each one of you to my bus. I got to tell you, I just absolutely L.O.V.E. new guests. My name is Roberto, and I am not from Mexico, hee, hee, but I sure had some of you fooled." He holds his right hand in front of his mouth as he slightly touches his upper lip while exhaling a happy gasp. He is a manicured man with sharp black hair; his sapphire shirt is buttoned just to the bottom of his chest, and neatly tucked into his very tight white capri pants. Matching sapphire low-cut Converse press the accelerator, and the shuttle bus whips down a few streets. Soon, the bus pulls into the resort and each guest is once again sprinkled with kindness by the driver.

There is one couple who may have seen a few pride parades in person and the driver winks and tells them, "Oh my, now you two know the shuttle runs every day. Just let me know if you need me to take you anywhere."

Nave walks to the check-in, and a heavyset young woman sweeps her hair away, and with a welcoming smile takes his information. She types, fills out a card, and hands him a small folded brochure.

She says, "Okay Mr. Craft. You will have a poolside suite on the third floor. Let us know if there is anything we can do during your stay."

Nave and Lynn (Craft) enter a suite and the woman who seems to be of the very earth she walks on, opens the white loose curtains. He looks at her and realizes when an eagle is seen at the zoo, it is majestic and beautiful. Then people pass to the next animal. At times, when we are next to a flowing river, tall evergreens sway and we hear a screech above—another witness this sight in nature. We are captivated in an appreciation of freedom, and stand still in wonder of such. She steps her bare feet onto the patio, and he wonders if six days will be enough to quench her thirst for the sun. Their bags are only opened to retrieve shorts, and soon there is a drink in one hand and Lynn grasping the inside of Nave's arm while they walk the sandy beach. The sun creeps slowly to give the coastal town a long warning that the night will come. Then, in the battle of when night rises and challenges the array of colors left to fade from the sun, the last rim of dark red is washed by the dark blue wave in the distant sea. Now the cabanas chime with festive Mexican music; food can be found if one simply follows the scent, and drinks are abundant at each turn. By the time the moon hangs like a disco ball, there are many pale-skinned tourists dancing to lyrics they can't understand—perhaps only a few words. A ridiculous joy is to watch a group of adults scream as La Bamba plays, and all partake in a conga line. Hanging lights will eventually dim, pit fires smolder until staff douses each one, and in the distance a glow burns hot just yards from the ocean. Nave and Lynn lie looking to the sky.

A spraying sound, the noise of chaise lounge chairs sliding across concrete, and the frequent closing of a metal gate against the latch awaken pool-view guests if the sliding doors are left open to first hear the breeze of night. Lynn walks along the beach knowing this portion of her trip will be alone. She will not know of where he is, how he is, or when he will wake next to her.

The night that has past took with it two men in an old CJ7 Jeep. Away from the resort and before light shines over the first peak, the Jeep is hidden in an outbuilding seventy-five miles out of Cabo San Lucas. Nave's vacation resort is now a hot, isolated shack. The GES, who escorted Nave, has left and now Nave lays his maps, intel, equipment, and satellite GPS locator on a 1970s school desk. He goes through the routine of opening his case, and validates his location. He is verified and tech support advises communication is positive. The case closes, sweat droplets hit heavy on the desk, and Nave stands. He opens the rollup door, and drives the CJ7 across the dirt path. Heading west until he can only travel north or south. With the sun to his right, he sees the waters of the Pacific to his left. Half a day passes, and he is in a remote town that has an eerie silence to it. Nave enters a home, and walks around back. A door is closed, yet he walks in. Nave closes the door and a man is slumped over a desk silent. Nave stands quietly; on the wall is a key rack. Nave quietly takes a keychain with one large Ford truck key.

He then throws the key high, allowing it to land hard on the desk. A fraction of a second after the crashing sound, and the man jolts from his chair. "AYEE LOCO WEDO MUTHA FUCKA!" the man exclaims. He takes a big deep breath and asks, "Gringo, now if you scare me to death, how I supposed to hep you? EH, tell me that amigo." He curls his hand in a motion, and tells Nave to come to the desk. "Okay amigo, I no see you here, I no know you, and you no return here, K? I have for you. Here I make all things bueno, and you no have any trouble. Oh no, no, no, I tell you true my freend. I work many year for operation, and I know who you are. You know I am, Si? Like you! I no make mistake. But you no make mistake. I give you time to be. You be there or no work, Si?" The two spend hours looking over routes through the cactus, unknown trails, and then a pickup location well up the coast. Nave knows, as the man advises, there is no room for error to carry out this operation. Nave leaves and returns to the small town outside Cabo. He pulls into the gift shop. He walks past the armed men, and appears to be mingled among the few tourists. The shop is small, has trinkets, and is more of an all-purpose store as he sees now. He walks each aisle. He views the drink cases, the windows, and the cash register. Just behind the cashier, a mirrored clock shows a gun, and a button device. The hall leads to a room near the end of the cooler case, and the center of the store has genuine Mexican cacti, shark teeth, snow globes, key chains, and Mexican blankets. Of course hats and sombreros lay abundant atop the shelves. He gets a few items and departs. He drives away and returns to the dry, hot shack.

His slightly tanned, mildly burnt skin has come by way of lying against the
nearby hills. He thinks about how he could have gained the same color lying beside Lynn. She enjoys the comfort of a chaise lounge, drinks delivered, and a cool shrimp cocktail. In the heat of the day, she can simply dip her thin body in the pool or retire to the room.

Saturday morning the dirt blows across the cracked concrete drive of the gift shop. A small lizard darts like a pinball chasing small insects. An old Jeep Cherokee runs with three men inside as their rifles rest on the hood. No cars are yet parked, and the neon, "Open" light has yet to illuminate. Then, the quiet is severed by the bellow of a high-performance exhaust pipe heard well before any sight of the car. Like an alarm clock, the men hear the exhaust, and exit the Cherokee. Hundreds of yards away, lying in a crevice just near the top of a hill, a pair of black binoculars peers in the direction of the gift shop. Each man is a focus in the glass. Then a white and black 1998 Toyota Supra pulls to the back of the store. A small man exits, and hands each guard cash. Then he unlocks a door, and soon the store is open for happy tourists to take a little part of Mexico home. The sun has few clouds to interrupt its scorching rays. Nave maneuvers to find little shade on the hill. Then midway through the heat of day, a cab drives up the street. It eases into the parking lot, and stops near the second pump. In the binoculars, he has a clear view of the back of the cab. The woman stays in the car, and then the second pump slides about three feet toward the middle of the island. There from the hole, crawls a person who is first facing away wearing a hoodie. As the man turns, his face is now pressed against the other end of the binoculars on a pane of window glass with Nave on the inside, and Ponds on the outside; they are face to face. Yet, Ponds has no knowledge of who is looking from the hills several hundred yards away. It's clear for a second, and then Ponds enters the cab.

Nave still wonders why it is so much trouble to use an underground route when it is so close to the same building. The only explanation would be the pure paranoia and concern of satellite imagery. Nave leaves the hillside with great relief from the heat.

The cab pulls into the carport of the house of Ponds's ex-girlfriend, and soon departs. Ponds enters, and the home is quiet. The screen door creaks, and then shuts behind him. Water boils on the stove, and hamburger meat simmers on a back burner. The refrigerator is slightly open, and Ponds is getting no answer when he calls out for his girlfriend. She is rumored to be an ex, as a cover for her to stop being constantly associated with him; yet they are very much still together. He makes his way through the house, and the back door stands open. He stays back, and looks to the open door; his mind replays the water. The meat. The open fridge. Slowly, comes a Glock 9mm from his waist. He turns toward the kitchen, and from behind him, footsteps hit the tile floor near the rear door. He turns, raises his gun, and suddenly . . . he pulls back at the last second as a Doberman pinscher excitedly rushes him.

His girlfriend stops, and yells, "What the hell, K? You paranoid asshole. One day you are going to shoot me I know. Fuck!" She pushes past saying how she has to get the water off the stove, and she just had to go chase Dante. The dog, however, doesn't care that Ponds nearly shot them both. The dog only knows he wants to play, and see who has come back.

Ponds spends Saturday and most of Sunday with his girl, and late Sunday night he is on the couch with her and tells her how he has to go on another trip. He explains how he might be more than a month this time. She is used to this, and asks no questions. She is satisfied with the arrangement as when he departs Mexico, she is often set up in a luxury penthouse in Las Vegas. There, she dances through the night, makes cash she hardly needs, and enjoys the companionship of her other dancers as they party with affluent clients.

Late Sunday night, the Ford Ranger drives near the pumps. The Cherokee sits running closer to the building, and moments later the Ford drives away.

An underground steel door opens. Ponds reaches, and turns on a light. The small quarters are adequate with a one-bedroom- styled layout and no windows. He pours a drink, sits at the counter, and flings his shoes toward the door. He then shuffles to the one room, and flops on the bed. Quiet is not the absence of sound. It is more the level of what sound is present. Underground, in the dark, and nothing on, there is still the hum of silence. As his eyes adjust to the darkness, the faint red light of a digital clock becomes brighter. The sound now is louder with the thump of Ponds's heart.

It increases, and is felt pulsing through his veins; each throbbing causes his eyes to strain and his throat tighten as his voice quivers to ask, "You are here, aren't you?"

The sound of the Supra echoes from the distance. The Supra pulls to the back, and the Cherokee remains as it did through the night. The guards are inside, the parking lights are on, and the guns are on the hood. The man looks over, and yells for the men to get their asses out of the truck and in place. None of them exits the truck. He moves his short, chubby body toward the truck, and then opens the driver's-side door. Against him, the guard falls. Each lies lifeless in his seat. The chubby man races to the building, and opens the back door. He first checks the safe, then the cash register, and then proceeds over to the rack with the sombreros. He struggles, but slides the rack over. He removes a few tiles, and lifts a door. The reality sets in that Ponds is not there. In minutes, there are men at his girlfriend's house, men racing around the area looking for him, and the chubby man is on the phone with Gutierrez organizing locations to seek out Ponds.

Gutierrez tells him, "Ponds is on the run. No one knows about the shop and no one would know how to get in through the pump. I want Ponds, and I want him in front of me alive. His tramp dancer slut told us he mentioned having to be gone for a while."

In the girlfriend's home, a dog lies with its belly flat on the floor. His eyes are dark, and look toward the door, and then back to the woman. Perhaps the dog looks to the door for Ponds, or any other who may take him. As the dog has licked the face of Ponds's girlfriend, Dante knows she will never rise to walk with him again. The dog moves once the running pool of blood touches his paw. Her cooperation would not have saved her, as her mortality is a mark of retaliation. She is left for any chance Ponds will return; he will be greeted by the slain action of this lifestyle.

Gulls glide inches above the ocean's waters. A few boats sway off the breaks. The sun prepares the canvas with its first coat of creamy dim color under the coastal clouds. The headlights of the CJ7 need to shine less. Hollow hum of the tires can be heard through the bikini top, which is open on the sides. A tightly wrapped, heavy green wool army blanket lies behind the seat. Motionless in the blanket, Ponds will stay unconscious for many more hours. Nave turns off the paved road, and drives across the dry dirt. He runs head-on into the blinding sun. Swirling and rising behind him, is the dust stirred by the past. Ahead is an abandoned car off the trail road. He stops. Nave crawls to the back of the Jeep, and carefully uncovers a portion of Ponds's arm. He exposes, and dilates the veins on the inside of his arm. The needle impales one vein, and a calculated amount of narcotics is introduced. Nave steps out of the Jeep, and walks over to the old Lincoln Continental. The paint departed many years ago. The tires are brittle and flat. Only a portion of the windshield remains, and a variety of bullet holes have been scattered against every panel of the car. He lifts the trunk. Nave reaches inside, and removes two five-gallon gas cans. He empties each into the CJ7, and returns the cans to the trunk. Soon, he continues deeper into barren desert. In an hour's time, he travels beyond any signs of life. Ahead, he watches the horizon float in the mirage of wavy abstracts across the desert floor. In the distance between the mirrored mirage and his Jeep, he sees the reflection of metal. As distance decreases, he observes the object form into a row of cars at a crossroads. The Jeep slows, and Nave knows his escape routes are limited. He eases his right pant leg up to gain easy access to an H&K compact 40mm. He lifts the worn seat cover of the passenger seat to assure the HK416 is positioned when needed. The seat back is also Velcro, and has a combat-level bulletproof vest inside. Now one hundred yards away, he can see it is the Mexican Army and law enforcement. He lowers his pant leg, and slowly rolls toward the men ahead.

His Jeep stops twenty yards away from the first car. A large man and two others approach the Jeep. The large man is likely the boss, as the two others flank him with rifles in hand. Dry wind carries dust through the man's thinning black and silver hair. His face is pockmarked from acne as a much younger man. He confidently walks to the window, and hands Nave a bottle of water. His appearance is one of gratitude. The two with him would contradict any welcome or trust. He opens a conversation with Nave.

"Hola, Señor Gringo."

Nave nods. The man leans against the door near the hood and continues.

"See my American friend, I can no tell you how long it has been for me to see any American to drive across this place. Why you drive across this no place? AYE, no you answer. See Gringo, my airplane take picture from way up there. See strange dust roll through my land. So I think Gringo . . . wrong turn. I bring him water and see where he try to go. Si'"

Nave looks to the man then looks beyond to the other trucks and cars. Both trucks have three armed men. Dark windows hide who, or how many, may be inside. Above, is the sound of the airplane which likely followed him into the driest portion of the desert.

The Mexican man continues his tirade against Nave. He creeps in closer; now his face is even with the open frame of the driver's window.

He speaks quietly. "Tell me Gringo, you have any souvenirs from a little place in a small city? Maybe a souvenirs that Señor Gutierrez is missing? No? Señor Gringo you no come to desert to find nothing. No? You already find you souvenir."

Nave slowly positions his right leg to allow open area near his lower pant leg. He counts each time the militia guard looks away on the passenger's side, and for how many seconds. The guard near the head guy never looks away. Nave knows the dirt road he came in on is flat and relatively able to handle high speed. His focus lands on the gas cans in each truck. He debates about whether or not to utilize them for explosives or needed fuel for the gas-guzzling CJ7.

As he lines his every move, the man in charge turns and rests his back against the door as he says, "Señor Gringo, you friend, he my friend. You friend, tell me when he find out my plane see Jeep in my desert." The man steps away and his heavy, deep laugh shakes his robust torso. "How he know too much, he damn good. He have all good toys to know what goes on, aye loco amigo. See Gringo, he tell me you very good at, let's say making maggots disappear. You have maggot in you Jeep?" Nave knows his friend who studied the plan must have inner working with the Federales.

Nave looks to the man and replies, "What is your intent with me here now?"

The Mexican leader looks to his guards, and advises for both of them to return to the truck. Nave is surprised just as the man explains, "Our friend, he tell me. You maybe no right in head. He say you maybe kill everyone if we try to stop you. See Señor, you doing all of us a favor to get rid of this maggot. I just ask, I see to be sure it same maggot our government want to see disappear. You show me, and we grant you safe travel to go on." Nave opens the door, steps out, and pulls the seat forward. The lump in the army blanket lay wet and sweating behind the front seat. Nave pulls a portion of the blanket back. A clammy, pale face with dripping hair and closed, drugged eyes reveal what the man sought. He looks to Nave and places one hand on Nave's shoulder.

He tells Nave, "Señor, you promise my government. You promise me, Ponds will rest in this desert of hell. I ask you, put marker so my people will know he will place his feet on any Mexican dirt never again. You finish this today amigo. You make friend with me, when our maggot is dead."

Nave covers Ponds, and looks to the man and answers, "He has already started dying. He can't even be saved now, if anyone tried to save him. I am just delivering him to where he will finish the process."

The Mexican man and his guards sit at one of the trucks near the crossroads. In hand, are Dos Equis and cigars. The Jeep is camouflaged into the desert dirt as it drives against the glaring sun.

The Jeep reaches a spur in the road that leads to an old building. The building has long been removed, and only the concrete steps that lead to a shallow opening remain. The space is only 4four feet high, and approximately five feet by six feet. Nave parks near the steps, and sets two chairs on the concrete floor. The sun is slightly past the highest part of the Mexican sky. He uncovers Ponds, and pulls him up from behind the seat. He rolls him near the back of the Jeep, and dumps him onto the desert ground. The sedatives have begun to wear off, and he can be heard making a childlike croupy cough. His larynx is chalky dry, and his lips have but a few moist drops left from the sweat when he was covered. Nave pulls the green strings from a long vinyl bag. From inside, he retrieves a canvas popup for shade. The popup only covers one chair. The other chair is hard to even look at as the sun radiates off the shiny metal. Nave pours half the bottle of water over Ponds's face. He awakens, yet he is still dopey. Nave sits him in the hot seat While Ponds comes to be more alert, he sees Nave using a pick. He is chipping up two holes in the concrete floor.

Nearly incoherent, Ponds snidely exclaims, "You dumb fuck. You are actually going to pick at the concrete and bury me under it? Dumb fuck, why not just dig a fucking hole in the dirt up there?" Nave just continues. Soon, there are two small holes, each near a twelve-inch opening, and about a foot deep. Between the two holes, is about an eighteen-inch piece of concrete remaining. Nave slides Ponds near the holes. Ponds still has no energy to even attempt to fight. He nervously asks, "What the fuck are you doing, you crazy bastard? Look, if you are going to kill me, just fucking do it and get it over with." Nave takes the bare feet of Ponds, and places them in the hole. Under the popup cover, is a large blue water container. Next to it, is one yellow bag of quickset concrete mix. Nave goes to the Jeep, grabs a five-gallon bucket, and returns to Ponds. The fear is unsettling in Ponds as he eagerly tries to command his legs to lift his feet from the small holes. He continues to try regardless of the certainty that he can no longer move anything from the waist down. He has little control over his arms and has become so weak; even speaking has become a huge effort. Nave mixes the concrete, and pours each hole to come level with the existing floor. Then Nave sits under the popup now shared with Ponds.

A long pause as Nave looks to Ponds and explains, "See, in the many years of tracking the ones I have, I have to say you are one who seemed to find a way to slip by. Each time I learned more, and discovered how enormously sick you are. See, and here is the most disturbing part, you truly enjoyed what you did. So many kids, so many times. You never had any remorse."

Ponds mumbles, "Hell, I gave those foreign kids a life. So why shouldn't I get a little payback? Look Mr. Righteous, if not for me those kids would be abused in their own country and never have anything after. They just kill them when they are used up, or simply cast them out to live on the streets. Here, they had a pampered life. Shelter, food, money, and when they were used up, they could turn to the good ol' USA to give them free shit the rest of their lives."

Nave stares at him and says, "Ponds, you are not even what I would call sick. You are just evil. Your greed, and your disregard for a child prove it. The thousands of young lives you permanently scarred and used just so you could live a lavish life. You may have plenty of time to relive your good deeds as you see them. See, when I came to the conclusion that you challenged the devil himself as to who was more of a piece of shit, I had to come up with a way you could see hell, even before you got there. So here is what is going to happen. You can't feel it, because I paralyzed you from the waist down. Now that is going to wear off slightly in a few hours. But the concrete is setting up, and soon your feet will be solidly in place here in this floor. As you come around, you may feel like you have been here before. Yes, you have. Before, this was merely a few slabs of foundation; this was the same building you used to store your Mexican boys before having them smuggled over through El Paso. So I figured it to be appropriate to spend the last days of your pathetic life, right here. Once the concrete is solid, you are going to come around a little more. Of course the nice popup shade deal here will be gone, and tomorrow it will get quite warm. The days are long this time of year and with no water, your body will quickly shut down. This will give you plenty of time to think about the last twenty years. The heat will surely bring visions of the past. Maybe hallucinations will haunt you as the many faces return to your mind. Kaleb Ponds, your life is ending here. No telling how long you will endure the desert, but be assured, Hell's heat will creep against your skin. The sizzle of your naked flesh will be slow. Those tears you are dropping will no longer run once your body is depleted of any moisture. Finally, you will lose feeling in your legs, your upper body will attempt unsuccessfully to flop once more, and only your mind will be left to see the brightest sun go dark. My deepest hope is that you are still alive as the buzzards circle then land around you. They will pick relentlessly at your blistered flesh, tugging, scratching, and clawing to fight over your warm body. You may even be able to see as they tear away piece by piece, and consume you as you continue to depart. That is if they do not take your eyes first."

The begging voice of Ponds is continuous. He yells, he cries, he summons a god whom he has only cursed before being delivered to the gates of hell. It is typical to reform only when one is faced with the ultimate outcome of one's fate.

The night cools. A weary, drugged man struggles to find comfort on the concrete floor. With his feet solid, the lack of circulation creeps with tingling numbness up his legs. The stars clustered thick soon fade as the sun delivers the new day. Swollen, dehydrated, and in a collapsed sprawl of human waste, he lies still on the solid, ever-warming floor. As the hands of Nave's watch turn past three, the sun has begun its chase toward the ocean waters. Before the shadows hide the signs of Ponds's agony, Nave walks near the motionless body. Deep gouges around his legs, and the skin of his shins stick under his nails. The concrete is stained with blood and skin. A strained attempt allows only one eyelid to weakly lift. His face finds shade, as Nave leans near him. With nothing said, Nave rises, and Ponds's one eye watches Nave's feet walk up the steps. Nave departs leaving Ponds to his final place there in the Mexican desert.

Nave returns to the shack, and calmly sits his briefcase on the desk. He enters his code, the red light illuminates, he places his left thumb on the scanner, the red light turns green, and the case opens and he sends the notice: **"NES 1912; GHOST has been eliminated! 10-17!"**

From a poolside room, a woman forwards an announcement to all ES agents. "C.O. announcement: 10-100, Level 5, Ghost. Repeat, 10-100 Level 5 Ghost. NES 19-12 confirms and reports Level 5 Ghost is 10-07. Script available in 24 hours on all ES computer updates. This notice is confirmation Level 5 Ghost is 10-07. 10-17."

Two days pass, and a dirt cloud follows a fleet of trucks toward the eternal concrete grave of Ponds. The trucks stop, and at the edge of the steps, the large Mexican man stands smiling. He holds a small bag that was delivered to him with one tooth. He places his dark sunglasses back on, and the trucks leave the decaying, animal-scavenged body to become part of the desert.

In a stuffy Virginia office, Morrow receives a secured message from Judge Clark. Morrow shakes his head, and calls Holcomb. Morrow is somber when he admits, "If remorse was in me, I would be untrue to myself. There is not a feeling of pleasure, yet relief is not always synonymous with joy. He terminated that life to rest eternally in hell, and I hold no guilt in that satisfied emotion."

Holcomb offers his wisdom, "Think now of the many who will not suffer from that man's hand, and know his departure was the only definite remedy."

Chapter 24
Cravings

Lynn is sitting on a chair near the counter when Nave walks in from work. He slowly walks around the counter, and stands in front of Lynn. He smiles. She smiles. He leans back against the counter, and she dips a crispy, thin taquito into thick, creamy guacamole. The one she holds is only part of the now nine remaining.

She laughs and says, "Don't say a word. I know this is not my usual dining choice, but your sister stopped by, and that aroma of fried corn tortillas just sucked me right in." Nave just laughs, and helps himself to share a few. They walk out of the garage door, and she helps him take the bags out of his truck from being away for a week. Hanging from the garage ceiling are their road bikes. He suggests they pull them down, and get out for a while. They load the bikes, and drive down to the Legacy Trail. In many sports or activities, Nave typically gears down to enjoy the time with Lynn. Bicycling is not one of them. Lynn's daily routine often involves an early morning spin class, and in her spare time she rides her bike long distances. Yes, she has a collection of tight, colorful cycling outfits. Nave simply throws on a pair of shorts. The two enjoy the closing, bright, westerly curtain as they return back to the truck. During the drive home, Lynn says she has her dreaded, annual, female exam tomorrow and asks Nave to join her. Nave looks and tries to wiggle his way out of it. Unsuccessful is he as Lynn already told his mom he would be coming with her. She works in the same hospital where the appointment is to be, and Nave knows he should at least say hi to his mom while he is there.

The next day, they sit in the waiting area as Lynn fills in her personal information.

She flips a page and says, "Oh my god! Used to be one simple page of questions, and now it is box after box after box. So freakin' stupid."

Nave sort of laughs and replies, "Taquitos, tossing all night, and now grumpy. Where is the, 'Are you prego box'? You might want to check that one."

She elbows him and exclaims, "Hush, mister. I am not prego."

The heavy wood door opens, and a familiar face greets them. It is Lindsay, the young woman from Colorado. She took Nave's advice, and contacted his mother about pursuing her nursing career.

Lynn looks to her then to Nave. She asks, "You two know each other?" He informs Lynn that Lindsay is the girl from Colorado who he referred to his mom. Lynn goes in the room alone, and Lindsay comes out to the waiting room.

Lindsay sits next to Nave and quietly says, "I have no idea exactly who you are, or what you really do. All I do know is you helped change my life, and I just wanted to officially say thank you. And that your mom is totally awesome."

Nave smiles, nods, and tells her, "Lindsay, the only way to get stuck is to stop moving forward."

After sitting awhile, he sees Lynn come out. She dips her head, and winks at him. She sits next to him, and holds the same clipboard she used earlier.

He asks, "You have more crap to fill out?"

She quietly answers, "Oh, I marked something wrong the first time." She holds it conspicuously and deliberately in his view. There in the box where she had originally placed an X in the NO box preceding the question, 'Are you currently pregnant?' were three dark lines across the Xed NO box. Now, it has the YES box with a happy face inside it. This is the first time Lynn has seen Nave's eyes become glassy. His smile assures her he has only exhilaration of what he dreams will come. The two walk through the hall, and to his mother's office. She stands and attempts to advise she wants to take them to lunch, but Lynn insists she look at her form. Her mouth opens wide, and one hand holds the clipboard while the other reaches around the two of them as she hugs them in close. Lynn stands with his mom as Nave walks to the door to hold it open.

Lynn stops talking, covers her left ear, and her expression tightens. She looks to Nave and a slight squint of her eyes. Then as quickly as the good news fills the room, Nave's earpiece chimes, "GES 1912; 10-19, Level 2 target; Salt Lake City, UT. GES 1912; advise 10-40 status." Lynn steps back, looks to his mom, then to Nave. With an assured smile, she tells him, "I think just the girls need to go to lunch. After all, I bet you have a few things to tend to this afternoon." Puzzled and wondering, the questions drip from his curious expression. She reaches for his hand in the lobby, turns him, takes his soul with her lips, and his breath with her passion. Her eyes open as she kisses him then says, "Come back to me always. More than myself, we all need you." His confused, inquisitive look is met by her soft, compassionate expression. She squeezes his hands as she tells him, "Yes, Valerio Nave, for every part of who you are, I have love!"

Made in the USA
Las Vegas, NV
03 May 2021

22423839R00281